# STRINDBERG'S STAR

# STRINDBERG'S STAR

JAN WALLENTIN

*Translated by*

*Rachel Willson-Broyles*

VIKING

VIKING
Published by the Penguin Group
Penguin Group (USA) Inc., 375 Hudson Street, New York, New York 10014, U.S.A. • Penguin Group (Canada), 90 Eglinton Avenue East, Suite 700, Toronto, Ontario, Canada M4P 2Y3 (a division of Pearson Penguin Canada Inc.) • Penguin Books Ltd, 80 Strand, London WC2R 0RL, England • Penguin Ireland, 25 St. Stephen's Green, Dublin 2, Ireland (a division of Penguin Books Ltd) • Penguin Books Australia Ltd, 250 Camberwell Road, Camberwell, Victoria 3124, Australia (a division of Pearson Australia Group Pty Ltd) • Penguin Books India Pvt Ltd, 11 Community Centre, Panchsheel Park, New Delhi – 110 017, India • Penguin Group (NZ), 67 Apollo Drive, Rosedale, Auckland 0632, New Zealand (a division of Pearson New Zealand Ltd) • Penguin Books (South Africa) (Pty) Ltd, 24 Sturdee Avenue, Rosebank, Johannesburg 2196, South Africa

Penguin Books Ltd, Registered Offices: 80 Strand, London WC2R 0RL, England

First published in 2012 by Viking Penguin, a member of Penguin Group (USA) Inc.

10 9 8 7 6 5 4 3 2 1



Originally published in Swedish as *Strindbergs stjarna* by Albert Bonniers Forlag, Stockholm

*Publisher's Note*
This is a work of fiction. Names, characters, places, and incidents either are the product of the author's imagination or are used fictitiously, and any resemblance to actual persons, living or dead, business establishments, events, or locales is entirely coincidental.

LIBRARY OF CONGRESS CATALOGING IN PUBLICATION DATA
Wallentin, Jan, 1970–
[Strindbergs stjärna. English]
Strindberg's star / Jan Wallentin ; translated by Rachel Willson-Broyles.
p. cm.
ISBN 978-0-670-02357-8
1. Signs and symbols—Fiction. 2. Secret societies—Fiction. 3. Murder—Investigation—Fiction.
I. Willson-Broyles, Rachel. II. Title.
PT9876.33.A24S8713 2012
839.73'8—dc23 2011043888

Printed in the United States of America

TO SAMUEL, LYDIA, AND HENRY

**Excerpt from my diary in the year 1896.**

*May 13th.*—A letter from my wife. She has learned from the papers that a Mr. S. is about to journey to the North Pole in an air-balloon. She feels in despair about it, confesses to me her unalterable love, and adjures me to give up this idea, which is tantamount to suicide. I enlighten her regarding her mistake. It is a cousin of mine who is risking his life in order to make a great scientific discovery.

—*Inferno,* August Strindberg

That which has been is far off,
and deep, very deep; who can find it out?

—Ecclesiastes 7:24

# STRINDBERG'S STAR

☥

# The Invitation

His face had really withered. The makeup artist's tinkering couldn't hide that fact. Yet she had still made an effort: fifteen minutes with sponge, brush, and peach-colored mineral powder. Now, as she replaced his aviator glasses, there was a sickly shine over his grayish cheeks. She gave him a light pat on the shoulder.

"There, Don. They'll come and get you soon."

Then the makeup artist smiled at him in the mirror and tried to look satisfied. But he knew what she was thinking. A *farshlept krenk*, an illness that was impossible to stop—such was growing old.

He had rested his shoulder bag against the foot of the swivel chair. When the makeup artist left, Don bent down and started to rummage through its contents of bottles, syringes, and blister packs. Popped out two round tablets, twenty milligrams of diazepam. He straightened up again, placed them on his tongue, and swallowed.

In the fluorescent light of the mirror, the hand of the wall clock moved a bit. Thirty-four minutes past six, and the morning news murmured from the closed-circuit TV. Eleven minutes left until the first studio guests were on the couch.

Then he heard a knock, and a shadow appeared in the doorway. "Is this where you go for makeup?"

Don nodded at the tall figure.

"I'm off to channel four later," said the man, "so the girls might as well apply enough to last."

He took a few steps across the yellow-speckled linoleum floor and sat down next to Don.

"We're gonna be on at the same time, right?"

"Yes, it seems like it," said Don.

The swivel chair creaked as the man leaned closer.

"I read about you in the papers. You're the expert, aren't you?"

"Not really my area of specialization," said Don. "But . . . I'll do my best."

He got up and removed his jacket from the back of the chair.

"In the papers it said you know this stuff," said the man.

"Well, then it's got to be true, right?"

Don put on the corduroy jacket, but as he put the strap of his bag over his shoulder, the man grabbed it. "You don't have to act so fucking important. I'm the one that found everything down there, aren't I? And by the way, there's . . ."

The man hesitated.

"By the way, there's something I think you could help me with."

"Oh?"

"There's . . ."

He cast a quick glance at the door, but there was no one there.

"There's something else I found down there. A secret, you could say."

"A secret?"

The man pulled Don a little closer, with the help of the shoulder strap.

"It's at my place in Falun, and if it's possible I'd really like for you to come up to my house and . . ."

His voice died away. Don followed the man's eyes to the doorway, where the presenter was standing and waiting in a light brown suit jacket and a frumpy skirt.

"So . . . I see you've gotten to know each other?"

A stressed smile.

"Perhaps you two can talk more afterward?"

She pointed out toward the hallway, where a cue light was glowing in red: ON THE AIR.

"This way, Don Titelman."

# 1

# 1

# Niflheim

With each step, Erik Hall's rubber boots sank deeper into the mud, and his legs were tired. But it couldn't be much farther now.

When, through the fog, he could make out the clearing past the last trunks, he came to a halt, and for a moment he felt uncertain. Then he caught sight of the ruins of the old fence. The rotting stumps stuck up like warning fingers in front of the slope down to the opening of the mine shaft. He slid down the incline to the ledge in front of the mouth of the shaft, pulled off his three dive bags, and stretched his back.

It was cold here, just like yesterday, when he had managed to find his way to the abandoned mine for the first time. The heavy pack of tanks with the inflatable buoyancy vest was still lying where he'd left it, and the same horrible, rotten stench was still in the air.

The fog had reduced the light to dusk, and it was hard to make out any details as he leaned over the steep shaft. But when his eyes had adjusted, he could make out the supports that started at a depth of about thirty yards. They braced the walls of the shaft, and an image of sparse, blackening teeth flashed by. Like looking down into the mouth of a very old person.

Erik took a few steps backward and carefully inhaled. The smell seemed to subside as he got farther from the hole.

He gave himself a pat on the back. He'd been able to make his way in this darkness and find the right route yet again; there weren't very many people who could pull it off.

Anyone could use a GPS navigator to get from Falun to an address out by Sundborn or Sågmyra. But finding the right place three miles straight out in the wilderness—that was different.

Most—in fact, all—abandoned mine shafts were supposed to be noted on the maps. The surveyors from the Mining Inspectorate had seen to that. But this hole had apparently been overlooked.

Erik heard a faint buzzing, as some flies had started to gather around him. They made their way in curiosity down into his bag to see if there was any food.

But in the first bag there were only spools of rope, snap hooks, and bolts. The double-edged titanium knife with a concave and a sawtooth edge. A battery-powered rotary hammer drill, the climbing harness, and the primary dive light that he would fasten to his right dive glove.

When Erik had dumped everything out on the yellowed grass, he opened the side pocket of the bag. In it were the Finnish precision instruments in hard cases. He unpacked a depth gauge, which would measure how far down he sank under the surface of the flooded shaft, and a clinometer to estimate the gradients of the mine paths once he got there. The flies had increased in number; they hovered around him like a cloud of dirt.

Erik waved the insects away from his mouth, irritated, while taking the regulators and long hoses that would keep him alive out of the next bag and checking the pressure of the tanks. Then he moved backward a few steps, but the cloud of flies followed him.

Half standing in the gravel, he pulled off his green rubber boots, then his camouflage pants and his Windbreaker. With bugs crawling across his face and neck, he opened the cover of the last bag. Under dive computers and a headlamp waited the bulky wetsuit and the rubberlike skin of the dry suit. Glossy black three-layered laminate fabric, specially developed for diving in forty-degree-Fahrenheit water.

He pulled on the full-cover neoprene hood. Now the flies could reach only his eyes and the upper part of his cheeks. Then he took out the bag that contained his fins and mask. At the opening of the shaft, the rotten-egg stench almost made him change his mind, but then he attached a nylon rope and began to lower the bag.

Forty, fifty yards—he managed to follow its jerky descent that long—but the line just kept going. Only after a few minutes did it reach the water that filled the lowest part of the shaft.

He secured it with a few loops around a block of stone, and then he went to get the bundle of climbing gear and hooks. When he got back to the shaft, he sank down to his knees.

A strident roar from the hammer drill finally broke the silence, and he could soon attach the first bolt. He pulled—it would hold. He drilled bolt number two.

Then he lifted the hundred-pound pack with tanks, the buoyancy compensator, and the hoses onto his back and fastened the strap of the climbing harness across his chest and did a few tests of the self-locking rappelling brake that would control the speed of his fall down into the shaft. He swung himself over the edge, the brake hissing as he dropped.

There were blurry pictures on the Internet from urban explorers in Los Angeles who, without a map, hiked their way through mile after mile of claustrophobic sewer systems. You could find texts from Italians who dedicated themselves to crawling through rats and garbage in ancient catacombs, and from Russians who described expeditions to ruins of forgotten prisons from the Soviet era, hundreds of feet below the ground. From Sweden there were video clips that showed dilapidated mine shafts where divers swam in pitch-black water. They crawled through tunnels that didn't seem to end.

Some called themselves the Baggbo Divers and hung out outside of Borlänge. Then there was Gruf in Gävle, Wärmland Underground in Karlstad, and several groups in Bergslagen and Umeå. And besides them, there were people like Erik Hall, who went diving on his own and most of all wanted to keep to himself. It wasn't recommended, but people still did it.

Because they shared tips about equipment and shafts that were worth exploring, all of the mine divers in the country knew of each other. Year in and year out, it was the same people who did it. Without exception, they were men.

But a month or so ago, a group of girls had started putting up pictures of their mine dives on the Internet. They called themselves Dyke Divers. No one knew where they came from or who they really were, and for their part they didn't answer any questions. At least not the questions that Erik had sent as a test.

At first when he was surfing around the girls' Web site, he had found only a few grainy photos. Then clips of advanced diving had shown up, and yesterday there had suddenly been a snapshot from a mine shaft in Dalarna.

The picture had shown two women in diving suits down in a cramped mine tunnel: pale cheeks, bloodred mouths, and both had shining black hair trailing over their shoulders. Behind them they had spray painted:

545 feet, September 2

Under the photograph, the girls had listed a pair of GPS coordinates, which marked a place near the Great Copper Mountain in Falun. The position had been only ten or fifteen miles from Erik Hall's summer cottage. They added:

Flooded shaft from the 1700s we found on this: /coppermountain1786.jpg/map, blessings to the county archive in Falun. After the scrap iron in the water, there are tunnels for whoever dares to pass.

No country for old men ;)

The self-locking rappelling brakes lowered him gently into the depths. The cloud of flies was still circling up by the opening, but down here in the dark, Erik was hanging alone. He breathed only through his mouth now to avoid the smell of sulfur.

When he let his eyes drift around, it was like sinking down into a different century. Rusted-away attachments for ladders, half-collapsed blind shafts, notches cut by pickaxes and iron-bar levers.

There was no room for mistakes when lowering yourself down into a mine. But he tried to persuade himself that this shouldn't be difficult, just a vertical hole and dirty support posts that had managed to withstand the strain of the rock for hundreds of years.

Still—older mine shafts were never truly safe. What looked like a wafer-thin crack could run deep into a rupture. And if the wall gave way, it would mean that one of the one-ton boulders hanging above him could suddenly come loose and tumble down.

How much farther?

Erik broke a glow stick and let it fall. The glowing flare disappeared in the dark, but then he heard a splash much earlier than he had dared to hope for. The stick glittered green far below, bobbing on the black water.

The depth meter on his wrist indicated that he had already lowered himself some 225 feet, and the cold had only gotten worse. Frost glistened on the rock wall in front of him, and the next glow stick landed on an ice floe.

Then he discovered that a small ledge stuck out just above the water. It was about ten yards to the right, so he swung himself along the rough boulder and landed.

Now to the most important part.

He took out a little bottle of red spray paint from the leg pocket of his suit and with a few quick movements, he sprayed a large E and an H. Under the letters, Erik Hall wrote: SEPTEMBER 7, DEPTH OF 300 FEET, then snapped a few pictures.

He pulled off his neoprene hood and ran a hand through his curls. Several more flashes. He examined the results on the camera's display.

His hair was a bit thin, now that he was over thirty, but it was hardly something you'd notice. The dark circles under his eyes made more of a dramatic impression than anything else, Erik thought to himself.

Then he sank back down into a crouch in the stench and the cold. He tried to forget that no one knew where he was and that no one would miss him if he drowned or disappeared in the tunnels far below ground.

The Dyke Divers had left bolts where he could secure his navigation line before his dive. When it was fastened, he pulled on his flippers and mask and put the regulator in his mouth for a first test breath. Before he had time to exhale, he had already taken a large step down into the water. The roll of line he was holding in one dive glove spun quickly, and above him he could see how the strong wire cut through several layers of ice as it followed his sinking body.

Below the surface, the better part of the light from his headlamp was swallowed by the dark walls. But the water was relatively clear, and the beam carried farther than he had dared to hope.

Erik braced himself against the wall of the shaft and pushed out into the emptiness. The safety line followed him, winding through the water like a tail.

The bottom appeared in the light from the lamp on his right wrist. Under him were remains of the litters that had been used to carry the ore out of the tunnels. Erik moved his fins carefully and floated weightless above a wheelbarrow. His underwater camera began to flash and take pictures of the iron gear that had long ago been forgotten and left behind. Precision tools, sledgehammers, chisels, an ax, cracked pump rods, and farther off . . . something that looked like a track.

Erik let his body sink, and he landed next to the narrow-gauge rails. The depth gauge read sixty-nine feet under the surface of the water. Even with a slow ascent to avoid the bends, he still had plenty of air left.

He sailed above the rails, which led him away from the middle of the shaft. He had the sensation that he was moving into a narrower space and slowed his speed. That was when he caught sight of the timber-framed opening of a tunnel, where a yellow scrap of fabric was speared onto a hook.

Erik glided forward a few more yards, and he illuminated the scrap with the light from his headlamp.

It wasn't fabric hanging there by the entrance to the tunnel, it was a strip of bright yellow seven-millimeter neoprene. Triple seams, made to be highly visible in cloudy water. The girls must have cut up an old wetsuit in order to mark the right way in.

The tunnel was perhaps two yards high, and a rusting mine car stood in the middle of it. Above the car there was a small space where it looked like he could pass.

Perhaps this was the beginning of a long system of tunnels and shafts—without a diagram or a map, it was impossible to know. But according to the Dyke Divers' pictures, it would lead to someplace that was dry.

He managed to make his way over the rusted-down mine car and tried to increase his speed gradually. With a third of his air in reserve, a total of forty-five minutes of dive time remained. Fifteen minutes tops in this direction, before he had to turn around and make his way back to the surface.

The farther he got into the tunnel, the more it began to slope upward. His clinometer showed a gradient of eleven degrees upward, and it was only getting steeper.

Only about a hundred yards more. Then the tunnel would presumably be at a higher level than the flood, and it would stretch out, dry and full of air. Or . . . the tunnels, because now he had come to a fork. The one that continued to the left seemed navigable. The right-hand one was barely a yard wide, dilapidated and tight.

He couldn't see very far into the dark passage with his headlamp. But the light was more than sufficient to show the yellow strip of neoprene, which indicated that the Dyke Divers had taken the difficult path. Slender female bodies, and there had been several of them, could help each other. He was alone, as always, and wouldn't even have enough room to turn around, if he should be in a hurry to get out.

Erik let his glove stroke along the frosty ore and hung there, weightless. Then he chose to continue to the left, but quickly felt like giving up, because only a bit farther he noticed that this tunnel also quickly began to narrow.

Ten yards, twenty, thirty. Soon he would be able to brush both walls with his fingertips. At forty yards his shoulders grazed stone. Forty-five. Two iron supports made a narrow doorway. He twisted his body to the side and managed to force his way through.

But the tunnel became increasingly narrow, and before long he reached two more supports, this time so close to each other that he would have to tear one out if he wanted to keep going.

Erik directed his flashlight to where the support was attached to the ceiling and the floor. It wouldn't be possible to dislodge. The right support's floor attachment seemed to have rusted away. Two bolts had detached at the ceiling . . . and two still seemed to hold. He grasped the right support and moved it carefully. It moved an insignificant amount. If he were to really put his weight into it . . .

Erik hung suspended above the narrow-gauge rails.

Then he let his headlamp search the darkness as far into the tunnel as possible. To turn around now . . . he shoved on the support again, and it unexpectedly came away from the wall in a cascade of gravel and small rocks. His view became clouded, and he curled up to protect himself, expecting the immediate collapse of the rock. After a while he began to search through the silt with his gloves. With lumbering movements, he managed to squeeze his way through.

After the bottleneck, the tunnel widened again. He had to hurry now. Maybe the Dyke Divers' tunnel and this one would converge again, just a bit ahead? Surely he had gone another ninety or hundred yards in just a few minutes. Hundred twenty, hundred thirty. It shouldn't be long before he reached the surface, because the upward slope was still just as pronounced.

He was so busy keeping an eye on the narrowing walls that he didn't realized until it was almost too late that he was about to swim into an iron door. It was completely rusty, with gaping holes, and it hung from the tunnel wall on crooked hinges. Through one of the openings he could see the bolt that kept the door from opening.

Erik let his light play over the brittle brown metal . . . and what was that? A lime deposit?

He swam a little closer.

No . . . not lime. White lines of chalk. Someone had written large, shaky letters, an incomprehensible word:

NIFLHEIM

Niflheim . . . maybe it was the name of the mine itself?

Erik placed the fingers of his diving glove against the rusty surface and gave it a careful nudge.

The door moved, if only a bit.

He pushed harder, and through the water he could hear the hinges creak.

Erik took a deep breath from the regulator. Then he pressed both of his diving gloves against the door and pushed with all his might.

Creaking, it swayed suddenly as the hinges came loose from their attachments. As it fell it swirled up a cloud of mud, and the water turned brown.

He pushed himself forward, but didn't see the stairs that rose behind the iron door and when his forehead hit the bottom steps, the diving mask was wrenched off and the regulator torn out of his mouth. The sudden cold gave him such a shock that he immediately swallowed water in a choking gulp. He started to fumble blindly for his backup hose, but couldn't find it. With his eyes shut tight, Erik flailed about and his lungs burned for air.

Air—

He desperately raised his head up and was suddenly above the surface of the water again. Snorting, spitting, and when he instinctively inhaled through his mouth and nose: that nauseating stench.

He hyperventilated so that he wouldn't fall forward and immediately throw up, and then crawled up the last few steps of the stairs and collapsed; just breathe through your mouth, just through your mouth now . . .

When his breathing calmed, he rolled over on his back and rested, until he slowly managed to sit up.

Erik noticed that he had dropped the lifeline that indicated the path back to the original shaft. He had no energy to return. The water must clear up first.

The smell of rotting made it hard to think.

He pulled off his fins and the mask, which had ended up hanging around his neck. The continuation of the mine tunnel ran away into a nightlike darkness, narrow and damp. He stood up on his reinforced-rubber dive shoes and started to walk.

The ore was even and regular where the tunnel had been burned out of the rock. The tunnel branched off suddenly, and he went to the right. Then there was another branch, but here the right side was filled with rocks. Left this time, then, and then right again when it branched into three. But it was a dead end, so back out to the fork. Which tunnel had he actually come from? At a loss, he stood in the smell of decay and death.

He moved, bent forward, farther and farther into the labyrinth. There were no longer any signs of mining in the tunnel, only clusters of stalactites that hung down from the tunnel's low ceiling. It was cold, a bitter cold that penetrated even the three-layer laminate of the dry suit.

What if he never made it up again? How long would it take before someone wondered where he was? Would anyone start looking for him? Erik Hall hit the tunnel wall with his glove and the beam of light wavered.

Mom had been gone for a long time, and for some reason it struck him to think about what he would leave behind in the lonely cottage. The extent of his fame: three old newspaper clippings.

One of the blurbs, a few inches long, said that he had scored eleven points for his school basketball team in a game long ago. The second was a picture from when the local paper had visited Dala Electric, although he was a little bit hidden from sight in that one. Then there was the achievement itself: a short quote from the big evening paper, when they had done a summer report on the mine in Falun. In that one he'd actually gotten his whole face in. He suddenly remembered: Dyke Divers; he couldn't forget why he was here.

Erik stopped.

This really must be the end. He looked at his depth gauge, which showed an inconceivable depth of 696 feet. Over 150 feet farther down than the girls, and he had done it without help from anyone.

He took out the spray can with stiff, frozen fingers and shakily sprayed another set of initials: E-H, 212 METERS. Then he thought for a second and added: AD EXTREMUM—at the limit.

He took a few pictures with his underwater camera and then let the light of his headlamp sweep over the tunnel walls. There was something there—

He took a step closer.

Another door? He really ought to turn back.

Yes, it was another iron door, the same kind, the same bolt, this one on the inside, too. The same . . . chalk?

NÁSTRÖNDU

The thick air streamed into his lungs. Náströndu?

He gave the door a light push.

It immediately gave way, swinging wide open on screeching hinges.

When Erik got control of his breathing again, he finally dared to move forward and peek in.

A stairway wound steeply downward, just behind the door.

*Ten extra minutes.*

He set the timer on his dive watch and his rubber shoes squeaked as he took a first step.

The stairway formed a tight spiral, as coil after coil led him deeper and deeper. At the opening at the end was a large cave, surely sixty feet high.

There was a slow drip of water that fell down into an overflowing pool. In the middle of this pool rose a stone, and on top of the stone was something that resembled a sack.

The air was heavy to breathe; it flowed like mud and the smell was worse than ever.

*Just a quick lap around, and some pictures.*

He tried to move as silently as possible, but the scraping of the gravel echoed through the cave. He stopped to calm himself down and listened to the drops that were falling.

The light from his forehead swept over the walls. A vein of copper glimmered to the right, all the way up to the ceiling of the cave.

Erik gave a start when he saw something that resembled an arch-shaped opening to the left. But when he came closer and let his glove glide over the hard surface of the rock, he realized that he had only been tricked by the play of shadows. He shone the light to the left once more and then . . . but there *was* something there! The same shaky lines of chalk—but this time whoever had written them had striven for more than isolated words.

Erik could barely decipher the writing. He took out his camera. It flashed, and he looked disbelievingly at its screen.

On his way back to the stairs, it occurred to him that perhaps he could take a souvenir with him. Something from that sack, maybe, the one sitting over there on the rock in the pool . . . ? He waded out into the waist-high water. When he finally reached the sack he saw that it was covered with something that looked like a moldy net.

Erik took off his gloves in order to get hold of it.

The net was a wet, slippery tangle of gray and black strings. He tried to lift them away and caught sight of an entangled object. He grasped its shaft of shining white metal.

But he couldn't get the shaft loose; it seemed to be attached. He felt farther up along the sleek surface and encountered three tied ropes.

Erik took out the titanium knife and cut through the first rope fastening. It snapped. Snapped? Was the rope so old that it had become petrified?

He took hold of the second tie and made another cut. Another sharp snap, and now the whole sack started to move. Despite the cold, Erik felt a wave of feverish warmth. He cut off the third tie and let out his breath.

When the shaft came loose, he thought at first that it looked like an unusually long key. But when the light from his headlamp ran along the object, he realized that it was actually some sort of cross. It had a shaft and a crossbar, but above the crossbar there was an eye. It shone white in the darkness and had the oval shape of a noose.

With his bare hand, Erik grasped the mess of strings and tried to pull them aside to get to the contents of the sack. The strings seemed to be sewn on, so he got a solid grasp and pulled.

It was too late by the time he realized he had used too much force. With his tug, the whole sack came up into his arms, and he fell over under its weight. His head disappeared under the icy water of the pool. When he finally managed to sit up again, a twisted face stared at him in the light from his headlamp.

Paper-thin skin was drawn tight around the dead eyes of a woman, and above the bridge of her nose, in her forehead, gaped a hole as large as a coin.

Then he felt the three cut-off stumps under the water. Those weren't ties he had cut off, they were the fingers of the woman's hand. He instinctively tried to move backward, but her head followed him as though she were a rag doll. He pulled back again and realized that the strings he was holding were the corpse's hair.

And when he breathed in through his nose, the odor of the body was apparent through the stench. The woman smelled like blood and iron and the summer warmth of barn walls. A smell that Erik could place at once. She smelled like Falu red paint.

# 2

# *Dalakuriren*

*Dalakuriren* was a newspaper with hearty feature columnists and caustic political columnists, but when it came to news, it definitely did not have the leading editorial team in the country. Still, the news director had some degree of lingering aptitude: He could answer the telephone.

The tip had come in at three thirty on Sunday afternoon, just when writing fluff articles from the towns of Gagnef and Hedemora felt most hopeless.

The crackling cell phone line had made it difficult to understand details, but the main message from the freelance photographer calling in the tip had been simple: This was the story of a lifetime. In broad terms, the story was about—at least as the news director understood it—some girl (*a teenager?*) who had been found dead (*a sex murder?*) in a mine shaft (*a spectacular sex murder?*).

The person who had found the body and called the police—apparently some sort of diver, according to the freelance photographer—had managed to rattle off a whole series of numbers before the connection was broken, numbers that the operators had finally been able to interpret as GPS coordinates. And now the better part of Dalarna's rescue teams were set in motion, out toward the location in the forest: three police patrols, a command car, two ambulances, plus the fire department, and with any luck, also some officials from the Mining Inspectorate, who knew all that stuff about mines.

After a frustrated lap through the Sunday-empty editorial office to find a reporter who could go, the news director found *Dalakuriren*'s extra resource—a lanky intern from Stockholm.

Two minutes of conversation later, the intern had tumbled away down the stairs with the yellowed newsbills, out to the staff cars in the courtyard.

The news director said a silent prayer and then set a course back to his desk. Which other papers had received the tip? He half ran past the rows of pale gray editing screens where tomorrow's paper had already begun to take shape. Which pages would need to be redone? The front page, of course—but after that: Was this just a Falun thing, or would it turn out to be something really big that made it onto the national pages?

He began to write the short text for the Web edition of *Dalakuriren*. This would be snatched up right away by TT, the Swedish news agency, he knew it. The red TT flash would then set all the other papers in motion, and at first, people everywhere would cite *Dalakuriren*'s report:

**BREAKING NEWS OUTSIDE FALUN:**
**MURDER VICTIM FOUND 700 FEET UNDERGROUND**

⁎

With the phone clamped between his shoulder and cheek, the intern skidded onto the forest road just south of Falun. The gravel from the freelance photographer's car sprayed up in front of him. It was hard to drive and listen at the same time, but soon the intern understood the photographer's directions; their destination was apparently some sort of rest stop.

Finally a straight stretch opened out, and when he saw the flashing lights far ahead, he realized that he had found the right place.

Several picnic tables had been turned over into the ditch and lay there with their built-in benches, looking like upside-down beetles. The police must have cleared them away to make room for all the rescue vehicles. The rows of vehicles had been forced to park so tightly that the hoods of the ambulances almost blocked the forest road. A bit farther on, the fire department's ladder trucks stood tilting down into the shoulder, and only after the intern had turned past them did he find a place to park.

The intern yelled and waved to the freelance photographer to get out of his car, and with squelching shoes they entered the gloom of the spruce forest. Soon they could hear the police German shepherds just ahead of them, and all they had to do was follow the barking through the thick fog.

The mine shaft was already cordoned off; thin fluttering plastic tape blocked off the better part of the clearing around it. At the edge of the shaft stood half a dozen policemen and a few firemen, engaged in what seemed to be a muddled discussion about what should be done next.

Behind them sat a lone figure on a boulder. The floodlights that the rescue crew had aimed at the shaft made the black dry suit shine. His diving hood was off; his rough, craggy face was red; his eyes were swollen when he looked in the intern's direction.

The freelance photographer nudged the intern in the side, and the intern gathered his courage, bent down, and slid under the plastic tape.

"You're the one who found her, huh?"

At first it didn't seem as though the diver understood the question. He just sat quietly for a moment and looked down at his big hands, but then he nodded stiffly.

"What happened down there?" the intern whispered, as he sneaked a look over at a nearby policeman.

"Something . . . something completely hellish, I think," the diver answered.

The intern imagined a pale, naked body, a girl sprawled in claustrophobic darkness. He couldn't help breathing a little faster. "So . . . how old was she?"

"How old? Well, I don't know."

The diver squinted uncertainly as their eyes met.

"The body was like a little girl's. Completely soft, just as if she were still alive. And she didn't actually weigh much. It was just that I slipped as I was lifting her, so she ended up on top of me. She had something in . . ."

"What did she look like, did she have any injuries?"

"Long hair . . ."

The diver waved, an attempt to explain with his hand.

"It was like a tangle in front of her face. I grabbed it, because I thought it was a bunch of loose strings."

"But did she have any injuries?"

"Yes, yes! There was like a hole above her eyes . . . it was . . ."

A flash from the camera; the freelance photographer had crouched down a few yards away. For the first time, the diver looked at the intern with definite interest, and a twitch appeared in the corner of his mouth.

"Hey . . . is this going in the paper?"

At the editorial office, the news director started to type the intern's quote.

**BREAKING NEWS: GIRL RAPED, MURDERED IN MINE SHAFT**
**THE DIVER'S OWN WORDS**

"You can add 'only in *Dalakuriren*,'" said the intern, because now he could see that the police were guiding the large diver into the forest.

The ambulance personnel followed after them with their stretchers empty.

Then came a period of contented waiting. *Dalakuriren* hadn't only been first, it had also gotten furthest with the story.

The intern and the freelance photographer had set up camp next to the trunk of a pine, where they tried to huddle together to protect themselves from the evening chill. And now a number of other teams began to gather in the dark. Swedish Radio and TT were there; the evening papers, of course; and next to the floodlights, TV4 and state channel affiliates had set up their cameras and tripods. Now and then the reporters went up to the rescue commander next to the stinking hole in order to update their reports, but the information kept changing.

First it was one of the local sport diving clubs that was going to help remove the murdered person from the shaft. Then the matter was passed along to the recovery divers from the coast guard in Härnösand. But at seven thirty, some high-up official in Stockholm must have happened to turn on the TV, because suddenly a special group from the National Task Force was supposed to solve the problem. Even though the Stockholmers had ordered a helicopter, it was easily three hours before they were on the scene. At that point, it was already a little past eleven o'clock.

Up till then, all the media outlets had had to cite *Dalakuriren* and the intern's short interview. *Dalakuriren*'s assistant editor-in-chief had placed a basket of celebratory pastries on the news director's table.

Once the task force had arrived in their black combat suits, the scene was transformed. The rescue command from Falun had to move away from the shaft, there were new cordons, and heavy boxes made of reinforced plastic were lined up on the yellow grass next to the edge of the mine's entry. The Stockholm divers checked their oxygen tanks, and the TV cameras captured how fit bodies slid into rubber and neoprene.

The Falun police stood like spectators with their arms crossed as the first pair of divers started to lower themselves into the mine, and when they reemerged, there was no time for them to react before the National Task Force commander arranged his own improvised press conference. The journalists gathered in a flock around him under the floodlights. The freelance photographer held up the camera with his arms straight up, aimed it down, and got a picture of someone with close-cropped hair, whose face was furrowed and resolute.

"Okay, listen. Let's get some things clear," said the commander. "We understand that some of you from the media have started to issue reports before you even know what we're dealing with."

"Are we supposed to ask permission or something?" interrupted a reporter from the state channel, which had done live reports based on *Dalakuriren*'s information at 6:00, 7:30, and 9:00.

A guy from the big evening paper also became angry:

"What we're dealing with? What do you mean what we're dealing with? We're dealing with a woman who was murdered way down in a mine shaft, and that's all we've said. That's what the guy who found her said."

"Well, listen," said the commander. "I don't know how you all got that information. But let's start from the beginning. For one thing, that's no woman down there in the shaft."

The journalists squirmed.

"Like I said, not a woman. It's a man."

The intern felt something cold trickle down his spine. Then he heard himself protesting: "But it was a girl! That's what he said, the guy who found her."

"I don't know who *you've* been talking to," the commander said curtly, "but the body down there, it's a man. And that man has been dead for several days, maybe longer, maybe *much* longer. So this is what will happen. Before our divers bring up the body, it will be wrapped, so that we can safeguard forensic evidence. You should all try to remember that none of us knows anything about *why* this man is dead. According to our divers, there's nothing that points to a murder."

"Is there anything that indicates it isn't one, then?" ventured the intern. The commander's jaw tightened, and it looked like he was planning to answer. But then he wrapped up instead:

"That's all, thanks, and you guys should try to keep to the facts from now on. We're going to move our cordon out into a circle of about two hundred yards, out of respect for any next of kin. So you can start packing up."

But, despite the blockades, the next morning both of the country's evening papers showed the picture: a man's corpse being lifted out of a mine shaft, wrapped up to the chin in the task force's body bag. His long hair framed a bloodless face, and the flash from the camera had illuminated the whitened strands into a wreath of light, like a halo. But what the buyers of this issue would presumably remember most was the deep notch that had been cut just above the bridge of the man's nose like a third eye socket.

# 3

# The Æsir Murder

It had been a very quiet morning meeting at *Dalakuriren*'s long center table as they worked through the list of potential follow-ups and, more important, decided who would do the job.

No one had said anything about the mix-up with the girl; that kind of whispering took place around the paper's coffee machines. Along with the whispers about how the intern from Stockholm would be allowed to continue shadowing the police investigation.

But it didn't really matter who took care of the reports from now on, because by now the evening papers had flown in their teams, and *Dalakuriren* would soon be left behind.

Erik Hall, the diver, lived in a summer cottage outside of Falun. From the road, the intern could glimpse the barred windows of the sunporch, but in order to get closer, he would have to pass a fence as high as his chest. And a weasel-like figure with a brown leather jacket was standing guard just inside the gate. It looked as though the Weasel was writing something on a piece of cardboard, printed letters in red marker: PLEASE SHOW RESPECT! PRIVATE PROPERTY! Then he wedged the cardboard into the gate and ran back toward the porch, where a door opened up and closed behind his narrow back.

By the time the other media had found their way to Hall's cottage, the exclusive story had already been sold. The diver wasn't answering the telephone or letting any other journalist inside.

Instead they had to sit and brood outside the fence for an hour or so, until at last the Weasel came slinking out from the sunporch with his photographer on his heels. All the cameras flashed as they tried to get a picture of the diver's shadow behind the windows, but no one had any luck.

On his way out through the fence, the Weasel waved happily at his competition and ran off toward his car; and just as he passed the intern he whispered the words "special issue."

The new papers came out at four that same day. The exclusive interview with Erik Hall and the write-up of the murder made it onto the big evening paper's newsbill, plus the front page and pages six, seven, eight, nine, ten, eleven, twelve, thirteen, fourteen, fifteen, sixteen, seventeen, eighteen, and the center spread.

The first page was almost coal-black with ink: a dark, pixelated photograph that depicted the shaky chalk marks at the bottom of the mine shaft. To be on the safe side, the quote in the picture had also been written out in plain text, both in Old Norse and in translation:

UM RAGNARÖKKR

Sal veit ek standa sólu fjarri
Náströndu á, Norðr horfa dyrr
Falla eitrdropar inn of ljóra
Sá er undinn salr orma hryggjum

Skulu þar vaða þunga strauma
Menn meinsvara ok morðvargar

ON RAGNARÖK

I know a hall that stands far from the sun
On the shore of the dead. The doors face north.
Drops of venom fall in through the smoke-hole.
This hall is braided with the backs of snakes.

Perjurers and outlawed murderers
Must wade through heavy streams there.

The headline on page six:

**WELCOME TO HELL**

Page seven:

**NIFLHEIM—THE KINGDOM OF HEL**

Page eight:

**SACRIFICED IN A PAGAN RITUAL?**

Nine:

**NÁSTRÖNDU—THE HALL OF MURDERERS**

And so on, and then a big lead-in to the introductory article:

> FALUN—His life ended on the shore of the dead.
>
> The wound between his eyes must have been made with brutal force and precision. Three fingers on the right hand have been cut off.
>
> On the north wall of the crypt, in white chalk, the murderer has drawn the door to Niflheim—the kingdom of Hel, the Nordic goddess of death. Hel's Kingdom. Hell. The underworld.
>
> The mystery that the police must now solve: Was it a human sacrifice?
>
> Read an exclusive interview with diver Erik Hall, 38, who reveals the truth about the ÆSIR MURDER.

The other evening paper was reasonably quick to respond and actually managed to produce a whole new thirty-six page supplement for the next morning.

**RITUAL MURDER IN MINE**

*The bloody religion—the victims and rites of the Æsir faith*

The most hard-hitting subject matter featured a survey of pagan churches around the country and their potential links to extreme-right and neo-Nazi groups.

That same morning, the TV4 sofa went nuts over the mythological angle, while the state channel's morning program let two New Age ladies explain that the Æsir faith involved sacrificing only fruit, flowers, and bread nowadays, and anyway, they said, the correct name was *Forn Sed.* Then a professor of criminology came on and gave a warning about jumping to conclusions, making the point that most murders were committed by people close to the victim. Then came the weather.

At *Dalakuriren,* the mood had become rather subdued. They'd been the lead, but now they were spinning their wheels. Æsir murder? Was there even such an expression? Who knew anyone of the Æsir faith in Falun, or for that matter in Grycksbo or Bengtsheden?

The intern from Stockholm and the other reporters had called every contact they had at the Falun police to find out more about the investigation. But at the police station over on Kristinegatan Street they just pressed their lips together in anger over the unfortunate publication of that crazy verse and the words Niflheim and Náströndu.

The next morning, the state channel dropped its skeptical stance and joined the ranks of the tabloids. They had somehow managed to shake the diver Erik Hall out of that cottage, and they'd flown him down to Stockholm for a studio interview.

At Hall's side on the red cushions of the morning show sofa sat a grayish academic named Don something . . . Titelman? The intern had to rewind the clip on his computer to be able to read the name displayed. Yes, Don Titelman, associate professor of history, Lund University.

But there didn't seem to be anything new when Erik Hall once again told the story of his remarkable dive down into the mine, so the intern fast-forwarded through Titelman's long-winded exposé, in which he seemed to want to trace the neo-Nazis' fascination with Norse mythology back to the Thule Society and someone called Karl Maria Wiligut.

Just another boring expert, thought the intern, and he slunk disappointedly down the stairs to *Dalakuriren*'s morning meeting.

# 4

# Bubbe

There was only one person Don Titelman had loved completely and unconditionally, and that was his grandmother, his *yidishe* Bubbe. She was the first person who had treated him seriously. And he remembered that he had felt chosen when, for the first time, she had turned to him as a confidant. He had been only eight years old then.

*

Bubbe's 1950s house, with its scent of mothballs, stuffy closets, and rotting seaweed, was Don's memory of summer. Neglectful, his workaholic parents were in the habit of dumping him there in Båstad as early as the beginning of June and then reluctantly bringing him back to Stockholm again in September. He was usually at least two weeks late for the beginning of the school year.

The house had been in shabby shape. The plaster on the front had fallen off in large chunks, and her yard had slowly become covered in rotting fruit, which neither of them had the energy to pick. His excuse had been laziness, but for Bubbe it had been her legs, which couldn't carry her anymore.

The last few summers, she couldn't even manage to go up the house's only staircase, and Don had had the whole top floor to himself. Despite the dust and the boarded-up windows, it had been better to sleep there than downstairs, because during the night Bubbe had never found any peace.

He had listened to her monotonous ritual every night from the bedroom above the stairs. First those creaking steps on the parquet, then the heavy sigh that revealed that she had sunk down into the corduroy sofa. She would usually sit there for a while, and he knew she would lean forward and let her fingers run along the scars and pits on her calves. Then the sound when she once again got up, and then another creaking lap around the room, a sigh, and the squeak of the feathers as the sofa welcomed her for another bit of rest.

And then it started over again, making up the rhythm that had rocked him to sleep every night.

She had been transported to Ravensbrück in July 1942, where the medical experiments had already begun.

The SS doctors had wanted to test the germicidal effects of sulfa powder on severe infections that followed gunshot wounds. They had said that the experiments would help the German armed forces and therefore must be very realistic. The first guinea pigs had been fifteen camp prisoners, all men.

The doctors had cut open their calf muscles, from the tendons of their heels up to their knees. Then they had rubbed a solution of gangrene bacteria into the wounds in order to start a nasty infection. The bacteria had been cultivated by Hygiene-Institut der Waffen-SS, the Schutzstaffel's institute of hygiene. The thought behind cutting up only the lower part of the men's legs was to make it possible to have time to amputate at the knee once the gangrene started to spread.

The open wounds had been dusted with sulfa powder and then sewn up. Curious, the SS doctors had waited to see what would happen, but soon they had to declare that the wounds healed far too quickly. Experiments didn't mimic what happened on the front lines at all, and the conclusion was that they hadn't tried hard enough.

So they had formed a new experimental group, this time of about sixty women. All of them had been young, under thirty, and one of those chosen had been Don's grandmother, his Bubbe. The concentration camp doctors had cut deep into both of her calves, from the tendons of her heels up to her knees. To make the injury similar to battle wounds, they hadn't only rubbed gangrene bacteria into the wounds; they also pressed in shards of glass, dirt, and sawdust.

Bubbe's legs had swollen up with pus, and she had lain in feverish dreams that not even the screams of the other women had been able to wake her from. But then the sulfa powder had begun to work, and after a few days, it had become obvious that none of the women would die of their infections. Thus the experiment had still not been sufficiently realistic.

The head doctors, Oberheuser and Fischer, had then traveled away to a weekend conference in Berlin, where they discussed their failed attempts with colleagues.

The German doctors had soon agreed that bacteria, glass shards, dirt, and sawdust were not enough. One must also cut off the flow of blood. In the case of actual gunshot wounds, they had noticed, several of the most important blood vessels were always injured. When they cut open the legs in this controlled manner, the blood had still been able to flow, something that had presumably prevented the gangrene from getting a deadly grip.

The first suggestion had been to simply shoot the women in the legs with machine guns. At least in that case, the experiment would not lack realism. But after a certain amount of deliberation, they had criticized that as a less practicable method. The women's wounds would presumably differ and thus not be completely scientifically comparable.

Instead someone came up with the idea of securing rubber bands around the women's ankles and under their knees after cutting open the calves again. In that way they could completely cut off the blood supply to the gashed calf muscle, and the conditions would be favorable for gangrene.

This had proved to be an accurate analysis.

Five of the women in Bubbe's group had quickly developed gangrene, which wandered up from their legs toward their upper bodies. And although they were so young, in their twenties, their bodies had given up after only a few days.

One of them had lain tossing and turning on a cot near Bubbe's. Don's grandmother had told him about how that woman's legs were transformed into swollen columns bursting with bloody pus. During the night her blood vessels had completely eroded, her skin peeled away, and the gangrene spread up to her thighs and genitals.

Even if one of the SS doctors had been awake, there wouldn't have been time to amputate. In the morning, they had made the last medical notations, and then they took the woman out of the ward to shoot her. But for Bubbe it had been *ein shrekleche zach,* a horrible thing, that she hadn't even bothered to protest; she had only felt immense relief over being rid of the woman's horrid odor.

In late fall of 1942, the SS doctors in Ravensbrück began to tire of their experiments with sulfa powder and gangrene.

Instead they decided to turn to new experiments, ones involving plastic surgery. The goal had been to invent new methods that could be used to make the wounded German soldiers more presentable after the war was over.

There had been several different experiments: from cutting off and transplanting parts of muscles and bone to prolonged investigations of how quickly one could get a broken bone or a damaged nerve to heal. Don's grandmother and the other surviving women from the gangrene experiments were useful here, too.

With Bubbe, the German doctors had cut off strips of her calf muscles, all the way to the bone, to see if the tissue might regenerate naturally. The result had been a disappointment.

Then they had broken her tibia in four places to see how fast the skeleton could heal. The nurses had been careful with the cast. After several weeks had passed and the bone had almost grown together, the cast was opened and the results recorded. After that they had rebroken the healed places so that the experiment could continue.

At first Bubbe had received low doses of morphine, but toward the end, when the situation in Ravensbrück had become more and more chaotic, anesthetics were often forgotten. But still she had been lucky, *sach mazel;* she always wanted to emphasize that.

One of the women in the group had had one shoulder blade removed in some type of transplant experiment, and after that, she had never again been able to raise her arm above shoulder height. Others had had entire body parts cut off: a fully functioning arm along with the shoulder and clavicle, a young woman's thigh that was cut off up to the top of her hip bone. A Polish woman—Bubbe had seen it herself—had had both of her cheekbones removed, so that her face had collapsed completely.

Each experiment, as would later be demonstrated at the Nuremburg trials, completely lacked any medical value.

In the last year of the war, in the spring, the Red Cross buses had arrived from Sweden to rescue concentration camp survivors. Bubbe had been one of those whose back was marked with a big white cross. She had been taken to Padborg, and from there on to Öresund. On April 26, 1945, she had been carried off the Helsingborg ferry on a stretcher. At that time she was twenty-eight years old. It took three years before she was able to walk on her own again, and the cavities in her legs had always remained. Along both of her calves ran the gnarled scars. As an eight-year-old, Don had been allowed to feel them with his fingers, and he had thought they were like the branches of a dying tree.

Each summer had continued in the same way, while the apples rotted in the yard. She had told her story in a muddled mixture of Yiddish and Swedish, and he had listened, because he loved his grandmother. She had called him *mayn nachesdik kind,* my treasure, my happiness, while the Germans were *yener goylem,* people who lacked souls.

When she got tired of her own stories, she told him about the mass executions in Lublin or the carbon monoxide gassings in Sobibor, about Zyklon B in Treblinka and Auschwitz or the high-altitude experiments in Dachau, where the SS doctors dissected the brain tissue of living people to see if it was possible to see the air bubbles in their blood.

And each story had been stored in Don's memory like razor-sharp shards. But no matter how deeply the stories had marked him, they were not his most frightening memory of Bubbe's 1950s house.

On the top floor one summer's day, he had happened to open the cupboard that contained his grandmother's hidden collection. There had lain worn leather cases with the Schutzstaffel's symbol, a dagger with the *Wolfsangel* symbol, and bronze medallions with the pinwheel cross of the swastika. She had bought yellowed portraits of Gestapo and Wehrmacht officers and several copies of the Schutzstaffel Honor Ring for herself. Under the pile of Nazi symbols was a large crystal plate on which someone had engraved Himmler's black sun, *die schwarze Sonne.* Its twelve rays twisted out like tentacles, and Don thought it looked as though the tentacles were searching for him to suck him in.

In a box he had found the auction newspapers, with her purchases circled in red ink. He never dared to ask her why she had brought this sickness into her own home and didn't know whether Bubbe would have been able to give him an answer.

To him the cupboard with its ominous objects became a whirlpool of darkness, from where the horror of her past flowed freely into his present. For hours he would stare into this abyss, spellbound by Himmler's black sun, until there was no longer any distance between Ravensbrück and himself.

Back home in Stockholm, Don had not dared talk about the collection or about Bubbe's whispered stories. He had written some of them down in the colorful notebook that his elementary school teacher had handed out. But he had never let anyone read them, and with time her words settled deeper and deeper. The summer he turned eleven, Don had refused to go back to the house in Båstad. He had a baby sister, and he didn't want, or dare, to be alone with Bubbe and her ghostly cupboard anymore. His dad and mom had pleaded with him, but finally they had let him stay home in Enskede with his own key. And so it was eleven-year-old Don who answered the telephone when they called from the hospital down in Skåne to say that Bubbe was dead.

After that moment, Bubbe sank away into the great silence. Her house had quickly been sold, and Don's dad hadn't said a word about the Nazi symbols or the cupboard.

It had been as if his dad—now that Bubbe was finally gone—had seen an opportunity to transform them into a family without a history. He had forbidden books about the Holocaust, and if anything about the war was on TV, it was immediately turned off.

The silence about Bubbe metastasized with time, until life in the house in Enskede had consisted only of squeaks from solitary silverware and monosyllabic conversations.

In the end, living at home had been like drowning, and Don, in a hurry to get out, had left his sister behind.

Perhaps it was a strange choice, considering Bubbe's stories, but right after secondary school, Don decided to study to be a doctor. He found he needed to devote himself to something practical, or else he could easily slip away, losing the boundary between reality and dreams.

He had completed his education without taking any notes. He immediately memorized what was said in the lectures, and he had hardly needed to open his books before he could recite them from cover to cover. After his internship, he first tried to specialize in surgery, but he had fainted when it came time to cut with the sharp blade of the scalpel. Instead he chose to devote himself to psychiatry, and that was when he finally found the drugs that could soothe and heal the shards of his own memory. They could at least temporarily stop the stories that had continued to consume him since he was eight.

At first Don tried only small doses of sleeping pills and mild tranquilizers, but after a few years he had switched to benzodiazepines and morphine. Just before he turned thirty, he had become so dependent that they kicked him out of the department of psychiatry at Karolinska Hospital. The fact that he later managed, in the early 1990s, to secure a position at the hospital in Karlskrona may have been due to the shortage of doctors and that they neglected to call his references. It was on a cloudy August day in that sleepy town that he first met the brownshirts from the National Socialist Front.

He had read in the local paper about the young men who used the *heil* greeting and yelled about a vigorous Sweden. But it hadn't been until he ran into them himself, up by the apartment buildings in Galgamarken, that he confronted the stories face-to-face.

The neo-Nazis had been handing out brochures with the yellow Vasa sheaf on them, but on their flags fluttered the swastika. The SS symbol, the iron cross, and the German eagle were all raised toward Blekinge's rain-heavy clouds. The black sun stretched its tentacles toward him from one of the largest streamers. While he told himself it was only a graphic symbol, for him, on that day, it was as if Bubbe's cupboard had flung open again. From its whirlpool of darkness gushed the streams of all his fears, and at that moment he knew he would never be free.

He had sunk down into a crouch on the grass, cradling his head in his hands, his heart clenched. And then, when he leaned forward on his fingertips, he could feel how the very ground beneath him began to tremble. In the next moment everything around him went dim, as he was drenched by the wave of unrestrained memories and pain.

# 5

# Copper Vitriol

The intern from Stockholm looked down at the floor, hunched his shoulders as much as he could, and then took a circuitous route past the bathrooms in order to avoid walking past the permanent reporters' corridor.

The morning meeting at *Dalakuriren* had been agony. One of the oldest pros from the crime office had cast the first stone.

"I'm ashamed," he had said, holding up the intern's thin four-columner.

Then everyone around the table, except for the news director, started picking on him.

Where were his own leads and ideas? Why hadn't the intern gotten hold of a good police source? Why hadn't he gotten further with the part about neo-Nazis and the Æsir faith—it was day four now, after all. And why, why, why hadn't he gotten an interview with Erik Hall himself?

Impossible?

Really? Well, this morning that diver sat on a *TV sofa* and told them about everything that happened. So it really couldn't be completely impossible, could it?

The intern had sat there staring at his coffee mug and hadn't dared to say anything, fearing that his voice would break. In the end even the lady with the smoker's cough from the family pages had joined in and declared how embarrassing it was that an inexperienced intern had been put on the country's hottest story, and that she'd heard that even the free papers in the Stockholm subway had produced more unique information about the Æsir murder.

"And they don't even have their own *reporter* on site here in Falun," she had concluded.

After he'd slunk away from the morning meeting, the intern had shut the door to his own office and fallen into his swivel chair. He felt like he was going to throw up. Reluctantly he realized that he should probably give up, and went to go tell the news director.

The director was on the balcony smoking. When he saw the intern walking toward him, he held up a small piece of blue paper against the glass. On the paper was a scribbled telephone number. The news director's mouth let out a puff of smoke and then formed one word: "Call."

The intern sat dejectedly at the edge of the desk, pulled the beige push-button phone out of the mess, and dialed the number. After a few rings, a sharp, piercing voice answered.

"So *you* were the one who wrote the article in today's *Dalakuriren*? Well, you can expect anything at all from the evening papers . . . but that our own *morning paper* would start speculating about murders and Nazism and pagan rituals and I don't know what else . . . that is truly deplorable."

The intern mumbled something about how it was unfortunate that the reader thought so, but there *were* those lines about Niflheim and Náströndu and not least, a murdered guy in a mine.

"A 'guy,' you say," said the surly voice.

"Yes, that part in particular is something the police have made quite clear," said the intern.

"Now, it just so happens that I *know* someone who has actually seen this 'guy' you're talking about," said the voice.

The intern clutched the phone to his ear and grabbed a coffee-stained notebook.

"You . . . you mean you know someone who's seen the murder victim? Does he know who it is, can he identify the man, is it someone from Falun?"

"Well, I *really* have no intention of going into any details, but you can think of it as a tip in case you're entrusted with writing more about this in the future. I have a friend, a *close* friend, who happens to be a *pathologist* at Falu Hospital. And from what he's said about the autopsy of the 'guy,' this case is totally unique. Or more accurately: The case is *almost* unique."

"I don't really understand what you mean."

"Vitriol," said the voice.

"Sorry?"

"Copper vitriol."

The intern wrote down the words, circled them, and added three question marks.

"Copper vitriol, you said . . . ?"

"You're not even from Dalarna, huh?" the voice said and hung up.

When the news director came back in from the balcony, the intern was still holding the silent phone.

"So what was it about?"

"It was some reader who wanted to talk about copper," said the intern.

"They're fucking nuts, the whole lot, everyone who calls."

"So I . . . ?"

"You've started off with this story, so now handle it."

The first thing the intern did when he returned to his office was try for about the hundredth time to get hold of Erik Hall.

The picture of the diver was all over the Internet now, and every Swedish journalist seemed to have gotten an interview.

Then, on the fifth ring, when he had almost given up:

"Hall?"

"Oh, it's just the local paper. Hey, can't you call later this week, there are so many people calling right now."

"But we would really like . . ."

"Wait, *Dalakuriren* . . . ?" Hall's voice changed. "Weren't you the one who claimed that I had said something about it being a woman down there? A little girl? In that case you don't need to call at all, you with your shitty journalism."

Again the intern was sitting with a silent phone in his hand.

He looked dejectedly down at the first page of the notebook. There, circled in black ink, it just said:

Copper vitriol???

The phrase "copper vitriol" got thirty-three hits in *Dalakuriren*'s index of articles, and apparently it was something you ought to have heard of if you worked at a local paper in Falun.

He began to read the first fragment of a sentence that the search engine had found:

. . . which was found in 1719, well preserved in **copper vitriol**. Fet-Mats was . . .

According to the article, the man's real name had been Mats Israelsson, a twenty-year-old mine worker who had lost his way and disappeared in Great Copper Mountain. It had happened one March evening, just before Easter, when he had just become engaged to a woman named Margareta Olsdotter.

The intern rubbed his temples. In March of 1677, no one had spent much time on large-scale search-and-rescue operations in order to find one isolated missing mine worker. The only one who hadn't given up was Mats's fiancée, Margareta, who would have time to become aged and bent during her search.

She had been waiting for forty-two years when by chance, in 1719, a team of miners had found a dead man at a depth of 480 feet. He had been lying in something called the Mårdskinn shaft, in a hole filled with water and . . . *copper vitriol!*

The intern's eyes came to a halt. He read on:

The deceased had looked as though he had drowned very recently, and his body was still completely soft. Those who had found him were surprised, because no one had been reported missing in the mine recently, and moreover, this particular shaft had been closed off since the great mine collapse of 1687.

Once they had managed to carry him up into the daylight, their confusion increased—no one was able to recognize the dead man's face. What they had before them was a large young man of about twenty, heavy and in good health (other than being dead) and with a body that seemed completely untouched by the passage of time. A week or so later, when there was a mine meeting and the corpse was displayed, an old woman stood up, shaking with sobs.

Margareta Olsdotter had immediately recognized her betrothed, and three of the mine worker's elderly friends also identified the dead man as Mats Israelsson. It had been recorded in the minutes of the mine meeting that the only thing that distinguished the youth who had gone down into the mine in 1677 from the one who had come up in 1719 was his hair, which had continued to grow after his death, meter after meter, shiny, wavy, and black.

"This is starting to seem like García Márquez," the intern mumbled. But at the next paragraph he stiffened.

The key to the puzzle had been *the high levels of copper vitriol* in the air and water in the Mårdskinn shaft.

Copper vitriol had long been known for its ability to preserve lumber—among other things, it was used as an ingredient in Falu red paint. Now it kept a corpse from rotting for forty-two years.

The intern had a dry feeling in his mouth. What was it that the Stockholm policeman had said again? *The deceased has been down in the mine for several days, and maybe much, much longer.* He scrolled further:

Mats Israelsson's body had been so well preserved that it hadn't even decayed when it was lifted to the surface. Year after year, the vitriol-brined skin had remained just as soft. The Royal Board of Mines had become so fascinated with the case that they had exhibited the youthful corpse for general viewing as a matter of curiosity. At first Mats Israelsson had been kept in a barrel; after that, when public pressure had increased, he had been propped up vertically in a glass case. Mats stood there outside the mine, staring at the visitors for thirty years; even the famed "father of taxonomy," Carl Linnaeus, came to see him.

Each year the case had been opened to cut the growing hair on his head, but otherwise the mine worker had been left alone. Finally, in 1749, some kind-hearted clergyman had buried Mats Israelsson's body under the floor inside Stora Kopparberg Church. But . . .

The intern started to feel impatient.

. . . in the beginning of the 1860s, when the church floor was being relaid, Fet-Mats had been found again, his appearance still just as youthful. This time his body was placed in a wooden box and put aside in the main office of the mine. The mine worker stood there collecting dust until 1930. Then he was buried one last time, and was given a granite memorial.

When the body was placed in the coffin, more than 250 years had passed since that March day in 1677, but Mats Israelsson's eyes had still been open and clear. Some said that there was something in his eyes that expressed a vague amazement. Others maintained that the only thing you could see in the miner's eyes had been centuries of sorrow.

The intern added a short sentence in the notebook:

Copper vitriol???

The corpse could have been in the mine for a long time.

In that case, how would the police go about finding out who the murder victim was?

The intern sat for a long time, thinking, chewing his pen until it broke; he sighed at his own incompetence. Then he simply typed the words "post mortem identification" into the search engine on the Net and looked at the hits sullenly.

The first one was about some advice from the Medical Products Agency about identifying unknown tablets and capsules. Scrolled. There, down a bit: "Blood banks help identify victims of tsunami," an old news article. He clicked on it and read:

> An extra session of parliament decided yesterday that the PKU registry may be used to identify Swedes who died in the disaster in Asia. The registry is primarily necessary to identify dead children, who may lack dental records.

*Dental records.* There it was. They searched dental records, of course.

The intern felt his headache fade slightly. Here he actually had his very own source: the dad of an old friend from high school, who ran a private dental practice at Karlaplan, in the posh part of Stockholm.

He dug out the number, called, and ended up at reception. Just after he'd been transferred, he could hear the whistle of a dentist drill slowing down.

"Dental records? Listen . . . we have nothing to do with those. That's handled by specialists at the National Board of Forensic Medicine . . . and I have no idea how far back their registry goes."

His friend's dad sounded a bit stressed.

"So how do you contact the specialists, then?"

The sound of steps, as the dentist walked away from the phone; then a door closed.

"Well . . . you'll have to call them, I guess."

The intern sighed.

"No, wait . . . Listen! There's actually a guy I happen to know a little up at the National Board—he was pretty strange even when we were at school . . ."

"Yes?"

"If you want, maybe I could check with him when I'm finished?"

It was less than half an hour before the dentist called back with an excited voice:

"Listen to this. The Falun police, along with the help of the national police, have requested the dental records of every Swede who has disappeared or been missing all the way back to the midfifties. They haven't had a single match. They also requested help from Interpol for an international search. Nothing there, either. Apparently the National Board has established that it could be a case of a corpse from who knows how far back . . . They said something about the body being really abnormally well preserved. I don't know if I really understood, but it was something about the salts in the mine that stopped the body from rotting; it was only the hair that . . ."

"Did they say anything else?"

The intern had already begun to write.

"Yes, apparently he had pretty strange clothes on too, coarse fabric, a suit with a vest, a shirtfront with a separate collar. No ID or driver's license or loyalty card, nothing. You know, they actually said that the police haven't found a single object made of plastic on that guy. Ivory shirt buttons, pants buttons made of horn, shoe soles that were made of some sort of natural rubber."

"Maybe he'd been kidnapped from a house in Östermalm. Old money and wealth," said the intern with the phone tucked under his chin, writing with both hands now.

# 6

# Up into the Light

The next morning—*Dalakuriren*'s leading news:

**DALAKURIREN EXPOSES**
**THE SECRET POLICE INVESTIGATION**

Then came the introduction, with the intern's name in a bold byline:

> FALUN—Today *Dalakuriren* exposes the secret police investigation of the so-called Æsir murder.
>
> According to the police's new theories, the victim has most likely been lying in the mine shaft for a very long time—possibly for centuries.
>
> According to several independent sources, the body of the murder victim has been submerged in the preservative copper vitriol, which has protected the body from decomposition.
>
> Police investigators now assume that this is not an active murder case but rather a crime for which

the statute of limitations has long run out. Officially,
the police do not want . . .

It was still as cold in the clearing as the intern remembered from last time. It was as though the fog and the cold were somehow rising up from the shaft opening itself, followed by the stench of the underworld.

As the rescue-service pump began to work, the nauseating smell became even worse. The horde of journalists began to move back as the water was sucked noisily into the colossal cylinder tank.

At lunchtime the forensics team rappelled down into the drained tunnels and began their work.

Quite soon, as the police spokesman would later explain to the intern and the other journalists, they had come across a pile of newspaper, sticky with copper vitriol.

The pile had been near one of the mine walls in what the evening papers had called the hall of murderers. It was still possible to read one of them; narrow columns with headlines in smeared black type:

**The great German offensive.**
**The advance finally stopped?**
**Only minor progress reported by the Germans.**

Farther down:

**The question of provisions. The rationing plan for next year.**
**A scarcely hopeful statement from the minister of agriculture.**

And on the next page, the entire masthead was still there:

**Southern Dalarna's Newspaper—7 June 1918**

After that, they had begun to suck up the water from the pool around the stone where the diver said he had found the dead man.

In the sand on the bottom they had found a large awl with a broken red handle, and you didn't need an extensive forensic education to realize what had hacked the deep hole in the vitriol-soaked man's forehead.

A few hours later, the police technicians and the journalists would learn that the only prints that could be gathered from the handle had come from the dead man's own fingers.

"So it's not even certain that it was a murder? It could be a *suicide*? It might not even have been a story a hundred years ago?"

The Weasel from the big evening paper was waving his hands as though he couldn't get air. The police spokesman nodded calmly.

"Fucking goddamn Dalarna," said the Weasel, shoving his way out of the press conference to call home.

His editor reserved half a page for the story in the afternoon edition. The other evening paper chose to fill the space with a lighthearted column.

That evening the newspapers called their correspondents home from Falun. Time to pay the hotel bill and come back to Stockholm.

This wasn't front-page news. It was something that could be discussed in science programs and explored on the culture pages—but as an explosive story, the Æsir murder was definitely banished to the archives.

Far, far, *far* back in the archives.

# 7

# A Secret

It was nearly five o'clock on the intern's last day, and there was a send-off for him at *Dalakuriren*'s meeting table. He said his good-byes and sneaked off toward the stairs to the parking garage. When he'd made it halfway, he heard footsteps behind him, then felt the news director's hand on his shoulder. Through labored breaths, the director offered him one last job. The intern had already opened his mouth to say no, when the news director spat out the three crucial syllables: "Erik Hall."

Here's the thing, the news director said when he had managed to catch his breath—that tiresome diver had called time and again the past week, asking what was going to happen with the *Dalakuriren* interview. What was up, were they still interested?

The mine story was dead and buried. But now something for the Saturday supplement had not come through, and there would be a gaping hole between the ads. Maybe the article didn't need to be too long? Just a little weekend profile with the Dala diver who had been in the mass-media limelight for such a short time.

The diver hadn't said anything unexpected, but it was enough to get five thousand characters, one page in *Dalakuriren*'s Saturday section. The intern hadn't planned to put his byline on some portrait of a hero anyway, so now there was just the part about the pictures . . .

The intern turned off his computer and walked with his head held high through the reporters' corridor. He sauntered past the coffee machine and turned left where he found the photographer leaning over an evening paper at the scratched layout table. The photographer was a part-timer just out of high school, hired so that she could gain experience. She had a ponytail and was quite heavily made up, and her childishly round cheeks revealed that she could hardly be twenty years old. The intern asked her to take a few pictures that felt fresh. Nothing with that diving suit that had been in every paper.

The photographer nodded, excited for the opportunity. She heaved the heavy camera case up onto her shoulder, grabbed her denim jacket, and disappeared down toward the staff cars in the parking lot.

*

"Welcome to Svartbäck," said Erik Hall. "You'd like some coffee, right? I've just put some on."

Hall was already waiting for her by the gate to his yard. And now, as they walked along the raked gravel path, the photographer felt the diver's hand on her back. With a firm shove, the hand pressed her up the steps to the glassed-in sunporch.

Inside, behind the barred French windows, she quickly took off her shoes. It felt like something you didn't need to ask about here. The green-painted planks of the floor shone, and from the inside of the cottage came a sharp scent of cleaning products.

The diver showed her to the kitchen. Erik Hall took the pot off, filled two cups, and handed one to the photographer. Then he suggested that she sit on the wooden bench.

Once the photographer had squeezed her way onto it, the diver shoved the oak table toward her, so close that it almost blocked in her legs. He sat down with his legs spread in an armchair on the other side of the table.

She should probably hurry back. But maybe, she thought, it would be worth a few extra minutes of chatting to get the diver in a good mood. Because at first he was really not in high spirits.

Apparently everything had been wrong: The other papers had misquoted him about the technical details of mines and diving, which made Erik Hall appear uninformed. Then, when he had tried to correct them, he had been ignored repeatedly.

And there was more he wanted to say—this was just the beginning. But who was going to listen?

Take *Dalakuriren*, for example. The paper hadn't even bothered to send their reporter here, had they? Journalists were so damned sloppy and completely lacked professionalism.

Then Erik Hall had spoken at length about professionalism, and about how he had worked at an electrical company in Falun that hadn't had the correct attitude either.

The photographer had nodded and agreed until Hall started to ask about her more private circumstances. Then she had pointed at her empty cup and said that she'd like to find a place with good light.

"Well, we can go take a look at the suit; surely you want a picture of that," said Erik Hall.

He shoved the table a bit with the weight of his body so the photographer could manage to wriggle her way out.

In the hall outside the kitchen, the diver unlocked a blue-painted country-style door. It led to a dining room where the afternoon sun was still shining in. Through the row of windows, you could see down toward the grass behind the cottage, which became a pine-wooded slope beyond the yard.

"How lovely," she said.

"Mom was the one who fixed up the whole shack. She and I were always here in the summers. I want it to be like it was then."

The photographer nodded.

"It's a great place. If you go down the hill, you can swim. Sometimes there are too many water lilies and algae, but it's been good this year."

The diving suit was hanging on a hanger by the short wall of the room. It had been hooked up on an open door like a human body without a head.

"That's the one you people usually want me to wear. Shall I?"

He made a motion as though to start taking off his sweater, but the photographer quickly told him not to bother:

"No, you know, this is about you and not the diving, so we want more personal pictures. Maybe from the kitchen, or if you have some place where you usually . . ."

She took hold of the suit and opened the cracked door. It smelled completely different in there; musty. A sagging bed with some glossy magazines spread out on top of soiled sheets and the pale gray light from a computer monitor.

"The kitchen is probably better," said the photographer.

Once again she felt the diver's hand on her back as he led her out.

The light was good in the kitchen. The thin linen of the curtains would work as a filter, perfect for the type of pictures she wanted to take. A bit dreamy, sitting at the kitchen table, Erik Hall with his heavy head leaning on one hand. Personal, that was what the intern had said, after all.

The photographer worked quietly, and for a long time the only sound was of her breathing as she changed position and the rhythmic click from the camera's shutter.

"You seem to know what you're doing, anyway," said the diver.

She gave him a quick smile, just a few more pictures . . .

Hall continued: "Hey . . . there's actually something I could tell you that would change this whole story."

"Mm-hmm," she mumbled, clicking one last time.

"You seem to be a girl who doesn't give it away. You can keep a secret, I mean."

"I see."

She put the cap on the lens and let the camera fall down and hang against her stomach.

"So what is it, then?"

"Well, maybe it's kind of a bit silly, but . . . there were a few things down there in the mine that I didn't . . ."

The diver looked away from her, out through the kitchen window toward the gravel path and the fence around the yard.

"You know, I was in quite a bit of shock when I came up, so I threw everything down into one of my bags. And the police . . . when I came back home, they had just put the bags outside my door. They hadn't opened them, I think, because, you know, the things were still there. They haven't asked any questions, either, and I . . . it just didn't occur to me to tell them. It felt so strange to say something, you know, several days later."

"Oh? Things like those old newspapers that the police found down in the mine, or what?"

Hall sneered. "Aha . . . now it's a little more exciting, huh?"

He looked at her in silence for a long time, and finally she had to look away.

"Wait a second."

The diver got up and disappeared out into the hall. When he came back a few minutes later, he was carrying something that looked like a wine-colored terrycloth towel.

He placed the bundle on the kitchen table and unrolled it slowly. Deep inside the red lay a bone white cross with an eye: a shape the photographer immediately recognized.

"That's one of those ankh-crosses, right?" she said.

Then she wrinkled her forehead.

"But isn't it made of plastic?"

"Plastic? No, no . . ." said Erik Hall.

He held it out to her so that she could feel it. Well, wasn't it made of plastic? Very light, cast in one piece, like a cheap toy.

"The key to the underworld, I've read," he said.

"What?"

"In Egypt, the ankh was also called Osiris's key, the key to the underworld. It's all over the Internet, if you just look."

The photographer bit her lip.

"You're saying that that plastic ankh was down in the mine?"

"It's not a plastic ankh!" the diver hissed. "I found it down there; he was still holding it in his hands."

She looked from the diver to the ankh and back again.

"So that's your secret?"

She noticed that the diver swallowed and that his eyes somehow became shinier.

"Yes, isn't it fantastic?" said the photographer.

But she could hear that this didn't sound very convincing, and the diver didn't seem to think so, either:

"I don't get you journalists. This lends a whole new dimension to everything. What was the ankh doing down there, right?" He placed the object on the towel again and quickly began to wrap it up.

"I will fucking kill you if you say anything about this."

At first the photographer wasn't really sure if she'd heard correctly, but then came a silence that was so uncomfortable that she rushed to pack up.

"It seems like a cool job, though," the diver ventured when they had gone out to the sunporch.

"Indeed," said the photographer.

She put on her tennis shoes and felt in her jacket to find her car keys.

"Hey—" he began.

The photographer turned around in the doorway.

"Couldn't we get together in town sometime, just you and me?"

She smiled quickly, without answering.

Not until she had gotten outside the gate to the fence around the yard did she notice that her hand was trembling as she went to unlock the car. But on her way home, when she called the intern, she still couldn't help telling him about the diver's latest discovery.

# 8

# Northbound E4

The window next to Don's table was greasy, and the odors of reheated children's meals, mini-weenies and meatballs, interfered with the taste of his coffee. Perhaps you had to expect such things if you chose to turn off the European highway to go to a motel restaurant, and anyway, life was essentially a *tsore,* a torment, as Bubbe would have said.

Don had unfolded the printed-out *Dalakuriren* article and placed it beside his tray. He glanced down at the picture of Erik Hall. It wasn't particularly flattering.

After their short morning conversation a week or so ago in the makeup room at the television station, Hall had called countless times to remind him of his secret discovery from down in the shaft, and his invitation to the cottage in Falun.

His muddled calls to Don had come late at night, and there didn't seem to be any civilized way to get the diver to give up.

But then *Dalakuriren* had published a whole article about the diver's secret and disseminated it to tens of thousands of subscribers. At the same time, the person who'd written the article didn't seem to put much confidence in Hall's strange story of the found ankh. It appeared to be a cheap trick by someone who just wanted to make himself appear interesting: forced, belated, and false. In the morning, the diver had called Don at home, sounding thoroughly dejected. It *really* had not turned out as he'd imagined, and no matter what that journalist had implied in the article, the story about the ankh had actually been true.

In addition, there was yet another thing he'd found down there in the mine. A document that was difficult to decipher, which Don could perhaps help him with. So once again, when would the researcher from Lund be able to come? Don answered with something evasive and hung up.

But then he suddenly felt the need, from deep within him, to go up to Falun after all, if only to put a stop to the diver's endless nagging.

He had taped the usual note to the doorjamb of his office at Lund University: In illegible handwriting he had written the message "temporarily out" to all the tiresome students. And at the very bottom—if, contrary to expectation, someone managed to decipher all the digits—was the number to a cell phone that was permanently off. Then he had gotten into his Renault, outside the Department of History offices, and in some magical way, he got its motor to sputter to life.

Don took his eyes from the *Dalakuriren* article and slowly put down his cup. The ankh had caused his memory to start up, and it couldn't be stopped: the ankh, a cross with a handle, *crux ansata,* the original cross, the symbol for the planet Venus. A hieroglyph that could mean vital force, water and air, immortality and the universe. Although those were only theories, of course; not even the Egyptologists knew what the ankh stood for.

One theory was that the ankh symbolized a womb; another was that it had originally been created as a picture of Egypt, where the vertical shaft was the Nile while the eye represented the delta of the

Nile valley. Someone who was more practical had suggested that the ankh quite simply depicted a sandal.

On the other hand, if the Rosicrucian Order was to be believed, the symbol of the enlightened, the ankh, could be used as a key to open the gates to the inside of the earth. But who believed the Rosicrucians?

Unfortunately, the answer was a surprising number of the students who came to Don's seminars in comparative mythology. And for them, it wasn't just the mysteries of the Rosicrucians that were tempting. Why not Atlantis or flying saucers in Roswell? Why not out-of-context theories about the ten Sephiroth that formed the tree of life in Kabbalah, or a day-long seminar on the lost civilizations of Lemuria and Agartha while you were at it?

When he left Karlskrona after his breakdown at the neo-Nazi demonstration up at the apartment buildings in Galgamarken, Don had stayed with his sister at first.

She had always been a loner, just like him, but by this time, she had become more or less a complete recluse. Once a brilliant student of mathematics at the Royal Institute of Technology, she had drifted into a shady programmer subculture that had gotten her a lot of money and some major legal problems, under the label of cybercrime. She had never been convicted, though, much due to the fact that she'd been able to vanish to a place where nobody could bother her anymore.

In her home, his sister had taken care of him during that phase when he had totally lost his grip. It was she who had forced him to find a way to challenge those inner demons, and now afterward, he realized that he had truly been saved by exchanging his medical career for the prolonged studies at the dusty history department in Lund.

Bubbe had filled her cabinet with Nazi symbols like a child who couldn't stop picking at a scab. For Don, his studies became a way to tear the wound open in order to find a way out of the darkness of that 1950s house. In his research, he had wanted to dig his way past the symbols that, for him, had been charged with such fear. By confronting them, he had hoped to be delivered from his past and to find some retribution for his grandmother's fate.

He had devoted the first part of his dissertation to Heinrich Luitpold Himmler's organization Ahnenerbe, the research department that the chief ideologue of the Holocaust had set up in order to rediscover, or rather reawaken, the mythological legacy of the Germans. Don had followed every tentacle, every sick thread of an idea, to its miserable end: from the use of made-up runes to the idiotic ideas about the spear of fate; from the theories about a lost Aryan homeland at the end of the world, Ultima Thule, to the swastika itself. The symbol for the sun and the cult of Mithras that German romantics falsely linked to the Aryan people and thus equally falsely to the Germanic people.

After the shattering of each myth, it all seemed more and more absurd. It turned out that not even Hitler had believed in Ahnenerbe's theories. Like everything else, Don could still recall the quote word for word:

> Why do we call the whole world's attention to the fact that we have no past? It isn't enough that the Romans were erecting great buildings when our forefathers were still living in mud huts; now Himmler is starting to dig up these villages of mud huts and enthusing over every potsherd and stone axe he finds. All we prove by that is that we were still throwing stone hatchets and crouching around open fires when Greece and Rome had already reached the highest stage of culture. We really should do our best to keep quiet about this past. Instead Himmler makes a great fuss about it all. The present-day Romans must be having a laugh at these revelations.

In his continued research, Don had dissected the myths surrounding the S rune, the *Wolfsangel*, the sun cross, the SS honor ring, the

Thule Society, Karl Maria Wiligut, and so on, and then finally: *die schwarze Sonne,* the black sun, a crystal plate in a cupboard a long time ago.

In the end, he had been able to prove to himself rationally that every Nazi symbol had either been made up or used completely incorrectly: a set design for the masses that supplied made-up bloodlines in order to justify wiping out those who were different.

But the one who held the emotional core of his fear, the eight-year-old boy he had inside of him, didn't seem to notice his discoveries and could never be reached by the power of argument. Finally Don had given up, because he couldn't get any further, and he was left with agony and a rage that he still didn't know how to shake.

After his dissertation, Don had widened his scope from Nazism to a critical study of symbols and myths in general. But his research had been misunderstood in an unfortunate way.

At first there had been only a few people who noticed that the Department of History had started to offer speculative courses on ancient legends. But once the rumor had started, the country's most stubborn New Age students streamed to Don's lectures. For them, this was a place where you could get financial aid to become absorbed in the occultism of the past. And what these incense-scented people could concoct about an ankh in a mine shaft, as a symbol for the keys to the underworld, was something that Don preferred not to think about.

He blinked suddenly and shook his head. Then he got up from his chair and kept his eyes on the view.

*Sheynkeit,* beauty.

There was beauty in what was simple. So what was the simple solution to the ankh in the mine? Presumably something much more ordinary than what that diver would like to believe.

Don pushed open the glass door of the motel restaurant and walked down the wheelchair ramp toward the parking lot. He stopped next to the old Renault 5 and took a few last breaths of fresh air. How much farther could it be up to Falun? Five hours?

Don opened the car door and lifted his black shoulder bag from the seat. After a minute's search, he found the right box and pulled out the blister pack. Pushed out five light brown capsules, times forty: two hundred milligrams of Ritalin. Crushed them with his teeth to make them take effect more quickly.

It would come about the time he got to Gränna, he thought, that tickling feeling of alertness. Then maybe another helping at Mjölby, before he turned off toward Motala and Örebro.

Then continue on Route 50 until he began to approach Falun. According to the directions, he should look for a sign that said Svartbäck. A right on a gravel road, and left six hundred yards after the fallen barn.

Then, the diver had said, he just had to keep an eye out for a fenced-in yard and a sunporch.

# 9

# *La Rivista Italiana dei Misteri e dell'Occulto*

A gust of wind rattled the bedroom window. A few drops of rain hit the pane, and then came the dull rumble.

Erik Hall was sitting in his bed and had drawn the blanket up over his knees. On the nightstand next to him was a bottle of gin and a half-empty glass. The tired springs made the mattress sag into a hammock under his heavy body, and as the thunderheads darkened the sky out there, all the light slowly disappeared.

That cunt of a photographer really had given it away; everything he'd told her had been there, distorted and crooked, in *Dalakuriren*'s article.

The ankh, the words about the key to the underworld, and then above that: the picture of his face, which no one would ever be able to take seriously again. Coming back one week later and suddenly telling about an Egyptian cross that he'd discovered down in the mine . . . She had made him look like a fucking clown.

Erik let the bitter liquor roll around in his mouth.

A fucking clown . . . was that what the girls in Dyke Divers had thought when he'd sent them his pictures of the ankh?

A fluttering flash of light, short pause, and then thunder and the black masses of water.

He had only to close his eyes to be back down in the vault, to hear the cracking sound as the ankh was cut away from the fingers of that hand, and to stagger backward again, crashing down into the cold water of the pool.

There was a sudden hiss as Erik drew in air between his closed teeth, in order to be able to find his way back out of the depths of the shaft.

He opened the bedroom door into the dining room and tried to avoid looking over at the corner with the diving bag, where the ankh lay rolled up in its wine-colored towel. But he couldn't help it.

The bundle was so light as he lifted it up out of the bag, and he let the tips of his fingers grope through the terrycloth until they brushed the shaft of the ankh.

Way down below the slope of pines, beyond the haze of rain, was the lake. If he were just to go out in the storm, down the dark path, and then throw in the ankh, deep, deep . . . then wouldn't that cunt, the Dyke Divers, and all the readers of that fucking paper be satisfied? Yes, he might as well throw himself in too, while he was at it. One thing was certain: No one would look for him.

But then the towel loosened, exposing the perfect white metal, which no one would voluntarily throw into a lake. Erik let his fingers stroke along the eye to the sound of the hammering rain. A chill crept from the ankh, as though it had lain in a freezer; it shot through his fingertips, through his wrist, up to his arm, and he felt a longing for light.

Even though it was only late afternoon, it could easily have been midnight, and the glow from the low-hanging porcelain lamp was only strong enough to light up a small part of the kitchen table.

He sat down on the sofa with his back to the window and carefully laid the ankh down in the middle of the pale circle of light.

It was perhaps a foot long, and as far as he could tell, it was cast in a single piece. But the metal was not entirely smooth: Some sort of decoration twined over its cold surface. Striations a millimeter high, too finely made to be able to read with the bare eye against all that white.

He had tried a magnifying glass and a strong flashlight, without result. When he gave up, he let the ghostly ankh lie hidden, so he didn't have to look at it, until Titelman came. If that bastard was ever going to come.

He looked over at the notebook by the telephone where he'd written down the researcher's number in smeary pencil. Maybe he should call again . . . maybe he should . . . but wait . . . *a pencil*?

Erik pulled himself along the bench, toward the telephone, and got hold of the notebook and pencil. He began to wind the next torn-off page around the shaft of the ankh.

When the thin paper was pulled tight enough, he took the pencil and let its blunt tip begin to stroke back and forth across the designs.

A flash just behind his neck made the pencil jerk in his hand, and he reflexively turned toward the window. He could barely make out the fence through the haze, and he started to count: a hundred one, a hundred two, and the crack came at a hundred three, two humongous pot lids struck together. The thunderstorm would come right over the house if it continued like this.

When Erik's gaze returned to the notebook paper wrapped around the shaft of the ankh, he saw that the pencil must have continued to sketch entirely of its own accord. In the light layer of pencil lead, a row of meandering symbols stood out:

अग्नमिीळे पुरोहतिं यज्ञस्य देवं
रत्वीजम होतारं रत्नधातमम
अग्नः पूर्वेभर्र्िषभिरिड्यो

A dry feeling spread through his mouth, and now he watched as the pencil began to move faster and faster, as though it were guided by someone else's hand.

When the first page was full, his hand—even though he truly didn't want to see more—automatically ripped another sheet from the notebook and twirled it into place around another part of the shaft, and the tip of the pencil began to work again. It wasn't possible to stop it.

पूर्वेभिरृषिभिरीड्यो नूतनैरुत स देवानेह वक्षति

The pattern was everywhere: the shaft, the crossbar, the eye; and soon sheets with snaking symbols lay spread out all over the table.

Erik shook his head in order to rid himself of the feeling of paralysis, of being only some sort of . . . *onlooker*?

Then there were two flashes in quick succession, and in the subsequent thunder he finally managed to stop—*drop the pencil*—and slowly, slowly, get his hands to start moving once again the way he wanted them to.

And what he wanted most of all right now was to shuffle the sheets of paper with their winding symbols together into a pile in the middle of the table. In the hazy light it was difficult to really see what he was doing. The only thing he knew for sure was that all of this had to go away immediately.

Erik crumpled the bunch of scribble-covered papers between his hands and carried it all over to the stove. There he sank down into a crouch, opened the door, and threw it in. He lit a match, guiding the burning flame, and let it go. At first nothing happened; then there was a crackle, and the paper burned.

He sank down until he was sitting, hugged his knees, and saw before him how that damn ankh actually disappeared in the lake, not just an impossible thought, it ought to be done now, right away; he never wanted to touch it again. Maybe it was just the liquor, but over by the table there had—

The sudden pain caused him to jerk his head to the side.

*What was that?*

He felt the back of his head with his hand.

Why, there was something that . . . had *burned,* like an electric shock, from the base of his neck like a projectile up to his forehead, and as Erik turned around toward the kitchen table and the barred windows: *Was there someone there?*

He could see only a faint reflection of himself; the sheets of rain had blurred the windows into a mirror. Another flash of lightning, and now the thunder was directly above him.

He stepped to the shelter of the wall alongside the window and the wooden bench and carefully widened the gap in the curtain so he could peer out.

S*omeone there?*

At first he couldn't even see the yard through all the misty fog, but then his eyes adjusted themselves, and he could make out the contours of the sunporch.

Erik let his eyes wander down the drainpipe toward the waterlogged grass, farther along toward the nearest gatepost, and there was . . . *a hand?*

A black figure rising up over the gate in the fence.

The curtain trembled as Erik slid back in toward the wall.

*Titelman?*

Soon, from the window, a white rectangle began to appear against the kitchen floor of the cottage, and Erik slowly pushed himself away from the wall. His fingers left marks: two fans, ten damp prints.

When he ventured up to the gap in the curtains again, the thunderheads had broken up outside the window. Through the haze, he could make out the sun, and the pouring rain had been wrung out into a light mist. And there, in the drizzle at the gate, stood . . . *a woman?*

She was dressed in a transparent plastic poncho, and under the hood he glimpsed a face that was half turned away. Erik could follow her slender silhouette all the way down to her tall boots through the slats of the fence.

In the time it took for his eyes to wander back up toward the woman's face, she must have had time to turn her head. Because now she was looking straight at him, there in the gap of the curtains, and although he should have been impossible to see, their eyes met. She was very young, and it was as though she had waited for him to finish looking.

"*Signor Hall?*"

The words were spoken at the same instant that Erik opened the outer door of the sunporch.

He took a few steps out onto the stairs and looked over toward the woman through the last flickers of rain. She waved at him.

*"Mi scusi, uscire un attimo?"*

Her voice was so delicate. Yet the words carried straight across the yard, as though she were standing right next to him, whispering into his ear.

*"Signor Hall?"*

He touched the tender spot on his neck and had a strong sense that the best thing to do would be to turn around, shut the door, and lock it. But then he noticed that his body had already begun to move forward between the puddles in the gravel path.

She continued to wave, smiling at him. Erik noticed with surprise that he was actually smiling back and that his own hand was raised to wave. This was just a girl, after all . . . a young girl, couldn't even have turned twenty. A teenager standing at his gate. Now there were only a few steps to go.

*"Scusi per l'intrusione, Signor Hall . . ."*

The woman stretched out a hand; it was so small, and as they shook hands, Erik noticed that the edge of her light pink blouse was sticking out from under the arm of her cardigan. Now he really must try to say something:

"Speak English?"

She took off the hood of her poncho and looked at him with smoky green eyes.

"Oh yes, of course," answered the woman, smiling sweetly.

Her hair was cut short; it was almost stubble. He let his eyes slide down to the woman's neck, following the fine veins, and he could almost make out her slow pulse. Then her voice made him look up again:

"I am terribly sorry for the intrusion, Signor Hall. Well . . . my name is Elena Duomi . . ."

"Elena . . . ?"

"Elena Duomi. I work for the Italian magazine *La Rivista Italiana dei Misteri e dell'Occulto.*"

Erik's hand stiffened as he was about to unhook the hasp that held the gates closed. After that photographer, he really couldn't handle any more journalists.

"Yes, well, I really . . ." he began before the woman interrupted him with her lightly accented English:

"It's been a very long journey here, and I wonder . . . would it be possible to come in for a little while for an interview? And maybe you would allow me to hang this up to dry somewhere?"

She shook the soaked poncho and smiled again. She had a wide mouth, soft lips, no lipstick.

"Well, Signor Hall . . . certainly that would be possible, right?"

He looked down at his hand, which was still holding the hasp.

"How did you know where I live?" he said.

"Oh, it was the police, they helped me. We had already written about *l'uomo sotto sale* in the last issue, but our readers' interest has been so great . . ."

She took a step closer.

"That's what we call him, *l'uomo sotto sale,* the salted man, that magically well-preserved man that you found down there in the mine. As I said, I have already gotten the police's version, and . . ."

The woman glanced up at him and then gently took his hand and helped him lift the hasp out of its position. Erik hesitantly pulled the gate open.

"I've already been to look at the shaft where everything happened," the woman continued once she had taken a few lithe steps onto the gravel path. "I realize that it's short notice, but a meeting with you, Signor Hall, and getting the story of your dive . . . that would really entice our readers. You should see the letters to the editor!"

Once again, Erik touched the tender spot on his neck and tried to organize his thoughts about the small girl. In the end, he could only grin at it all, and he nodded at her to follow him up to the cottage.

While Elena Duomi pulled off her boots, Erik went ahead of her into the kitchen. There he took the ankh from the table, in order to avoid making a fool of himself again.

He turned it between his fingers and looked around. Then he decided on the pile of newspapers next to the stove. He slid in the ankh and nudged the shaft so that it disappeared into the middle of the pile. He had just managed to get up when he heard her steps.

They sat down at the kitchen table. Elena opened her bag and took out a small gray Dictaphone, which she placed between them. Then she pressed RECORD.

"Exclusive to *La Rivista* . . . Italy's weekly magazine about mysteries and the occult: an interview with the Swedish diver Erik Hall."

When the Italian journalist began to ask all the questions that he had gotten so many times now, the answers came so automatically that Erik could take the time to examine her face more closely. She was perhaps not quite so young, after all. There was something sad about her, and sometimes her eyes seemed uncertain, flickering around along the kitchen walls as though they were searching for something.

But soon Erik no longer had time to think about how Elena looked, because Italian journalists were apparently terribly scrupulous. Despite his halting English, she managed to walk him back and forth through the mine paths and write down observations that not even the police had cared about.

The Italian woman was most interested in the vault where he'd found the corpse of the vitriol man. She asked questions about the chalk marks but already seemed to know that the verses about Niflheim and Náströndu came from *Völuspá* (*The Prophecy of the Seeress*) in the Icelandic *Poetic Edda*.

And not only that. From her questions, it was soon clear that the Italian woman knew considerably more about the ancient Scandinavian doctrine of hell than he did, even though Erik had had time to search out a lot of information before the Æsir murder theory had fizzled out.

When she finally paused, and he looked out through the kitchen window, Erik noticed that it had already become evening. He began to contemplate how long he would actually be able to get her to stay.

"No, now you must have something to drink."

Elena had been in the middle of a question when he'd interrupted her. She waved him off, but Erik had already stood up.

He started to clatter around in the cupboards and happened to catch sight of some candles in verdigris-covered candlesticks. He placed them on the table and lit them.

Then, back at the cupboards, he finally found the three bottles of Pata Negra that Mom had left behind a long time ago. He usually preferred liquor, himself, when he wanted to get sloshed, but he could make an exception.

He filled two glasses to the rim, and handed one to her between the burning candles. For an instant he thought she was going to refuse it, but then she lifted her hand.

"*Grazie*, thanks."

The Italian woman took a large gulp and closed her black-lined eyes. When she looked up again, the nature of the conversation changed.

They began to talk about what the vitriol man could actually have been doing down there in the mine. What were Signor Hall's own thoughts on it? What did he think about the dating and about the newspapers that had been found? Elena nodded thoughtfully, almost submissively, at his answers, and when Erik switched over to whiskey, she didn't bat an eye.

This was just a little girl, he thought, no matter how much she had made up her eyes. A sexy little Italian, who for some unfathomable reason was sitting in his kitchen.

And now, as the night drew near, it came with a stifling warmth. A sticky physical heat, which, along with the liquor, made his face begin to run with sweat. Erik had just dried off the salty moisture with his sleeve when the Italian woman took a newspaper clipping out of her bag: the article from *Dalakuriren*'s Saturday supplement.

"That last bit, with the ankh . . . is it true?" she said, pointing to the concluding paragraph.

He must have had a stupid look on his face, because she laughed. "One of the policemen translated it for me; he seemed to think that it was something you had probably just . . . made up? Is that right?"

Erik felt himself grinning.

"Well, I believe you, in any case!" said the Italian woman. "Besides, I've already called my editor, who says that this story about the ankh makes everything so much more exciting. So he actually insisted that I bring back at least one picture."

He barely heard her; his thoughts had drifted to the photographer cunt. The Italian woman tried again: "Just one picture, and then I'll go. I really think I can't leave here without it."

*Can't leave here without it.* Erik looked over toward the pile of newspapers.

"Yes, the ankh would make a good picture," he said.

"I would really appreciate it."

He swayed a bit as he got up from his chair, steadied himself with the help of its arm. The sweat came faster along his back, down toward his buttocks.

The Italian woman turned off her Dictaphone and placed it in her bag. Then she positioned herself very close to him: "I can help," she whispered, "if you just tell me where the ankh is."

Erik felt the Italian woman's breath against his ear and couldn't quite make out why she was suddenly so anxious. But he understood this much: Once he had shown her the ankh, she would leave him and go.

"Okay . . . but in that case, you'll have to do something for me first," he said. He looked down at her and saw that she was nodding. She was smiling, actually.

"Come with me out into the fresh air for just a little bit—"

Erik didn't wait for an answer; instead he continued with a thickening voice:

"If you come out with me, I'll show you something, and then you can take your pictures of the ankh. As many as you want."

When he heard her voice, he had to ask again, and it took a minute before he realized that she had actually said yes.

She looked so fragile, standing and waiting on the gravel path at the bottom of the stairs to the sunporch. When Erik approached the Italian, he made an attempt to seize her with an arm around her shoulders, but she slipped away.

Then he heard himself say something incoherent about the house and Mom, and he was surprised when the small woman laughed and pretended she had understood.

He gestured toward the fence that led around to the back of the cottage, and when she walked ahead of him, he felt how he just wanted to grab the soft movements of those hips.

Just behind the house was a small shed, and Erik fetched a few towels and brought them out into the moonlight. Then he motioned to the Italian woman to follow him over to the opening in the fence, which led them down to the path toward the pine slope.

They made it up to the edge of the forest before she suddenly stopped and looked up at the moon.

*"Quanto è bello."*

The Italian woman seemed to hesitate for an instant, but when Erik gave her a little nudge in the back, she complied after all, continuing into the darkness.

As they walked side by side on the narrow forest path, she began to ask questions about the ankh in her bright voice. How had it looked? Had he inspected it? Then she asked several times whether he had found anything else he hadn't told the police about down there in the mine. Even if Erik had wanted to, he couldn't answer any longer, because his throat had constricted as it always did when he was this close.

He fumbled for the Italian woman's hand in the dark and felt how he managed to graze her fingers. But then she quickened her steps, and soon the hill leveled onto the strip of beach by the lake.

The white water lilies covered the silky smooth surface out to the end of the T-shaped dock. Usually they were done blooming by September, but this year the petals were still there, with their slippery stems firmly rooted in mud and sludge.

Erik placed a bare foot on the damp planks of the dock, and he had gone out a bit before he noticed that the Italian woman didn't intend to follow him. He continued by himself out to the metal ladder down into the dark water. There he turned around.

Elena was still standing on the beach with her arms crossed as he began to take off all his clothes. He couldn't make out her expression.

"So—you want to see the ankh, Elena?" he called to her. "If you really want to see it, you have to come and swim with me." Then Erik turned, naked, out toward the water. He stood there for a long time and let her get a good look.

"Signor Hall . . ."

The whisper sounded very close. But now his body was already in motion, and the surface of the water rushed toward him.

He didn't know how long he would sink; the liquor made his body feel like an armored suit of lead.

Then his arms made a first instinctive stroke, and then another, and then he exploded up through the surface of the water. Erik rolled over to float on his back and opened his eyes. After he'd blinked a few times, he realized that that really was the Italian woman standing naked out by the ladder, with a black bandage around her snow-white upper arm.

She raised her arms from her chiseled waist and the triangle between her legs. Elena dove quickly off the edge of the dock and did the crawl stroke past him out to the middle of the lake.

Not until he got a cold swallow of water did Erik notice that his mouth was hanging open. He tried to swim up to her, to get hold of her body, but he soon had to give up, and then it was as though everything slowed down.

The Italian woman swam out of reach on her back, and there they were, drifting around slowly in the lake. Neither of them said anything, and she didn't seem to be in any hurry. They just lay there, floating, under a distant moon, a minute sliver away from being full. Her breasts floated weightless on the water, and she didn't seem to care when he looked.

But then everything started to move again, and Elena was the one who got out first. She took one of the towels and wrapped it around herself. Then she walked over to the grassy spot by the edge of the woods above the beach.

Erik hurried to follow her. Once he had plowed through the lukewarm water up to the ladder and managed to get his feet to take the three steps up, he had to take another look to make sure that the Italian woman was actually still sitting there.

There was a row of wet spots from his footsteps on the planks of the dock up toward the grass, and soon he would be there. Erik sank down into a crouch next to Elena and made another attempt to clasp his arm around her shoulders. She moved backward rapidly, and there was something sharp about her voice as she said, "You promised me an ankh."

"Yes, yes," he mumbled and tried once again to get hold of her.

"So first you will go and get it."

Her eyes shone black under her long lashes and after one more clumsy attempt, he realized that he had no choice other than to get up again.

Bare-chested, with a towel around his hips, he staggered up toward the cottage. When he came back down the path after some time, he had another opened bottle of wine with him. Erik waved it in greeting, but when he approached the Italian woman, he realized that the gesture had been meaningless. Her eyes had already riveted themselves onto the object he was carrying in his other hand: an ivory-colored cross with an eye.

*"Bentornata,"* she mumbled.

Erik released the ankh into her outstretched hands.

And so they sat there, a short distance from each other, above the lake's water lilies, the beach, and the dock. The Italian woman was still naked under Erik's towel, and she inspected the ankh while he swigged wine.

At some point, he made an attempt to move the bottle to her lips, but she moved away quickly without even needing to look up.

It took such a fucking long time—he couldn't understand what the little Italian was doing. She rotated the shaft, turn after turn, as though she were pretending that she could read those winding inscriptions. At times he thought he even heard her mumbling a few syllables, but when he looked at her lips her mouth appeared to be closed.

"It's my ankh, you know. I found it," Erik said in a low voice.

Elena turned in his direction, and he could have sworn that she showed her teeth like a beast of prey. Nothing was left of the Italian woman's ingratiating manner; her perfect face was closed and cold.

"You know, I have one other little secret . . ."

Erik moved closer.

"Another little secret that I found down there. That only I know about."

She lifted her eyes from the ankh.

"But it will cost you more. A kiss. It's gonna cost you a kiss to see it."

The Italian had time to laugh before she covered her mouth.

"A kiss," he said thickly. "A ki . . ."

And in one sweeping movement, Erik laid his arm over the Italian woman's shoulders and pressed her face to his mouth. But then he felt a sharp elbow in his stomach and lost his breath, and she was free again.

"Just a little kiss," Erik tried once more.

*"Where?"* he heard the Italian woman ask.

No more ingratiating voice; it was sharp, cunning, pointed. His mouth chomped a few times, empty, a sour taste, a sick feeling. Suddenly all that dark stuff came pouring up through him and buried everything in its way:

"It will cost you, do you understand, you cunt?!"

He heaved himself up onto her; it was such a violent movement that he surprised himself. He pressed his lips to hers, forced open her mouth, and shoved in his tongue. But it wasn't until Erik had swung himself up so he was sitting on the Italian woman's chest and had pressed her arms down into the grass with his knees that he realized that this was how it would have to be.

*"Pezzo di merda!"*

He got a good grip on her mouth with one hand, and with the other he determinedly pulled the towel from her breasts. For a split second, Erik lost control of one of the Italian woman's hands, and although he half managed to block the blow, her smack made his cheek burn like fire. How could that little hand hit so hard?

Now he completely lost his cool; he could smell the stench of that fucking mine and see the photographer with her ponytail and her cunty pictures.

Once again Erik forced the Italian woman's arms to the ground, and he moved his crotch up toward her mouth. But just as he managed to loosen the towel from his own hips, it was as though his head broke. An intensely piercing noise; a circular saw of shrill tones that cut right through his forehead.

He rolled heavily to the side and held his ears, as though that could stop the pain. Sharp nails digging and rooting inside his head, it was as though . . . Then he noticed that the pain disappeared when he rolled away from the Italian woman and, blinking, he fumbled again for her escaping body.

Somewhere a glass shattered.

Although he had actually managed to sit up just before she took aim, Erik Hall never saw the broken bottle whizzing toward him.

He would also never know that the force behind the Italian woman's blow was so great that the razor-sharp edge of glass cut through his temple as though it were made of butter and that it then ripped a bloody ravine through his right eyeball and the right side of his brain, until it sank, trembling, into the inside of his nasal bone.

A gentle breeze blew through the tops of the pines above the supine body. A few soft lapping waves, and then, closer and closer, the sound of a stuttering car motor.

# 10

# Don Titelman

Don had just managed to force his Renault to a bumpy stop outside Erik Hall's summer cottage when the roar of a motorcycle ripped the night apart. In his rearview mirror, he saw the red light flicker away just above the asphalt before it disappeared in the dark, on its way south.

The roar of the motorcycle diminished to a far-off hum, but Don had always had a great sense for sounds, and what he heard now was a large, horizontally opposed boxer engine with a low center of gravity. A vibrationless two-cylinder four-stroker, which at 8,000 rpm could give a max speed of more than 250 kilometers per hour. A machine made by Germans. A BMW.

He straightened his knees to get rid of the stiffness and try to move on to other thoughts—but his inner calculator was already rolling.

Bayerische Motoren Werke. The company that had manufactured the first working turbojet motor. Mounted into a Swallow, a Messerschmitt ME 262, on July 18, 1942. The test flight in Niedersachsen in 1944, and from 1945 onward thrown into the last desperate defense of the very heart of the disease: Stuttgart, Ulm, Munich, Innsbruck,

Salzburg. The last superior weapon aside from the V-2 rocket. It was . . .

Don banged his wrist on the door frame, and the sudden pain stopped the babbling of his memory. Then he heaved himself out of the driver's seat and slammed the fussy door behind him. Clapped the flakes of rust from his hands and looked over toward Erik Hall's fence.

He didn't really know what he thought the diver's cottage would look like, but he hadn't counted on it being completely dark. It was only . . . yes, it was eleven o'clock, and the sunporch was lit only by the moon.

But it would be unusual if the diver were asleep. The last week's phone calls from Erik Hall had come at night several times, when the diver woke him up with some new, incoherent theory about his strange ankh.

He could knock, in any case. *Knocking at doors unexpectedly, that's what people do in the country,* Don thought.

He let his hand slide along the rails of the fence on his way up to the gates. Someone had put a lot of love into the cottage; you could see that even in this darkness. Don lifted the hasp and gave a shove, and the gate opened, rustling against the gravel.

Now that the motorcycle was gone, he could hear only a quiet rush, and rainwater dripping into a barrel from a drainpipe. Don had run into the thunderstorm on his way up, but it seemed to have left this area a long time ago, and it was remarkably warm for evening.

He walked up the gravel path through the moonlight and caught sight of his reflection in the windows of the sunporch. He tried knocking when he had gone up the steps, but there was no answer from within the cottage. He leaned his forehead against the glass pane in the door and peered in.

Don knocked again; not hesitantly this time but rather a solid pounding that Hall wouldn't be able to avoid hearing, if indeed he was in there, somewhere in the dark of the cottage. But no answer: only the whispering of the wind through the leaves and the dripping noise from the overflowing rainwater barrel at the corner of the house. He had almost given up when he quite spontaneously tried to push down the handle. There was a creak as the unlocked door swung open.

Don remained standing hesitantly on the stairs for a second, but then he took a step onto the sunporch, into its scent of red wine and burned candles.

"Anyone there?"

The Mora clock ticked quietly.

"Hello?"

Don stood there in the dark for a second, wavering.

Then he felt that he had traveled way too far to just turn around, and he knocked hard on the interior door. But still only silence, except for the pendulum's monotonous rhythm in the old clock.

He continued to call out as he walked through a parlor with pink velvet easy chairs. Then he came to a long, narrow room with a view to the back of the house.

When he turned around he caught sight of another doorway, which turned out to lead to the kitchen. There he saw the orange light of the coffeemaker shining. So the diver couldn't be too far away, after all.

There were two glasses, candles, and a few bottles of wine on the table in front of the wooden bench. When Don turned on the porcelain lamp, he saw that one of the bottles was still half full.

And then his heart fluttered as he caught sight of a tall, thin figure in the window. Not until he moved one hand did he realize that the blurry figure was he himself.

He'd always had a hook nose, a real *yidishe noz* that stuck out from his face like a broken-off hanger. He had bought his aviator glasses a few years ago, when the sharpness of his vision began to disappear, and that must have been about the same time that his hair had become thin and peppered with gray. He had been a bit stooped since his teenage years, but he couldn't remember when he'd become so thin, or when the skin on his hands had become so yellowed. The corduroy jacket didn't help; in fact, it intensified the tired forward, downward, curve of his shoulders; and the only thing he might possibly have been satisfied with, his new Dr. Martens boots, weren't even visible in his reflection in the window.

Then there was a clatter from the refrigerator, over by the stove, and Don's heart racheted up in pace even though he soon realized that it was only the refrigerator's compressor chugging to life.

And the quick patter of his heart soon turned into that fluttering under his sternum that had become so familiar these days. An overwhelming anxiety that would soon be followed by a dry taste in his mouth and great difficulty swallowing.

Don dug his hand into his bag and found a packet of Russian-bought clonazepam. This would be his first time trying these particular pills, but it would have to do.

He took six flat two-milligram capsules, which landed on his rough tongue, and he tried to get them down his throat. Then he realized that there was, in fact, wine, and he took a few steps toward the table, where he poured a glass. It tasted vaguely of iron, and as Don stood there drinking, he considered that this was not exactly something that a *choshever mensch*, a respectable person, would have done, as Bubbe would have said. But then again, it hadn't been his idea to come here to Erik Hall's cottage outside of Falun.

He placed the glass back and listened to the ticking of the clock.

He saw on his wristwatch that there was half an hour left until midnight.

Perhaps he could wait thirty minutes for the diver here in the cottage, if only he could avoid the pressing darkness.

He couldn't find any lights in the hall, but in the living room there was an old light switch of Bakelite.

The incandescent light made the row of windows flash, and when

Don looked over toward the short end of the room, he caught sight of a figure without a head or feet. It was on a hanger, which was hooked onto an open door.

He walked up and felt the rubbery fabric of the dry suit and wondered what kind of person would voluntarily crawl down into a labyrinth hundreds of yards underground. Then he heard the hinges creaking, and the door slowly swung open. For an instant he thought there was someone lying on the bed in there, but what looked like a body was a mess of blankets.

But everything suggested that the diver was nearby—a machine was on in here, too: a computer, whose monitor displayed the local paper's article about the ankh. On the floor there were magazines with other pictures, photographs of women with their legs spread, and a jumble of clothes, cups, and glasses.

The room was *ein chazzershtal*, a real pigsty, and Don was just about to let the door swing shut when his gaze fell on something that didn't really fit in.

On the nightstand, behind a bottle of gin, a sepia-toned photograph was leaning against the wall. It depicted some sort of . . . church?

He took a step into the mess, snatched the photograph, and took it with him out into the light of the living room.

Out here, he could see that it wasn't a church in the photograph; it was more like a cathedral. The building had three naves, with crosses on the very tops of their facades. A rose window, which was flanked by two tall spires, formed an arch above the closed side doors.

One side of the picture was somewhat faded, and three blurry figures, one of them the size of a child, stood on the cobblestone square in front of the cathedral. They must have happened to pass by just as the photograph was taken, which must have been a long time ago.

Don carefully bent the paper, which was remarkably rigid. And when he turned it over, he realized that it was actually a postcard.

There was no stamp or address on the dotted lines, but printed in the upper left-hand corner was

La Cathédrale Saint Martin d'Ypres

Where there should have been a closing, there was a print of a red mouth, as though someone had given the postcard a kiss with painted lips. And above the kiss, written with blue ink in neat handwriting:

*la bouche de mon amour Camille Malraux*
*le 22 avril*
*l'homme vindicatif*
*l'immensité de son désir*
*les suprêmes adieux*
*1913*

Don turned the card over and looked at the picture again. The cathedral in Ypres, a few years before World War I. And a few isolated lines in French. The twenty-second of April 1913, written to a beloved woman—it reminded him of a poem.

Something rustled suddenly over by the hall and the sunporch, and Don thought it must be the diver coming home, but then the first of twelve strokes sounded from the clock.

He tapped the postcard lightly against his palm, waited for the sound to stop, and then declared that the time was up. When he turned the light off in the living room, he could once again see the starry sky outside the row of windows. Over by the fence there was a clothesline with a few bath towels hanging on it, and down below that, there seemed to be a slope of tall trees.

There was something about these pills that didn't feel very good, and Don would have preferred to sit in a chair inside the cottage to rest. But out in the car would be better, and perhaps not as obtrusive if the diver were to end up coming home very late.

When Don had left the sunporch behind him and was walking back along the gravel path to the gate, he realized that he was still holding the postcard in his hand.

He absentmindedly put it into the torn inner pocket of his jacket, where it slipped all the way down and landed against the bottom seam of the jacket lining. At first he cursed, but then he thought it could just stay there until he met Erik Hall.

In the car, he lowered the back of the seat as far as it would go, and he lay there with his eyes closed and thought about the postcard, but the clonazepam had really made him start to feel thoroughly rotten.

He opened his eyes again and saw that the steering wheel in front of him had been stretched out into a strangely oval shape, and despite the short distance, it was difficult to find the car door so he could let in some air.

His fingers were soft as dough when they finally found the door handle, and he had to throw his whole body against the door to be able to get out. At first he just lay doubled over in the warm air, panting. Then it felt as if his legs began to fill with carbon dioxide, and he had to move somehow. Don forced himself to stand up and found that he had suddenly started to walk. He must have been reeling around for some time when he noticed that he had ended up below the cottage. In front of him, the moonlight showed him the beginning of a path. It snaked off through the night, or was *snaked* really the right word . . . ?

Don searched in his bag for something that would bring clarity, fumbling among bottles and plastic-sealed syringes, while his carbonated legs continued to carry him away of their own accord.

In the pine forest, the trees pressed in closer and closer, encircled themselves around him, pressed down over his head, as though they wanted to close him in a cave. And when he finally managed to get a few more pills out, he dropped the first one on the path, where he couldn't find it even though he dug in the ground with his fingers, and now he had slumped down into a sitting position, and how would he be able to get up again while he felt like this?

There was something on his chest, too, which felt heavier and heavier, and his breaths sounded dangerously shallow, panting and weak; he truly became frightened then, and he pulled up a random box in the dark and swallowed something without having any idea what it was, and soon after that he dropped off.

*

When Don's eyes opened again, he was lying on the forest path and looking up at the sky, and he thought it had completely lost its color. Hadn't it just been black? Now it seemed to have turned beige or, wasn't that a streak of blue? Was it morning already? And if it was: lucky that the diver hadn't seen him.

He sat up and looked around.

Yes, it was morning. A blackbird was singing somewhere, and it looked as though water was glittering at the end of the path. A T-shaped dock extended out into the water, and the surface alongside the dock was covered in a thick layer of green leaves and white roses. A red patterned shirt had been left at the very end of the planks. Don had the thought that perhaps the diver had drowned, and maybe that explained why the machines were on up in the cottage and why the door had been open.

But then he caught sight of someone who was lying asleep just next to the edge of the woods. The dew glittered around the diver, because that must be him lying naked there in the grass, right? But there was no glitter around his large head; the ground was just sludge there. It looked as if Erik Hall had lain down to rest with his face in a rust-colored puddle.

A few steps closer now, and the sun really began to shine, strong even though it was still only dawn.

Nothing was bending or moving in an unnatural way anymore. Still, Don thought that this had to be some sort of dream or hallucination, because it was as though someone had ripped off a large part of the diver's face—from his temple through his right eye socket and all the way into the root of his nose.

One eye was missing, or maybe it was there in the sludge somewhere. It was hard to tell, because from the curls on his forehead down to his neck, Hall's face was covered with something that looked like a cowpat of coagulated blood.

Don wanted to stop, but his legs just kept moving, and they lowered him to his knees by the diver.

At the same time, his hands, a doctor's hands, wanted to find something to do—but when he poked at all the red, his stomach turned, and he had to bend forward to force the vomit back down. Now his heart started to flutter away again, and he searched through the medicine in his bag, but all his fingers found was some angular object made of plastic.

When Don lifted it up, he saw that he was holding his cell phone. Pushed the power button; the battery was way down in the red. And while he continued to force back his vomit reflex, his fingers started to search for the buttons that made up the emergency number: one, one, two.

# 11

# Solrød Strand

The asphalt of the Øresund Bridge rushed by about four inches below the foot pegs of ridged aluminum. Elena was crouched in place on the motorcycle, behind the carbon-fiber windshield, with her thin chest pressed against the snow-white gas tank. Since she had retooled the suspension, there was hardly any cushion left between her body and the spinning tires, and as soon as a crack or bump in the road made the machine bounce, she had to answer the throw quickly with the strength of her thighs. She forced her mind to concentrate fully to stop the image from coming back. But then there it was again—the diver's body falling onto the grass, and all the blood that came from his face. And if the bottle in her hand hadn't been broken, it would have been easier to come up with an excuse. Then maybe she could have said that she had tried to use the least possible amount of violence, that the blow from the bottle had happened to land in an unnecessarily bad place.

But that wasn't what had happened.

In reality, she had purposely broken off the wine bottle against a stone before she struck its sharp edge with full force against the part of the Swede's head she knew was fragile and weak.

She could still smell the odor of his crotch, but she couldn't remember what it had looked like when the glass had carved its groove through his temple.

Her next memory was only noise: the creaks inside his face as she tugged and wriggled the neck of the bottle to get it loose from the Swede's nasal bone and eye socket.

Then came a few random fragments of having put on her cardigan and boots. It must have been at that point that she first noticed the sound of a sputtering motor approaching up on the road, above the pine forest.

Then she saw herself running on the dark path, and when she had reached the fence, she could remember being surprised that she was still holding the bottle in her hand. She had taken a running start and heaved it as far off into the underbrush as she could, and she'd heard it land in thick bushes. Then, when she'd turned back to continue to the cottage, she had been blinded by headlights. The unfamiliar car had slowed down and stopped on the road outside the sunporch. It was standing there waiting with its high beams on, and in her confusion, she hadn't been able to think of anything other than protecting her ankh.

She had started running again—this time toward the grove beyond the house where she had hidden her motorcycle. When she reached it, she had wrapped the pale metal of the ankh in her poncho and then pressed the bundle hard, hard underneath herself, against the motorcycle as it shot away through the coal-black night.

The next clear image was a blue sign that said LUDVIKA 10. She had stopped there and squatted in a grove of birches to pee. At this point her senses had become clear, and she realized that it had been a mistake to leave the cottage in a panic, without even trying to find the diver's other secret. But now it was too late to turn around, and no matter what they said, at least she had gotten the ankh.

She slid into her tight leather gear and put on her helmet. She let her glove twist the throttle lever, and was once more on her way.

When she'd left the Copenhagen area behind, she followed the directions: exit onto Cordozavej, then a left on Jersie Strandvej, until the radial-mounted brakes stopped the BMW in front of the last row of brick buildings. She pulled off the helmet and massaged her temples to quiet the buzzing sound that filled her head. She had started to hear it at dawn, and during her journey she had thought it was only background noise from the motor. But now it was turned off, and the humming just kept going. It varied in intensity, but nevertheless it was always there, like the whispering voices of your parents before you fall asleep.

She'd had the ankh pressed against her chest inside her leather outfit during the entire journey. Now she pulled down the zipper in order to feel it through the poncho. Although the metal should have been warmed by her body, it was still ice-cold.

Just as they had told her, next to one of the buildings there was a mailbox with a sticker: DF, an oval encircled by red arrows, the symbol of the Danish People's Party. She opened the lid and picked up an envelope.

Elena followed the walkway down to the long beach. The wind had started to pick up, and gusts from seaward swept plumes of sand from the tops of the dunes.

As she walked, she hesitantly pressed a finger first against her right and then her left ear canal. She tried opening her mouth wide and yawning, but the whispering and rustling in there still didn't stop. It had been a long time since her senses had surprised her this way, but she was probably just tired.

When Elena was absolutely certain that she was alone, she sat down in a little ravine between drifts covered with greenish yellow lyme grass. From here she could see the stripes of black seaweed and the glittering sea.

With a decisive movement she ripped off the edge of the envelope, stuck her hand in, and took out a prepaid phone and the slip of paper with the thirteen-digit German phone number. She set her watch at zero, even though she knew that the receiver would end the call when the allotted time was up.

Two crackly rings, and then that voice that had made her anxious since her childhood:

"*Ja?*"

"*Es ist das Echte.* The symbols are correct."

"*Eine erfreuliche Nachricht, Elena.*" Good news, very good.

"*Aber . . .*" But . . .

"*Ja?*"

"*Es gab eine Abweichung.*" There was an anomaly.

"*Das wissen wir bereits,*" the voice interrupted. "We already know about it. Don't worry, our friends have already promised to take care of that."

Her fingers loosened their grip on the cell phone. Looked at the clock, thirty seconds left.

"And there was something else."

More crackling. Then the voice came back.

"Elena?"

"*Ja?*"

"*Jetzt zurück nach Hause.*" Come back home.

A quiet click, and all that was left was the sound of the wind and the humming whispers.

She slowly took the battery out of the phone and thought about how he had called the place her home. Perhaps it was, but it would never feel like it.

Elena could envision how he had already turned toward the wide window and how the lines alongside his mouth had deepened, if only a bit. And it wasn't until she saw the image before her that she knew with certainty that she had failed.

She felt the chill of the ankh against her breasts under the leather suit. Elena stood up and brushed off the sand.

She threw the prepaid SIM card into a trash can on her way back to the motorcycle. The phone itself she threw over the railing of the Great Belt Bridge just before she reached Fyn.

Now the motorcycle would be able to make use of its lightweight construction with the boxer engine and magnesium rims: only 110 miles left to Flensburg on the German side of the border. Then the E45 Autobahn to Hannover, and then off toward North Rhine–Westphalia. Her body was aching by her upper arm, under the bandage.

# 12

# The Interrogation

The arched facade of Falun's police station was covered with oblong tar-colored stone slabs, and along the curve ran two rows of sound-absorbing windows whose white blinds were pulled down to keep out the rays of the morning sun.

In the corner on the second floor, behind slanted blind slats, was one of four interrogation rooms in the violent crimes division. An open notebook covered with keywords written in messy handwriting was lying on the fake birch veneer in the semidarkness.

In front of the notebook, someone had placed an ancient tape recorder with its record button depressed. But at the moment, its sound meter was only registering the hum of the ventilation system and the monotonous buzzing sounds that were coming from one of the fluorescent light tubes in the ceiling.

Leaning against the back of a chair that was upholstered in black fabric sat a bowed figure with a corduroy jacket, bloodshot eyes, and aviator glasses. Across from him, on the other side of the table, sat a surly Falun policeman with a cold and a mustache. And they had been sitting like this for several hours.

Then the Mustache straightened up in order to make another attempt to move forward:

"Perhaps we should start over from the beginning again, then. Why were you at Erik Hall's house last night?"

Don didn't even make an effort to try to answer this time. The policeman in front of him was clearly what Bubbe would have called a *shmendrik*, an idiot, and no matter how many times you explained something to this idiot, it seemed totally impossible to get him to understand.

The questions had begun as soon as the police arrived down by the dock in their yellow reflective vests. And maybe his explanation had been muddled at first, considering the amount of morphine he'd swallowed, but now he had repeated his version so many times that the only reason to continue asking questions was that the true version was somehow not good enough.

"You're not falling asleep, are you?" asked the Mustache.

Don took off his glasses and carefully began to clean them with his handkerchief.

The police had already heard him state that Hall had invited him there to inspect the ankh, which the diver claimed to have found down in the mine. That explained the phone records from the past week, which they seemed to have really become obsessed with. He had also admitted that he had drunk some of the wine, which explained the fingerprints on the glass, and this thing about going into the cottage without permission . . . was that really a sufficient reason to detain him for so many hours?

Don put his glasses back on his nose again, blinked, and made a face so they slid into place.

"The suspect refuses to answer."

The Mustache attempted, with difficulty, to make another note in his awful handwriting. Then silence descended once again, the hum of the ventilation system, the buzz from the ceiling, and finally Don had had enough:

"Well, why is anyone anywhere?"

The policeman looked up from his notebook.

"Or if you put it another way . . ." Don continued, fixing his eyes on a grease spot on the worn uniform, "maybe you could explain why we're still sitting here?"

The Mustache tapped his pen authoritatively.

"Because you reported a murder . . ."

Don gave the table a kick, but the policeman just continued stuffily: "And thus far everything is well and good. But when we get there, you're sitting there with blood on your hands . . ."

"But I've told you that I'm a doctor, and I was trying to examine his injuries."

"And with a bag on your shoulder, half of the contents of which is narcotic-class drugs and the other half is powerful sedatives. You stink of alcohol and you can hardly talk. The dead man stinks of the same wine. In the kitchen, where you'd been drinking, there are two glasses on the table, and when we check for fingerprints it seems that you've been rummaging around in several different parts of the cottage."

"I didn't . . ."

"Then, when we request phone records, Hall has called you several times in the past week and the two of you have had long discussions, and on his computer we find notes about that ankh, where he writes that you're very interested in learning more. And when we search through the cottage we don't find any ankh. How does that look, do you think?" When there was no answer, the policeman sighed. Then he paused and blew his nose, and then another few minutes went by under the blinking fluorescent light while he picked the snot residue from his mustache. *Shmendrik.*

Don let his memory rewind, and he was once again sitting in the dewy wet grass next to Hall's body, looking out at the white water lilies on the lake.

He had truly had all the time in the world to wash away every trace of blood and brain matter from his hands after his bewildered call to the police. But he hadn't had the energy to move during his entire long wait for the police; instead, he just sat there next to Hall's battered head in nauseated confusion. Even when he heard the sirens screaming up on the road he hadn't had the strength to get up. When he had seen all those shadows come running from the edge of the forest, along the path down to the water, he had thought that he would finally be able to rest. But instead he had been hauled up, hooked by a pair of strong arms.

They had lugged him up toward the cottage to a crookedly parked car with flashing lights and pushed him into place on the backseat.

From the garage of the police station, they had taken him into a corridor and to a room that had a bed with a plastic mattress. It wasn't until Don had discovered that there was no handle on the inside of the door that he realized he was locked up in a cell.

He had lain down and tried to sleep, but just when he'd managed to get his body to relax, the Mustache came back, along with a colleague. They had grabbed hold of his arms again and walked him up several flights of stairs to this interrogation room with its flickering light.

At first they had taken turns asking questions, but during the last hour, it had seemed as though the colleague was beginning to give up. A moment ago, he had excused himself and left the airless room to get coffee.

But the policeman with the mustache wouldn't leave him alone.

"So, Don . . . what were you doing at Erik Hall's house last night, besides taking pills?"

The policeman had picked a worn leather bag up off the floor and put it on the table. He dug through bottles and syringes with one hand while he looked at Don.

"You have, let's see . . ."

Then he started to line up the bottles methodically.

"Diazepam, Rohypnol, an unmarked bottle . . ."

"But I told you . . ." Now that Don saw his bag so close by, it suddenly became difficult to breathe, and he felt his mouth cement itself closed. Finally he got his speaking under control: "But I told you, I'm a doctor."

"Apodorm, Ketogan, another unmarked drug, and then these: morphine, Metadate, Xanax, Haldol, Provigil, something with Russian letters, fentanyl . . ."

"I have the right to prescribe to myself."

"Spasmophen, Ritalin, Nozinan, Versed, Subutex . . ."

"You can call the Board of Health and Welfare and . . ."

"Oxycontin, Serax, Mogadon, morphine, another bottle of diazepam, an unmarked bottle of capsules . . . ephedrine . . ."

The policeman finally turned the bag upside down, and a pile of loose blister packs fell out onto the table, followed by some plastic-sealed syringes and a rubber tourniquet.

Then he turned off the tape recorder and let an effective silence descend for a minute before he said, "You know . . . sooner or later we'll find the rest of that bottle you used to chop up Erik Hall's head."

Don tried to avoid looking at his collection of medicine and dug his nails into his palm to stop it from moving toward the closest bottle of Mogadon.

His heart was pounding so fast again, and why couldn't that policeman hear how much trouble breathing he was having? This *yentse tsemishnich,* this fucking mess.

He had to stop his whirling memory: Hall's battered temple, the frayed right frontal lobe, the eye that had slipped out of its socket, and the image of the stiffening blades of grass where the blood had recently dried.

Don looked at the policeman in front of him, who surely only had faint fragments of memories left by now, and who would soon surely need photographs to even be able to remember how the victim looked. For the Mustache, the image had already begun to disintegrate and be erased. For him, sleep would be no problem.

There was a knock.

When the door swung open, Don gratefully took a few deep breaths of the rich air that had been let in. The other policeman stood outside; after an hour and a half, he had come back with two steaming mugs of coffee.

But then Don noticed that there was yet another person out there in the corridor. A woman in a beige coat, with blond, upswept hair. It was hard to tell how old she was, but Don would bet on forty-five. The downward lines around her mouth showed that time had left its mark.

The policeman placed the coffee on the table inside the interrogation room, and the Mustache immediately began to slurp from his steaming plastic cup. Then he turned questioningly to the woman out in the corridor.

His colleague cleared his throat. "This is attorney Eva Strand; I ran into her asking questions about this case downstairs. She says that she's been sent here by the Afzelius law firm in Borlänge."

He waved the woman in. She took a few steps forward and then stood expectantly in the doorway. The other policeman laid a hand on the Mustache's shoulder. "The prosecutor is going to make the decision about the petition soon, so it's really just as well that Titelman has someone, right?"

The Mustache just kept slurping his coffee without giving an answer.

"If there isn't another one you'd prefer?" said his colleague, and it took a few seconds before Don realized that this question was directed to him.

"Another one . . . ?"

"Another lawyer you'd rather have?"

Don shook his head wearily. He was still having trouble understanding how he could have ended up here. The woman approached the short end of the table, grabbed the back of a chair, and turned toward the sitting policeman. "If I may . . . ?"

The Mustache muttered something inaudible, but she sat down

anyway. Then she extended her hand to Don. "Hi. My name is Eva Strand, and I'm an attorney."

Don shook her hand.

"We heard the news about the murder on the radio, and that someone had already been apprehended. I understand that you are Don Titelman?" He nodded, and it was as though he didn't want to let go of her warm hand. She let him keep holding it.

"From what I understand, you've sat here all morning answering questions? No phone call, nothing to eat, no coffee, nothing?"

Since Don didn't have the strength to answer, she turned to the Mustache. "Is that how I should interpret the situation?"

"Yes, but . . ."

"Then I think it would be appropriate to give Don here a little breakfast."

At first the Mustache just sat still, but when he saw that she was serious, he got up hesitantly.

"And all of this on the table . . . ?" the attorney said, gesturing toward the collection of medicine.

Now that the policeman had stood up, he seemed to recover some of his confidence.

"Well, you can see for yourself. Subutex—a heroin substitute. And these are all benzodiazepines, or tranks, as they're called." He started pointing at the bottles. "Here's something Russian. Here are three unmarked bottles. Here he has Spasmophen with morphine, and then a bunch of junkie stuff. You can see for yourself."

"Does he have a prescription for Subutex?"

"Yes, I guess there are some slips in the bag there. But . . ."

"Spasmophen?"

The Mustache nodded reluctantly.

"In that case, I suggest that you apologize immediately and give all of the prescribed medicine back to my client. I want a confiscation receipt for everything else, and then we will deal with this once we get to court."

Don was still holding on to the attorney's hand, and now he was sure that he never wanted to let go.

The policeman began discontentedly to put the medicine back into the bag, and then he pushed it across the table to Don.

"And then there was that part about getting him something to eat," said the attorney.

With a heavy sigh, the Mustache went over to his colleague by the door of the interrogation room. Once there, he turned around.

"It was Eva Strand, right?"

She nodded slightly but didn't take her eyes from Don.

"From the law firm Afzelius in Borlänge?"

She nodded again.

"Are you new there?"

"I don't know about new . . . I've been up here since last summer, when I moved here from Stockholm. I was with the criminal lawyers there for thirteen years. Why?"

"He just means that we so seldom see new faces," said the colleague in a conciliatory tone.

"We usually work together up here," said the Mustache.

"Oh . . . ?" said Eva Strand.

"That's all. So, welcome."

With that, the Mustache slunk off. His colleague gave a little smile after him as he disappeared down the corridor, then turned back to the attorney. "It's been a long night."

"I understand. For my client, as well. And now . . . if you could perhaps let us have some time alone?"

Don didn't release his grip on the attorney's hand until the police officer had let the door swing shut.

She took off her coat and hung it on her chair. Under it, she was dressed in a herringbone jacket with shoulder pads and a rust-brown high-buttoned shirt.

Don thought she was a bit reminiscent of a blond Ingrid Bergman:

an angular face and dressed like someone who'd stepped out of a movie from the forties. *Timeless*—maybe that was the word.

Eva Strand's eyes were blue and slightly transparent, and if Don hadn't felt otherwise from holding her hand earlier, he would have thought that the expression in them was cold.

Then he broke their eye contact and turned all his attention to his bag. After some rummaging among the white boxes, he finally got out six milligrams of alprazolam. Light blue, oval, notched pills. He washed them down with a gulp of the now lukewarm coffee.

"Well then, Don . . ." the attorney began. "Perhaps you could tell me what it was that happened."

He started at the beginning: the encounter in the television studio, Erik Hall's late-night calls, nagging him to come up to Falun to look at the diver's strange ankh. He told her a bit about his own research and tried to emphasize how little he actually cared about mystical objects and that his trip to Dalarna had been something of a snap decision. He said a few words about the motorcycle that had driven away, and it wasn't until he arrived at the part where he entered Hall's cottage that the attorney stopped him.

"So it wasn't locked?"

Don shook his head.

"And then you took the opportunity to go in?"

"Well, he was the one who wanted me to come."

She made a note and gestured to him to keep going. So they went through the story of why he had drunk the wine and how he had maybe walked around the cottage a little bit to have a look around.

"Did you find anything?"

He blinked.

"Why would I have found something?"

"Well, you went there to look at an ankh, right?"

Her pen had stopped. He was irritated and slightly confused. "How should I know where Erik Hall had put his damn ankh?"

"Maybe he told you on the phone?"

"I wasn't exactly walking around looking for it, if that's what you mean."

"I don't mean anything," Eva Strand said, smiling slightly. "But as I understand it, the police are concerned because the ankh is gone."

Under the table, Don fingered the lining of his jacket.

"Well, the police have searched through my clothes, of course, so it will be quite difficult for them to claim that I've stolen anything."

"Have you?"

"What?"

"Stolen anything."

The postcard was still lying there untouched; it was barely noticeable through the stiff fabric of the jacket.

"No. Like I said, this is all just an idiotic misunderstanding."

"That's good."

He sighed and continued to tell her about the blood on his hands and how it had just been an automatic attempt to help Erik Hall. When he finally fell silent, she drew a line and then flipped thoughtfully back through her notes.

"If I understand you correctly, you broke into Hall's cottage, had his blood on your hands, and were drugged when the police arrived on the scene?"

"Drugged, I . . ."

"And your fingerprints are all over the cottage, and you claim to have heard a motorcycle—a BMW endurance racer, if I wrote it down correctly—drive off just as you arrived at the scene, but you have no proof of that. In addition you take narcotics to such an extent that you could easily be labeled an addict." A short pause, then she set down the notebook.

"Well, at least we know what we have to work with."

Then the attorney looked over at the blinds inside the triple-pane windows but turned her head back when she caught sight of her own reflection.

"So what do we do now?" he asked at last.

"Is there anything else I need to know?"

He looked up at her between his fingers.

"I . . ."

"Yes?"

"I've actually been convicted once before."

"I see."

"But it was simple assault, a suspended sentence. A neo-Nazi demonstration that . . ."

When his voice caught, she grasped his fingers gently and pulled them from his face.

"Hey, Don. We can deal with that later. Is there anyone who should know that you're here?"

He thought of his sister, but then he shook his head.

Then he could feel that the alprazolam had finally made his eyes start to feel heavy. He let the wave of drowsiness and calm wash up through his chest. The weariness soon made him lean forward, and he let his cheek fall to rest on the birch veneer of the table.

The attorney took his hand as his breathing became slower and slower.

She sat patiently with him until his rest was interrupted by the sound of a knock. When Don peered up, he saw that the Mustache and his colleague were once again standing over there by the interrogation room door. Their faces were dark.

"Yes?" said Eva Strand.

The colleague squirmed a bit.

"Well, we've just heard from the prosecutor that she got a call from down in Stockholm."

"Oh?"

The Mustache interrupted: "Well, shit, what a way . . ."

"It seems," his colleague continued, "that the suspect is to be moved."

"Moved?" said Eva Strand.

Don got up on his elbows with difficulty, his back sunken, his hair gray and scruffy. He was still having trouble understanding that this conversation was about him.

"And quickly, it seems," said the Mustache. "Some guys who will be taking care of the transport have already come over."

"The National Police?" asked the attorney.

The Mustache raised his eyebrows and answered with a snort: "Sure. That would have looked great, if the National Police had decided to come here and stick their noses into a local murder investigation."

His colleague walked up to Eva Strand and showed her the prosecutor's decision.

"Perhaps your client can explain it."

He looked at Don. "It's two guys from Säpo." The Swedish Security Service.

# 13

# The Dream

After the long hours in the interrogation room, Don was blinded by the powerful sunlight, and he couldn't make out his own crooked shadow until he had blinked a few times.

Then he looked down at his handcuffs, and when the light flashed on the metal, he started to wonder how even a *shmendrik* could think that it was worth the trouble to lock his thin wrists together. But judging by the Mustache's firm grip on his upper arm, the risk that he would attempt escape must be considered imminent, even out here on the sidewalk in front of the Falun police station.

The two men from Säpo were standing by the parking lot, waiting next to a metallic-colored station wagon. One of them had sparse, thinning hair, and now and again he smoothed it in the wind. They were dressed in blue jeans and pale gray jackets, and attorney Eva Strand was standing in front of them and waving some papers indignantly. But when the thin-haired one discovered Don, he seemed to lose all interest in her questions and set a course for the entrance of the police station.

As he handed Don over, the Mustache attempted a sarcastic remark about Stockholmers. But the man from Säpo didn't seem to be in the mood for small talk; he just silently took over the grip on Don's arm.

As they walked past the attorney, Don felt his legs suddenly wobble underneath him, and the thin-haired man had to support him so that he could manage to get into the backseat of the car at all. Then he sat there helplessly and looked out at Eva Strand through the tinted windows.

She still didn't seem to want to give up. He could see her talking on her cell phone now. The men from Säpo just seemed bored, standing there with their arms crossed, waiting out her conversation.

After a bit, the back door on the other side was opened. "Is there room?"

Don nodded gratefully as the attorney moved into the seat next to him. She fastened her seat belt and placed her papers into her bag, with her legs pressed together under the close-fitting suit skirt. Then she turned to him and asked, "Are you sure there's nothing you've forgotten to tell me?"

But Don had no answers, and then the thin-haired man walked once around the car and slammed all the doors.

When the motor had purred to life and they began to move forward, they passed slowly in front of the Mustache. The last thing Don saw was how the *shmendrik* turned around, scratched his head, and then trotted back to the entrance of the police station.

At the first red light, the back-door locks slid down and locked.

"You really must tell us where you're planning on taking us," said Eva Strand.

But the man from Säpo just looked disinterestedly at her in the rearview mirror, and then his eyes moved back to the traffic light just as it turned green.

"This must all be some sort of misunderstanding," she said to herself.

The car began to roll again.

Her fingers drummed against her handbag. Don noticed that the skin covering the attorney's hands was very thin; it lay like a veil over her veins.

Then she continued to put her frustrated questions to the men from Säpo, but after a while Don no longer had the energy to listen. Instead his thoughts wandered back to the long interrogation. But no matter how he turned the conversation over in his mind, he couldn't understand what he could have done differently.

It must just be an idiotic misunderstanding. *Nor Got vaist farvos.* Only God knows why. Soon he would presumably be back in his airless room in the Department of History in Lund, among piles of mixed-up lecture notes and unread student essays.

Don dug out a blister pack of comforting Halcion, mild sleep aid, pushed out a few white tablets. Then he placed them on his tongue, swallowed, and glanced down at the edge of the window, with the depressed lock button.

*"Also . . . die Türen bleiben geschlossen, bitte."*

Once again that disinterested look in the rearview mirror from the thin-haired one. Don let his head fall back against the seat, closed his eyes, and repeated quietly to himself:

*"Die Türen bleiben geschlossen, bitte. Und wenn den Juden Wasser so gefällt, gefällt ihnen Jauche noch viel besser."*

In the darkness behind his eyelids, he slid in through the doors to the 1950s house, and it was summer again, and he was lying on a mattress that smelled like dust and listening to his grandmother's voice. He used to lie like that at Bubbe's feet, under the glass table, his eyes closed while she told stories. *Die Türen bleiben geschlossen, bitte*—the words came from a deserted train station in the beech forests of Poland, where her freight car had stopped on the long journey from the Warsaw ghetto to the concentration camp Ravensbrück.

One hundred degrees, burning rays of sun in through the rusted gaps in the narrow metal walls. They had sat silently in there, waiting, for five days, forgotten on a sidetrack in the railroad chaos of the Holocaust.

Bubbe had with her bare feet trampled the bodies of those who had already suffocated, in the short instances when she wasn't being lifted up toward the ceiling by the pressure of those who still had energy to stand. The Germans had managed to squeeze almost two hundred Jewish men, women, and children into the freight car, behind the bolts of the sliding doors. August, the dog days, and they had received nothing to drink. But when the screams had become too difficult to bear, one of the Germans had enough.

They had heard a fire pump start up, and a few seconds later water had flooded in through the gaps. But the gesture had been meaningless, because the rusty metal had been so hot that most of it immediately turned to steam.

But the commander had been enraged, *toyt meshuge,* about this wastefulness, and the man who had sprayed them was beaten like a dog. Then Bubbe had heard these words:

*"Die Türen bleiben geschlossen, bitte. Und wenn den Juden Wasser so gefällt, gefällt ihnen Jauche noch viel besser."* The doors will remain closed, and if the Jews like water, they'll like piss even better.

Then the SS guards climbed up on the roof of the car, like a flock of ravens in their black coats. Once there they unbuttoned their pants and pissed down into the holes in the rusty metal roof. And Bubbe had been so thirsty—*a shand!* what shame!—that she clawed her way up over the children's backs to fill her mouth with the Germans' warm urine.

The car gave a sudden lurch, and through his sticky eyelashes Don managed to make out a sign that said ENKÖPING 25.

Then his stomach acid must finally have dissolved the triazolam in the white Halcion tablets, because the next time he closed his eyes, it was as though someone had pulled a plug.

When he once again had the sensation of being awake, Don noticed that his body was falling slowly. He was sinking, floating like a feather down through an abyss, past the rounded walls of a tunnel. And when he finally got his sticky eyelashes open, he saw that a blue-violet light was glittering from the inside of the walls.

He floated like a shadow past the trickling light, but then a great void opened up under him. He was sucked down into it faster and faster, until he finally landed in a deep layer of dust.

He had sunk all the way up to his calves into the powdery blanket, and when he moved his boot, the dust was swept along with it; it spread through the violet light like a fan of ash.

Don took another step and it felt as though he could sail and could put his foot back down however he liked, as though he no longer weighed anything.

His feet paddled forward in slow motion, across the surface of the dust, and at the very end of the void he could see the edge of a pool. A stone rose out of the water in the pool, and there, on the top of the stone, was something that looked like a bundle. No, not a bundle . . . there was someone sitting there, someone whose face was hidden in lank black hair.

Then Don heard a voice he thought he recognized come from the stone. It was piercingly unpleasant, but at this distance it was impossible to make out her words.

He must . . . go in the cold water; he waded out to the stone and was soaked up to his waist. At the same time, ice-cold fingers slid up through his throat and tightened along his trachea.

When he finally got close, he stretched his hand out to the long hair that hung in front of the woman's face. But then he stopped himself, because he thought of Bubbe for some reason, and how he had never seen his grandmother's black hair loose, only tied up in a knot. And he was aware that he knew the meaning of every word that he heard muttered, but still he couldn't understand:

*"Di nacht kumt. Red tsu der vand, di nacht kumt."* Night falls and I speak to a wall.

"Bubbe? Grandmother?"

Don was almost sure that he really had spoken the question, and yet he hadn't been able to hear his own voice.

At that second, a white light began to expand from the lank hair, and when he looked up above the crown of the woman's head, he saw that a rectangle of lights several meters high had towered up behind her back.

*"Loz mich tsu ru, Don. Loz mich tsu ru."* Leave me alone.

He wanted very much to say that he would never leave her, but the ice in his throat wouldn't release its grip.

*"S'iz nisht dain gesheft,"* said the piercing voice. None of your business.

Bubbles of new words collected under the knot in his trachea, but he couldn't get an answer to force its way through the ice. It lay like a lid in his throat.

*"S'iz nisht dain gesheft, Don!"*

At the same instant that Bubbe's scream died away in the void, it was as though someone had blown a powerful breath through the white rectangle behind her, and a cloud of shining dust loosened from its surface.

The cloud of dust swept through the air, past Bubbe on the stone, and just as it washed over Don, it was as though someone seized him. He could feel himself being dragged upward and backward by his arms and now he soared back up toward the tunnel again.

When he turned his head to see what it was that was holding him, he saw that the dust had been molded into a figure with a face of light. The face had two holes for eyes, and there was something black on its forehead that spun very quickly.

Far below him he could hear the piercing voice once again:

*"Don, du kenst mir nisht pishn oyfn rukn meynendik as dos iz bloyz regen!"*

Closer and closer to the tunnel now; soon he would be out.

*"Don, du kenst mir nisht pishen oyfen rukn meinendik as dos iz bloyz regen!"*

Then he felt an intense pain just above his eyes. And when he looked back up toward the bright face of dust, the black thing on its forehead had begun to rotate more and more slowly, feebly, sluggishly, and even before it had stopped moving, he recognized the shape of a swastika.

"You really must have taken a wrong turn, now."

The attorney's voice through the darkness.

"I don't think so," the thin-haired man answered.

Don got his eyes to open and turned his aching neck. Eva had moved up to the edge of the seat; she sat with her hand on the back of the driver's seat.

"But you should have continued up toward Bergsgatan to get to the police station. Now we've driven way too far."

*"Du kenst mir nisht pishen oyfen rukn meinendik as dos iz bloyz regen,"* said Don.

The attorney gave a start and turned to him.

"A Yiddish expression. *Du kenst mir nisht pishen oyfen rukn meinendik as dos iz bloyz regen.*"

The thin-haired man's eyes in the rearview mirror.

"You can't piss on my back and make me think it's only rain."

The attorney faced the front again: "I demand to know where we're going now."

But no answer, only the dull sound of the car's tires against the asphalt streets of Stockholm.

Don could vaguely make out the voice blaring from the speakers at some demonstration when they rolled past the light sculpture at

Sergels Torg. Then he saw the entrance of the department store NK through the tinted glass of the window, shadows of all those people with shopping bags on their way home. The wide stairs of Dramaten, the theater, and after that, out toward Strandvägen and the boats.

After they had crossed the Djurgården Bridge and continued toward Skansen, the thin-haired man suddenly turned left up a winding avenue.

After they had passed the majestic oaks along the driveway, the car stopped in a turnaround in front of a turn-of-the-century villa that was covered in dark brown wooden shakes. The roof was irregular, with narrow slopes of glazed green brick. The granite foundation flowed into the surrounding terrace with no transition, which gave the sense that the house had somehow naturally grown out of the original Swedish rock. Through the rear window, Don could see two men come out of the front door of the villa. One was wearing a dark suit and looked as though he was in his sixties. The other was short and had a wide head that seemed to rest directly on his shoulders, which caused him to resemble a toad.

Then the locks popped up, and the man in the dark suit took a few final steps forward and opened the back door on Don's side. He said that his name was Reinhard Eberlein, and even in this first short phrase, Don could make out a slight German accent.

# 14

# Eberlein

A wide hall of stairs with low-hanging chandeliers opened up inside the front door of the villa. The glow from the candles' shafts of imitation candle wax made Don think of a cave of stalactites, but instead of bulging granite, the walls here were covered in oil paintings.

A scent of dust and national romanticism: Zorn's Dalarna girls looking at their reflections in the water, Liljefors's flight of birds, and of course the main attraction—a door-shaped painting by Carl Larsson, centrally placed above the wide, ostentatious staircase. A girl with a parasol, two towheads dressed in frocks. At the very bottom, the title of the painting: *My Loved Ones.* On a tray under a gilded mirror lay several letters, stamped with the German eagle.

The man who called himself Eberlein had hooked Don's arm and led him forward across the creaking parquet. It was presumably the pale gray tone of his face that made Don place him in his sixties, but now he had begun to wonder, because the German was moving as lithely as a cat alongside him. His body thin and sinewy under the elegant suit, a slender slope to his shoulders, and on his pointed nose sat a pair of nonreflective eyeglasses. Below the round, rimless glasses, his mouth was a shade too red, and his lips seemed to have become stuck in an inward smile.

Ahead of them, the other man, who still resembled a toad more than anything else, had already made it halfway up the stairs with Eva Strand. Don's eyes followed the way the attorney's hand slid along the white-glazed railing on her last few steps up toward the balustrade of the upper floor.

The two policemen from Säpo didn't seem to have any intention of following them farther into the house, and the last thing Don noticed, once Eberlein had guided him so far up that he could look back down at the hallway, was that the thin-haired one was slowly lighting a cigarette.

On the upper floor, the Toad led them through a suite of bright parlors that could have been models for a Svenskt Tenn brochure. A birch spiral staircase twined up to a darkened corridor, and at the end of it there was a pair of closed double doors. Eberlein took out two miniature keys, which he had apparently managed to take over from the thin-haired Säpo man. Then he unlocked Don's handcuffs and gently rubbed his wrists. A heavy scent of cologne rose from the German's body.

"I hope you realize that you have nothing to be afraid of." Don heard the accented intonation in his ear. "This will only be a matter of a few questions, asked with utmost friendliness. An exchange of information, if you will."

The German touched him lightly on the arm.

"This way."

The double doors opened into a vaulted library. The shelves along the high walls of the room stretched from floor to ceiling. Endless rows of the black spines of books, which ended in a wall-to-wall carpet so thick that it would swallow all sound. It was like finding oneself in a cocoon. Centrally placed under the glass lamps was a dark-stained table, and Eberlein indicated that he wanted them to sit at it.

Green leather seats, brass rivets. Don sank onto the chair, and, hunching down, pulled his leather bag closer to him on his lap. Then he heard someone behind him, probably the Toad, lock the two doors. With a breath that sounded somewhat strained, Eva Strand also took a seat at the table and started to search through her papers.

"As I said, this will just be a purely informal conversation," Eberlein began, and he brushed Don's bent back lightly as he walked by.

The cocoon of the library crept a bit closer, and Don could feel Eva trying to get him to wake up with a little nudge. But when he remained silent, she answered in his place: "We don't understand what this conversation is meant to be about."

Eberlein pulled out the chair on the other side of the table, adjusted his dark pants, and sat down. Then he twined his fingers together in front of him, and a pair of yellow-green, very deeply set eyes was directed at Don from behind his nonreflective glasses.

"First I would like to welcome you to Villa Lindarne, which is part of the German embassy nowadays."

"So you have orders from the embassy?" said Eva Strand.

A sudden smile swept over Eberlein's face.

"The ambassador is what you could call a good friend, but I personally came here to Stockholm only this afternoon. And I would be grateful, as I said . . ."

He gestured toward her pen.

"Grateful if we could keep this conversation as informal as possible."

The attorney hesitated for an instant, but then she shrugged her shoulders and put down her pen.

"I'm here to ask a few questions on behalf of a foundation," said Eberlein. "There is great interest in Germany in a thorough investigation of this matter, for, shall we say, historic reasons."

"A German foundation that receives help from the Swedish Security Service?" asked Eva Strand.

"Yes, for a short meeting of utmost friendliness."

Eberlein smiled again, but this time the corners of his mouth didn't quite follow in his pale gray face.

"In this case, everyone will profit from cooperation."

"I have a difficult time imagining that the prosecutor in Falun knew about the purpose of this journey."

"I can assure you that everything has been done properly."

"If this is about the death of Erik Hall . . ."

"This matter does not only concern that," said Eberlein. "I am more interested in investigating exactly *what* Erik Hall actually brought with him out of that mine."

There was a gravity in the German's eyes, behind his glasses, that made it hard for Don to look away.

"Did Erik Hall make any suggestion to you that he found any type of document or object down in the mine, besides the missing ankh?"

"He has . . ." the attorney began, but she was interrupted by a cracking voice.

Don swallowed in irritation, trying to get his voice to work: "Why do you want to know?"

"That, Don Titelman, is a very long story."

A cough made Eberlein glance over toward the Toad, who had sat down on a stool with his back leaning against one of the bookcases.

"Far too long," Eberlein repeated.

It looked as though he was waiting, but when Don didn't say anything further, the German tried again.

"The fact is that the ankh Erik Hall happened to find completely by chance is an object that we have good reason to believe actually belongs to us. You could say that *everything* that was in that mine is a clue to a historic mystery that the foundation has spent many years trying to solve. But now Hall happens to have left us, and you seem to be the only one who can guide the matter farther."

"I really have trouble understanding why you think I could help you with it," said Don.

An irritated breath from the Toad in the darkness.

"I only met Erik Hall once," Don continued in his rough voice, "and the only object I know of is that ankh. Other than that, all I know is what has been in the papers."

"It's too bad we had to start our conversation like this," said Eberlein.

"Is it?" said Don.

"Yes, because from what I understand, you're not telling the truth."

Don squirmed in his chair, as though he were adjusting his jacket.

"No, let us start over instead," the German continued. "As I understand it, you had long telephone conversations with Erik Hall the week before he died. And we have heard that there were notes on Hall's hard drive that said that he found at least one type of document down there in the mine, and that he told you about it."

"That doesn't really sound familiar," said Don.

"We've also learned that Erik Hall spoke of some type of 'secret' that he brought with him out of the shaft. Whether he meant the document or some other object by that, we don't know."

"Some object other than the ankh?"

That was the attorney's voice.

"That's what we've come here today to attempt to clear up," said Eberlein.

Don let his eyes slide over toward the Toad, who was sitting with his wide face leaning backward, looking up at the ceiling. Then he heard Eberlein's voice again.

"Did Erik Hall mention anything to you about an object shaped like a star, or an area north of Svalbard?"

Don shook his head.

"And no other documents?"

"No, like I said . . ."

"So what did you talk about?"

"He only called late at night," Don said, squirming again. "He mostly nagged me to come."

"I would like to ask you to think very carefully now," said Eberlein. "Something that might seem utterly meaningless to you might be of great interest to us. The slightest clue . . ."

Don managed to avoid the German's eyes by looking down at his lips. Somehow they were too red to fit with the rest of his face.

"But like I said. Nothing."

Eberlein snapped the fingers of one hand, and the Toad got up awkwardly and waddled up to the table. In his hand he held a paper with faded blue handwriting.

"Does this remind you of anything?"

Looping curves, by the same hand that had written the text on the postcard in Don's pocket.

"No," Don said and tried to shrug his shoulders, but they suddenly felt heavier.

At this point the attorney broke in.

"I am having a very hard time understanding the point in continuing with this. It is perfectly clear that my client doesn't know anything, and furthermore, he has no interest whatsoever in speaking to you. A conversation, you said—in this country this is what we call an interrogation. Now you must see to it that the police from the Security Service take us back to Falun immediately."

The attorney shoved back her chair and stood up.

"And furthermore, Eberlein, or whatever your name is, a great deal of what you have confronted my client with is protected by investigational confidentiality. I can't understand what the Swedish police are thinking to let outsiders have access to this sort of information."

Though Don had also stood up by now, Eberlein remained sitting at the table with his head lowered. It seemed as though the German were thinking about something. After a long time he turned his gaze back to Don.

"Imagine that, I believe your attorney is right."

"She is?" said Don.

"Yes, she's quite right that this should not be considered an interrogation." The inward smile spread again; red lips, gray teeth. With a few lithe steps Eberlein came around the table and laid his hand on Don's shoulder.

"This is no interrogation, and in addition I completely understand why you are reluctant to say anything, the way your situation looks. But since you seem to be the last link . . ."

The German absentmindedly fingered the corduroy fabric of the shoulder of Don's jacket, as though he were thinking it over one more time.

"Since you seem to be last link to Erik Hall and his discoveries, I suppose we can take the time to turn it around and see if we can come to a greater understanding of each other. I'll tell you a story, and you can help me with the end."

"How am I supposed to do that?"

"We'll figure that out when we get there. You'll see."

Eberlein patted Don's arm and said in a slightly lower voice, "I actually think that you, as a researcher, will quite soon come to be as interested as I am in trying to find an answer to this mystery. I mean, once you've come to see it in the right light."

When Eberlein had gotten Don and Eva to sit down again, he walked over to the Toad, next to the bookcase. He crouched down and whispered something. Then the Toad got up with a displeased grunt and disappeared from the room.

"Just wait a little bit," Eberlein said, smiling at Don again. "I believe you will think it is worth the trouble."

# 15

# Elena

It was in her early teens, when her special talents had subsided and disappeared, that Elena had learned to never again make any demands. But on her eighteenth birthday, one of the lower section leaders at the foundation had handed her an apartment key. The key had led to an attic apartment a few blocks away from the large banking hall.

Tall timber-frame houses with bricked gables that were shaped like stairs around a cobblestone square with a walled-in well. Behind one of the solitary windows, at the very top, she had been able to lock the door after herself for the first time.

At first she had interpreted the key as an indication from Vater that he was going to release her to a different life. But everything had stayed the same. It had only been a fifteen-minute walk from the attic apartment to his management office, and work had continued there as it always had, in the shadow of the castle's north tower.

Wrapped up in a blanket in her kitchen alcove, she tasted a spoon of honey out of the jar she must have accidentally left on the table when she departed so hastily for Sweden.

The movement of her arm up to her mouth was the only sign of life in the dreary two-room apartment. She had assumed that furnishing it was pointless.

She could make out her bedroom in the dark on the other side of the door frame in her kitchen alcove. The bed, which she hadn't had time to make, the bureau with the narrow mirror, and the portrait of the Holy Madonna. Otherwise nothing. But in the other room, she had made more of an effort, hung up the boxing bag on a chain and screwed her training equipment onto the wall next to the weapon cabinet.

Elena licked the shaft of the spoon with her tongue. A taste of golden sugar and summer, *miele di acacia.*

She still hadn't had time to catch up on sleep after the long journey back down toward the mist of the Teutoburg Forest, bordering the stinking industrial valley of the Ruhr. For twelve hours, she had watched the asphalt rush past beneath her, lain with the cross glued between her heart and the snow-white tank of the motorcycle.

She thought, as she took another spoonful of honey, that the ache in her thighs from the long hours might be good for her somehow. It was so seldom these days that physical pain affected her; her training with the cheerless men from Sicherheit had at least had that result. Nothing was capable of affecting her anymore.

On the road from Denmark down to Westphalia, she had called the management office once more and was met with questions about Hall and someone they'd called Titelman. Elena had tried to remember everything that had been said in the summer cottage in Falun, and now, at her kitchen table, she went through it yet again to see whether there had been something important she might have missed after all.

She got stuck as soon as she thought of her first encounter with the diver, when she'd said she was a journalist with *La Rivista Italiana dei Misteri e dell'Occulto.* Not even in that instant had she been able to push aside her longing for what she had lost. And she had chosen the name of an Italian New Age magazine just because they had once, so long ago, published a little news item about what they called her astral gifts. But had she really been able to read back then? Like everything else from her first years, that memory was blended with the sensation of dreaming.

When Elena had finally gotten enough of the sweet flavor, she screwed the lid of the honey jar into place and let the blanket slide from her body. Then she got up and walked past the drawn curtains in the window, up to the mirror above the bureau.

She followed the boyish lines from her cheekbones down to her makeup-free mouth. Tousled her short hair, and although she immediately tried to push away the thought, she knew very well who she resembled.

*Miele de acacia,* the honey's flowery vanilla flavor.

She leaned her forehead against the mirror to push away the thought of the solitary woman who had once had to leave Vater's banking hall, denied by her own six-year-old daughter.

But now, behind the honey, came the familiar taste of ricotta; honey and ricotta, the floury cookies she and her sisters had used to take along to the beach. The taste of lemonade, the heat of the Gulf of Naples, and all the smells. The stench of the mountain of garbage that trickled in through the gap in the balcony doors in the run-down apartment complex. She remembered that she had tried to reach up to close them when the smell had been at its worst. But the door handle had been far too high on the balcony door for a child's fumbling hands.

And then her mother's face came toward her; that bright oval above a rayon dress, like an extra shimmering skin around her body. When Elena heard her sisters' laughter, she searched in vain for some way to turn herself back through time in a spiral, so her life could go in a different direction on that particular day. The day when her gifts had been put to the test for the first time.

# 16

# Strindberg

Dusk had begun to fall, and a drizzle came in over the green-glazed brick roof on the hill, wrapping the crowns of the oaks and the rugged rocky knolls of Skansen in a cloak of moisture. But inside the windowless heart of the villa, the crypt-shaped library, you couldn't tell night from day. Warm incandescent light came down from the glass lamps above the table, and all that could be heard was Eberlein slowly drumming his fingers against the lid of a large metal box. Between the German's well-manicured nails, Don had just managed to make out the label that was riveted in place:

**Strindberg 1895–97**

The Toad, who had just brought the metal box in, had once again sat down on his stool over by the bookcases, and his face was half-hidden in darkness. Next to Don, Eva Strand had leaned backward with her arms and legs crossed, her mouth drawn into a line. Then the fingers stopped drumming and Eberlein broke the silence.

"Now then, to help you see the matter in the right light . . . may I begin with a question: Are you familiar with the Taklimakan Desert?"

There was a displeased sigh from the Toad over in the corner.

"The Taklimakan Desert," continued Eberlein, taking no heed, "is an ocean of sand that stretches from the roof of the world, the Pamir Mountains, 115,000 square miles straight into northwestern China. Arctic cold in the winter, and once summer comes, the sand can be transformed to a kiln on certain days, with heat that can reach over 122 degrees Fahrenheit. Hell on earth, it is said. In any case, it's a place that's impossible to live in, and up until the end of the 1800s, the area was only marked on maps with a white spot, a *terra incognita* as large as Germany. At that time no one knew anything about its interior, not even those who lived near the desert. The only information about it was a few lines in the manuscripts Marco Polo left behind in the 1300s; fanciful stories about ancient cities buried under sand dunes hundreds of yards high. The first person who ventured out in that absolute emptiness came from a remote place up in northern Europe. His name was Sven Hedin."

There was a creak as Don changed position in his chair. His mind was still somewhat numb and sluggish from the sleeping pills he had taken in the car, and being in this library gave him the distinct feeling of having tumbled down Alice's rabbit hole.

"You are familiar with Sven Hedin's journeys, I presume," said Eberlein.

The faint smile of the German, which followed this question, was so annoying that Don made an effort to sober up: "I maintain a deep and indelible memory of Adolf Hitler and consider him to be one of the greatest men in the history of the world."

There was yet another mumble from the Toad, but Don just shrugged his crooked shoulders. "That's what Sven Hedin wrote about Hitler at the end of the war. 'I maintain a deep and indelible memory of Adolf Hitler and consider him to be one of the greatest men in the history of the world.' He was ennobled—Hedin, that is."

"Well, where Sven Hedin stood politically has nothing to do with this. I can assure you of that," said Eberlein.

Then the German pushed the box aside and leaned forward over the table.

"No, this is about something that occurred long, long before the war, when Hedin had barely turned thirty and was still a young explorer. In the beginning of 1895 he stood at the edge of the Taklimakan Desert. In order to get there, he had traveled by railroad car from Saint Petersburg to Tashkent in Russian Turkestan, and from there he continued across the frozen steppe in a fur-lined horse cart, and then he went by foot, along with Kyrgyz nomads, through the eighteen- or twenty-thousand-foot mountain passes of Pamir. That in itself was a truly remarkable journey at the time. On the fifth of January 1895, he finally reached the oasis city of Kashgar, the site next to the Taklimakan Desert where the caravan routes of the Silk Road have converged since thousands of years ago. With his one-man tent, his tools, and his weapons, he disappeared into the sea of sand on the twenty-second of January with a few camels and some servants and donkeys. At that time, he knew nothing about the violent sandstorms that can redraw the desert in a few hours with their whirling sand, nor had he heeded the warnings he had heard in Kashgar about the supposed existence of strange voices out in the emptiness; voices that bewitched wanderers and caused each one to get lost in the labyrinths of the desert.

"Everything went as planned on the first and second nights, and when the group camped under the open sky, Hedin sketched the geometry of the terrain with his charcoal pencil so that he wouldn't lose his way. But on the third night, the sandstorm came. According to what Hedin wrote later, it raged for all of seventy-seven hours. When the black dust finally settled, the whole landscape around their camp had been transformed. The storm hadn't just moved the three-hundred-foot-tall sand dunes—they were obliterated by the wind, and where there had been sand before, there were now petrified trees stretching their branches toward the sky. When he had been wandering among the trunks for a while, Hedin discovered some white bars sticking out of the sand, and when he came closer, he saw that he was standing at the remains of a fence with widely spaced posts. Along with his servants, he followed the fence as it stretched to the west, and after only a few miles, they reached a group of empty houses, the remains of a city that the strong winds had swept clean of hundreds, or who knows, perhaps thousands of years' worth of layers of sand. Hedin later wrote that his servants demanded to leave the place, which they called the Ivory Houses, but for his part, he danced around with joy and was convinced that he'd found another Pompeii.

"In some of his first notes, Hedin wrote that the houses appeared to be built of wood, more specifically poplar. Poplar, in the middle of a sea of sand! But although the white facades felt hard at first, they fell apart like cracked glass when he tapped them with his riding whip. Hedin also painted some pictures showing that some of the walls were covered in frescos: naked praying women, with something that Hedin interpreted as an Indian caste mark painted on their foreheads. Men with peculiar weapons, and at their sides, Buddha figures with the lotus flower in their hands. Hedin came to the conclusion that he found himself in something that had once been a temple. Today we know it as Dandan Oilik, the buried city. But what is less well-known," Eberlein continued, "is what Hedin found *under* the buried city on that first day. In a letter, which we have access to, Hedin describes quite dramatically how by mere chance he stepped through the floor in one of the grandest buildings and crashed headlong down onto a stone mosaic in what seemed to him to be a much older burial chamber. He never succeeded in dating it. Around the greenish black heart of the mosaic lay twelve wrapped-up bodies, mummies that had been preserved and dried out by the desert air long ago. Then, when he walked closer, he found an ivory-colored cross in the shape of the hieroglyph called the ankh on the chest of one mummy. On top of the ankh, on its crosspiece, someone had long ago placed yet another object: a star made of five staffs protruding from a hub. The shape that the Egyptians called *seba,* which they regarded as a symbol for the god Osiris, ruler of the extreme periphery, the god who holds the keys to the very underworld."

Eberlein stopped speaking and observed Don for a long time as though searching for answers.

*"Ver volt dos geglaibt?"* Don said at last.

Eberlein didn't release him from his gaze.

"I mean, a star and an ankh in a sunken burial chamber under a sunken city . . ."

Don's eyes were burning, twenty-four hours without real sleep.

"*Ver volt dos geglaibt?* Who would have believed that?"

Eberlein gave a weak smile. "But you see . . . Sven Hedin never *tried* to convince anyone of the import of his discovery in the burial chamber under Dandan Oilik. The fact is that he considered the whole story embarrassing until his dying day. Because you can't very well tell people about sensational, historical objects that you found and later happened to . . . lose."

He coughed, took a handkerchief from his jacket pocket, and wiped his lips. "Dreadfully dry air in here, isn't it? Perhaps you would like something to drink?"

Eva Strand's expression didn't change, but Don nodded. The German turned to the Toad, who got up from the darkness in the corner, mumbling. When he waddled out into the corridor, he left one of the library doors ajar, and Don could glimpse the red rays of the sunset in the villa windows beyond the corridor and the spiral staircase. Then he heard Eberlein's voice again.

"We know that Hedin brought the ankh and the star back with him to the oasis at Kashgar, because they're noted on his inventory list from the excavations. What happened later was presumably largely due to Hedin's personality. He was nearly obsessed with correctly describing, by himself, each object that he discovered, before he packed them in shipping boxes to be sent back to the scientific academies in Stockholm. But with the ankh and star, that proved to be impossible. Despite a few primitive tries, Hedin didn't even succeed in determining what material the objects were made of. To hide this failure from his colleagues, he then sought the advice of an acquaintance who was living in France at the time. He placed the ankh and star in a sealed brass case, along with a letter in which he described the discovery and asked for a technical assessment. The parcel is noted in Hedin's papers, and it arrived, as far as we have managed to ascertain, from Kashgar to the Hospital St. Louis in Paris on February 2, 1895. The hands that loosened the rivets of the box were wrapped up in strips of linen to relieve certain chapped rashes that had been brought forth by long nights of experiments with alchemy. They were hands that, for a month's time, could hardly hold a pen."

Eberlein's face seemed to have become younger somehow in the soft incandescent light from the glass lamps; the grayness was on its way to disappearing, and now it was just as though he were waiting for Don to say the name:

"Strindberg?"

A nod. Don tried to keep his mouth closed, but he couldn't help laughing with a hoarse hack, which disappeared into the wall-to-wall carpet and the leather-bound books. But the German's eyes didn't yield; he just continued:

"It might seem like an amazing coincidence, but you must understand that the Swedish upper class at this time was a very limited circle. Besides this, Strindberg was a person whom Hedin knew had access to the analytical laboratory at the Sorbonne, which at the time was one of Europe's most technologically advanced facilities."

Don glanced at Eva, but she only rolled her eyes. Then he turned back to Eberlein and said, "But just the thought that Sven Hedin, of all people, would send something to August Strindberg . . ."

"Yes?" Eberlein asked.

"You know that they were mortal enemies, don't you?"

"Oh, but that animosity came later! And it's possible," continued

Eberlein, "that it's connected with the way Strindberg handled Hedin's two objects. No, up until 1895 they had a good relationship."

Eberlein smiled again.

The sun must have already gone down, because the light in the vault of the library hardly changed as the doors swung open and the Toad came back. He placed the tray on the table with a bang. A silvery tea kettle, three gold-rimmed cups on gold dishes, and alongside them a discreet pile of white cotton, which Don realized after an instant must be several pairs of thin gloves.

Eberlein got up and walked around the table, and there was a clinking sound as he arranged the porcelain with a few dainty movements. The steam from the cups spread a soporific scent of poppy and cinnamon, and Don sneaked a few fingers into his bag to hunt for two capsules of energizing amphetamine derivatives. The German meditatively raised the porcelain cup to his red lips.

"In any case," Eberlein said when he'd taken a sip, "Strindberg's experiments with the ankh and the star went very poorly. He was, of course, something of a charlatan when it comes down to it, a poet-chemist, as he himself wanted to be called. When it came to determining the origin and properties of a material, his knowledge was entirely too superficial. In addition, Strindberg was somewhat moody during this period, and after a month of failed experiments, he grew tired of 'Hedin's desert things,' as he called them. Because he didn't want to admit that his experiments had gone badly, he just sent a short explanation in which he lied and said the ankh and star had quite simply disappeared, misplaced at Café du Cardinal in the second arrondissement. Sven Hedin became enraged, of course, but from his position in the deserts of Central Asia, he could hardly do anything about it."

Eberlein walked up to the table and let his nails glide over the metal box, down onto the back of it, where some sort of lock gave a click.

"No, *August* Strindberg never got anywhere with the ankh and star."

Then he unfastened two more hinges on the sides, and the lid swung open.

"He who wishes to get the story straight loves a collector, isn't that right, Titelman?"

Eberlein stood with his hand on the back of his chair and looked down at the contents of the box.

"Yes, we love a person like August Strindberg, someone so convinced of his own importance that he dates laundry bills, shopping lists, and the tiniest inferior sketch to be kept for posterity. More than ten thousand letters are said to have been preserved, to Nietzsche, Georg Brandes, Zola . . . and then there are the letters that Strindberg sent to his cousin Johan Oscar, or Occa, as his family called him, in the late 1800s. The friendship between them was actually so close that August later became godfather to Occa's son Nils. Now, it just so happened that by this time, in the early spring of 1895, this Nils Strindberg had grown up to become one of the most promising physicists and chemists in the country. We know that Occa mentioned his son's findings about electrical resonance in a letter dated February 2, 1895, and that only a week or so later, Strindberg sent a series of physical questions directly to Nils's address at the university college in Stockholm. Nils wrote a detailed answer, which is also preserved, along with another dozen letters. During that entire spring, he became something of a confidant, even almost forsworn, to August Strindberg in his alchemic research. After a while, the tone becomes more personal, and in one of the last letters, from June 1895, one can read Nils's complaints about how Stockholm is so dreary in the summer, when all scholarly work has been put aside. In answer he received a parcel from his godfather in Paris that contained two objects: a cross that ended in an eye, and a five-pointed star in Egyptian style."

There was a clatter as Eberlein put down his porcelain cup. Then he sat down once again at the table, across from Eva and Don, pulled the metal box a bit closer, and slowly started to pull on a pair of cotton gloves.

"What I intend to show you now is something that we brought primarily as a basis of comparison for Erik Hall's discovery in the mine. But I expect it might be able to serve another purpose."

Eberlein twined his hands together to pull the white fabric tight between his fingers.

"In the note that Strindberg sent with the package, he didn't mention a word about Sven Hedin or the Taklimakan Desert. All he wrote were a few short lines requesting a careful analysis of the ankh and star and a quick answer. The first thing the photographically inclined Nils did when he inspected the objects . . ."

From the metal box Eberlein took a thin, rectangular carton that appeared to be made of cardboard. He placed it on the table and loosened its string so that he could open the lid. On the very top was a layer of grayish padding, which Eberlein loosened and spread out before them. Then he stuck his hand down into the carton again and brought forth a number of fragile plates of glass, which he carefully began to lay out on the soft padding.

Don leaned forward so he could see.

At first it was difficult, with all the light that was reflected in the dark glass, but when Eberlein provided a shadow with his hand there was no longer any room for doubt.

On the oxidized silver of the glass plates shone an ivory-colored cross with an eye, and beside the cross lay a brightly glittering star, with five arms sticking out from its center.

Beside the objects someone had placed a ruler. Looking at it, Don could tell that the cross was 16¾ inches long, including its eye, with a crosspiece of 8⅜ inches. In another of the pictures there was a handwritten note that the *seba* star had been measured at 4⅓ inches in diameter.

"It feels different when you see it, doesn't it?" said Eberlein.

By now, Eva had also leaned over the table. She grabbed hold of the gray padding, pulled the glass plates closer, and studied them. Eberlein shook a pair of thin gloves loose from the pile of cotton and handed them over. She slipped them on and lifted up and examined the delicate glass.

"Collodion negatives," Eberlein said after she had been looking for a while. "The emulsion is made up of guncotton dissolved in alcohol, ten seconds of exposure. Good definition, isn't it?"

Don met the mirror image of Eva's eyes in the dark fragment.

When Eberlein lifted away the next layer of padding, they could see a bundle of yellowed notes on the bottom of the carton. They appeared to be bound with wire, and on the top page was stamped: STOCKHOLM UNIVERSITY COLLEGE—BERZELIUS LABORATORY. Under the stamp came rows of numerals and abbreviations, carelessly written more and more densely in dark blue ink.

The German placed the bundle of papers on the table next to the glass plates. Then he unwound the wire, loosened the first page, and gave it to Don, along with a pair of white gloves.

"From the experiments in mid-June 1895," said Eberlein.

Don was able to recognize a few chemical terms, but the rest of the text ran off in impossible, meandering handwriting.

"Arends's stenographic system," Eberlein said. "Nils Strindberg always used shorthand when he was working alone in the laboratory. What you're looking at concerns some of his early experiments with acids. He later attempted to use chemicals to affect the surface of the metal, but he didn't get any results there, either." Eberlein turned some papers to the side.

"This is from later at night, when he had begun to examine the inscriptions on the ankh. Nils Strindberg used a magnifying glass and a microscope, but his notes on this are rather muddled, because he couldn't explain how someone had managed to carve the etchings into the ankh. He couldn't do anything to its surface at all, not even when he used one of the Berzelius Laboratory's instruments for testing hardness, which had a diamond tip. Another thing that surprised him was the exceedingly light weight of the object."

Eberlein pointed at a column of crossed-out numbers.

"The ankh and the star hardly gave any reading at all on the laboratory scale."

Turning a few more pages.

"Several days later, he actually began to ask himself whether the objects were composed of metal at all. It was true that they reflected incidental light and they had a luster of metal, but no matter how hard he tried, he could get the ankh and the star to conduct neither electricity nor heat. Nils Strindberg tried to heat up the objects one at a time on the wire gauze of his Bunsen burner, but they didn't seem to be affected even at 2700 degrees Fahrenheit. Nor did he need tongs to remove them from the flame, for he writes that the objects were still cool, almost chilly, after being warmed for half an hour. It wasn't until June 27, 1895, that he had the breakthrough he'd been waiting for."

Eberlein searched ahead a bit through the pile with his white cotton fingers. At last he seemed to find the right place, and he put aside the pages he'd skimmed.

The notes that lay before them now were very different from the earlier ones; they were filled with rough sketches that appeared to have been jotted down in great haste. In several places the ink had been blotted into dark blue puddles.

"You see," said Eberlein, "the Bunsen burner at the Berzelius Laboratory had a maximum temperature of approximately 2700 degrees, but on the evening of June 27, Nils Strindberg had set up a cylinder of pure oxygen at the air intake to see if he could push the temperature up a bit more. In a moment of carelessness, or plain laziness if you prefer, he warmed the two objects up simultaneously for the first time, and he had placed the star on the crossbar of the ankh. Just when he was about to make the blue flame turn white via the gas valve—the objects melted together completely unexpectedly. At that time the temperature had only reached . . ."

"Two thousand, two hundred twenty-eight degrees," said Eva Strand. She pointed at the number next to the exclamation point.

"At 2228 degrees"—Eberlein nodded—"on the wire gauze in the flame of the Bunsen burner, the objects melted together. Nils Strindberg writes that it was as though the star suddenly just sank into place totally seamlessly, in the crossbar of the ankh, as though the two objects were really just two parts of something that had once been a whole. Yet on earlier attempts the star and ankh had been completely resistant to heat."

Don felt a wave within him; the dextroamphetamine capsules must finally have dissolved and begun to work. A quickly increasing alertness made his mouth feel dry.

"You can see for yourselves," said Eberlein, pointing at one of the sketches.

In the middle of the sketched ankh there were indeed five thin lines, the rays of a star that had been affixed to the handle under the eye. Alongside the picture was a vertical note, written in pencil. Don turned the paper and read:

> At the point of intersection the navigational instrument becomes fluid, like quicksilver.

Don looked up at Eberlein:

"Navigational instrument?"

He looked down again at the fused ankh and star, which Nils Strindberg had so hastily sketched at different angles all over the sheet. At the very bottom of the page was a version in which the ink had run out into a smudged blue hemisphere, like an arched halo above the horizontal object.

"He was able to depict the reaction better on the next page," said Eberlein, switching pages.

Here Nils Strindberg had taken the time to make two considerably larger and more detailed drawings.

In the upper picture, what Don had interpreted as just a blot of ink had been sketched as a gray-blue sphere that arched like a dome above the fused ankh and star. Seven points were marked in a familiar pattern at the highest part of the sphere, and there was another penciled note next to the topmost point.

The North Star in the Dragon's Wing

"The Dragon's Wing," said Eberlein. "Nils Strindberg's name for the constellation we call Ursa Minor today. The Little Bear, or sometimes the Little Dipper."

From there, his fingers followed the seven points on the sphere above the ankh and star, from the square of the dipper up to the end of its handle. "First the double stars Pherkad and Kochab lit up. This one is Anwar al Farkadain, and here is Ahfa al Farkadain. Then come Urodelus and Yildun, and at the very top here is Polaris, the Polar Star, or the North Star, as Nils Strindberg calls it. The star that is always fixed above the north pole of the earth." Eberlein sat silently for a minute and studied the drawing. Then he said:

"According to Strindberg's notes, the pattern of these seven points appeared out of thin air just above the ankh and star, almost immediately after the objects had fused for the first time. At first he thought it was a case of some stray sparks from the Bunsen burner, and he couldn't understand why they remained suspended there. Then, after a minute or so, the constellation was joined into this first celestial sphere that he's drawn over the ankh and star. He later wrote that it was like watching a halo form out of nowhere."

"The *first* sphere?" asked Don.

Eberlein nodded toward the lower drawing.

Don passed his tongue over rough lips and slowly moved his gaze. In the next picture, there was indeed another sphere. Under the starry sky with the Little Dipper, Nils Strindberg had drawn yet another half circle above the ankh and star, a smudged gray lower dome, covered in contours that could hardly be misunderstood.

"He's drawn the northern hemisphere?"

"He's drawn the other sphere," said Eberlein.

And the German followed the lines of land with a cotton-clad finger:

"The Siberian coast along the Arctic Ocean. The Kola Peninsula. The fjords in northern Norway, Svalbard and Sjuøyane. The ends of the glaciers in Greenland and the Lincoln Sea. The Canadian north coast, and the tundra in Alaska at the Bering Strait. And here—"

His finger moved back toward the middle of the lower sphere.

"The North Pole."

"So what is that?" said Eva.

A thin line ran from the North Star toward a point several inches below Eberlein's finger.

"That," said Eberlein, "is a ray of light. At the end of the reaction, it fell from the North Star down toward the northern hemisphere, and Nils Strindberg seems to have assumed almost immediately that it served as some sort of guide."

Don lifted the yellowed laboratory papers to get better light from the glass lamps.

The ray that fell from the North Star ended in a small X just north of the contour that Eberlein had called Svalbard. But now that the light was brighter, Don could see that there were actually several small X's in this particular area, drawn in pencil and carefully numbered. They seemed to correspond to a list in the right margin:

pos. 1 (29/6): lat. 82° 50' N long., 29° 40' E
pos. 2 (30/6): lat. 83° 45' N long., 27° 10' E !
pos. 3 (1/7): unchanged.
pos. 4 (2/7): unchanged.

pos. 5 (3/7): lat. 83° 10' N long., 34° 30' E !!
pos. 6 (4/7): unchanged. !!!

"After several attempts, Nils Strindberg managed to measure with surprising accuracy where the end of the ray pointed," Eberlein said when Don looked up. "As you see, small but regular changes in position occurred from the start, and it took a long time before he was able to map a pattern."

The German flipped past several pages of increasingly detailed drawings of the sky, the hemisphere, and the ray, until he arrived at a carefully organized chart. He followed the dates and the positional notations with his finger:

"This is, as far as we know, the first proper compilation that Nils Strindberg made of the movements of the ray. It was in the beginning of August 1895, and he must have learned to sketch quickly by that time, because the reaction with the spheres lasted only about ten minutes at each attempt. After that time, the ankh and star fell apart once again into two cool, perfectly shaped objects, and it was as though they had never fused." Eberlein let the chart remain in front of them as he began to collect the glass plates on the gray padding.

"As you can see," he continued, with his head bent, picking among the glass plates, "there were about fifty attempts, during which the sequence of events was always the same. Nils Strindberg laid the star on the handle of the ankh on the wire gauze of the Bunsen burner and adjusted the flame to the correct temperature. When the ankh and star fused together into a single instrument, the seven points always began to shine. At each attempt they formed the pattern of the Little Dipper, with the North Star at the zenith above the star, which was fused to the middle of the ankh. After another minute or so, the celestial sphere appeared, soon followed by the dark half circle of the northern hemisphere. The terminus of the reaction was always the bright, thin ray that fell from the North Star down to a point in the vicinity of the eighty-third parallel, north of Svalbard and Spitsbergen. And if you look there in the list, the distance between the positions as they changed is small; they are within a radius of approximately seventy miles. In the end, Nils Strindberg came to the conclusion that the change in position returned regularly, and that the ray moved about every third day. It was almost as though it was following something within this limited area north of Svalbard. Like an indicator searching for a target."

Eberlein folded the padding around the glass plates. Then he laid them carefully back in the carton.

*"Ver volt dos geglaibt,"* Don said quietly.

# 17

# The Awakening

The frozen instant had slashed its way into Elena's dreams time after time, forcing her to wake up in a cold sweat. And even now, when she had sat up on the edge of the bed and looked out into the darkness of the attic apartment, she couldn't get the image to disappear completely.

The memory of the woman whose face was so like her own; the short black hair, the high cheekbones, the wide mouth. Her mother was still there, on her knees on the marble floor at the bottom of the stairs in the banking hall, her arms open, calling for Elena to come. Then the lingering echo of her own short answer, the voice of a six-year-old, squeaky and thin in the great room:

"*Wer ist sie, Vater?* Vater, who is that?"

And when she had seen the guards coming, she gripped Vater's bony fingers even harder. Because of course she knew quite well who it was, who had finally come to the bank in Wewelsburg to fetch her. But that woman had come far too late.

*

Elena first dared to whisper her deepest secret to her mother at the age of five. That she had the ability to look into other people's thoughts, see all their dreams and hopes in distorted, brilliantly colored forms.

At first her mother had laughed at her and passed everything off as a child's fantasies. But when Elena drew pictures of the strange perversions and desires of adults, her mother's smile had faded away.

That spring so long ago, when all Elena wanted to do was play with her sisters, she had been dragged to her first series of parapsychology tests.

Like a circus monkey, she had been made to demonstrate her ability to read hidden series of numbers. The *ganzfeld* experiment, in which her eyes were covered and she was forced to wear headphones full of white noise. And then: the long journey to the man in the north and the language that sounded so dirty and hard. The memory of panic as her head was put into something that was like the opening of a washing machine. Her hair twisted together with metal clips and the top of her head covered in adhesive wires, the first measurement of a little girl's extraordinary ability to perceive astral wave patterns and electrical activity.

She had been abandoned there in Wewelsburg with Vater for more than a year, as one winter had turned into another. Until one early December morning when a woman had come back, as though dropped from heaven into the banking hall, to bring her home.

And even if she was ashamed of it, Elena had always felt that she had asked exactly the right question after that long period. Because what right did that woman have to believe that a six-year-old, after all that had happened, would still want to recognize her own mother, or, for that matter, that she would be willing to leave?

During this first year in Wewelsburg Elena had been transformed into another person. The strangers had treated her as a princess, giving her all she had ever dreamed of. Vater had prized her psychic abilities and tenderly helped her to explore the immensity of their scope.

Over and over during that year she had been told that her mother had been richly compensated. And, in the dim light of the banking hall, the denial had seemed a fitting retribution against someone who had so carelessly given her child away.

After that morning, the woman had never come back. And it wasn't until she was a teenager, as her abilities slowly died away, that Elena happened to find out what had occurred.

That her parents had been in a hurry on that summer day, that her sisters hadn't been buckled in, and that the serpentine road across the mountains down to the coast had been muddy from prolonged rains. That a pickup had come into a curve at an excessive speed, and that the brake pads of the Citroën had been badly worn.

It was just an unfortunate coincidence, they had told her. The deadly plunge down to the sea had just been one of those things that was no one's fault. And any possibility that she would find answers had disappeared along with it. But why would a child who was given away seek answers?

Elena pushed the pillow up behind her and looked toward the attic apartment's only window, but the image of the heartbroken woman still wouldn't disappear.

Inwardly, she tried to get the six-year-old on the stairs of the bank to look up at Vater instead. See the happiness in his eyes; it had always been there during the first years. Think of their work with the sparkling dust under the glass windows of the lead boxes and the geometric patterns that had once sparkled up at her so clearly.

Not until later, when she was so much older and her senses had been mute for a long time, did Elena understand what she'd helped Vater and the foundation see.

But they hadn't been able to get much further, not even with her help. The material they'd had to work with in the lead-encased glass cylinders had been no more than a few flakes from the source that had been closed for so long.

Then Elena felt how the six-year-old slowly began to move her gaze down the stairs toward her mother's face. She did all she could to stop the chain of memories. She wanted to remain in the long silence before the question came:

*"Wer ist sie, Vater?"*

In that drawn-out instant, Elena could count the windows in the large banking hall, see the winter light that fell pale against the smooth gray stone tiles. The seams at the shoulders of her mother's coat, her open, inviting arms, and her tense smile. Then the images rolled on again.

Yet something was so different this time, because there was a sudden crackle, and the soundtrack of the memory changed. The child's question disappeared in a distant murmur of voices, the same voices she'd heard during the long motorcycle trip from Falun to Wewelsburg.

Elena threw off the blanket and ran across the floor to the kitchen alcove. Because she knew only one way to get the persistent dream to come to an end, to get all these grim things to be quiet and die away.

She pulled out the top drawer and turned on the gas stove. Then she placed the tip of the knife into the burning flame and heated the metal until it glowed red.

She rolled the bandage off of her chalk-white arm, exposing the row of red burn marks. There was a sizzling sound as she pressed the blade of the knife against her bare skin.

Inside the pain, it was as though someone had turned up the volume of the murmuring voices, and Elena felt heavy vibrations coming from a point just behind her forehead. Then, with what sounded like a tape being played backward, she heard syllables, a soft voice that she knew so well.

*"Devi darmi la, Elena.* You must give it to me. *La croce.* The cross. *Elena, dammela."*

The tip of the knife in the gas flame again, trembling this time, letting it burn away her skin until everything inside her went black. She sank to the floor and pressed her hands to her head, but she could no longer find silence.

# 18

# The *Eagle*

The last page of Nils Strindberg's laboratory notes had been pieced together from several different sheets of paper, and when Eberlein had unfolded it in front of Eva and Don, it covered the better part of the surface of the table under the glass lamps.

As in the earlier drawings, a lofty celestial sphere arched above the ankh, with the constellation of the Little Dipper at its center. This time, the geography of the northern hemisphere had been drawn under the sky with meticulous precision.

From the first hasty sketches, in which the contours of the coastlines had hardly been discernible, Strindberg had advanced to the detailed projection of a map in which the prime meridian ran in a straight line from Greenwich in London up to the Arctic and the North Pole.

A bow-shaped grid spread east from this line toward Svalbard and Spitsbergen, and just north of the islands there was a shaded circle with the note:

Each 3rd day new ray position
+always returns within the circle:

lat. 82° 10' N—84° 20' N

long. 21° 0' E—39° 20' E

the radius of the area (approx.) 65 nautical miles = 120 km

"There are some things," said Eberlein, "that indicate that Nils Strindberg had contacted the engineer by the middle of July 1895. But the first time this map is mentioned is in the memorandum from their meeting in Gränna in the beginning of August. As you can see, the young physicist was quite sure by this time that the ray moved only within a radius of about 120 kilometers. No matter what the North Star pointed out, the goal was just north of Svalbard, and it would theoretically be possible to reach it via a short journey by air, over the ice."

Don rested his head in his hands where he sat, bent forward and looking down at the glued-together sheets of paper. At the topmost point of the coast of Svalbard were a few half-faded lines, written in more pedantic handwriting than Strindberg's, that began with a question:

Strong northeasterly winds?

"We don't know what Engineer Andrée thought of this first meeting with the twenty-two-year-old physicist from Stockholm, with his map and his Bunsen burner, but Nils Strindberg describes it as a disappointment."

Eberlein carefully smoothed out a wrinkle that had formed in the paper along the contours of the English Channel, and then he continued:

"Strindberg believed, of course, that Andrée had been serious when he spoke of a hot air balloon journey to the North Pole, and at first it seemed that he was. Over a simple lunch at his home on this beautiful August day, Andrée told him about the perfect flying conditions in the Arctic. About the midnight sun, whose light would make navigation easier, and that the journey in the gondola would be warm and pleasant. He described the system of drag-ropes and sails that would make it possible to steer the balloon, and the mild summer weather they could expect. Nils was, of course, familiar with the engineer's plans; the papers wrote of nothing else at that time, and indeed, that was also the reason he had come to Gränna. But in his notes after the meeting, he writes that Andrée's enthusiasm seemed to fade the longer lunch went on, and that the conversation petered out after a while. When Strindberg finally got ready to demonstrate the reaction with the Bunsen burner, Andrée remarked that he wasn't particularly interested in antiques and works of art, and at first he explained away the spheres as a cheap trick. Then he began to place the blame on a lack of money. Before the Royal Academy of Sciences, Andrée had claimed that the entire expedition would cost only 130,000 kronor, although that amount was very much on the low side. Now he admitted that he might have idealized the project a bit to get Oscar II and Alfred Nobel each to contribute a donation. By the time the coffee arrived, with cognac and cigars, it was already clear to Nils Strindberg that Andrée's North Pole plans were a charade, a way to attract free publicity. It also came as something of a shock to him that the engineer had flown a balloon a total of only nine times, and that most of the flights had ended in wrecks. Andrée claimed that he still suffered from back pain after a landing on Gotland, where he had been carried by the wind from Gothenburg earlier that spring."

In order to have space to unfold the glued map, Eberlein had moved the metal box to the edge of the table. Now he lifted it back and placed the box in front of him, alongside the lines for Normandy and Brittany. Don looked at Eva as the German once again undid the catches on the lid. She twisted her arm toward him and pointed at her watch. Then he noticed that she was shaking her head slightly.

"That the expedition happened at all," Eberlein continued, "was due only to Nils Strindberg. In a letter dated the seventeenth of

August, he asked his father, Occa, how one might go about getting a large sum of money to make Andrée's project a reality. Occa, who was a wholesaler specializing in trade between Hamburg and Berlin, strongly advised against it at first, but in the end he arranged contact with a group of German businessmen. On the third of September 1895, Nils Strindberg and Andrée stepped off the train at the newly built Bahnhof Berlin Zoologischer Garten, and after a demonstration of the Bunsen burner and the spheres, they were able to convince the Germans to put up the finances, a sum of 2 million kronor. This was a time when the interest in Egypt had reached feverish levels, and the Germans were surely inspired by the unparalleled discoveries the Englishmen had just made in the Valley of the Kings. The financiers quite simply hoped that Strindberg's navigational instrument would turn out to be a treasure map." An inward smile passed over Eberlein's face, and then he continued.

"But there were a few conditions. For one, the businessmen demanded that the *main purpose* of the balloon trip would be to explore the area that the North Star pointed out above Svalbard; whether they also happened to reach the North Pole was of less interest. The second condition was that the Swedish donors must not know of their investment, because they didn't want to risk their defense-industry contacts with the Nobel firm. They assumed, not entirely without reason, that Alfred Nobel would protest if he found out that German interests were trying to influence Andrée's North Pole expedition. The third and final condition was that all information about the Bunsen burner, the ankh and star, and any discoveries in the designated area would be kept secret and would *for all time* be preserved by a foundation with its headquarters in North Rhine–Westphalia. Engineer Andrée refused to sign at first, but was eventually convinced by Nils."

Don watched as Eberlein opened the lid of the box and took out a small green-checked book. The cover of the book was of a smooth material, similar to oilcloth. Inside the cover, the pages seemed crinkled and bent, as though they had been exposed to a great deal of moisture.

"On the thirtieth of May 1897, after two years of preparation, the expedition's ship headed in toward Svalbard and the cliffs of Danskøya through rotten, broken-up ice. I don't know if you've seen the pictures, but they seem quite unprepared, Andrée and Strindberg, standing there side by side on the deck of the gunboat *Svensksund.* Two slender men with gold watches and suits, their hands inside the lapels of their jackets. The only person on the expedition who had much experience with physical labor was Knut Frænkel, whom Andrée had demanded they bring along for the sake of his physical strength. The intent was probably that Frænkel would be able to pull the four-hundred-pound sled if, contrary to expectations, they were to touch down some distance away from their target. For five weeks, they waited for the right winds. Nils Strindberg passed the time by playing the violin and writing letters to his fiancée, Anna Charlier, while the sailors from the *Svensksund* varnished the balloon's fabric and made it watertight. They hadn't had time to take the balloon, which Andrée and Strindberg had ordered from the manufacturer Henri Lachambre in Paris, on a test flight. On the eleventh of July, the weather finally changed: the wind was blowing to the northeast."

Eberlein opened the green-checked oilcloth book. Don recognized Nils Strindberg's handwriting, but here it was in plain text, no shorthand.

"This is his travel journal, begun at lunchtime just before their departure."

The first page was damaged, a thin flap that Eberlein carefully turned aside. In the upper corner of the next page was the note:

Danskøya, Virgohamna.<br>
11 July 1897<br>
Written in the shelter of the north side of the balloon house

A sketch showed that Nils Strindberg must have lit the Bunsen burner one last time and fused the ankh and star together to determine the position of the ray. Underneath there was a smudged note in ink:

1:27 P.M. Greenw. time
The current position of the ray:
lat. 84° 10' N—long. 30° 45' E
estimated distance from Danskøya: 352 miles
wind according to Frænkel: 16 mph NE, strong gusts

Next to the note of distance were a jerky "attested" and a big A.

It looked as though the page had been hit by a few drops of water just as Strindberg was writing, because the ink in the words that covered the rest of the page had almost bled out. In what Don managed to decipher there was only speculation about the lifting capacity of the balloon and its noticeable frailty.

Eberlein's voice from the other side of the table: "The front of the balloon house had been torn down, Andrée and Frænkel had already taken their places in the gondola, and the carrier pigeons were tied on in their cages—and still, these last expressions of doubt. When it comes to the departure, we must rely upon the eyewitness accounts: how Strindberg nodded at Andrée to give the order to cut all the ropes, and then came three sharp snaps as the ropes that anchored them were hacked off. The balloon stood still for a second, but then Frænkel began to raise the three sails. The ground sank away beneath them, and they hung weightless. When they had almost made it up out of the balloon house, the wind took hold and the craft rolled one last time back toward the wall. But then it climbed to a height of a hundred fifty feet and drifted out over Danskøya and Virgohamna. They had waited until their departure to christen it. The businessmen had insisted on a German-sounding name, the *Eagle,* instead of Nobel's suggestion, *Le Pôle Nord.*"

Eberlein flipped forward a few pages in Strindberg's oilcloth book.

3:33 P.M. Greenw. time
The Eagle, past Danskgattet

At the top of the page, Don saw some notes on the weather. They were followed by words about beer and sandwiches, a sketch of birds flying next to the gondola, and a note that Andrée had just stood up on the ballast ring to piss. A short memo that his last greeting to his fiancée, Anna, had been sealed and thrown down as they passed over the island of Vogelsang. And after that, underlined twice:

Frænkel knows!

Don looked up at Eberlein.

"The part about Frænkel was a surprise to Strindberg. All the measurements had been carried out in Andrée's berth on the *Svensksund,* and the Bunsen burner had been smuggled aboard in a closed canvas sack, along with the ankh and star, just before their departure. The idea was that the secret would be kept from Knut Frænkel, as with all other Swedes, but he must have learned about the existence of the instruments somehow. Strindberg seems to have suspected Andrée; there's a bit about that further on."

Eberlein moved a cotton-clad finger across a few words that had run together a bit lower on the page.

"It's remarkable, actually," Eberlein continued, "that Nils Strindberg had time to devote energy to this question. The flight was already a catastrophe. When they got out over the harbor, a gust caught the sail and forced the balloon down toward the waves. They had flown so low that the gondola hit the surface of the water with a thud, and once Andrée and Strindberg had finally emptied nine of the sandbags they did float up, but by that time the balloon had rotated half a turn around its own axis so that it began to go backward. This spinning movement caused several of the important drag-ropes to come unscrewed from their anchors, and they no longer had a way to steer. But instead of cutting the expedition short, Andrée and Strindberg seem to have been gripped by panic at the prospect of losing the ankh and the star in the sea, so they continued to dump out sand. The *Eagle* climbed uncontrolled to a height of nearly two thousand feet. But when they felt the wind, their courage returned, because it was blowing stronger and stronger to the northeast."

Eberlein pointed to some figures:

Curr. pos. according to A. (approx.) 79° 51' N—11° 15' E
Estimated distance to the ray's pos.—336 mi
40 knots, approx. time—8 hrs.

"The glaciers and cliffs of Spitsbergen were behind them now; there was black sea below, and Nils Strindberg wrote that he noticed a steamer trying to follow them. They all helped splice the remaining drag-ropes with more rope, but the *Eagle* was now flying too high for this to allow them to steer. They soared into increasingly dense fog; it started to become very cold; and the balloon's thin silk fabric cooled down. The low air pressure caused them to lose hydrogen much faster than expected, yet Strindberg still took it for granted that they would reach the ray's position before evening."

Eberlein picked up a few final objects from the bottom of the metal box: a handful of black-and-white film negatives encased in glass, which he lined up on the table with his cotton fingers. Then he pushed one of the glass plates over to Don, so that the photograph ended up next to the crinkled page of the diary.

"The first picture Strindberg took from the gondola," Eberlein said.

The negative inside the glass was almost empty of subject matter, except for a thin black line.

"You must remember that the colors are inverted," said Eberlein. "They're approaching the white edge of the pack ice."

Then he pushed over another negative—two bright spheres and a black ray. Below the lower sphere they could see the fused ankh and star above the dark flame of the burner.

"Strindberg took this photograph an hour or so later, down in the sleeping cabin in the gondola. The balloon was now traveling at an altitude of 2,300 feet. Everything was dripping with moisture from the clouds, and that was probably why he dared to light the Bunsen burner and check the position of the ray. The tiniest stray spark would have been a catastrophe, and the *Eagle* would have turned into a fireball."

"What is that?" Don asked, pointing to some white marks in the lower corner of the negative.

"Points of the compass and the time," said Eberlein. "Strindberg's camera was equipped with a mechanism that marked each picture. This was taken just after midnight, dawn on the twelfth of July, and the position of the ray hadn't changed yet."

He turned ahead another few pages in the journal, and Strindberg's handwriting became messier with each page.

"It was the cold from the clouds and the loss of gas that caused the balloon to begin falling. On the morning of July twelfth, ice had started to form on the load-bearing net and the drag-lines, weighing the *Eagle* down by more than a ton. The gondola hit the ice every fifty feet, and as you see, he had difficulty writing. Their course had become more easterly, and they argued about how they could get the balloon to struggle on, up toward the mark made by the Bunsen burner. Around eleven o'clock, Frænkel and Strindberg went to bed, but they didn't get any sleep."

Eberlein pointed at several lines:

the rustling of the lines in the snow—
the perpetual flapping of the sail

The next page:

pole buoy sacrificed

"The day after that, the thirteenth of July, they had thrown everything they could do without overboard. The North Pole buoy with the Swedish flag, which they had brought along for looks, wasn't difficult to sacrifice, but they also started to get rid of quite a lot of provisions. That night one of the drag-lines got caught in the blocks of ice, and they had to stay there for several hours. When they finally managed to get it loose, the sun had come out, and the warmth allowed the balloon to lift. Once again they tried to climb to reach the higher winds and continue to the northeast. But once they got the sails in order, all the warmth had disappeared, and the balloon sank again. There are no notes from that day—Strindberg writes further on that he was far too seasick from thudding against the ice. Their luck didn't change until July fourteenth."

Eberlein lifted yet another glass-encased negative from the table. In this picture they could see the spheres again, but something was different here: a hazy ring of light encircled the Bunsen burner, the ankh, and the star.

"It was taken at two in the morning," Eberlein said, pointing at the numbers on the lower edge of the negative. "They had anchored on a floe of ice, to rest awhile, and the midnight sun was so weak that Strindberg must have had to use his magnesium flash to be able to take a picture at all. The burner seems to have been five or ten meters from the balloon; as you can see, it's possible to make out the contours of the gondola through the spheres."

Don angled the negative toward himself but didn't see anything other than the thin ray from the star, which fell onto a lower dome that arched over the silhouette of the ankh.

"When Nils Strindberg came back to the balloon, Andrée had taken their position with his sextant and was ready to give up. But when Strindberg showed him . . ."

Eberlein flipped a few pages ahead in the journal, then stopped, wrinkled his forehead, leafed a few pages back again, and found the spot:

14 July
1:47 dawn Greenw. time
ray changed position!
double measurement after problem with safety flame
lat. 82° 59' N—long. 31° 5' E
new approx. distance: hardly 27 miles!

"As you see," said Eberlein, "the ray had moved. Actually, it shouldn't have been a surprise for Strindberg. He had, after all, estimated during his calculations at Stockholm University College that the shift happened about every third day. The balloon had left Danskøya on July eleventh, and now it was the fourteenth, and the new position that the North Star pointed out was at a distance of less than thirty miles. They made one last attempt to get the *Eagle* to lift off and threw everything but dry rations, rifles, snowshoes, and the sleds out of the gondola. The lighter weight allowed them to float slowly just over another eighteen miles to the north. At nineteen minutes past seven, they decided that they had come close enough. After he had landed the gondola, Andrée began to empty the balloon of gas. Nils Strindberg lifted out the camera, brushed the snow off of the leather-covered beech frames, and took eleven pictures of the giant silk cover as it sank down onto the ice. The next morning, they assembled the sleds and thus began their hike, the last few miles to the goal of their journey."

Don bent forward over the journal and carefully began to turn its pages.

On the pages after the last indication of their position was something that looked like an inventory of what they had brought along. Several of the articles had either been scaled down in weight or crossed out entirely. It ended in a circled note:

6 bottles champagne, gift from the King

When he was about to keep browsing, Don noticed that the page with the list was strangely loose against the bound spine of the book, as though it were poorly attached. Then it came completely loose, and he thought it seemed like the last pages had been ripped out. All that was left now was a single sheet, folded up on top of the back cover. He looked at Eberlein, who seemed to have been waiting for his discovery:

"Isn't it odd?" said Eberlein. "Of a hundred twenty bound pages, the last thirteen were missing when the journal was recovered at the end of 1899."

The German pushed a glassed-in negative across the table. It seemed to be the last thing he had to show them.

"The foundation managed to develop a single exposure from the last roll. It was found next to Nils Strindberg's body, stored in a copper cylinder in the pocket of his felt jacket."

Within the glass plate that Eberlein had placed before them, Don and Eva could see a negative with black cracks through it. An inverted picture of something that looked like black flakes of sleet. Behind the snow, a white hole shone in the dark ice.

"Did they come to a hole in the ice?" asked Don.

"Not a hole," said Eberlein. "Look at the edges."

Don lifted the negative again. The edges of the hole in the picture formed a perfect circle. When he compared it to the figure with binoculars that was standing next to a small flag at the opening, he realized that the hole in the ice was very large, surely 150 feet in diameter.

"Strindberg must have been the one to take the picture," said Eberlein, "he was the only one who could use the camera. But we haven't been able to determine whether it's Frænkel or Andrée who's standing there looking down."

Don tried to invert the colors of the negative, to see it as it must have looked on a July day in 1897. Far away, a circle-shaped, black abyss in the white ice, and right at the edge, the silhouette of the binocular figure. It was as though someone had carved a tunnel straight down into the earth's interior with a welding torch.

Eberlein gestured toward the markings at the lower edge of the picture.

"Eighty-two degrees and fifty-nine minutes north, the morning of July fourteenth, 1897. They are at the exact location the ray indicated. It must have taken them twenty-four hours to get there after leaving the balloon."

Don put down the negative and loosened the final, folded sheet from the oilcloth book. He looked up at Eberlein, who nodded. So he unfolded the sheet in front of him and smoothed it flat. A row of columns with numbers ran across the page: date stamps, amounts of precipitation, air pressure, and wind speed.

"This is taken from Frænkel's meteorological calendar," Eberlein said.

Then the German turned the sheet over. On the other side, smudged across the tables, ran bled-out, blotted ink with isolated discernible words, out of context, sprawling:

All is lost!!!
Nor strangers were already the opening
Andrée and the burner execution! Knut is bleeding
belly! morphine, six panes
I myself have sought shelter since the morning

In the voices above me

the gate down open! and they know!

the ankh? and the star!

is sucked down

the vault, the walls

followed us all the way here?

what will become the Eagle?

the elder was called Jansen, but it was the younger who

cannot turn back without

Anna, I

dearest sweet Anna

"He's writing to his fiancée." Eva's subdued voice.

"To Anna Charlier." Eberlein nodded. "That's the last clue we have."

When Don, too, had lifted his eyes from the sparse lines, Eberlein pulled the paper away and returned it to the very back of the checked oilcloth book, with the printed weather notes facing up, and closed the cover.

"And especially in consideration of Anna Charlier, one can say that the end of the story was needlessly tragic. If I may . . . ?"

Eberlein took the last negative from Don's hand and placed it back in the box along with the journal. Then he continued. "The bodies of Frænkel and Strindberg were found two years later. They had fallen a hundred fifty feet down into a crack in the ice. Andrée's corpse was never recovered, but Strindberg's last notes suggest that he may have been murdered. The only documents that are left from the expedition are Strindberg's travel journal and a few photographs. You have seen almost all there is to see, and it all fits in a metal box."

"Andrée . . ." Don began.

His tongue didn't really want to move, but it had to be said anyway: "Andrée's body was found in the final camp on Kvitøya."

"Kvitøya . . . ?" said Eberlein.

"Yes, Kvitøya," said Don. "Andrée's body was there."

His cracked voice was stronger now.

"You must know of the discoveries on Kvitøya. The final camp, where they found the bodies, the equipment from their long hike across the ice. All of Nils Strindberg's photographs that they've successfully developed, and . . ."

"As I said," Eberlein interrupted, "that part of the story is tragic, and quite unnecessary now, afterward."

He looked down at the table and began to collect the rest of the glass-encased negatives.

"The Swedes didn't know where they should look, of course," Eberlein continued with his head bowed, "but the German financiers were aware of the coordinates of the target area, and as early as the summer of 1899 the foundation sent out the rescue expedition that found the gondola next to the scraps of the balloon. In the sleeping cabin, on top of several blankets, were the final calculations that Strindberg and Andrée must have done before they set off toward the location of the ray. All they had to do was follow them."

"And when they arrived?" asked Don.

Eberlein looked up.

"No hole, no ankh, no star. No Bunsen burner. Nils Strindberg and Knut Frænkel were found dead, as I said, thirty meters down in an ice crevice. Frænkel had been shot in the stomach. The copper cylinders containing some of the pictures I've shown you were still in Strindberg's knapsack, along with his oilcloth book. Frænkel had hidden his meteorological paper in his glove. With that, they knew then about as much of this story as we know today."

A silence settled in the vaulted library, broken only by the quiet clinking as the glass negatives fell into place in the metal box. Then the attorney asked, "You said something about Strindberg's fiancée, Anna Charlier?"

"A precautionary measure," Eberlein said quietly. "A precautionary measure that went rather too far. The financiers behind the foundation believed for a long time that it would be possible to find these 'strangers' who were responsible for the men's death and get back the ankh and the star. They didn't want any questions from the Nobel concern and the Swedes about the fate of the expedition. Moreover, by way of the conditions of the contract, they now considered themselves to be the sole owners of the ankh and the star, and all potential discoveries. Falsifying a few documents was no problem. They were familiar with Andrée's handwriting; that's how they created his two journals from the hike. The same with Strindberg's shorthand notes and Frænkel's meteorological papers. The falsified pictures from the expedition were probably the least successful; they do rather give an impression of having been staged. To divert interest from the upper northeastern latitudes, they then let the clues lead to the southwest. The selection fell on Kvitøya, east of Svalbard, an isolated place that could be prepared in peace and quiet. The final camp was built there, and finally they put out three very badly knocked-around bodies along with a series of objects they had recovered from the gondola. So that the Swedes would be able to figure out who was who among the corpses, they sewed Strindberg's and Andrée's monograms into the clothes. The work continued during the summer months at the turn of the century, but it wasn't until thirty years after the trail had been laid that some walrus hunters from Ålesund happened upon the boat hook marked 'Andrée's Polar Exp. 1897' that had been set out. Then the bodies were transported in a funeral procession through central Stockholm. And that was the end of that."

"But Andrée's family—Nils Strindberg's Anna—they must have seen that the bodies that came home from Kvitøya in the coffin were completely different people?" Don asked.

"After thirty years there wasn't much left to see," said Eberlein. "Besides, the remains were cremated without an autopsy. A great scandal at that time."

"And Anna Charlier?" Eva Strand's voice again.

"The whole operation was excessive, of course," said Eberlein. "Why would it have mattered if the bodies had never been recovered? It was unnecessary, quite simply. And for Anna Charlier's part, she never stopped mourning for Nils Strindberg. Fifty years later, her heart was buried in a silver keepsake box at his side, in the memorial park at Norra Begravningsplatsen. The fact that her heart is lying there all alone has always struck me as awful. May I . . . ?"

Eberlein started to fold up the large drawing of the spheres. The glue crackled as the paper strained over Nils Strindberg's drawing of the northern hemisphere.

"After making Svalbard a secret, the German businessmen continued their investigations. With time, of course, their pace became slower and slower, and the foundation became more of an archive, the keeper of a secret, a historical mystery, still looking for answers."

He placed the folded-up sheet in the metal box, and there were two snaps as the pins of the lid closed. And the table was once again empty.

"Today, the founders are dead, naturally, but the mission of the foundation remains, and the contract that was once signed with Strindberg and Andrée is still considered to be valid. And you can understand that Erik Hall's discoveries have engendered great expectations. I don't think I'm exaggerating when I say that my employer in Germany is prepared to go to great lengths to become enlightened in this matter."

"You want Strindberg's navigational instrument back," Don said. Eberlein smiled.

"The foundation wants what belongs to it back. What it paid for once upon a time."

The yellow-gray eyes behind the nonreflective glasses.

"You, Don Titelman, happen by chance to be the last link to Erik Hall, to the ankh, the document, and the other object he seems to have found . . . perhaps a star?"

Don squirmed in his chair, and he felt his hand go down to the postcard inside the lining of his jacket.

"You must be interested in becoming enlightened too, aren't you?" said Eberlein. "The ankh is gone . . . trouble with the police. Maybe we can be of help. If it's a question of money . . ."

Eberlein's voice thinned out as, in his mind, Don saw the double doors open, saw himself walking down the spiral staircase, out through the bright parlors, past the oil paintings, the gilded mirror, the front door of the villa. Then he opened his eyes:

"It strikes me, now that you mention it, that Erik Hall may have mentioned something about a star . . ."

Then Don's eyes fastened on Eberlein's smiling mouth. The lips slightly too red, and astonishingly gray teeth.

"Something about a star, yes," Don continued, "there were so many different versions."

Eva Strand turned to him.

"You shouldn't . . ."

"Yes, and not just a star, incidentally," Don said. "Actually, Erik Hall also talked about a document that he found down there. It was such a modest discovery that I hardly remembered it. A few lines on a letter, or maybe it was some sort of card." Then he looked into Eberlein's eyes . . . the expensive suit, arrogant German upper class.

"Did he tell you what the lines contained?" Eberlein asked tonelessly.

"Well, it's a little hard to remember . . . the contents were so incoherent, like a code, almost," said Don.

"A code?"

"Yes, or maybe a poem. There was a year among the words, and the name of a place."

"So what can you remember?"

"I . . ." Don began.

"Yes?"

"It depends on how you look at it, but perhaps you could say that I can remember a total of four words, a place name, and a year. Hygiene-Institut der Waffen-SS, the concentration camp Ravensbrück, 1942."

# 19

# The Postcard

The wall-to-wall carpet stretched into a dark rectangle around the table with the closed metal box, and when Don let his eyes slide up to the library ceiling in the silent room, he thought the book spines at the top must be almost fifteen feet up.

If he could only find some way to blast himself past those last eight inches of old turn-of-the-century insulation and the outermost layer of roof tiles, he would be able to see out over the open night sky, maybe even glimpse the tower of Seglora Church.

One potential aid in an attempt to break out might be the brass ladder on wheels, which stood at an angle a few yards from the shrunken form of the Toad, but somehow the ladder seemed far too slanted. Besides, it would be impossible to climb up the wall, Don realized, because the rows of bookshelves had quite obviously begun to lean inward, and it was as though the whole room were closing in on him.

Eberlein was grinding his jaw in the light of the glass lamps, and the movement spread up toward his temples, where the German's thin skin expanded as though from a rapid pulse.

Then there was a scrape as the Toad suddenly got up from his stool over by the brass ladder.

On his way to the table, he avoided looking directly at Eva and Don, and when he reached it, he immediately bent down and whispered something to Eberlein.

It was impossible to hear what the Toad was saying, but from the harsh melody, Don understood that the words were in German. Eberlein looked straight ahead while he listened, with his eyes directed at a point far behind Don, over toward the locked double doors.

When the Toad had stopped speaking, Eberlein nodded quietly. Then he got up and straightened the glossy fabric of his suit pants. He said, "I must make a phone call."

But the smile that followed this time was weak and didn't extend to his eyes. The German's face, which had been so illuminated during the long story, was once again pale gray and rigid.

After the doors had closed behind Eberlein, the Toad sat down across from them at the table. Eva Strand had already begun to collect her papers, and now she placed them in her purse along with her pen.

When her hand came up again, she was holding a red cell phone. She looked questioningly at the Toad, but he just shrugged his shoulders. After a few seconds, the screen of the phone had woken up, and the attorney quickly dialed a number. While waiting for the call to go through, she fixed her eyes on Don.

Then he saw her forehead wrinkle; she looked down at the phone, another attempt, dialing more slowly this time. There were no signal bars alongside the numbers. The Toad's bulging eyes widened slightly.

"You have a landline in the house, I assume?" Eva said.

At first there was no reaction, but when Don repeated the question in German, the Toad shook his massive head.

Don watched as she made yet another attempt, but then his thoughts began to slip away. The amphetamine seemed to have fried a crack into his memory, and where the pictures had earlier been so clear, everything was cloudy and distorted now.

The photographs he'd once seen from the final camp on Kvitøya—Strindberg's buried body under the mound of stones, Andrée's logbook, the skeletal remains of Knut Frænkel—were now double-exposed against Eberlein's glass-encased negatives.

He let out a dry cough, a laugh that he managed to smother as it issued from his throat, as he thought of the sketched spheres, the ray above the northern hemisphere, and Eberlein's careful movements with his cotton-clad fingers. It was like finding himself in a hall of broken mirrors, and to get out of there Don did what seemed easiest: opened his shoulder bag and took out six milligrams of Xanax.

He had just screwed the lid back onto the bottle when there was a click from the lock behind him, and the double doors once again let in light.

Eberlein was back.

"You can't have had much luck," Eva said as the German approached the table.

He looked at her uncomprehendingly.

"Your assistant claims there's no landline. And it's not possible to make a call in here."

She showed him her cell phone.

"No, that's true," said Eberlein. "It must have to do with the bugging protection; there's some sort of jamming station in the house, from what I understand. As I said, this villa belongs to the German embassy these days, and they do have their special rules."

The attorney put her cell phone into her handbag and pushed her chair back.

"Telephone or no, it's time for us to go, if you don't have any further questions. I truly hope that we have reached the end of this strange excursion."

She directed these last words to the thin-haired Säpo man and his colleague, who had by now also come into the library.

"I'm afraid that's not what is going to happen," said Eberlein. He placed his hand on Don's shoulder once again and pressed it lightly. "Even if I would personally like to trust what you said about Ravensbrück, it doesn't seem to have made much of an impression in Germany. They're talking about giving you a choice. A choice that I would prefer to discuss privately with you."

"I don't understand," said Eva Strand.

But Eberlein had already given the signal to the men from Säpo, and the thin-haired one now came up alongside her and grasped her arm.

At first it seemed that the attorney intended to refuse, but then she gave up and stood with surprising difficulty. Her joints seemed completely stiff; the high-buttoned blouse was wrinkled; blue veins wound under her pale nylon stockings.

Eberlein held up her coat.

"It will only take a few minutes," he said.

Eva took her coat without answering, placed her handbag over her shoulder, and looked at Don for a long time.

"Whatever he says," she said, "we'll soon be back in Falun."

When the double doors had closed behind Eva and the two men from Säpo, Eberlein sat down on the chair next to Don's. A scent of cologne, that heavy aroma, and a gaze that was impossible to avoid. The hand that the German placed on his knee was narrow, thin at the wrist, as though it belonged to a woman.

"There are so many modern systems these days," Eberlein said.

Don looked over toward the doors, but the soft voice lured him back.

"Today, what used to be a simple lock can consist of a device that scans the iris of an eye or senses the lines in a fingerprint. In the case of fingers in particular, some of these systems can be so advanced that they can even tell whether the skin is warm or cold, in order to determine whether the finger is on a living person."

In vain, Don tried to feel the sensation of the Xanax.

"But as with everything, there is always room for cleverly executed forgeries."

Eberlein patted him on the thigh.

"A person who wanted to make a copy of your fingerprints could, for example, brush the porcelain cup you used in this library with finely pulverized coal. Then one could lift the lines of the prints from the cup with something as simple as transparent tape. With the help of a needle, one could then etch the lines from the tape into a thimble-size mold, which one could then fill with a thin layer of gelatin. When the gelatin had solidified, it would conduct electricity and warmth, just like your own skin, and one would have a false fingertip that could deceive any fingerprint reader at all."

"I have always been partial to the mechanical," said Don.

"There is quite a range of conceivable uses," Eberlein continued. "One would be to press a few copies of your fingertips against the broken bottle that's presumably lying somewhere in the underbrush down by Erik Hall's lake. One would then, of course, be obligated to turn the bottle over to the Swedish police right away, because such an important piece of evidence would be downright illegal to keep for oneself. A murder weapon with the perpetrator's fingerprints—something like that must be considered conclusive evidence."

Don felt himself nodding.

"But of course, it is a work-intensive procedure," Eberlein sighed.

He let go of Don's thigh with his hand and leaned back in his chair.

"Yes, it sounds complicated," said Don.

"Perhaps one wouldn't even be able to find that broken bottle that killed poor Erik Hall. In that case, it would be unnecessary work, to say the least."

Don nodded again.

"Perhaps there wouldn't even be a reason for us to look. Perhaps you and your attorney could come up with a suitable suggestion that would make everything I said superfluous." The light disappeared as Don slowly closed his eyes. Then he tried to get his thoughts moving by rubbing the side of his nose, and at last he said, *"Wovon man nicht sprechen kann, darüber muß man schweigen."* Of what one does not know, one cannot speak.

Eberlein smiled.

"You can think about it until tomorrow morning."

Don could hear the Toad moving over by the double doors, and then the sound of a light knock. When he opened his eyes, he saw that both of the men from Säpo had lingered outside with Eva Strand. He hesitantly got up from his chair and sneaked a look at the clock; it was midnight.

"It will be somewhat confined and inadequate lodgings for the both of you, I'm afraid," said Eberlein. "But you will have to be satisfied with what the house has to offer."

Then Don felt the Toad's hand on his back, and he found that he was slowly beginning to move out of the library, on his way to the winding spiral staircase.

# 20

# The Syringe

They had followed the Toad's waddling back through the corridors on the lower floor. Via a dining room with a ceiling mural that depicted two eagles in flight against a white and blue sky, they had arrived in a grandiose kitchen. There the Toad had unlocked a door that led to the windowless pantry. After asking Eva and Don to step in, he had handed the keys to the thin-haired Säpo man.

Cupboard doors covered in gold-marbled wainscoting, linseed oil–stained shelves above a sink and basin. Bowls of whisks and ladles were mirrored in a gleaming zinc splash guard, and two heavy freezers were humming next to the gray-checked laminate slab of the counter. Behind a tinted glass door with a small lock, they could see a wine cellar with bottles resting in delicate metal racks.

The Toad had nodded toward them and in the direction of the two mattresses on the floor, and then there had been a rattle as the thin-haired man shut and locked the door.

At first Don had been able to hear people mumbling in Swedish out there, but soon the whispers had stopped. Perhaps the two Security Service policemen had fallen asleep, because it had gone from midnight to two thirty.

During the hours in their stuffy cubbyhole, Don and Eva had time to turn Eberlein's threat over and over. When Don told her about it, Eva hadn't believed him at first. Then she had declared that of everything that had happened since they'd left the Falun police station, perhaps this bit about falsified fingerprints was the least surprising. Don had said something about the German tradition of combining confusion with ruthless methods, and along with mounting fatigue, a sleep-drunkenness had crept up on them, and soon half-stifled laughter could be heard from the pantry.

But now Eva stood up from the plastic-covered mattress and walked up to the long counter.

She opened a few cupboards at random and finally found a large drinking glass, which she filled with water. Then she seemed to change her mind and poured it out in the sink. Don followed her eyes over to the glass door and the dim rows of bottles in the wine cellar.

"Your research was in history," said Eva, "about Nazi symbols, wasn't it?"

Don nodded, but she had already turned away and started to search through the drawers under the counter.

"So what do they usually say is the symbolic meaning of a knife?"

"Of a knife . . . ?"

He searched his memory and found that at least some scraps were still left.

"A knife usually denotes victims and revenge. Death."

Took a deep breath and continued with eyes closed: "To cut with a knife can symbolize releasing something, like in Buddhism, a sign for the liberation of the self, of cutting away all ignorance and pride."

He heard Eva clattering around in the drawers.

"For Christians the knife symbolizes martyrdom. Bartholomew the Apostle, for example, was skinned alive by a knife.

"For the Nazis, knives were connected with the swastika. In the emblem of their predecessor, the Thule Society, the swastika was intersected by a dagger. Men in the SS received double-edged daggers when they were admitted, and they were to protect them with their lives. They had some bizarre idea that one became noble this way, in a direct line of descent from the knights of the Teutonic Order."

There was a clatter and then silence, but Don had just begun.

"In Old Norse mythology, the goddess Hel had a bed that was called sickbed, a dish called hunger, and they said her knife was called . . ."

"Thanks, that's enough," said Eva.

"They said her knife was called famine."

When Don looked up, he saw that Eva had turned toward him. In her hand she held a small, sharp table knife.

"But what I wanted to know . . ." said Eva, walking over to the door into the wine cellar. "What I wanted know was whether a knife could be regarded as a . . ."

She stuck the blade into the lock.

"As a key."

There was a pop as the thin catch in the glass door broke.

"That will be something to write about in *The Lawyer*," said Don.

"Well, there are limits to what a person can tolerate," said Eva. She wedged the knife into the molding, got the door open, and disappeared into the darkness.

Don had almost managed to doze off when he heard her heels approaching again from inside the wine cellar. The glass door swung open, and Eva carefully placed a dusty bottle on the counter. Black, with a rounded shape, and on its label Don could read "Graham's Vintage Port."

"A fine collection the ambassador has put together," said Eva. "This one is from 1948."

Then she took two shimmering green glasses from the cupboard above the counter and placed them next to the port wine bottle. Don followed her movements from the mattress.

"One of the truly great . . ." she continued, as she pulled off the strip of the seal. "One of the truly great vintages, isn't it?"

This was a question that was way beyond Don's knowledge.

"Well, you can pretend you're not interested . . ."

Eva pulled out the cork.

"But I'm telling you that the forty-eight is exquisite. This port wine could have aged another fifty years without harm. It is completely timeless."

She poured and handed one glass to Don. He could tell that she was paying careful attention to the expression on his face as he brought it to his mouth.

"This is how Lisbon tasted just after the war," said Eva.

Don thought it was like drinking syrup as he took his first sip. A strong and almost incomprehensibly concentrated taste of coffee and caramel.

"It was an unusually cold July that year," Eva continued, after having let the port wine roll around her mouth. "An oppressive, dry warmth came in the beginning of August, and the grapes matured quickly. If I remember correctly, the heat was so intense that the harvest had to be moved, but most of it still dried up. It tasted very sweet even then. The forty-eight was already a classic by the early sixties, and it was compared with the 1942, which was also a very good year."

She let her tongue slide over her sugary lips.

"For port wine, maybe," said Don, putting down the glass. "But you certainly know a lot about vintages."

"Well, I've been taking a couple of classes," she replied, with a slight blush. "It's a hobby that eases the conversation with clients sometimes."

"A couple of classes . . ." chuckled Don.

Then he awkwardly got up from the mattress and made an attempt to shake the stiffness out of his arms and legs. In the splash guard, it was like looking at the mechanical movements of a scarecrow. He could also see Eva's reflection there; she was standing with her hip against the counter. Under the speckled herringbone pattern of her jacket, her brown blouse was hanging askew, and a gray strand of her light upswept hair had come loose and was hanging down by her eye.

"See for yourself what you can find," she said, nodding toward the forced glass door.

"There must be something else we can do," said Don, irritated.

But she just shrugged her shoulders.

It was cold inside the wine cellar, and raw air streamed toward him when he entered the corridor between the protruding necks of bottles. Built-in lights gave a dull illumination, and a gold corkscrew and two crystal glasses stood on a wine cask. Alongside the cask, a staircase ran down to something that seemed to be a lower floor. Don threw a glance over his shoulder and could discern Eva's waiting figure through the tinted glass. But then he decided to go down there anyway.

The lower part of the wine cellar had walls of coarse-pounded brick. Along them ran rough planks, closely spaced, which were filled with rows of grimy bottles. A few plain lightbulbs hung from the high ceiling on cables of twisted fiber.

Don wondered how the attorney had been able to find what she was looking for so quickly, but supposed, without being any great connoisseur of wine, that the best must be kept farthest in. So when he had come to the end of the wine cellar, he stood on tiptoe and took out a bottle from the middle of the top row. It looked ordinary, and it was marked with the year 1999. The next was better, a Bourgogne from 1972, and the third seemed very promising, from 1959.

"If someone saved something for so long, it must be good," Don mumbled to himself.

Then he looked back up at the empty place on the shelf, where the bottles had lain.

The attorney was still leaning against the counter when Don came back up to the pantry. She looked more tired now than when he had left her, and she didn't seem to care about the port wine bottle anymore.

"This story must come to an end," she said.

"There's something down there that you have to see," said Don.

He led her back into the wine cellar, closed the glass door after them, and made sure that it closed properly. After they had walked down the narrow corridor, past the cask with the crystal glasses, they came down to the lower wine cellar. On the floor, standing in a line, were fifty or so bottles, which Don had removed from the top shelf.

"Well, you're not skimping," said Eva Strand.

Don pointed to a wooden box eighteen inches high, which he had emptied so he wouldn't have to stand on tiptoe as he picked through the bottles. Eva took a few steps forward, looked questioningly at him, and then climbed up on the box. With her fingers on the top shelf, she peered into the opening that had been formed when the bottles were removed.

"You see it, right?" Don asked.

Eva nodded. Then she stretched an arm in to feel around.

"I can't reach," she said.

"It looks like it's made of glass," he said.

"I can't . . ."

After one last try, Eva gave up, pulled out her arm, and looked down at him.

"So what were you planning to do now?" she asked, still keeping her balance with her fingers on the top shelf.

"Help me remove the rest of the bottles," said Don.

Eva looked at him skeptically, but finally she handed down a Bordeaux. Then another, and another, and when the top shelf was empty, together they lifted away the rough board that the bottles had lain on and began the work of emptying the next row.

Soon the far end of the wine cellar was covered in bottles, and when they moved away yet another board, they no longer needed the wooden box to reach.

Now they could see it, what had earlier been concealed by the shelves up by the ceiling: a small cellar window, its blue and red mosaic glass streaked with dust and dirt.

Don kicked the wooden box so it broke, and then, with difficulty, he pried off a plank. Two rusty nails were still sticking out of it, and he held it in his hand like a weapon.

"And if they hear?" said Eva.

He looked at her and felt the nails with his fingers.

In silence they continued to clear away the shelves until they got down to the bottom board, which turned out to be screwed into the brick wall. Don thought this was actually a good thing, because maybe then it would be able to bear his weight. He motioned to Eva to support him, and when he got a grip on her shoulder, he carefully braced his boot against the bottom shelf. Then he took a step up but swayed backward, and she had to help him so that he wouldn't lose his balance completely.

The small cellar window was now within reach, just three or four inches above his head. Don rocked on the sagging board, and it seemed to hold. So he stretched out his hand.

"Give it to me."

She gave him the board with the protruding nails.

"And you'll have to support me," he said.

Nothing happened.

"And you'll have to . . ."

He felt her hands on his back.

A firm grip on the board, the nails turned to the front. He didn't know how hard he should hit, so first he tried a light knock.

There was a rattle as the tips bounced back from the mosaic glass.

Then he tried again, harder this time, a short, powerful swing, and the pane cracked, falling in blue and red shards down onto the stone floor. The sharp sound of broken glass, and Don felt Eva give a jump. After a long silence, she hissed, "Well, that was discreet."

Don pulled the arm of his jacket as far as he could over the knuckles of his right hand, then began to knock away the last sharp fragments from the edges. He could already feel the night air trickling in.

When most of the shards were gone, he released his grip on his jacket arm and stretched his hand through the window. About four inches down, his hand ran into something moist, and when he brought it back into the wine cellar, Don saw in the glow from the lightbulbs that it had become black with dirt. He showed Eva.

"I'm not sure that this is a good idea," she said.

Her hair was a mess, her eyes edged with red.

"Do you have a better one?" Don asked, climbing down.

He didn't receive an answer.

The benzodiazepine in the Xanax capsules had really kicked in now, and it was with a sense of remarkable calm that Don moved back toward the glass door, out to the pantry.

His black bag still lay on the plastic mattress, and the light from the ceiling was reflected in its shiny leather. He lifted it up by the strap and then went over to the locked kitchen door to listen.

No steps, no voices, nothing.

He looked at the clock. It was three thirty, and it would still be dark outside the villa.

A quick run down the avenue of oaks, and he would come to the road that went past Skansen. From there to Karlaplan, and then to the central station. Change to the subway running north, to the only place that he knew was safe.

Don placed the strap of the bag over his shoulder, made sure it was hanging securely at his side, and with a final glance out toward the pantry, he pulled the glass door closed behind him.

The attorney was waiting for him in the brick vault. She looked up at the gaping cellar window.

"It's way too narrow," she said. "You'll never get out, and even if you did, what would you do then?"

"I have a vague idea," said Don.

"That sounds reassuring," said Eva.

Her arms crossed over the herringbone pattern.

"Better than staying here," said Don. "What do you say?"

Eva looked over toward the stairs to the upper floor. Then she said with a weak smile, "An attorney must look for alternatives in a process and never lead her client into a dead end where the door locks behind them."

She looked at him; he had managed to stand up, balancing on the lowest shelf.

"Good luck."

Don had taken two white towels with him from the pantry. Now he wound them around his hands, stretched them toward the frame of the window, and grabbed hold. When he realized that the strength of his arms wasn't enough, he called for help.

Eva gave him a shove upward, and then he braced his boot against one of her shoulders.

"This does not feel dignified," he thought he heard her say, just before he really got a good grip and managed to heave himself up so he landed with his chest halfway out the window.

There was a sting in his stomach from some shard of glass that he had been too careless to clear away. Then he moved his head and looked around, out into freedom.

To the right, a few yards away, he glimpsed the wooden shingles of the villa's facade. To the left were branches and leaves, a garden shrub, Don thought, heaving himself a little farther out. Then he managed to wriggle his legs up from the cellar window and crouched with his back pressed against the dark wall.

A whisper from down in the wine cellar. "How does it look?"

Don moved as quietly as he could back to the window. He looked in. Eva Strand's face down there, anxious now.

"I didn't think you were serious," she hissed.

"You were a great help anyway," said Don.

She nodded and looked aimlessly around in the empty brick vault.

"So you're staying there?" Don asked.

"I . . ."

He stretched out his hand.

Eva uncrossed her arms and took a hesitant step forward. Don gripped her wrists and succeeded in lifting her up onto the lowest shelf.

He leaned backward and braced his boots against the outside of the window frame. She was surprisingly light; it was like lifting a child.

When Don had managed to pull her almost halfway out of the window, he heard Eva cry out suddenly. He immediately released her hands, and he saw her give a jerky kick with one leg, as though she had become caught in something. Then she finally managed to get loose, and she crawled behind him, in among the branches next to the wall of the house.

He saw that she was stretching one hand down to her leg to feel it. Showed him her fingers. He couldn't make it out in the dark, but when Don took her hand he realized that it was covered in blood.

"I cut myself on something. You could have been . . ."

The words disappeared in a moan before she managed to continue. "You could have been a little more careful to remove all the glass."

Don couldn't think of an answer. Instead he took off one of his towels and pressed it to the spot she had shown him: Just under the crease of her knee, a four-inch gash ran diagonally down her calf. She held herself up with the help of his hand, and he felt her grip become harder with the pain. They sat like that for a few minutes until

Don thought he heard a faint rustling, which soon turned into the sound of steps.

"Someone's coming," he whispered.

He heard her trying to hold back her breathing, short puffs through her nose, her lips pressed tight together.

Don crawled forward through the shrub, crouching, and moved a few branches aside so he could see.

Out on the terrace, illuminated by the villa's floodlights, stood the thin-haired Säpo man. He had taken out a cigarette, and soon Don could see the flame from within his cupped hand, and then the glow from his first drag.

The thin-haired man had stopped only about thirty feet away from the bushes where they sat hidden in the dark, alongside the wall. Don could smell the pungent scent of smoke. Some distance away, in the turnaround, he could see the metallic-painted station wagon. The Säpo man slowly finished smoking. Then he shook another cigarette out of the pack, coughed, and stuck it between his lips.

Don began to search through his bag, trying in vain to find some sort of weapon. He could hear Eva carefully changing position. Her movement against the wall shouldn't have been noticeable, but something about the thin-haired man's posture changed. He took the cigarette from his mouth and threw it on the ground. Then he turned around, with his gaze aimed in their direction. As Don looked into the policeman's eyes he was sure that they had been discovered. But as the thin-haired man slowly began to move forward, toward the bushes, he realized that there was still time.

He looked down at the small plastic tube he had taken out of his shoulder bag, and he was surprised at how well he knew all of its corners and compartments. Then he tried to back up toward Eva, but the small movement was enough for the thin-haired man to see.

Don felt himself being lifted up by his left arm and hauled out into the sharp light on the terrace. Somewhere along the way he must have succeeded in getting in a kick to the Security policeman's leg with the Dr. Martens boots on his flailing feet, because something caused his grip to loosen, if only a shade.

In that short instant, Don managed to twist himself around so that he could get the plastic tube up to his mouth. With his teeth, he ripped the cover from the syringe, and then he stabbed the long needle haphazardly into the policeman's neck.

There was no doubt he had hit his target and stabbed deeply, because the thin-haired man cried out and let go. But when Don looked up from the granite terrace, there was still something that didn't make sense. The Säpo man remained standing up.

At first, Don didn't understand what had gone wrong, but then he discovered that the plunger of the syringe still wasn't depressed. The needle must have hit the carotid artery, because it was bobbing in time with the man's heartbeat. The policeman fumbled clumsily along his neck with his hands, and Don tried to gather the strength to get up.

But then he caught sight of a herringbone-patterned figure limping into the light. The thin-haired man didn't have a chance to see her, because she was approaching from behind. And when she was just behind his back she slipped her hand onto the syringe in the man's neck from the back and resolutely pushed the six milliliters of Leptanal in with the plunger.

The policeman had time to turn around and look deep into the attorney's eyes. Then he swayed, stumbled a few yards to the side, and collapsed.

Eva Strand was crouching next to the supine body with her hands against her bleeding leg.

Don ran up and started to search through the Säpo man's jacket pockets. He cursed and swore until he finally found the key to the car. Together they stumbled toward the turnaround, she with her arm over his shoulders.

Don unlocked the station wagon from a few yards away. At the same time, Eva's legs gave out, and Don had to carry her the rest of the way. After he'd thrown her into the passenger seat, Don went around the car panting, tore open the other door, and sat behind the wheel. After one failed try, he turned on the dome light to find the keyhole. He turned the key—the sound of a powerful motor, something that could carry them away.

The hand brake off, the car rolled off toward the avenue; then Don pressed the gas pedal hard. At the last second, he had time to swerve around the large tree trunk that came rushing toward them, and the wheels finally spun them away.

As they sped along Djurgårdsvägen, Eva began to cry out when the car jolted, and Don stopped at the 47 bus stop. Searched in his bag again and took out six purple tablets. But as she swallowed them, he realized that it was way too much.

He patted her comfortingly on the thigh and looked down at her leg.

Her nylon stocking was completely wet and dark, and when he took her shoe off, it was full of blood. He wrapped the last towel around her as hard as he could and knotted it.

Eva leaned her head against the back of the seat. Don released the brake, looked in the rearview mirror, and decided at the last minute that he would probably make it out before that clattering truck drove by.

Strandvägen, he thought. Strandvägen, Hamngatan, central station. Dump the car and then the blue line northbound.

# 21

# The Ankh

A sharp morning light hit Elena as she pushed open the door that led out to the small square with the walled-up fountain.

It was no longer possible to make out any signs of last night's dreams in her face. She had been extra careful around her eyes, and she took a chance and powdered her cheeks with rouge. It was a balancing act, because she knew that Vater didn't want to see any signs that she had become an adult. To avoid provoking him further, she had put on a loose-fitting tracksuit and a pair of jogging shoes.

The ankh lay like an icicle in her backpack as she reluctantly began to move through the city in the direction of the banking hall. But then she couldn't help increasing her pace, and despite all of the weight inside her, her steps were light and springy as she ran along the familiar cobblestone streets. At Landgasthaus Ottens Hof she turned in at the gate between the timber-frame houses, which would lead her to Wewelsburg's town square.

As she jogged the last bit up to the large bank building, she couldn't resist peering up over its roof toward the silhouette of the castle. As a child, she had taken it as a sign that she had truly come to a fairy-tale place—her own castle!—but now it just stood there as a depressing reminder of everything that she had lost.

Elena stopped at the glass entry hall and stretched her arm backward over her shoulder, to fumblingly reassure herself one last time that the backpack really did contain what she had promised him. Then she drew as much air as she could into her lungs and stepped into the great marble hall of the bank.

When she approached the reception booth in the echoing room, both of the guards greeted her tersely, as usual. One of them pushed out the tablet to take her fingerprints, even though she had known them since she was a child.

As soon as she touched the tablet, there was a buzz in front of her, and an opening appeared in the bulletproof glass. Her jogging shoes moved up the staircase, their shuffling the only sound, and Elena tried to stop all the thoughts that would lead way too far.

Then the stairs finally came to an end, and she turned off into the corridor, to the right. She followed its long carpet to the elevator that brought her up to the waiting room outside the management office.

Here sat the young assistant with his freckled face and chalk white hair. He gave her a measured look; she was expected. Elena looked up at the oil paintings above his head, matte black in their golden frames. Generations of severe faces, all their sharp looks directed down at her, as she took the last steps up to the handle of the door. Then, without the slightest sound, the door to the management office swung open.

The oak-paneled walls, the polished surface of the parquet, and the rows of safes where the lead capsules with the sparkling dust had long been closed up in the dark, waiting.

Elena stopped a bit away from the desk at the panorama window. Although Vater had his back to her, she knew that he was listening to her breathe.

As always, his eyes were fixed on the castle. Above the oversize north tower, the clouds were moving in. It had started to become overcast; iron-gray clouds against the white sky.

His thin body stretched so high above the back of the electric wheelchair that it looked unnatural, as though an adult had been placed in a piece of furniture made for a child.

"Elena . . ."

"Yes, Vater."

She was speaking to his back.

"You have performed a vital service for the foundation, but you also made several big mistakes."

"I realize that, Vater."

"It was a great show of confidence for us to send you. The task was simple but of vital importance. And you couldn't keep from . . . making a mess."

He paused so that she could attempt an apology, but she realized it was better to remain silent.

"So what is the ankh without the star, Elena?"

There was a squeak as the rubber wheels of the wheelchair began to move, turning him around toward her, while he continued.

"Only junk. A completely worthless antique."

He rolled past the edge of the polished leather surface of the desk and came out onto the shiny floor. Then Vater tilted the lever on the arm of the chair backward, and the hydraulics in the electric wheelchair's seat and leg rest brought him to a standing position.

She had never truly been able to get used to his oblong face, which was completely hairless, or his flat cheekbones and closely set teeth in a mouth that was way too small. In order to avoid the hazy reflection in his unseeing eye, Elena looked up at the other one, which was black and piercing.

She had always thought that his sickness had made Vater like a spider, with wire-thin arms and legs. But never as much as now, as he rolled even closer and directed his one eye down at the backpack, which she held open in front of her.

"Only junk," he said again. "A knickknack."

With his long fingers spread out like a rake, Vater stuck his hand into the backpack.

*"Es weigt ganz leicht, ja?"* He held the ankh up in front of him. "I said it would be light, didn't I?"

His spider fingers turned the shaft of the ankh as Vater mumbled his way through its inscriptions.

"I call on you, divine creator, invoker . . ."

". . . the giver of fortune," she filled in.

The cataract-filled eye, and then the other one, sharply looked down at her.

"That remains to be seen, doesn't it?" he said. "There is only silence from Stockholm so far."

"Titelman . . ." Elena began.

"We ought to have forced the Norwegians to keep it safer," Vater interrupted. "It cost us ninety years. Ninety years, or many more, if this really is all that was down in the mine. Although if the son was so attached to the ankh that he carried it with him until he died, then he can hardly have thrown the star into the sea."

"Hall said . . ."

"Of course he did!" said Vater. "Erik Hall *said* something. That he had found something more. Perhaps we should ask the Swedish police to ask one more time. A few more details, maybe, without having to take a detour through that Titelman?"

Elena looked down at the floor.

"The Swedes have placed Hall's body in a morgue, I've heard; perhaps you would like to go back yourself and conduct an interrogation. If you can awaken your delicate senses, maybe you could even get something out of him."

Elena pressed her lips together and said nothing. In the silence of the room, she could still sense the sound of the night voices inside herself, but it was too weak to be worth mentioning to Vater.

"We have lived as though in slumber, Elena." Then Vater turned the lever and the electric wheelchair angled him back into a sitting position.

"And soon our entire advantage will be gone. These last years have been borrowed time. You must understand . . ."

From the door came the sound of loud knocking. Vater stopped talking. Then the handle was pushed down and the assistant came in.

*"Ein Anruf aus Schweden,"* said the assistant. A call from Sweden.

*"Ja, bitte?"*

Elena saw that the freckled man was squirming. Then the assistant finally gathered his courage: "Something has happened."

# 22

# The Station

Eva Strand tried to sink back into the forgiving sleep, but the pain had grown too severe.

Eyes still closed, she wanted to pull her leg toward herself in order to determine the extent of her injury, but it was as though the signals didn't get through.

She grasped her left thigh with both hands and managed to pull her knee up to enough of an angle that she could feel along the back of her calf. The tips of her fingers brushed some sort of cloth, a bandage that had been wound so tightly that it almost cut off all circulation. When she carefully pressed along the four-inch wound, she could feel the contours of the small pieces of tape someone must have put there to hold the edges together.

At that moment it slowly began to come back. Titelman being thrown down on the granite terrace and the thin-haired policeman's back just about thirty feet away from her. Stuck in the side of his neck, a pink syringe that bobbed in time with his pulse.

Who that woman who performed the next action was, she didn't know. She herself had never done anything reckless in her whole life, but still the images in her memory said that she, Eva, was in fact the person who had gotten up out of the shrubbery along the wall of the villa and, in one decisive movement, pushed in the plunger of the syringe with her palm.

When the thin-haired man had collapsed and, surprisingly enough, lost consciousness, her legs had given way too. She recalled thinking that this was hardly what one should expect of a law-abiding Swedish lawyer.

After that, the pain had taken over, and her last memory after having swallowed those pills was of the car's jerky escape across the Djurgård Bridge, and then everything had faded away.

Eva turned her head, opened her eyes, and blinked a few times. In the dim light she could make out looping golden embroidery on silk fabric; petals and stalks in Indian style, stretching up toward a concrete ceiling.

She moved a bit closer to be able to reach out and touch the tapestry. It quivered, hanging loose against the wall in front of her.

When she looked down at her feet, she saw a wrought-iron bed frame and more embroidered fabric. Above her head she could feel silk as well, and her palms were stopped by another wall. Between the bed and the far side of the room lay a thick Oriental carpet, exactly the right size to cover the floor, which was perhaps thirty feet square. More Indian fabrics in soft colors, and over by the door stood small crystal dishes with burning candles and sticks of incense. That explained the scent of sandalwood, but behind that there was a faint odor of something else. It smelled somehow like burned . . . rubber?

Eva felt a stabbing sensation in the back of her lower leg as she managed to sit up on the edge of the bed. She noticed that her high-heeled shoes had been placed neatly over by the doorway, and the carpet felt unsteady under the nylon-clad soles of her feet as she made a first attempt to stand up.

It didn't go particularly well, and she sank down again among the pillows. She sat still, waiting for the pain to subside. But then, in the sound of her own moaning breaths, there was suddenly something else: a metallic thumping noise that came closer and closer, and she thought it was impossible, but it was as though something very heavy was rushing straight toward her where she sat.

Eva clutched the mattress with her fingers and tried to push away the instinctive feeling that she had to move immediately to avoid being run over. Then her intuition took over and she shoved herself up off the bed with all her strength and took a few staggering steps on the floor.

She thought her leg could hold her despite the sharp ache, but no matter how much she looked around, there was nowhere to seek shelter from the noise that was now roaring into the room. It sounded as though something were pounding ahead against the joints of . . . *rails*?

Thundering, rattling, it could hardly be fifty yards away now, and she was about to be *run over* at any second! But how could it be possible? Wasn't she standing in a room, protected by four walls and a roof?

Then it was as though the sound was transformed into its own detached wall that pressed itself toward her. Eva held her arm up over her face and cowered.

For one eternally long second, the sound crashed by just above her head, and a few clouds of sand came loose from the concrete slabs of the ceiling down toward the epaulets on her blouse. Over on the floor, next to the doorway, the flames flickered from the rush of air, and then the roar rushed off.

In the silence that followed, Eva shivered.

The blue arm of a shirt fumbled its way in along the wall covering beside the door, and suddenly the room was flooded with light. With squinting eyes, Eva saw a short figure approaching her at the bed. The figure placed Eva's arm around its thin shoulders and helped her out.

"Sorry about that. Must be some sort of signal problem."

The voice was bright and feminine.

"But you did have to wake up sometime, after all, right?"

Eva couldn't think of anything to say as she staggered out through the doorway with her arm over the woman's shoulders. In front of them opened a weakly lit corridor with even more hand-knotted rugs: Kashmar, Shiraz, Karachi, Afghan. Once, a very long time ago, Eva had learned to recognize the Oriental patterns, and this was like stumbling through an auction hall.

The woman looked up at her. "For the noise," she said. "Sounds like hell in here otherwise, when some schmuck in the traffic routing office gets it into his head to redirect the lines." The curly black hair wasn't as gray as Don's, Eva thought, and there was a different calmness in her eyes. But the pale face, the pronounced wings of her nostrils, and her slightly bent walk . . .

"He's been sitting up waiting for you. It's almost seven o'clock."

"Seven," Eva repeated, and tried to comprehend the time. "In the morning, you mean?"

The woman stopped next to a doorway at the end of the corridor. She had a small nose ring, and the front of her shirt said MAJORNAS IK in white letters.

"Seven in the *evening*."

The woman made a face.

"You've been lying there resting ever since your friend got the exceptionally idiotic idea to bring you here."

Then she helped Eva across the threshold into a stripped storage room, where the cement shone bare and white.

It was like walking into a workshop: industrial metal shelves that ran along the walls, hard drives, cables, cardboard boxes, power supplies, projectors, boxes, broken motherboards, tangles of cords, empty PC chassis, circuit boards, binders, well-worn charts and plans . . . And in the middle of this chaotic computer warehouse was a bench with five flickering monitors, and the farther in they came, the louder the whirr of the fans was.

Eva was amazed at the relief she felt as she approached Titelman, who was sitting crouched down on a low office chair in front of one of the computer keyboards.

A pair of plastic cup-shaped headphones arched over his head, and he didn't seem to have noticed that she was standing behind him. His eyes were still fixed on the closest monitor, which displayed the text version of the radio news:

> 6:43 P.M., Thursday, September 14
>
> NATIONAL ALERT AFTER ESCAPE
>
> The National Criminal Police have declared a national alert for the forty-three-year-old man who, along with a forty-seven-year-old woman, escaped yesterday from a police transport between Falun and Stockholm.
>
> The forty-three-year-old is a murder suspect, based on reasonable suspicion; the forty-seven-year-old woman is wanted for aiding escape and for battery on an officer.
>
> According to police spokesman Johan Widén, extensive searches are under way in the northern parts of Stockholm.
>
> *Continously updated* > > >

The dark-haired woman gave Don a rough shove in the back, and he turned around, irritated. But then he caught sight of Eva, and a weak smile spread over the lined face.

"Run over by the train?" he said.

She looked down at her wrinkled clothes.

"Yes, I guess that's the least you could say."

Then she leaned toward the monitor and read the text.

"This forty-seven-year-old woman, that's supposed to be me?"

"Aiding escape and battery on an officer—yes, I think they mean you," Don said. "But you're the one who knows about the legal stuff." He took off his headphones and gave them to Eva so she could listen to the feature on the radio.

As it started, she began to grope in her handbag for her cell phone. She found it, and she steadied herself with her free hand against the surface of the table to ease the weight on her aching leg. After she had finished listening, she played the feature one more time, and her fingers drummed more and more quickly beside the keyboard. At last Eva put down the headphones and took a deep breath.

"The man from the Security Service who's helping Eberlein must have been forced to make up a story."

She started to dial a number on her cell phone.

"Who are you calling?" Don asked.

Eva looked up at him, surprised.

"My colleagues at the firm, of course," she said. "Someone has to help us figure out what is actually going on up there at the police station in Falun."

"You're not calling from here," said the woman.

The attorney looked questioningly from her to Don.

"What my sister means," Don said, "is that it might be better to wait a bit to call, until the searches in Greater Stockholm are finished."

Eva's hand, with the phone, sank down to the table.

"Your sister," she said.

Don looked as though he wanted to swallow his tongue.

"I wish it were possible to say something different," said the woman.

Don made a face at her to extend her hand, and his sister reluctantly obeyed.

"Hex."

"Hex?"

The woman didn't look as though she intended to repeat herself. Eva tried a smile:

"Eva Strand. Younger or older?"

"What?"

"Sister, I mean," said Eva. "Younger or older sister?"

"Well, what the hell do you think?" said Hex.

After an embarrassed silence, Don got up and helped Eva sit down in his chair.

"You have to let me look at that leg now," he said. "If you . . . ?"

He nodded at her to pull down her nylon stocking, so he could get to the bandage. When she hesitated, he said:

"Who do you think taped you up while you were asleep?"

Eva felt a blush come over her cheeks, but then she began to take her stocking off anyway, so he could get to the bandage. When Don had crouched down next to her leg, she bent down toward his ear.

"Perhaps you can tell me where we are."

"You're at my place, in Kymlinge," Hex said before Don could answer.

His sister had also sat down at the computers now; she leaned against the back of the chair.

"You don't need to . . ." Don said.

"In that case, you probably didn't need to bring her here," said Hex. "I really can't understand in the least what the point was supposed to be. You're just losing time."

Then she turned away and leaned forward, hunching over one of the keyboards. It looked as though she was starting to work on something, because soon several of the monitors on the bench had woken up.

"Do you live here?" Eva asked.

"Yes, does the lawyer have a problem with that?" Hex mumbled, without looking up.

Eva grimaced as Don reached the gauze over the pieces of tape; then she shook her head.

"No, I think it's lovely."

"How nice."

Don sighed.

"What my sister means to say is that she is very happy here, in an uninhabitable, condemned basement under the Kymlinge subway station, pretty much exactly between Hallonbergen and Kista. The blue line."

"Kymlinge?" said Eva.

"Most people react more to the part about how she lives in a basement under the subway," said Don.

"I didn't even know there was a subway station in Kymlinge."

"That's what's so great about it," said Hex, concentrating on the movement of her fingers over the keys.

"Kymlinge," said Don, as he began to wrap the bandage again, "was supposed to be a station on the blue line out toward Akalla, and the heart of a city center that was planned here in the seventies. The construction never happened, so the station just consists of a few concrete staircases and a platform. Above us it's mostly evergreen forest and a little snippet of platform, and . . ."

"Soon you'll have enough for a book," Hex muttered.

"So the train that came . . ."

". . . was on its way to Akalla, yes," said Hex. "But they don't usually switch over to the side tracks, otherwise that would really be a bad place to put your bedroom."

"Right, because now it's a great place," said Don.

In the closest monitor, Eva could see that his sister made a face.

"Thanks for letting us come here."

At first Hex looked as though she hadn't really heard, but then the tapping of the keys stopped and she turned her pale face toward Eva, as though she were noticing her for the first time:

"It's all right. No problem at all, actually."

A crooked smile and then Hex went back to her hunched position in front of the quickly scrolling lines on the monitors.

"It looks good," said Don, when he finally nodded at Eva to put on her stocking again. "Sorry about the window glass."

After she'd pulled on her nylon again, Eva neatly straightened her skirt over her knees and put on her high heels. She tried once again to put weight on her injured leg, and her mouth contorted with the pain. She let her foot relax and lie resting against the floor underneath the workbench of computers.

Hex had disappeared into her work, and Don sat quietly, his face gray with exhaustion. For a long time the only sound was the whirr of the fans.

"What's going to happen now?" Eva asked at last.

Don didn't answer.

"What's going . . ." Eva began again, but she was interrupted by Hex:

"Your Eva wonders what you're planning to do, Danele. She wants you to initiate her into your plans for the immediate future."

"I'm not his . . ."

"I was planning to . . . leave the country for a while," Don said without turning toward her.

"Leave the country?" Eva asked, confused.

"Danele is going to leave on a train tonight," said Hex. "I've promised to help him with the tickets."

"On a train?"

"Your friend has gotten stuck," said Hex.

"Yes, on a train," said Don.

"They've put out a national alert, and you're going to get on a train," said the attorney.

"Good God," mumbled Hex. "This woman of yours is like an echo. I can't concentrate if I have to listen to this."

She turned to Eva.

"I'm going to send Danele out of the country like the damaged goods he is. Don't worry about that. What you *should* worry about is how you're going to clear up this legal mess with the police. If you listen to what Don says, it doesn't seem like you've done much about it so far."

"It will probably be difficult to . . ."

"Yes?"

"It will probably be difficult to do anything if Don just disappears somewhere, I'm afraid," said Eva.

"Come with me, then," said Don.

He had gone to stand behind Hex, and he was following the text on the screen. Eva wondered if she'd misheard. But then he turned to her.

"Come along, and your colleagues at the firm in Borlänge can help us until we figure out what's going on. You must be in as bad shape as I am after what happened with that man from Säpo."

She raised her eyebrows.

"Okay, maybe not in quite as bad shape," said Don.

"You and I, Erik Hall's murderer and his forty-seven-year-old attorney, flee the police on a train on the way to where? South?"

"Southwest," said Don.

The clattering from Hex had ceased, as though the sister was also waiting for an answer.

Eva suddenly felt that she needed time to think, time to herself, and she gripped the armrests with her hands. With a swinging motion she managed to heave herself up off the low office chair.

Her calf burned as she shifted her weight into a first, tentative step. With clenched teeth she soon realized that she could actually endure the pain well enough to limp on her own over to all the junk that had been piled along the walls of the concrete room.

Behind her she could hear the siblings arguing. Hex was speaking brightly and heatedly, now and again interrupted by Don's hoarse voice, as it had sounded during the long hours in the locked pantry.

Eva couldn't stop a small smile from moving over her compressed lips as she thought of how Don had grumblingly related a few samples of the bizarre theories that flourished among some of his students. He said that the long story in the library had been a condensed horror version of a decade of seminars, but still he seemed somehow fascinated by Eberlein's story about Strindberg and the spheres. Eva ran her hand along the rows of empty chassis and tubes on the shelves; her fingers passed by dismantled transistor drives and cooling paste for processors, and she realized that she had to stop fooling herself. Because she knew very well whom he reminded her of. Whom he had reminded her of from the first moment, and that that was what made it so hard for her to think clearly. The same hacking laugh she had heard so long ago, the same fascination with the extraordinary, with myths and treasures hidden in forgotten documents. The same resigned and slightly sad look.

She turned back toward the two siblings and thought there was no more time to hesitate.

"I'm coming along," said Eva.

She had sunk down next to Don. He didn't answer, but she could see that he was relieved.

"Well, well, so it is possible to understand what you're saying sometimes," said Hex.

"But it will have to be some other way than by train," said Eva. "That sounds like an incredibly bad idea."

"I think you'll be satisfied," said Hex.

For a moment the only sound was the buzzing of the computers.

"Don?" said Eva.

Don hesitated, looked at his sister. "May I . . . ?"

Hex nodded. He cleared his throat:

"We'll be traveling in a private compartment, you could say."

"More of a freight car, actually," Hex interjected.

"A freight car?" said Eva.

"The apple of my eye," said Hex.

She tapped in a Web address and nodded to Eva to roll her chair closer so that she could see better.

As Eva moved closer to the screen, a green and white page lit up with text:

**Green Cargo—Logistics solutions—customer to customer**

"If you tell anyone about this, Eva Strand, I will haunt you for the rest of your life."

"That would be taxing," said Eva.

"Okay, it's like this."

Hex pointed at the green and white screen.

"In 2001, the Swedish State Railway was split up into six different companies. The old division for transport of goods, SJ Gods, would become, as they said, 'market-oriented,' and it was restructured into the corporation Green Cargo. It was quite a messy process, among other things when it came to the data system. I followed it with great interest and took the opportunity to snatch one of their approximately seven thousand railroad cars."

"You stole a railroad car?" Eva couldn't hold back the doubt in her voice.

"She borrowed a railroad car, you might say," said Don.

"Okay, *borrowed,* then," said Hex. "I gave myself access to Green Cargo's incredibly faulty system and made a slight change. You might call it creative bookkeeping."

"Creative bookkeeping?" Eva repeated.

"You really have to work on that," said Hex.

She clicked off the page with the Green Cargo logo and pulled up something that resembled a flowchart. Then she continued: "Anyway, it was really mostly a test, you know, to see if it was possible to manipulate the system. But the really great thing about the freight car is that Green Cargo still doesn't understand that I snatched . . . *borrowed* the car. In their transport system, it seems to be doing a completely ordinary freight transport when I use it, and when I'm not using it, I instruct the system to place it on a sidetrack with other unused cars in a freight yard here near Kymlinge. It only takes a few simple codes to show that the freight car is booked or in for repairs, and then they leave it alone. It's been like this for several years now."

She pointed at a blinking row of numbers.

**GC 21-74-2262098-9 Gbs**

"I usually call it the Silver Arrow," said Hex.

"But traveling in a freight car . . ." said Eva.

"It *was* a freight car," said Hex. "Now it's . . . well, something of a hobby, you could say. Holding areas for railroad cars are relatively unguarded, so I've devoted the last few years to renovating it a little bit."

"Don't be shy," said Don.

"Well . . . it has a compartment, anyway, like he said, and I can guarantee that it is an extremely peaceful way to travel. At first I mostly used it within Sweden, but once I realized the implications of the Schengen Agreement and the open borders, I've also gotten out to the continent quite a bit."

When Hex noticed that Eva was still shaking her head, she closed the flowchart and returned to her keyboard and the other monitors.

"You can think what you want, Eva Strand. But now I have to make some travel documents for you two, and if you want a ticket out of here, you should let me work."

Eva crossed her arms, pushed her chair back from the table, and followed Hex's hands for a while as they danced across the keyboard. She looked over at Don, but he sat waiting with his head resting against his hand. Then Eva could feel her leg really starting to ache again, and she slowly closed her eyes in an attempt to collect her thoughts.

"Green Cargo . . ." she mumbled to herself.

# 23

# The Car

Around two at night, the hard drives in the concrete room fell silent.

The sudden silence caused Eva to wake up. Hex stretched and yawned in her office chair before the row of darkening screens.

Then Hex turned around halfway and gave Don a nudge. When he had become somewhat responsive, Hex declared that it was time to get moving. The sender, addressee, and type of freight had finally been swallowed by Green Cargo's system, and the freight car was now scheduled to be linked into the European flow of traffic, with a departure time of 3:43 A.M. This gave them a tight time margin, but otherwise the trip would have to have been postponed more than twenty-four hours.

The drizzle blew in across Eva's face above the condemned cellar on the half-finished platform. Hex had turned on a powerful flashlight, and she led them across the subway tracks, up the incline, into a thicket.

Eva clenched her arm around Don's shoulder with all her strength for support, but still her high heels slipped under her, and the lashes from branches and twigs caused her to nearly lose her balance time and again. Then they came out onto a gravel road, and in the shine from the flashlight, a short distance away, they saw the rust-mottled wreck of a car leaning down into a ditch.

Once his sister had unlocked the doors, Don helped Eva into the rotted-out backseat. Hex had forced her way behind the wheel and turned the keys in the ignition, and after a few hissing attempts, the motor coughed to life. Only one of the windshield wipers worked, and to the sound of its stubborn squeaking they rolled off along the forest road in the darkness.

They came up onto the highway next to a gas station, and through the drops that ran down the side window they could see the Råsta garage, where the red Stockholm city buses stood in a line, waiting for the morning service to start. The lanes spread out empty before them, which Eva thought was lucky, since the brakes hardly worked as they turned off onto the little road toward Solna and the Råsunda Stadium.

They passed a bridge across double railroad tracks, and then she saw a cream-colored building through Don's window. High up on its facade was an illuminated sign of corrugated metal with the words SOLNA TENNIS CENTER.

The car slowly rolled into the tennis center's parking lot. The hand brake was pulled, and Eva removed the flimsy strap that had once been a working seatbelt.

Her high heels were on the asphalt, and her arm was once again across Don's shoulders. Then Eva looked over toward the trunk, where Hex was lifting out two large plastic cans.

They limped behind Don's sister toward a café, where there was an outdoor faucet for watering. Hex stopped at it, took out a small tool, and began to fill the two cans. When she was finished, she heaved one over to Don and turned off the flashlight, and then they prowled on along the wall of the sports center. They stumbled up over the top of a hill full of trees that had grown wild, and they slid down the other side until they were stopped by a tall fence. Hex searched along one of the fence posts, and after a while she found a wire hook. She lifted the wire and threw it aside, and a gap opened in the mesh.

"They use dogs, so move as quickly as you can," Don's sister whispered before she slid through the narrow opening with her plastic can.

Don helped Eva to follow her, and while she tried to put weight on her painful leg, she looked out over a large field of gravel that was crisscrossed by railroad tracks in an extensive, irregular pattern.

About a hundred yards farther on, they could see the long chains of railroad cars, and a lone locomotive moved slowly through the veils of rain. A sharp yellow light shone over the freight yard, and the far-off roar of a semi was audible from up on the highway.

Don put down the heavy can to rest. But then Hex whispered that there wasn't any time, and after she had looked to the right and left, she disappeared, crouching, across the first track. With her arm twined fast around Don's shoulders and her eyes directed downward so as not to stumble, Eva limped as fast as she could across the rows of concrete ties and puddles of water in the gravel. When she managed to look up now and then, she could see Hex swinging the can at her side to gain extra speed. The swaying shadow of Don's sister moved expertly across the series of tracks.

The first row of railroad cars had open platforms, and metal pipes were piled on them in shining pyramids. Hex set a course for the end of the row, where she stopped in the shadow of the protruding cylinders. When they reached his sister, Don tried again to put down his can, but Hex nudged him and pointed. In the yellow light, two tracks away, stood a lone freight car. Its sides were painted bright green, and the black name stretched across the green:

GREEN CARGO

Lines marking the sides of a door cut through the last two letters in the company name.

They looked small as they approached the heavy car, whose metal side stretched out a hundred feet on either side, with a roof that was twelve feet high.

Hex went first, a thin figure in a raincoat with the hood pulled over her head. Eva followed her in her gray-speckled two-piece suit, with one foot dragging in the gravel. She still had her arm across Don's shoulder, and she could hear him employ a long string of expressions in Yiddish to curse the weight of his can.

When they stopped, Eva released her grip on Don and looked up at the words above the freight car's massive axle:

21 RIV
74 GC
226 2 098-9

Hex took a thick key from her jacket pocket. She stuck it into the lock of the sliding door, and there were two creaks as she turned it. Then she took hold of the lower edge with both hands and pulled so that the door rolled to the side.

"How will we fit?" Eva heard herself say.

A compact wall of dark brown Masonite crates towered in the opening. They had been stacked from floor to ceiling, and they appeared to fill the whole car. The metal fittings on the sides of the crates shone in the light from the freight yard, and it looked as though it would take a forklift to move even the top one.

Eva's eyes looked to Don for an answer, but he was already on his way up to Hex to help her onto the tiny strip of empty floor in front of the piles.

It sounded as though his sister were undoing some catches, and a moment later she had managed to work the middle walls of crates aside. Behind this secret wall was a pitch-black corridor that was only about eight inches wide.

Hex turned around and crouched down. "Come on now, hurry up!"

Eva hesitantly took Don's sister's outstretched hand, and with help from Don she managed to climb up onto the edge of the car. Hex showed her how to move sideways so she would have room to squeeze into the corridor between the crates.

Her chest hit the walls of the passage as she tentatively began to move into the opening. For a short time, there was still light from out in the freight yard, but then she heard a rattling noise as the sliding door behind them rolled shut.

Without being able to see, Eva let her fingers slide along the crates as she carefully kept going forward. When she ran into the far wall of the car, the space was too small for her even to be able to turn around.

"Up to the left," Hex whispered.

The words must have been directed at Don, because now Eva could feel him stretching up to the ceiling above her, and then she heard a metallic click. There was a scraping sound from an edge dragging across the floor of the car as the left side of the Masonite wall was moved away tug by tug. Then there was a familiar sliding sound, like an old-fashioned train door being pulled aside.

Don's fingers around her wrist; he pulled her to the left, in through a doorway. Eva's heels sank down into something soft, and then Hex's voice: "Where the hell is it? There!"

A pleasant incandescent light was switched on, and Eva thought that she must have fallen into a time warp, because it was like coming home somehow.

A thirty- or forty-foot-long train lounge stretched out before them, with walls of close-set panels of glazed teak.

At this end of the deep red wall-to-wall carpet, next to a round table with mother-of-pearl inlays, were two chocolate-brown high-backed club chairs. Farther away there was a dining-room suite in ornamental cedar, with six comfortable chairs. Framed copperplate engravings of Indian palaces and patrician villas hung on the long wall on the left side, and along the wall on the right ran a sleek hardwood bookcase. It was crammed with tattered paperback thrillers.

Eva took a few steps forward and loosened a book from the bookcase.

"Agatha Christie," she said to herself.

"Yes, but it was a hell of a job."

Hex's voice made her turn around. Don's sister was still standing in the doorway.

"*Murder on the Orient Express*," Hex said. "Ingrid Bergman, Sean Connery, Lauren Bacall . . ."

Hex knocked on the frosted glass of the compartment door, above the brass bolt fitting. Then she slowly walked along the left-side wall of the lounge, and one after another she lit the wall lamps that were mounted alongside the copperplate engravings.

"And Albert Finney, of course, as Poirot. A hell of a job to re-create."

"I can see that," said Eva.

She pushed the Christie thriller back into the bookcase and tried to collect herself.

"Those were very special years—the thirties," she said then, and smiled.

At the very end of the wagon, along its short wall, stood a large mahogany cabinet, and now Hex opened its doors. Inside the cabinet was something that looked like a kitchenette: a small counter with two hot plates, shelves of spices, china, saucepans, and at the very bottom, two brushed-steel refrigerators.

Don had followed his sister, dragging the two cans along the carpet, and now he heaved them into the refrigerator on the left. When he opened the one on the right, Eva could see a few bottles of wine and several rows of jars and canned goods.

"It's been sitting here for a few months, but there's no time for you to get more," said Hex. "And use the water sparingly."

Then she walked back through the train lounge and opened the compartment door out onto the narrow Masonite hallway. From out in the darkness, they could hear snapping sounds, and yet another secret wall opened, and a light came on on the other side of the car.

Eva looked at Don, but he just nodded at her to follow.

When she reached the right side of the car and had pulled another frosted train door aside, she entered a cozy compartment.

Two sleeping-car bunks had been folded out from the wall. Alongside the lower one was a nightstand with a laptop on it. Both of the beds had reading lamps of orange porcelain, and as in the lounge, the floor was covered by a wall-to-wall carpet of the deepest red.

Hex had sat down on the edge of the bed with a thin leather briefcase on her lap. She opened the zipper, took an envelope from inside her jacket, and placed it in the briefcase.

"I think you should consider your credit cards to be temporarily deactivated," she said, zipping the zipper. "You can take the cash I had at home with you, and then we'll figure out a solution over the Internet."

Hex nodded toward the laptop. Then she turned around and placed the briefcase in a net hanger that was mounted above the bed.

"But it's not a gift, Danele," she said as she got up.

Then she walked up to Don, who had leaned against the compartment wall, exhausted. Hex took hold of the lapels of his jacket with her small hands and directed her gaze up at his face.

"Very soon, probably within a half hour, a locomotive will come tow you out from the Hagalund freight yard to the freight center in Västberga. There you'll be coupled into the Rail Administration's Friday transport to Helsingborg harbor. It will be a slow journey to Skåne; the tracks are usually full of other traffic. Then I've ordered a recoupling at 2:45 P.M.; that will be a French freight transport with lighter cars, so after Helsingør the speed will increase. You'll arrive after another ten or eleven hours. All the documents are in the envelope."

It looked as though Don wanted to say something, but instead he bent his bowed back to his sister and gave her an awkward hug. Hex took a step or two backward and smiled, embarrassed.

"You have my log-in info, so we can stay in contact via the computer, and make damn sure that you don't get caught in any customs check. You have a declared net weight of twenty-one tons plus two tons of cargo. I listed you as recycled goods on the NHM register."

"You have earned your name, Sarah," said Don.

Hex stiffened, but then she shrugged her shoulders.

"Yes, it's unbelievable that it works, but the control is so careless. Schengen is really fantastic. And you also need this."

She gave Don the key and stood before him, hesitating. Then she placed her hand against his cheek.

*"Ich vintsh dir glik, Danele,"* she said. I wish you good luck.

She turned to Eva. "You, too."

With a final light caress of Don's face, his sister walked over to the compartment door. Pulled it open and said, "Make sure to buy new clothes when you arrive. You two really look awful."

She disappeared out into the dark Masonite corridor. A minute or so later, the secret wall was closed from the outside, and then the dull noise as the sliding door slid shut.

Eva sank down onto the lower bunk of the sleeping cabin, and after a while she kicked her shoes off onto the carpet.

"Sarah?" she asked.

"What?" Don had taken off his aviator glasses and was sitting and leaning against the wall.

"You called her Sarah? Your sister?"

"Yes . . . no, I was just so tired. She doesn't like that name; it's an old story."

"Her name is Sarah?"

"Yes . . . or Chana Sarah Titelman, to be exact, but if I'd called her that, she would probably have thrown us off, both of us. She has some issues with her Jewish heritage, you could say."

"But you don't?"

Don looked away.

"You can't choose your family," Eva said softly.

He didn't answer, just sat there and rubbed his eyes.

"So why the name Hex?"

"It's the computer thing," Don said, "It's some sort of nickname."

"Have you traveled in this car before?"

"I'm not much for traveling," Don answered. "And my sister is not a very inviting person, if you haven't noticed."

"I really liked her place in Kymlinge, though," said Eva. "It's very intriguing, just like her."

"Yeah, cozy, isn't it?" said Don.

Then, after a moment of hesitation, he decided to continue.

"When she first found it, it was just an abandoned cellar filled with rubble. She used it as a primitive hideout, a getaway of sorts, after some highly organized series of computer attacks against bank-to-bank transfers that she happened to get involved in. After that experience, she has become somewhat suspicious of uninvited strangers."

"As a lawyer I can't . . ." Eva started, but Don just waved her off.

"Forget about it, it was a long time ago," he said. "Anyway, by now she seems to have gotten very fond of the place, and I guess she has settled down underground for good. She has always been a loner by default. Almost autistic sometimes, with a certain knack for advanced math and cryptology. Nowadays she claims to have gotten some legitimate use of her expertise as well, acting as a consulting agent in especially troublesome cases of online security. I doubt that anybody she deals with knows about her real identity, though. Ever since she was a child, she has been obsessed with designing her own private retreats, places where she can be totally self-sufficient and alone. This train, I guess, would be the prime example of that."

"Yes, it's wonderful," said Eva, and looked around the sleeping cabin. "Amazing, actually. And she is actually able to operate this thing from her computer?"

"Do you have any reason to doubt her?"

The situation was getting too bizarre, and Eva couldn't help but laugh. A gloomy gaze from Don cut her short, and instead she asked, "How often do you see each other, you and your sister?"

"We keep in contact, let's put it like that."

"And what about your family, do they . . ."

"Well, you know, it's complicated," Don interrupted curtly.

In the long silence that followed, he thought of everything he could have told her about Chana Sarah Titelman.

If it hadn't been so late, if he hadn't been so deathly tired, it would lead him on to that night of despair in 1994 when she had become older than he, had taken him into her home and cared for him, her older brother, as though he had been a child. What did he care what she called herself, or what she had decided to do with her life? She was the one who had carried him when he hadn't had the strength to stand.

"There are hot water bottles," said Eva.

She had pulled a drawer out from under the bunk and held up a rubber bed warmer.

At that moment, the car was shaken by a hard bump, and the movement spread through the compartment and made the frosted glass in the train door start to vibrate.

Don looked at the clock.

"The locomotive," he said.

From outside they could hear the rattle of chains, voices, and steps of people moving around the car. Someone called out, a sharp whistle, and there was another powerful jerk. Then everything was quiet.

Don's legs wavered as he tried to rise from his seated position by the wall.

"You have to get some sleep," said Eva.

She moved backward into the bunk, and he hardly had the strength to take the last few steps and lie down beside her with his face turned out toward the room.

The compartment window rattled again as the car was pushed a few yards backward on the track. They lay awake there for a few minutes before the locomotive finally started to pull. Eva could hear the noise from the joints of the rails, a rhythmic thudding through the bunk bed. She had almost fallen asleep when she formed one last whisper:

"But she still said something Jewish before she left. Hex, I mean. And whoever switched the subway wrong in Kymlinge I think she called a schmuck."

"There is hope," Don mumbled.

Eva thought she ought to be quiet, but she had to ask anyway. "Why did she call the car the Silver Arrow?"

Don turned toward her and switched off the orange lamp. Then he fumbled in the drawer where she'd found the bed warmer and brought up a blanket, which he spread over her and himself. He laid his head down and stared into the dark and tried to find a rhythm in the vibration of the car as it moved over the rails in the dawn.

"Don?"

The freight car stopped on a side track, another train pulled past, and the roar lingered at the wall as the train rushed away.

"Don?" Eva said again.

"That old rumor," he said thickly.

"What old rumor," she said.

With a sigh he turned around and tried to make out her face.

Then, in a whisper, he began to tell her about the ghost train that roves around deep down in the Stockholm subway. The dead gaze out at the living through its windows as its silvery cars open their doors at the platform. And if someone dares to step on . . .

The words came out of his mouth with drawn-out pauses.

The Silver Arrow, the Flying Dutchman of the underworld, only lets passengers off at Kymlinge, the station of the dead.

When he stopped talking, he could tell from Eva's breathing that she had fallen asleep. And at a quarter past six, as the freight car was towed out of Västberga heading south, Don, for the first time in forty-eight hours, also dared to relax.

The buzz of the slowly waking city, which they were leaving behind them. Inside the compartment, safe darkness, heavy wheels rhythmically striking the joints of the rails.

Don felt Eva grope for his arm and pull it around herself. He moved close to her body and then slowly began to fall asleep.

# 2

# 24

# Ypres

The plans to leave the city as it was, obliterated, as a monument to the power of the new era's weapons, had come quite far. But in a practical sense it was impossible, because the people who had lived in Ypres before the war soon demanded to be able to return home. And though they had been told that there was nothing to return to, they refused to change their minds.

In the fall of 1918 the authorities gave up, and temporary camps began to be erected in the trenches of scrap metal that had once been a city. At that point, all that was left of the central square, Grote Markt, were two ruins, burned black: the remains of a colonnade that showed where the cathedral had risen, and the broken bell tower of the medieval cloth hall. It was as though someone with a giant road grader had once and for all scoured Ypres from the flat Belgian landscape.

The cause of the city's misfortunes had always been its strategic position—placed like bait in the middle of the fertile fields of West Flanders, a short distance from the coast toward England, with Germany to the east and France to the southwest. A suitable area for deployment, with no natural obstacles, that through the centuries had been crossed by nearly every European army.

In October 1914, the Greater German offensive streamed in across West Flanders, heading for the coastal towns and northern France.

Before they got stuck, the Germans managed to surround Ypres on three sides, and from the surrounding low hills, they could bombard the city at will. One month later, in November 1914, over a quarter of a million people were dead or wounded, and the Allies still held the city. This first strike on Ypres was later called *der Kindermord,* the Massacre of the Innocents, because an entire generation of teenagers had been obliterated on the muddy fields of West Flanders. Barely six months later, in April 1915, the slaughter began again. After a few weeks of artillery fire, there was practically nothing left of the medieval Ypres.

The third blow became the iconic picture of the madness of World War I and has gone down in history under the name Passchendaele. Four months of pelting rain and bottomless mire, in which wave after wave of youths were thrown at barbed wire and machine-gun fire. The Allies' attempt to break a hole in the German front continued until November 1917, and its only result was that hundreds of thousands more people died. After this came a time of resignation and exhaustion, and both sides awaited the end of the war in the same positions they had occupied on the day the battles had begun.

With the help of reparations for war damages, which would be one of the reasons for the next big clash, Ypres began to be built up again during the fall of 1918.

For those who didn't want to forget, there was a marked path that led out to the trenches of World War I. It began at the monumental facade of the Cloth Hall and ran with yellow arrows along Meensestraat, where wave upon wave of young men had marched on their way to the fields of slaughter to the northeast.

A triumphal arch was built in memory of the British soldiers whose bodies had never been recovered, and it was named the Menin Gate. Fifty-five thousand names were carved into its stone panels. The other approximately half million fallen were buried in the hundreds of cemeteries outside the city walls. There they rest under white crosses, in straight rows that are miles long.

Saint Martin's Cathedral was rebuilt from the photographs that remained after the war, but the spire was redesigned in Gothic style. Soon it once again towered high over the merchant halls of Grote Markt, its defiant tip aimed at the sky from which the incendiary bombs had once fallen.

From the spire of Saint Martin's, one could make out a white light that was slowly approaching the southern city limits of Ypres. The freight terminal waited there like a yellow rectangle. Down on lively Rijselsestraat, the last bar had closed, and in the quiet night, you could hear the whistle of the train clearly, although it was still many miles away.

It rattled and shook inside the lounge of the freight car as Don unfolded the Belgian railroad company's blueprints on the surface of the table between the easy chairs. He had found it in the briefcase Hex had sent along, and it had an overview of the freight depot's rail yard. His sister had circled track number seven and written a note in ink about their estimated time of arrival.

Don had tried along with Eva to estimate how much distance there was between track number seven and the depot's exit, and they had ended up with a distance of about five hundred feet. The attorney had assured him that she would be able to run the short distance without help, but it was only after he'd examined her calf that Don understood that she hadn't just wanted to appear brave. Because where there had once been an ugly gash, there was now only a bit of scar tissue. Eva had already removed the bits of surgical tape. Don thought that he might have overestimated the depth of the cut and that his medical knowledge was out of date. Still, it seemed strange somehow, how quickly she had healed.

They had been traveling in the car for more than twenty hours now. Don had been awake since they passed Hässleholm. It had already been lunchtime then, and the sun had been very strong; it made the compartment stale and stuffy.

When they arrived in Helsingborg, he had risked opening the sliding door of the freight car to let in a little fresh air. From the sound of the sea, he had realized that they had been towed to a waiting area down by the harbor, and when he looked out, the gray-black water had been calm beyond the railroad tracks, at the end of the quay. He wondered whether he should go out and try to move around for a bit, but then he had heard Eva calling from inside the dark car. So he had let the sliding door roll shut once again in front of the opening of the Masonite corridor.

They had eaten a simple lunch. Vegetable soup from Hex's canned goods, a glass of white wine each, crispbread, and crackers. For dessert Eva had found a jar of preserved fruit, and afterward they had started up the laptop.

On the Internet, they had been able to follow the Swedish police's hunt for new leads, and Eva had sent off messages to the law firm in Borlänge to see if they might be able to get help there. But there had been no results yet.

And now, as they sat there before the layout plans in the lounge, the heavy freight car finally began to slow down.

They remained in the easy chairs, waiting, for over an hour after the train had stopped, for the last voices outside the car to grow quiet and disappear. By quarter to three, they could hear only distant cries from some blaring loudspeaker, in a language that sounded like a mix of English and German.

Don nodded at Eva to follow him out through the narrow Masonite passage. At the secret wall, he carefully lifted away the outer locks. Then he stood and listened again for a short time before he finally dared to turn the key in the lock of the sliding door and start to pull it aside with small movements.

When Don stuck his head out into the night air, he saw that the rail yard was lit only here and there, and that the path was open to the exit of the terminal, only a few hundred yards away. That was blocked by two simple wooden bars, and next to those was a dark sentry box. Two night-shift workers in yellow vests were squatting at the foot of a crane. They seemed to be busy with some sort of welding work, because there were occasional sparks from a white-blue flame.

Don helped Eva climb down from the freight car, and she landed with her high heels in the gravel. Then he dug around in the bag and found the cylinder-shaped inhaler that contained trichloroethylene. Took two slurping breaths and felt the liberating calm appear. He rolled the sliding door shut and breathed in the scent of rubber and diesel. Each step crunched as they began to move toward the yellow and black bars at the exit. Somewhere far behind them they thought they heard someone shout.

Don quickened his steps, and thirty seconds later they had managed to pass the sentry box and were on their way out into something that looked like an industrial area.

There they temporarily took shelter behind a Dumpster and waited for a while to see whether someone inside the freight yard had seen them.

But when no one appeared, Don took the map that Hex had sent along out of his shoulder bag, so that they could find their way to the central neighborhoods of Ypres. Eva pointed to an open place that appeared to be called Grote Markt, whose edges were marked by several red circles with the letter H on them.

# 25

# Saint Martin d'Ypres

Hotel Langemark was squeezed into a brick building from the 1600s that was so narrow that it had space for only a few rooms, despite being sixty feet high. It sported white-lattice arched windows; and like every building that surrounded Ypres' medieval square, Grote Markt, the building had been rebuilt from the ground up after the war, brick by brick.

A red and white canopy hung droopily over the hotel's outdoor seating, and it took a long time for the night receptionist to come down and open up. He just waved tiredly at them when Don tried to explain why they didn't have passports and identification.

In return for a cash payment up front, the old man unhooked a key from the cabinet behind the reception desk. Then without further questions, he limped ahead of them up a steep staircase to the fourth floor of the hotel. There he opened a run-down room that had wallpaper in a large pattern and whose barred windows looked out at the facade of Cloth Hall.

When the night receptionist had disappeared, they lay down side by side on the bedspread of the double bed, to rest a bit more before morning came. But it wasn't long before they had both fallen asleep, exhausted by the long train trip.

When Don woke up around nine and caught sight of himself in the hotel room's mirror, he realized that they really should take Hex's advice. The arms of his jacket were ripped from his climb out of the cellar window on Djurgården, and brown traces of dirt ran along his corduroy legs.

Eva didn't look particularly elegant either, sitting there in a chair in her wrinkled clothes. One lower leg was still wrapped in a bandage, and red flecks of blood were visible on her left shoe.

Don suggested that they try to get new clothes even before breakfast. When Eva nodded, he helped her up, and out in the hall he kindly offered his arm as support. But then Eva said a bit irritably that she could make it down the steep stairs on her own. And as they walked across the large square in the September sun, he noticed that she wasn't limping at all now.

Don had imagined that the matter would be quickly taken care of, but an hour or so later they were still walking around the lanes near Grote Markt looking for the right kind of clothes for the attorney. For his part, he had grabbed a salt-and-pepper suit in the first good store, and he had changed in the fitting room.

The old corduroy jacket with the postcard was now dangling in a yellow plastic bag in his hand, and Don was doing his utmost not to start complaining. The attorney turned out to have very particular taste and would not tolerate any objections. Not until they were on a back street far from the main street, Rijselsestraat, did they finally find a boutique of a sufficiently conservative type.

Because a group of older women were elbowing their way forth among the piles of clothes in there, Don stationed himself outside the boutique and waited until he saw Eva waving at him through the glass of the display window.

Up by the cash register, she had already put on the clothes she had picked out. The attorney seemed to have gotten stuck in some sort of 1940s style: wide trousers with creases, a white satin blouse, and a moss-green trench coat with a silk scarf.

The dirty two-piece suit lay in a pile on the counter, and Eva explained to the shop assistant in French that those old rags could be burned for all she cared. The assistant answered pointedly that *French* was not spoken in *Ieper* or the rest of West Flanders and that it was better to try English or, even better, *Flemish,* if one wished to get an answer. Then a girdle and some salmon-pink silk stockings disappeared down into a small package, which the assistant handed over, and the cash register jingled.

Fortunately, the attorney found a shoe store that turned out to be good enough a few doors down. And after Don had paid for a pair of tall, shiny boots of Italian leather with the euro bills that Hex had sent along, Eva was finally satisfied.

They slowly walked back over Grote Markt and sat down at the hotel's outdoor seating, in the shadow of the canopy. The continental breakfast was still spread on the table, along with a colorful tourist brochure that Don had picked up in the hotel.

On the front it said "Ypres—city of peace," and in the middle of the brochure, there was a map of the central parts of the city.

As Don looked out across the square and saw the busloads of tourists pouring out in the direction of Cloth Hall and the war monument, it struck him that he and Eva probably looked like a middle-aged couple on the run from a tour group. But because the idea had been to travel as anonymously as possible, that wasn't really a problem.

"'A more sacred place for the British race does not exist in the world,'" Don read aloud from the tourist brochure, to perfect the illusion.

Eva looked up from her breakfast and used her napkin to wipe her mouth.

"That's what Sir Winston Churchill said about Ypres."

He pointed down at the quote, which was blown up in large letters above a cemetery of white crosses.

*"Ieper,"* said Eva. "That's what Churchill said about *Ieper.*"

"The city is called Ypres in French, and that's what it was called by the French and English during the First World War," said Don. "And the cathedral here"—he flipped back to the map in the middle of the brochure and pointed to a small color picture—"its French name, as far as I understand, is Saint Martin d'Ypres."

"And I am certain that those who live here want to call it Sint Maarten," Eva said drily. "But if you were thinking about devoting yourself to sightseeing, I think that's a bad idea. It's probably better to assume that the Belgian police already have access to photographs of us." When she saw that Don was skeptical, Eva continued: "One of the partners at Afzelius hinted that the National Police sent out an international alert yesterday. I got hold of him from the hotel while you were sleeping."

Don looked out over the square as he slowly stirred his spoon in his coffee cup.

"I see," Don said at last. "Did the guy at Afzelius say anything else?"

"He asked questions about where we were, which I assume he had been requested to do if I were to make contact."

"And what did you tell him?"

"What happened. That we had left the country in a private freight car and that now we're in a small city somewhere in the northwestern part of the European continent."

Eva pushed her plate away.

"No, I hung up, of course. If you like, I can check with some of my old criminal lawyer colleagues in Stockholm, whether they want to help, but . . ."

She sighed.

"But I really don't know, Don."

He looked down at the traces of coffee grounds. Then they sat in silence for a while, until Don made up his mind: "I actually think that's Saint Martin's Cathedral that you can see over there."

He pointed at a Gothic spire that rose up just behind the enormous Cloth Hall. Eva compared it to the picture on the map, and then she nodded curtly.

"As I was trying to say . . ." she began.

"But that's not what the cathedral looked like *before* the war," said Don.

He stuck in his hand and pulled his old, dirty corduroy coat out of the yellow plastic bag, laid it across his lap, and felt along the inside of the lining to find the stiff contour of cardboard. He fished up the postcard with the aged photograph turned toward Eva.

"You can see here," said Don, pointing at the yellowed picture. "Before the war, Saint Martin d'Ypres had a much shorter square tower, and the rose window was much smaller."

Eva looked at the picture for a long time without saying anything. Then she put down her wineglass and took the postcard out of his hand. She turned it over carefully and sighed as she caught sight of the short lines on the back.

"And this . . . ?" she asked, without lifting her gaze.

"I found it in Erik Hall's bedroom," said Don. "During our last conversation, he mentioned something about another object he had found down in the mine, besides the ankh. Some kind of document that was difficult to decipher. I guess this is what he was referring to."

"You guess?"

"It was the only item in his room that was about a hundred years old and didn't reek of porn."

"So, you *did* do some snooping around at Erik Hall's house then," she said. "What else is there that you haven't told me about what happened?"

"That I was the one who hit him in the head with that bottle."

The attorney looked inquiringly at Don, without smiling. Then she turned her attention to the postcard: *"Les suprêmes adieux,"* she said. "The final farewells."

Eva placed it between them on the table, with the lines of blue ink facing up. She seemed to disappear in her thoughts for a while before she said, "La Cathédrale Saint Martin d'Ypres, you were saying."

Don showed her the printed letters in the upper corner of the postcard.

"A photograph taken a few years before the war," he continued. "No stamp, no address, just that short verse."

"And he's the one who wrote it," said the attorney.

"Erik Hall?"

"No," she mumbled, a bit absentmindedly, "no, not Erik Hall, it must be the man in the mine who wrote it, I assume."

"Yes, we could probably assume that," said Don.

"But why didn't you show this to Eberlein?"

He considered this but couldn't come up with a good answer.

Eva let the matter rest, drank the last drops of wine, and moved the postcard a bit closer. Then she read the words aloud, one by one, as they had once been written down over the shape of a red mouth.

*la bouche de mon amour Camille Malraux*
*le 22 avril*
*l'homme vindicatif*
*l'immensité de son désir*
*les suprêmes adieux*
*1913*

*"La bouche de mon amour Camille Malraux* . . . This is my beloved Camille Malraux's mouth . . . or lips, I suppose?" Eva said, touching the faded lipstick.

*"Cherchez la femme,"* said Don.

"So that's why we're here?"

"Well, we had to have some destination."

Eva mumbled the woman's name to herself again, and then she continued to read: *"L'homme vindicatif* . . . the vindictive man, *l'immensité de son désir* . . . his tremendous desire, and *les suprêmes adieux* . . . the final farewells. Written on the twenty-second of April . . ."

"Nineteen thirteen. One year before World War One broke out."

Eva slowly leaned back in her chair, and then she said with a crooked smile: "And this was what was so important to keep hidden from Eberlein and the Germans? A kiss and a few lines of poetry, written to a beloved woman almost a hundred years ago?"

Don shrugged. Then he took the postcard from the table and put it in his shoulder bag. He signaled to the waiter for the check.

"So what's your plan?" asked Eva as she stood up. "To try to find this Camille Malraux? Why would she still be in Ypres?"

"Can you think of a better place to start looking?"

She looked at him hesitantly.

"Do you really think this will improve your case? An old postcard?"

"There could be some kind of connection, right?" said Don. "The murder of Erik Hall, Eberlein's story, Strindberg's navigational instrument, and these few words directed a long time ago to a woman. If we found out more about her, maybe we could find some clue that could help explain the mystery behind the man in the mine, and Erik Hall's death. Besides, I really have a problem with walking away from dark hidden secrets. My experience is that they are better off being exposed to the light."

"It could be worth a try, I guess," said Eva slowly. "Right now we really don't have anything to lose."

"So you'll help me then?" Don made an effort to sound casual, as he took the roll of euros out of his pocket and unrolled a few bills.

"Well, why not?" said Eva. Then she smiled, noticing his surprise. "The client is always right, as they say. And after what happened at Villa Lindarne, I need to find out the truth behind this as much as you do. You've got me wanted for aiding escape and for battery on an officer, remember?"

She started to put on her trench coat.

"So where do we begin?"

"Maybe there's someone here in Ypres who knew this Camille Malraux," said Don, rising up from the table. "She must have died a long time ago, of course. She could have left behind papers that explain . . ."

He became quiet when he realized how far-fetched that sounded.

"You're awfully negative sometimes, you know," Eva said, as she took hold of his arm. "She might have good genes, Camille. Who knows, maybe she's still alive."

# 26

# Stadsarchief

At first, the stiffly smiling information officer in the overcrowded tourist center inside Cloth Hall didn't even try to understand Don's question. But then, probably mostly to get the line moving once again, the woman behind the counter suggested that they begin by searching for historical documents at the Ypres city archive. All the registers of births and deaths, marriages, immigration, and emigration were there. And not only those from the city of Ypres, but from all of Westhoek, the district of West Flanders.

The city archive was the starting point that most people chose for their genealogical research, the information officer said. In some cases, she had heard, such personal details as copies of wills, courtroom proceedings, and sometimes even personal letters could be found there. And Camille Malraux really was quite an unusual name, of course, at least in the Flemish part of Belgium.

Then the information officer depressed an angry red button on a small box, there was a beep, and a new queue number flashed up on the digital screen above her head.

Don convinced Eva to take a taxi with him out of the historical district, past the medieval walls. When they had passed a stone-paved bridge over a canal, the aspect of the city suddenly changed and became modern and lacking in character. It was as though the money for rebuilding hadn't been enough to include this area.

The city archive and city library shared an entrance in a box-shaped structure of red brick and glass on Weverijstraat. On the way into the entrance, there were signs in five languages advertising that there was more than 425,000 feet of shelves full of precious documents preserved here.

But the clerks' enthusiasm for shuffling off in search of documents didn't seem particularly great once they had found their way to one of the small offices for *Archief en Genealogie,* the archive for genealogical research.

The girl who sat yawning behind the gray plastic computer terminal could hardly be twenty years old. She seemed to be a temp worker, or else it had been a grave error to hire her. Skinny white arms, purple lipstick, and a black T-shirt on which the bloodred face of a goat shone behind the text CHURCH OF SATAN.

The girl put a piece of gum in her mouth and then yawned again, obviously bored, in the direction of the older man who had the misfortune of sitting in the chair in front of her. When he finally got up to leave, apparently without having received answers to any of his genealogy questions, the girl slipped out a small violet paperback book, which she began to read with great interest.

Don looked at Eva, and then he walked up to the small office booth and gave a cough.

*"Een moment,"* the girl said obstinately in Flemish, without looking at him.

"Yes, hello," said Don. "My name is Don . . . *Malraux.* I would like to . . ."

The girl shook her head, irritated, shoved a notebook with an attached pen toward him.

"Spell, please," she muttered.

Don tried to smile at her, but the girl had already started to read again. He wrote the surname MALRAUX in neat block letters. When the girl took the time to look at what Don had managed to produce, she sighed deeply.

"Jesus! . . . First name. Birthplace. Year."

"Her name was Camille," Don said quickly, while he still had the girl's attention. "My sister and I think that she might be a relative."

"Your sister?" said the girl skeptically, looking at the blond woman behind Don and then back at his swarthy face.

"Yes. Our family has Walloon roots."

"So what relation are you to this Camille?"

"It's a . . ."

"Are you her grandchildren? Second cousins thrice removed?"

"It's a bit of a long story, I'm afraid. Does it matter?"

"No, no," the girl muttered. "I don't give a damn. This Camille, she was born here in the Westhoek region?"

"Yes . . ."

"Yes, we think so," said Eva, sitting down beside Don with a resolute expression on her face.

"I see," said the girl. "When?"

Don sneaked a look at Eva.

"Sometime in the late 1800s, we think," he said.

The girl suddenly became interested in her fingernails and began to examine them thoroughly.

"You can look at the years between 1870 and 1895," Eva said.

"Eighteen seventy to ninety-five," the girl repeated. "In the city of Ypres, or one of the surrounding villages?"

"We . . ." Don attempted, but he was interrupted by an uninterested babbling:

"Boezinge, Brielen, Dikkebus . . . maybe Elverdinge? Hollebeke, Sint-Jan . . . Zillebeke?"

"We . . ."

"So, Zillebeke," the girl decided.

"We think we know that this Camille Malraux died in Ypres," Eva said. "She was still alive in 1913, we know that for certain. Perhaps she died during the war."

The girl turned unwillingly to her plastic-enclosed keyboard and brought up the civil registry of Ypres on the screen.

She tapped in "Camille Malraux" with one index finger.

"Ah," she said, without turning back to them. "There are actually two people with that name who apparently died during the war. One born in 1885 in Voormezele; her parents were named . . ."

"And the other one?" Eva asked.

"For the other one, there's no information about her parents' names or where she was born. French citizenship. It says she died in Ypres in 1917."

"So what else does it say?" Eva asked impatiently.

The girl sighed even more deeply, took out her gum, and threw it in the wastepaper basket.

"That's all there is. Not all the information is entered into the computers. Unfortunately. If you want more, then I'll have to go down into the archive to find her folder. It's rarely worth the trouble."

"I insist," Eva said curtly.

With a groan, the skinny girl got up from her comfy place at the keyboard. Then she locked the computer by hitting two keys and pointedly sauntered away slowly between the shelves.

When she came back just over half an hour later, she had two thin folders. The girl threw them down in front of Eva and Don and then returned to her book.

In the first folder, they found only a few brief statements. A woman by the name of Camille Malraux, née Holst, born in 1885, had married a Ronald Malraux in Onze-Lieve Vrouwkerk, Our Lady's Church in Voormezele, in 1905. No information about where this Camille had worked, whether she had children or siblings. A hospital record, a death certificate, and a short note that her husband had died early, in 1907.

"Worth the trouble?" the girl mumbled behind her book.

In the next Camille Malraux's folder, there were only two pieces of paper: the death certificate and a reference to all other documents having been moved to the woman's French place of birth, which was listed as Charleville-Mézières.

"Can copies of her French documents be ordered?" Don asked.

The girl pretended that she hadn't heard anything.

"We would like you to order copies of all the documents that exist about this Camille Malraux from your colleague at the civil register in Charleville-Mézières, in France," Eva said with emphasis on each syllable.

The girl gave up and placed her paperback book on the table in front of her.

"Something like that," she said, "takes a *very long time.* There's a whole pile of bureaucratic crap that has to be filled out, and it takes a lot of rubber-stamping."

The girl picked up the first Malraux folder from the table, the one containing the Camille Malraux who had originally been named Holst.

"I bet it's this one," said the girl.

"We want to order . . ." Eva began again.

"Do you plan to stay here in Ypres for long?" The girl smiled scornfully. "Because it usually takes several months to get documents from a different country. Particularly from a country like France. Besides, it has to be registered and . . ."

Don sensed that Eva was about to have some sort of fit.

He took out the postcard, which, after having carefully checked the seams, he was now keeping in the inner pocket of the new jacket. He placed it on the table in front of the girl and showed her the photograph of Saint Martin's Cathedral.

"You've done the tourist thing at Cloth Hall, I see," said the girl. "It's unbelievable that people actually buy sentimental crap like that."

"We inherited this, and it was actually purchased before the war," said Don. Then he turned the postcard over and pointed at the verse and the red print of the mouth. For the first time a trace of interest was aroused in the girl's eyes. She read through the lines.

"Yes, it seems to be from 1913, as you said," said the girl. "So what is this, a little love letter?"

She mumbled her way through the verse one more time.

"Well-chosen words," she said. "But borrowed."

"It was written by our grandfather to this woman, Camille," Don said. "We would be eternally grateful if you could help us. She was the love of his life."

"Are you really sure it had to do with love?" asked the girl.

She put the postcard down.

"I mean, *l'homme vindicatif, l'immensité de son désir, les suprêmes adieux* . . . He's writing that he's a vindictive man with unquenchable desires. But nothing wrong with that."

Eva became tired. "Are you planning on helping us or not?"

"With what?" the girl ventured.

"With filling out an application to Charleville-Mézières in France, so we can find out if there are any documents there," said Don. "We're prepared to wait."

"Well then, only because your grandfather had such good taste in literature," said the girl.

She dug a thick form out of a desk drawer, tapped her fingers, leaned over it, and slowly began to fill in the empty lines. When she had been writing for a while, the girl said, without raising her eyes, "You don't need to sit here and watch. Come back in a few days and maybe we'll have gotten an answer."

"Thanks," said Don; he took the postcard from the table and got up.

*"Dessin d'un Maître inconnu,"* the girl mumbled to herself. "Portrait of an unknown master."

"Sorry?" said Don.

*"Dessin d'un Maître inconnu,"* said the girl, looking up at him. "You didn't think your Swedish grandfather came up with those lines him-

self, did you? *Combla-t-il sur ta chair inerte et complaisante, l'immensité de son désir . . .* He borrowed every word, but you probably knew that already."

Don looked at Eva and then back at the white face with the purple lips.

"You only have to love Baudelaire," said the girl.

Then she continued to write serenely.

# 27

# In Flanders Fields

It had begun to drizzle even as Eva and Don had stood waiting for the taxi to come and take them back to central Ypres and Grote Markt from the city archive. And now, as the car was coming to a stop in the puddles on the square, the isolated drops had turned into a torrential rain.

Eva pointed over to the huddling crowds of tourists who had taken shelter under the archway at the entry to the war museum at Cloth Hall. Then she opened the door of the car and ran over to them, with her trench coat pulled up over her head.

While Don waited for the taxi driver to get his change in order, he watched Eva struggle to shove her way in among the tourists so she wouldn't get drenched.

Drooping flags were hung a short distance in front of the entrance of the museum. If they had been dry they would presumably have been light red, but, drenched with water, they hung as dark as blood. On the bloody flags was a blue and white cross, which was adorned by a bunch of poppies with stems made of barbed wire. At the very bottom, on a black border, one could read:

IN FLANDERS FIELDS MUSEUM
IEPER 1914–1918

When it was Don's turn to elbow his way into the crowd of tourists under the entryway arch, he was shoved out again and again by an older Japanese couple. At last he grew tired, caught hold of Eva's arm, and yanked her along between the packed bodies, and they went in through the doors of the museum.

In the next instant, everything was peaceful, and they found themselves in something that looked like the inside of a cathedral. Along the walls were pointed Gothic windows with lead that surrounded small pieces of light blue and pink glass like spiderwebs.

Don exhaled and drew a hand through his soaking wet, lank hair. Beside him, Eva used a handkerchief to try to save her mascara, which the rain had caused to run.

In the lofty hall, they heard the hum of subdued whispers, someone coughing, and then, distantly, the sound of shots and explosions from the film projectors that were rolling inside the dark exhibition halls.

Up at the ticket counter of the museum stood two wax models in period costumes. One of them wore a field uniform with buttons of brass from his throat down to the belt of his uniform. He had a small mustache on his yellowish face and blue porcelain eyes. On a small plaque was the name Robert Launer, German artilleryman.

At Launer's side stood a woman in a stiff, beseeching position, with a white veil over her artificial hair. She depicted someone who had once been called Roosje Vecht, a Dutch nurse who had worked in the camps behind the trenches and whose leg had been blasted off just after lunchtime on the twenty-third of January 1915.

When they had paid and gotten past the entrance gates, it was as though Eva's back stiffened. She had a mournful expression as she passed the long stone engraving with H. G. Wells's ominous words:

EVERY INTELLIGENT PERSON IN THE WORLD FELT THAT
DISASTER
WAS IMPENDING
AND KNEW NO WAY OF AVERTING IT.

The War Museum turned out to be enormous, and Eva moved through the choppy, black-and-white image sequences at an irritatingly slow pace. It was as though she wanted to draw all the death into herself, and she stopped for a long time at each short film to really take the time to watch it. For his part, Don thought that the dim halls gave a ghastly impression, with all their small arranged scenes and life-size wax soldiers. Contorted figures that were locked in an eternal crawl along the dirt, down in the narrow graves of the trenches.

After a while he began to be annoyed by the attorney's leisurely pace and all the heinous details she proved to be able to tell him about the battles. When it came to the art of weaponry in the First World War, he had really met his match. She knew technical details and advances that he hadn't known anything about. But when he asked, she only said that there are some things you just can't forget.

Her whispered commentary on the flickering pictures of machine-gun fire and torn-up bodies from the projectors made Don feel more and more discouraged. Yet when he looked up at an information map of the different sections of the museum, he saw that they had made it through only the first floor of four.

Then Don noticed a small symbol on the fourth floor that showed a silhouette of a computer. He pointed at it, relieved, and immediately suggested that he should try to get online to see if he could contact Hex.

The weight on Don's shoulders started to lighten as he moved up the stairs toward the upper floors of the museum. The sound of the volleys of shots and screams from the films disappeared gradually, and in the stone corridor at the top of the building everything was silent and peaceful.

An arrow pointed the way toward something called the Documentation Center, and when he arrived at its door he was met by a forbidding notice made of metal:

DOCUMENTATION CENTER RULES

Nothing is lent out.

Fragile documents must never be reproduced.

Always attain the express consent of the center supervisor.

Under the notice was a stern order that the computers were under no circumstances to be used for anything other than searching the museum's unique database of war graves.

Inside the room there was a row of archival cabinets and a few carrels with simple desks and desktop computers. Don soon realized that he was the only visitor. An older woman sat, watching, in a small glass booth, her dyed blue hair tied up in a severe bun.

He could feel the woman following his every movement as he cautiously tiptoed into the dead-silent room. He sat down at the nearest computer, and he could hear her get up with a scraping sound.

The woman came out of her glass booth with a binder pressed tightly to her chest. Above it was a plastic badge identifying her as 1ST OPZICHTER—1st Supervisor—and she scrutinized him with a displeased expression.

After first trying to get Don to return to the exhibit, the supervisor finally pressed a combination of keys that made the monitor in front of him wake up.

"Name?" asked the supervisor in a shrill voice.

"Titelman," said Don.

"Army?"

It was a question he hadn't expected, and he couldn't think of a good answer.

"Which army did the person you're looking for belong to?" she asked impatiently. "Belgian, French, English, or German?"

"The . . . Belgian," said Don.

She brought up a gray form with the title Casualty Database. Selected Casualties from the Belgian Army and typed in the name Titelman. Clicked on SEARCH. No results.

"You're a Jew, I take it," said the supervisor.

Don decided not to answer; instead he said, "There are some other relatives I'd like to search for." The woman waited there, hanging over his shoulder.

"I think I can do it myself, if you'll just give me some time?"

"Well, okay," said the supervisor. "We're closing in twenty minutes."

"That should be enough," said Don.

She took a few steps backward and stood there, not letting the screen out of her sight.

"So, thanks," said Don.

The supervisor tossed her head and walked, with her arms crossed over the binder on her chest, over to her private glass booth.

When he peered up over the wall of his carrel, he could see that she had sat in a position from which she could observe him.

But the supervisor couldn't see what he was writing, and Don began to tap in the codes to the server in Kymlinge, at Hex's place. After a while a smiley face appeared, but the corners of its mouth were turned down—the symbol that indicated his sister was temporarily away.

Don wrote a short message about what had happened since they'd traveled away from Stockholm in the freight car. At the end he added a line saying that it would be great if she were to see what she could dig up about a certain Camille Malraux, born in the late 1800s in a small French city called Charleville-Mézières. Then he cast a glance at his watch and saw that only five minutes had gone by.

Outside, the rain was still falling, streaming in long rivulets along the leaded panes of glass. There was a faint smell of cleaning agents in the room, and the silence began to be oppressive. When Don sneaked a look over at the supervisor, he saw her raise her eyebrows. Still, he thought that he would try to linger until she physically threw him out, in hopes that Hex would come home and log in.

To pass the time, he browsed the Internet.

With one of the Swedish evening papers' lead stories was the picture of a colleague whom Don had always despised. Under it, the headline screamed at him in bold:

**A FRIEND SPEAKS OUT:**
**THE TRUTH ABOUT THE NAZI EXPERT**

After he had clicked on the article, he could hardly handle skimming through all the distorted quotes.

It had only taken a day or so, but apparently he had now been promoted from a researcher of history to a pill addict and an essentially condemned assailant—morbidly obsessed with Nazi myths and symbols. He hit the mouse to remove the text from the flickering screen of the computer.

Then, with misgivings, Don went to the Web sites of the morning papers. It was almost worse there, and now he realized that the attorney had been correct.

The National Police said that they had cast a wide net, including outside Sweden's borders, and they claimed to find themselves in an intensive phase of the investigation which made outward silence absolutely necessary.

*"Oif tsores,"* Don mumbled. Not good.

Then he linked into Hex's server again, but his sister still didn't seem to have come back to her home under the subway. Without daring to look toward the glass booth and the supervisor, Don assumed that he could linger for at least a few more minutes. As he sat there, he thought of the words about Baudelaire in the city archive, and to pass the time, he typed the poet's name and the phrase "l'homme vindicatif" into the Internet search engine.

The very first link proved that the gum-chewing girl had in fact been right. It led to poem 178 on the Web site The Flowers of Evil, fleursdumal.org.

Charles Baudelaire
Une Martyre
Dessin d'un Maître inconnu

Alongside the poem was a short author biography, which Don scanned in the hope of finding some idea that could lead onward. But when that hope had faded, he returned to the poem, which seemed very long.

His French had never been anything to brag about, but as far as he could tell, what he was reading was a description of a necrophile: a man's longing to have violent sex with the corpse of a woman, rich with details, bordering on pornography.

He found the phrases from the postcard in the third and fourth stanza from the end:

L'homme vindicatif que tu n'as pu, vivante,
Malgré tant d'amour, assouvir,
Combla-t-il sur ta chair inerte et complaisante
L'immensité de son désir?

Réponds, cadavre impur! Et par tes tresses roides
Te soulevant d'un bras fiévreux,

Dis-moi, tête effrayante, a-t-il sur tes dents froides
Collé les suprêmes adieux?

After a big of digging on the Net, he managed to find a translation:

That vindictive man whom you were not, despite all
your love, able to satisfy,
has he slaked, with your compliant, lifeless flesh
the tremendous heat of his desire?

Compliant, lifeless flesh that soothes the heat of desire, Don thought. The man in the mine must have been *toit meshuge,* not right in the head.

Answer, corpse! Frightening head, lift
yourself up with feverish hands
in braids that have become stiff: tell me, has he kissed
your cold teeth in farewell?

"Feverish hands and cold teeth," Don mumbled to himself, moving his fingers to click it all away.

But then, although it was probably all just hopeless *narishkeit,* idiocy, and a dead end, he clicked on PRINT after all. A printer a few yards away started spooling and droned to life. The sound caused the supervisor to get to her feet surprisingly quickly inside the glass booth, and before Don had time to react, she had grabbed the long lines of poetry that the printer had spit out.

"Now I think it's time for you to go," said the supervisor.

Then she began to read the page on top.

"You are a sick person."

She stated this as fact, and Don felt that he couldn't do anything but nod.

With a sigh, he heaved his bag up onto his shoulder and closed the

Web browser. He saw that the supervisor was moving toward the carrel where he sat, but just as he felt her lean down over his shoulder to force him to log out, he was seized by one last thought.

"You have to let me check one more name."

He thought she was going to try to stop him, but instead the supervisor took a nervous step back. And now that the Web pages had disappeared, the only thing glowing on the screen was Casualty Database. Don placed a check mark next to Casualties from the Belgian Army. Typed the name into the search field and clicked.

No hits.

The supervisor collected herself again.

"Now I must ask you to . . ."

Don hesitated for a second, but then he checked Casualties from the French Army instead. Tapped in the name again. Had he spelled it correctly? Yes. He clicked on SEARCH.

⁎

Eva was standing in front of a glass case where one could observe wax models in French uniforms lying and writhing under gray-green, billowing smoke.

One of the models was grasping its neck with its fingers as though it couldn't get air. Next to the mouth of another was a glittering red pool, to show how the war gas caused vomiting that was full of blood. Eva seemed not to hear that he had come, although Don was now standing right behind her. That was strange, because he was breathing loudly and panting after having rushed through the dim halls of the museum.

Finally she must have realized that he was there after all, because Eva began to speak straight ahead, without looking at him:

"When they inhaled the gas, their throat and lungs were eaten away immediately. The few Frenchmen who managed to keep breathing died later when their lungs filled with fluid and blood. It's a fight against death, like drowning, even though you know the sky around you is full of air."

"Eva . . ." Don tried, but he couldn't wake her from the grotesque scene.

"The poison gas attack at Gravenstafel was against all rules of warfare," she continued tonelessly. "The French soldiers didn't know what was approaching them as they lay down in the trenches. The only thing they saw over by the German positions was a cloud of green smoke that slowly blocked out all the light. It grew to a height of a hundred feet and then began to roll forward slowly with the wind. When the cloud swept in over their trenches, the oily smoke sank downward. It was heavier than air and it ran over their faces, and after a few minutes there was hardly anyone who could see. The gas ate into their eyes, and when they tried to claw their way up over the embankments, they were cut down by machine-gun fire."

"Eva . . ." Don tried again.

"It was the first time gas was used on the Western front. A few weeks earlier the Germans had tried artillery shells of bromide against the Russians. Later they developed it further, of course, much, much further, with phosgene, lewisite, and sarin."

Don tugged her arm, but the attorney shook herself loose and pointed down at the small informational placard that stood level with their knees.

"At five o'clock in the afternoon," she read, "170 tons of gas was let out of 5,700 metal cylinders. Six thousand Frenchmen dead or dying, and finally a breach in the front. But the Germans were so shocked by the results that they never managed to exploit the gas to its fullest potential. They . . ."

"That's enough, Eva," said Don, grasping her shoulder.

In his other hand, he held the printout he had forced the supervisor to give him before he left her in the room of computers.

"You see," Don continued, "we had it wrong from the start." And he finally made eye contact with Eva.

"The postcard was written to a man."

She stood, silent, then shook her head.

"No, that's not possible. That lipstick, the kiss . . ."

"Yes," said Don. "The dead man in the mine wrote those words to a man he once loved. You can read for yourself."

He held up the copy from the museum's database of war graves.

| | |
|---|---|
| Name: | Malraux |
| First name: | Camille |
| Rank: | Sous-Lieutenant |
| Regiment: | 87 RIT |
| Date of Death: | 22/04/15 |

When Eva had read it, she said hesitantly, "But it could still be someone else. Just looking at the city archives, there were two women named Camille Malraux. And I don't think . . ."

"I'm completely certain, Eva."

"I don't think it fits."

She let her gaze slide back toward the glass case.

"Eva . . ."

"No matter what, it's an incredible coincidence," she said slowly.

"It could probably still be a love letter; maybe they were lovers. Maybe he considered Malraux to be his woman. Maybe they . . ."

"No, not that," Eva interrupted him. "Look at what day your Camille Malraux died."

Don looked at the date on the paper; then he followed her eyes down to the informational placard next to the display case:

THE BATTLE OF GRAVENSTAFEL RIDGE

22ND–23RD APRIL 1915

"So he was gassed to death," Don mumbled.

Eva nodded. Then she took a deep breath and shook herself, as though to wake up.

"But I still don't understand how you can be so sure. As I said . . ."

Don took the postcard out of the inner pocket of his jacket and gave it to her.

"So?" Eva said when she had read the short lines another time.

"Look at that last number," he said.

"Yes, the postcard was written in 1913. What about it?"

"The number 1913 isn't a year," Don said. "It's the number of Camille Malraux's grave."

"A grave?"

"Yes, the number of his grave. It was listed in the museum's database, right by his name. They also had records about the specific location."

"But . . . ?"

"He's lying in a war cemetery called Saint Charles de Potyze, outside of Ypres."

# 28

# Saint Charles de Potyze

Just inside the doors of Cloth Hall, Don was trying to protect himself from the gusts of wind, his thin suit jacket pulled tight around his crooked shoulders. It had already become evening, and by now the rainstorm had blocked out all the light over the large square. It felt as though the ice-cold dampness could sweep right through him at any time.

Out on Grote Markt, the pouring rain whipped back and forth. The grates in the street were bubbling, overflowing with water, and at regular intervals yellowish brown cascades full of cigarette butts and trash washed out over the pavement.

Over on Rijselsestraat, the shopping seemed to have finished up a long time ago. The small boutiques had pulled in their awnings, and all the display windows had gone dark.

The only living thing that was braving the downpour, against its will, was a lone dog. It stood forgotten, tied to a lamppost in the rain. Soaked through, it tugged and pulled at its leash, trying in vain to get free.

"I guess we really ought to go there and see if you're actually right," he heard a voice say behind him.

Eva had drawn her trench coat up around her neck and stuffed her hands deep into its pockets. It was hardly possible to make out the attorney's face in the darkness of the entryway.

"To Malraux's grave, I mean," she continued. "Number 1913, at Saint Charles de Potyze, if you remember."

At first Don didn't bother to answer, because he assumed she meant it as a joke. But it wasn't: "So we can find out if his body is really there."

"Tomorrow morning, in that case," Don managed to shiver out.

He couldn't see the attorney's eyes. He continued: "And what's the point, by the way?"

"What is the point of finding that Camille Malraux at all?"

Don was so cold he was shaking. It was as though the violent rain had blown all the enthusiasm out of him.

"Then we'll at least have tried to get as far as we can with the postcard, right?" she said.

"If it's the right Malraux lying there, then he'll probably still be lying in his grave when the weather is better and . . ."

But then Don saw that Eva had already raised her arm and was starting to wave at the line of taxis that were waiting out on Grote Markt.

They got no reaction at all from the first illuminated car. Its driver had become absorbed in a newspaper that he had hung up over the steering wheel. The next taxi was unlit and deserted, while the third in line emitted a sluggish blink from its broken headlights. And when the couple in the doorway didn't immediately start to move out into the torrent, the short light signal was followed by an angry honk.

Eva grabbed Don's arm and dragged him across the square in the rain. And although he squelched his way through the puddles as fast as he possibly could, his shirt had already become wet through under his jacket by the time he could finally throw himself into the backseat of the ivory-colored taxi.

A liver-spotted face looked at him with bloodshot eyes in the rear-view mirror. The hand that was resting on the stick shift was covered in blurry blue tattoos, and when Eva had closed the door on her side, the scent of liquor in the taxi increased quickly.

*"La nécropole Saint Charles de Potyze,"* Don mumbled dejectedly. After he had repeated the address in English a few times, the driver seemed to understand at last. They rolled away along Meensestraat, and Don glimpsed some senior citizens in raincoats who were pointing up at the forgotten soldiers' names on the arch of the Menin Gate.

When they had left Ypres behind and got out to the misty, gray countryside, the driver began to point out all the graveyards that the car passed slowly.

"This particular road, Zonnebeekseweg," he informed them, slurring in the front seat, "the English soldiers called Oxford Street when they marched out to their death in the trenches of World War One." Now all that was left was their white crosses, in long, hopeless lines.

The car swerved in its lane as the eyes peered back toward Don: "They say that the corpses lying out there can still smell the rain. The mud and mire trickle down through the collapsed lids of their coffins, and then the dead are seized with hope that they might still be alive."

Don looked over at Eva in the dark car, but her eyes were directed out at the mists of the cemeteries.

"The end comes far too quickly in war," the driver continued in his slightly slurred voice. "The soul doesn't have time to follow; the changes are too quick. One second, the screech of all the scrap metal, when every fiber of muscle is busy carrying on the rush forward. And the next second: everything is over. A soul can't handle change like that. It continues to crawl across the mud forever, even though it no longer has a body to crawl with. It refuses to see that its time is up, and that life is over forever."

The eyes in the rearview mirror again.

"You can see them crawling between the gravestones too, can't you?"

Don chose not to answer. The rain kept falling, and the driver slowed down alongside a low brick wall.

On the other side of the wall, white crosses ran in symmetrical rows toward a horizon of stunted trees. As they passed, the pattern between the crosses seemed to be vertical one second and diagonal the next, forming a long transverse incision.

The taxi was soon standing at the entrance of the cemetery: two white columns and a black wrought-iron fence. Iron swords had been riveted onto the columns, and their long, narrow blades were covered with laurel leaves.

Inside the wall they could see a melancholy monument to the memory of Golgotha. On a granite pedestal stood two women in pleated bronze mantles with their faces hidden by hoods. Above them in the rain rose the cross on which the Christ figure was nailed up. Under the sharp crown of thorns, his eyes were open.

"No rest for the dead in Flanders," said the driver, turning toward Eva and Don.

Don felt how his shirt had glued itself onto the small of his back like an ice-cold hand.

"And it's going to rain like this all night," the driver continued. "At least, that's what they said on the radio."

"Maybe you can loan us an umbrella, then," said Eva.

Then she grabbed hold of the shoulder bag, which was lying in the backseat, and tossed it over to Don so that he could pay. He took out a few bills and said to the driver:

"This isn't going to take very long. We're just going to check something, and we'll be back soon."

"I can't just stay here and . . ."

Don handed him 30 euros.

"But there are runs in . . ."

The driver received another few bills, and he bared a sparse row of teeth in his liver-spotted face. Then there was a powerful stench of liquor: "You can look back there and see if you can find something for the rain. I have no defense against the other thing."

Eva gave Don an encouraging look. He shivered once more and then opened the car door.

When he pulled open the trunk of the car and looked in, there really was an umbrella with a broken-off handle. When open, it displayed the text COLRUYT SUPERMARKT—*LAAGSTE PRIJZEN*, but at least it was quite large.

They walked as close as they could under the umbrella, and the gates creaked open.

A paved walkway cut a line between the fields of crosses that rose above the waterlogged grass. There must be space for several thousand graves here, Don thought, and he approached the nearest one.

A fine-meshed net of mold had covered the surface of the white concrete cross, but the plastic nameplate was still clean. Under the French name were the words that Don would soon come to recognize in his search along the numbered gravestones: *Mort pour la France.*

After they had wandered among the graves, stooping, looking at random and without success for number 1913, they finally managed to find a map of the cemetery. It rose up above a long stone bench like an altarpiece.

Don found a small plastic lighter in his shoulder bag, lit it, and held it up to the sign.

NÉCROPOLE NATIONALE FRANÇAISE
SAINT CHARLES DE POTYZE

Under the black text, the cemetery had been divided into four bright red rectangles, covered in miniature numbers.

Don started from the bottom and used the flame to search along the first hundred or so graves, and then he kept going up across the four fields. Finally, the lighter became so hot that he couldn't hold it, and he was forced to let its flame go out.

"Malraux's grave isn't here," he said to Eva in the dark.

"You must have simply missed it. Try again."

Don sighed. Then he started to point at the four fields, whose red edges were now only faintly visible:

"On this side are all the grave numbers up to 1800. And over here . . ."

He moved his finger:

"The next series of numbers begins here, from number 2101 to the last grave, 3567. No grave with the number 1913. There must be some problem with the numbers from Cloth Hall."

Eva took the lighter out of his hand. It had had time to cool, and she flicked it on again and began to systematically move it once more across the laminated map. Just under the black band that marked the far boundary of the cemetery, she found a bluish rectangle:

*"Le mausolée de Gravenstafel,"* she read, and let the light pass over the line of text.

Then the flame went out, and they stood silently in the falling rain. Don threw one last glance over toward the taxi as Eva grabbed his hand. Then he followed her along the paved path, farther into the darkness.

They passed the French tricolor, which was suspended just above the ground in the middle of the cemetery. A pond of dirty water had formed on its sagging surface.

Eva seemed to be in a hurry now, and she didn't bother trying to avoid all the puddles on the path.

At the edge of the cemetery stood a simple obelisk that marked a mass grave. Behind it rose a row of willows, like a wall, their branches trailing on the ground.

Just next to the trees, a small gravel path veered off to the left. It had presumably once been carefully raked, but now it looked like just a narrow, muddy trail.

As they followed the trail along the far side of the cemetery, Don noticed that the graves no longer bore French names. Here lay the bodies of Moroccans, Algerians, and Tunisians. Their stones ended in an onion-shaped point and had winding Arabic letters. But when it came to the years in which the Muslims died, they were no different from the Frenchmen's gravestones.

The muddy trail led them to a bunch of trees, and among the trunks they could see a temple-shaped building.

Perhaps the facade had once resembled Roman marble, but now the pillars were cracked. Rainwater poured down from the angled roof, and it formed a small lake in front of the wide staircase.

Eva dragged Don along with her in among the willows so that they could avoid wading the last little bit up to the mausoleum. There was no door, only a gateway with an inscription:

*Les crimes de guerre—La grâce divine*

"*Après vous,*" said Eva.

Don took a few hesitant steps past the pillars, into the gaping opening of the gateway. It was so dark inside that he couldn't even make out where the concrete room ended. The only thing he heard was his own breathing, which came creeping back toward him in a trailing echo. Then the sound of Eva's steps, and their breathing blended together.

"There must be some light in here, anyway," Don heard himself whisper.

He fumbled his hand along the wall toward something that was flickering red, and there was a crackle from up by the ceiling. Then a pale blue light woke from frosted glass globes.

"So, what have we here?" Don asked, just to have something to say.

The floor of the mausoleum was covered in tiles with ingrained flecks, and along the wall stretched a checked pattern of gravestones in the form of rectangular plaques. The names and dates of the dead were embedded in the concrete under a greenish web of mold.

It smelled like a public bathroom, and a hole in the middle of the floor was barely covered by a few rough-hewn planks. They had been nailed together into a hatch, and it looked like a temporary arrangement.

When Don had taken a few steps closer, he realized that the musty stench was coming from down in the covered hole. They heard a faint gurgling, as though from a water seal that was no longer holding tight.

He turned away from the gloomy wooden hatch and started to search through the numbers on the wall. Found the first plaque number in the left-hand corner of the room:

-1801-

MONTARD JEAN-LOUIS

MORT POUR LA FRANCE LE 22-4-1915

TUÉ À L'ENNEMI

Then he followed the checked pattern of the wall until he arrived at plaque number 1850. The series of numbers continued on the other wall, only to stop thirteen numbers too soon, with a plaque marked 1900.

Don looked at the leaky hatch in the middle of the tile floor.

"There must be another level," he whispered.

In the sound of the rain that roared against the roof of the mausoleum, they each took a side of the sloppily nailed-together planks. It took a great deal of effort for them to heave up the hatch, and when it had finally been lifted into a vertical position, Don was left to bear all its weight alone. Eva had let go and covered her mouth with one hand to keep out all the putrid air that was now streaming toward them. In the rectangular opening that had been hidden under the planks, a staircase descended into someplace pitch-black, where the lights were apparently completely dead.

Don pushed the vertical hatch away, and it landed on the floor with a bang.

He looked hopefully over at Eva, but she just shook her head. Then she signaled to him that he was the one who ought to go down.

He took a deep breath through his mouth and lit the lighter again. He turned the little plastic lever to max and climbed down with his Dr. Martens boot on the first step.

The staircase ran down along the bare wall on the right side of the lower room, and Don looked up at Eva, who still had her hand over her mouth. He listened to the pounding rain. Then he decided they'd come way too far to turn back now, and he slowly continued downward.

When his eyes had started to adjust to the light, Don realized where the abominable smell was coming from. A sewer pipe must have sprung a leak somewhere down here, because floating above the final step of the staircase was a brownish sludge that covered the floor of the lower level.

The flood had reached so high that its surface lapped above the lowest row of plaques. He hoped that the cement seams at the openings of the compartments still fit tightly.

"You don't need to come down!" Don called up to Eva.

There was only enough light for one, after all, and hardly even that.

Taking shallow breaths, he made his way down to the last dry step. He let the lighter go out so it could cool off again. The muffled sound of the rainstorm was far above him.

Then he struck the lighter again and leaned out from the wall to the left, so that he could examine the closest row of plaques.

"Nineteen oh seven . . . 1908, 1909."

The lighter burned Don's fingers, and he swore and shook his hand in front of him.

In the dark he tried to form an image of how the niches might be placed. The numbers went from left to right, and 1909 was the last one he had managed to reach. He needed to stretch another four numbers away to reach plaque 1913.

It would be very close to the limits of what he could do without having to wade out into the sludgy water.

He grasped the edge of the opening, which he could just reach above his head, with his hand, then leaned forward, hanging by one arm, as far as his stiff back would allow. He extended his other hand toward the wall of plaques and struck the lighter again:

-1912-

BELLEMÈRE GEORGES

MORT POUR LA FRANCE LE 23-4-1915

BLESSURES DE GUERRE

Don let the lighter go out and heaved himself back. Just a little rest. He closed his eyes and listened in the dark. Then he opened his eyes, one last try, just a little bit more.

He stretched out as far as he could with his arm. A harsh sound as the flame crackled to life. It flickered before him:

-1913-

CAMILLE MALRAUX

MORT POUR LA FRANCE LE 22-4-1915

TUÉ À L'ENNEMI

# 29

# The Glass Capsules

Elena knew very well that she wasn't the only person the foundation had fostered. After finding her, Vater had built up a network of para-psychological research centers all over northern Europe. The children who had been identified there as psychic-gifted had also been lured to Wewelsburg with promises of stipends and scholarships, but her powers had remained of superior quality, impossible to match.

The other children had had to work in small groups of twelve—for some reason, the most favorable combination. The foundation's men had then tried every method to develop their receptive abilities. Still the children's minds had proved to be hopelessly dull, and throughout the years she had remained Vater's first and most prized discovery.

He had given her his loving attention as one chosen and adopted. Even before Elena had been able to understand what they were, Vater had shown her the oldest sketches from deep within the source.

The visions had sneaked into the edges of the purely technical descriptions of the cavity that had been made by the scientists early on. Isolated, hasty drawings in the margins that seemed to have been written by a different hand.

But only a few of the original researchers had had any psychic aptitude for taking in the astral fields that were hidden in the underworld. And those whose notes had been affected had dismissed it as a phenomenon that lacked any rational weight.

Everything had changed when they had discovered that one of the involuntary sketches had the form of a self-recursive molecule that no one had ever seen before. It could have been a coincidence, but soon the incident had been repeated, in sketches of building blocks for materials of more and more bizarre quality.

The visions had seemed to appear without any internal order, and interpreting them soon became the foundation's most important project. The notes that remained after contact with the source ceased had been enough to fill many decades with meticulous scientific work.

Only afterward, when the meaning of each vision had been exhausted, had the men of the foundation tried to conjure up new discoveries. There had still been samples of the sparkling powder left, preserved in lead-enclosed capsules of glass.

This peculiar dust carried with it a trace of the spiritual energy that ruled in the underworld. A lingering shimmer, only perceptible to someone who had a sufficiently sensitive mind and soul.

This had essentially been Elena's gift, and she had helped them come further than anyone had dared to hope. Oblivious to her own history, she had, like an obedient child, been rewarded with unrestricted affection from her stepfather for all the detailed pictures she had been able to sketch during the first years.

Then, when her body had just begun to change into that of a woman, the powder in the containers hadn't spoken to her anymore. It had just lain there under the glass like gray flakes of ash, lifeless and mute.

When Vater pointed out that she was failing more and more often these days, Elena had defended herself by saying that she couldn't help it if the material in the glass capsules had exhausted its power. But when the other children produced new discoveries, she had been exposed and had to admit that her mind had become insensible and blunt.

It had been described as a remarkable favor that Vater had kept her with him anyway. For him, she had already served her purpose, and searching for a new role had been her way of trying to remain close to him, her only family, and to justify her existence. The bonds of love and fear that connected her to Vater had grown so strong that she couldn't envision another path.

Elena had learned to use her body as a weapon from the men in Sicherheit. She had proved to have remarkable talent for that too. They had taught her to control machines whose strength she could never have dreamed of. They had drilled her in close combat and laughed at her until she had learned to control the revealing play of her facial movements.

So in an unexpected manifestation of sentimentality, her stepfather had given her the task of bringing Erik Hall's discoveries home. Vater could have sent someone else, which in hindsight would probably have been a much better idea.

She had succeeded—and failed. That was the message that had been repeated these past few days. Now it would be her job to fix everything that had gone so inconceivably wrong.

And with the ankh in the vault of the banking house, the perceptions of whispers she thought she had heard went quiet again. They had disappeared along with her memory of another life. What remained was the lingering sense of entrapment, a feeling of having been trapped.

# 30

## *Les Suprêmes Adieux*

When Don had managed to get back up the stairs from the lower level of the mausoleum, he was forced to lean forward, support himself against his knees, and take deep breaths to get the sickly stench of sewage out of his lungs. And as he stood there panting in the bluish white light on the dirty tile floor, his thoughts wandered to what he had actually hoped to find.

A carved image of Strindberg's ankh and star? A clue? What had he hoped for? A sketch of the Bunsen burner's spheres, stuck between the plaque on the niche and the cement wall?

*"S'iz nor vi redn tsu der vant,"* Don groaned to himself and shoved the hatch back to reduce the nauseating smell. "It's like trying to talk to a wall."

Then he shuffled over to the wall of the mausoleum, where he sank down with his arms around his thin legs. And there he sat until a shoulder bag suddenly was dangled in front of his face.

"You might need this," said Eva.

Don took the bag from her hand and searched greedily inside it until he found a Bulgarian antianxiety medication, which he didn't even remember having taken with him from his office in Lund.

When the colorful pills landed on his tongue, his mouth was filled with the bitter taste of chloral hydrate. Then he swallowed and took a quick breath from the trichloroethylene inhaler. All to hasten the chemical calm.

His inhalations must have caused his eyes to roll back for a few seconds, because Eva seemed nervous when she shook his arm.

"So what's down there?" she asked when he had once again managed to focus his eyes on her.

"Nothing," said Don.

"Isn't Malraux buried here?"

Don cracked his neck and looked up at the glass globes on the ceiling.

"I thought it couldn't be a man," Eva mumbled. "So we'll just have to . . ."

"Yes, Camille Malraux is down there," Don interrupted. "*Gants geshtorben,* completely dead, as long as his niche isn't empty."

Eva crouched down in front of him. After a minute of silence she said, "And there was nothing else?"

"Go down and see for yourself, if you're so interested."

"The dates were right? The spelling of his name?"

"It just said, *'Tué à l'ennemi.'* Killed by the enemy."

He looked at her and smiled faintly.

"A dead end, you could say."

Eva sat still for a bit without saying anything. Then she got up and went over to the dark opening toward the cemetery, where the rain just kept on pouring down. She rested one hand against a mold-speckled pillar, and with the other she smoothed a strand of her upswept hair. Don closed his eyes and listened to the patter of the rain.

"Camille Malraux," he heard Eva say. "Camille Malraux, *tué à l'ennemi.* Killed by the enemy. A postcard sent to a beloved man who died in the war."

He heard the scrape of her boots, and when he looked up, the attorney had turned toward him.

"What does it mean?"

A drab green trench coat, her thin arms crossed. Her handbag hanging over her shoulder, her sullen face.

"That we have a taxi waiting," said Don.

He placed the strap of his bag over his shoulder and began to gather the strength to stand up. Eva remained standing like a shadow in front of the falling rain.

"Eberlein was so eager to know what you had found at Erik Hall's house."

Don sighed and leaned back against the wall again.

"He probably thought it was about something else. Maybe the diver knew more than what he told me. It was only by chance that I happened to find that postcard; it doesn't really have to mean anything, does it? Erik Hall could actually have written it all himself. Maybe he had a burning interest in World War One."

"Still, there is a Camille Malraux," said Eva, "who is lying in niche number 1913 in the Saint Charles de Potyze cemetery outside of Ypres. And the date is correct; he died on April twenty-second in a gas attack at Gravenstafel."

She left the opening of the mausoleum, walked back to him, and extended her hand.

"Let me look at it again."

Don took the postcard from the inner pocket of his jacket. It had almost been destroyed by the rain; the edges of the paper had softened and begun to disintegrate. He turned it over and saw that at least the ink hadn't begun to run. Then he gave it to her, and she mumbled her way through the lines one more time:

*la bouche de mon amour Camille Malraux*
*le 22 avril*

*l'homme vindicatif*
*l'immensité de son désir*
*les suprêmes adieux*
*1913*

The tip of her nose had taken on a reddish tone from the cold. Thin lips, lines in her forehead, the transparent eyes moving from left to right.

Eva turned the card over and looked once more at the picture of the church.

"Could it be some sort of wordplay?" she said. "A code?"

"It could be a nonsensical old postcard that the man in the mine had planned to save until he was old, until he happened to kill himself with the help of an awl instead," Don said. She didn't smile.

*"La bouche de mon amour Camille Malraux,"* Eva said. "This is my beloved Camille Malraux's mouth."

She fixed her eyes on Don, and it looked as though she was expecting a little help. Finally he took a deep breath and made an effort: "Maybe they're sitting together at a café on Grote Markt. World War One is raging, but there is still hope. The man in the mine has an old postcard of the cathedral as it looked before the battles began. It means something special to them. Maybe they promise each other something. The man asks Camille Malraux to press his painted lips to the postcard, and then he puts it in his pocket, to save it. Much later he writes these phrases as a reminder of their love. Something like that?"

"Yes. Who knows?" said Eva.

But at least she seemed satisfied that he had made an effort, because she sat down on the tile floor at his side.

"And what then?" she said.

"The date he chooses is the day Camille Malraux dies, April 22, 1915—the gas attack at Gravenstafel. He adds 1913, the number Malraux lies buried behind. And then he writes the phrase *les suprêmes adieux,* because now he has said good-bye for the last time to someone he loved."

"But we don't really know that they loved each other in a purely physical way," Eva said. "They could have been just good friends, right?"

Don looked at her with surprise.

"But what does that matter?"

"It doesn't, I just wanted . . . keep going."

"In any case, there are only two lines left. *L'homme vindicatif* and *l'immensité de son désir.* The vindictive man and his tremendous desire."

"Yes?"

"That part about tremendous desire does seem to indicate that there was some sort of attraction," Don said. "And vindictive . . . maybe vindictive toward the Germans. Although I think it's really just *meshuges,* meaningless. A few lines of verse that preserve the memory of a poem they both liked."

"Baudelaire?"

Don nodded.

"Yes, it's from Baudelaire, just as she said, that girl in the city archive. I looked up the poem in the war museum before I found the note about Malraux's grave."

"And?"

"I don't know. All three phrases were in the same poem in *Les fleurs du mal, The Flowers of Evil.* Baudelaire was prosecuted and sentenced because of it, and parts of the collection were banned in France until the fifties, because it was considered to be so incredibly perverted."

"Times change," said Eva.

Don closed his eyes and tried to find his way back, in the catalogue of his mind, to the image on the screen in the war museum.

"I didn't have very much time, but of course I thought that there had to be something that could link them together; Baudelaire and the man in the mine."

"Yes?"

"But what I had time to pick up was just that they shared a morbid fascination with hell. The man wrote Niflheim on the wall of the mine, of course, and Náströndu, 'the shore of the dead.' Baudelaire praises the devil in the foreword of the collection."

He saw Baudelaire's lines before him again; at the very top it said *Au lecteur.* Then he made an attempt in his poor French:

C'est le Diable qui tient les fils qui nous remuent!
Aux objets répugnants nous trouvons des appas;
Chaque jour vers l'Enfer nous descendons d'un pas,
Sans horreur, à travers des ténèbres qui puent.

"It's the devil who . . ." he began.

"It's the devil who controls our movements," Eva whispered. "In all that is repulsive we find delight. *Chaque jour* . . . Each day we sink deeper into hell. And we move through the shadows and the stench without fear."

He nodded.

"About like that."

There was flickering up by the ceiling, and then the light in one of the glass globes went out.

"Which poem did the lines on the postcard come from?" said Eva.

"It was taken from a long exposition about necrophilia, a detailed description of a man's longing to have sex with the corpse of a woman."

"What was it called?"

"'The Martyr.' *Une Martyre, dessin d'un Maître inconnu,* drawing of an unknown master, just as the girl said. *Un cadaver sans tête épanche, comme un fleuve,* a headless corpse whose blood runs down onto fabric that drinks with the thirst of a meadow, and so on and so on."

He took a breath. "Shall I take the postcard?"

"Not yet."

A gust of wind tore at the willows outside the mausoleum. Another of the lights seemed to have become tired; it ticked with a snapping sound.

"The martyr," Eva mumbled to herself. "Maybe he means Malraux."

"A martyr for his country," Don said, "sure. Or maybe he's referring to himself, that he, the man in the mine, was martyred, and endured sorrow and loss for his French second lieutenant. That that was what made him take his own life."

Eva had sunk down with her head in her hands. Don was going to ask if something was wrong, but maybe she had just been sitting and thinking, because she said, "How did the poem go, word for word?"

"Do you want it in Swedish?"

She shrugged.

Don closed his eyes and recited from memory:

That vindictive man whom you were not, despite all
your love, able to satisfy,
has he slaked, with your compliant, lifeless flesh
the tremendous heat of his desire?
Answer, corpse! Frightening head, lift
yourself up with feverish hands
in braids that have become stiff: tell me, has he kissed
your cold teeth in farewell?

When he opened his eyes, he saw that the attorney was looking at him, puzzled.

"Did you say: 'in braids that have become stiff: tell me, has he kissed your cold teeth in farewell?'"

"That's how it was translated."

"Sounds strange."

"Maybe you have to be strange to translate Baudelaire the right way," said Don.

She sat thoughtfully, holding the postcard up to the light. Whispered through the words again.

"*Les suprêmes adieux.* Kissed your cold teeth in farewell. So . . . how did the end go in the original text?"

"The original text?"

"How does the poem sound in French?" asked Eva.

"Do you really want to hear it?"

"If you stop trying to do French *r*'s."

Don closed his eyes and found his way back to the supervisor and the humming computers of the research room. Then he began to read from the image in his photographic memory:

Dis-moi, tête effrayante, a-t-il sur tes dents froides
Collé les suprêmes adieux?

It was quiet. Then: *"Collé les suprêmes adieux?"*

Don nodded.

"Nothing about a kiss? *Une bise, un bisou, une baiser*?" He shook his head.

"*Coller*—it's really more like 'glue,'" said Eva. "Those last lines literally mean 'glued his final good-bye to your cold teeth,' or maybe, 'to your cold mouth.' What could the man in the mine have wanted to glue to his beloved's mouth?"

Don looked up at her, questioningly, as she stood up.

"Could it be that . . ."

"You don't think . . ."

". . . that the lip print on the postcard was made *after* Malraux's death, when he had already been interred? Maybe the man in the mine opened the niche and then sealed it again? In that case, what else could he have wanted to hide with his lover down there?"

Don clawed at his hair.

"I think you should go out to the taxi and ask if he has any tools," said Eva.

⁎

By the time Don had finally managed to make his way back out to the gates, his boots were covered in mud.

The taxi was dark, and he thought, a bit relieved, that the driver had probably fallen asleep. But then the headlights came on and the sudden wave of light blinded Don. He raised his hand to his eyes and had to grope his way forward in order to knock on the driver's window.

The window was rolled down: "And your friend?"

"She's still there," said Don. Spoke loudly to be heard above the rain.

"You know what time it is? I've been sitting here waiting for almost an hour."

"Yes, we . . ."

"Have you seen the dead?"

"They are where they are."

The driver moved his lips, but his words were drowned out by the downpour. Don continued as loudly as he could:

"It's just that . . . we need to borrow some tools."

For an instant he wondered whether the man had heard the question, but then a sparse row of teeth appeared again from inside the car.

"You can rent some," said the driver, looking at him with eyes heavy from liquor. "For three hundred euros you can take what you want from the trunk."

Don wondered whether he could make up some excuse to tell Eva, but then he took out Hex's roll of bills and started counting them under the umbrella.

"Two hundred fifty," he said.

"Three hundred if you're going to dig around in the cemetery. And another three hundred if you want me to wait."

A bluish red tongue moved quickly over his row of teeth.

Don walked a short distance away, swore to himself, and counted once more through what he had.

"Three hundred for everything," he said when he came back, looking down at the taxi window again.

The driver took the crumpled bills from his hand and then bent forward and opened the trunk from inside the car.

When Don turned around to go have a look, he heard one last croaking yell. He looked back and saw a hand stretching out through the window with a small business card. Apparently he was a good customer. When he had taken it, the driver immediately rolled up the window, presumably to retain the dry warmth of the car's interior.

Under the spare tire in the trunk there was a wrapped-up bundle of big chisels, which Don tucked into his waistband. After some rummaging, he also managed to find a black rubber flashlight whose bulb was nearly burned out.

It went out several times on the way back through the cemetery, and when it did work it emitted an orange-red glow that only reached a few yards in front of him.

When he approached the entry to the mausoleum, he could see that Eva had managed to move the wooden hatch away from the lower level on her own. The stairs were visible again, and the smell from down there had already started to come back.

"*A groyse shand,* a great shame," Don mumbled as he walked up to her and held up the tools.

Then he chose a long chisel with a wooden shaft and aimed the flashlight at the top step.

"The dead should not be disturbed," he said.

"I can go myself," said Eva.

He could feel his chest tightening and took one more turn through his shoulder bag to dig out two Tramadol. Then he saw Eva disappear down the stairs, and he realized that he didn't have a choice.

The flashlight was truly bad. After a few seconds it went out, and he had to shake it to get the light to come back. He could see Eva squinting up at him in the orange-red beam of light. She was standing on the last step above the flood.

"So where is Malraux's plaque?" she asked.

Don moved the light along the wall, a few yards across the brown water.

*"Tué à l'ennemi,"* Eva whispered.

He extended the long chisel to her.

"Here you go."

But it was only a meaningless gesture, because he knew very well that he was the one who would have to go down into the dirty sewer water. Don felt with the tip of his shoe for a first careful step under the surface and then the icy cold water ran in under the laces in his boot.

He pushed his foot down completely under the surface, and with a few more squelching noises his leg had sunk down to the knee.

"It's probably not particularly deep," Eva informed him from behind.

Don heard himself grunt out some sort of answer, and then he quickly moved all the way down the stairs.

The sludge covered him up to his waist, and he struggled with all his might not to breathe through his nose. At the same time, he was forced to hyperventilate to keep his body going.

He waded back along the long side of the staircase, and when he got up to Eva, he handed the black flashlight up to her.

"Maybe you can help me out and aim the light."

An orange-red beam swept over the ceiling, down along the wall, and landed on number 1913 and the name Camille Malraux.

Don waded over to the plaque through the thick sludge and held the chisel up in both hands so that he wouldn't drop it, now that the cold was making his arms shake. It felt as though something under the water was clinging to his legs, hanging there around his ankle like a slimy rope that was trying to hold him back.

"You never cease to amaze me, Don Titelman."

Don didn't know if he had just thought the words himself or whether he had really heard Eva's voice, but now he was finally close enough to support himself against the plaques on the wall. Looked back toward the attorney, where she was crouching on the dry portion of the staircase.

After he had searched around Malraux's plaque with his fingers, Don found a small opening that seemed promising. He drove the large chisel into it as far as he could, which was an inch or two. Still, he leaned backward with all his weight and tried to break it as quickly and as hard as he could.

A chip crunched loose from the concrete, and the splash was so big that he got water in his face.

*"A bisel naches!"* Don swore.

But then he was forced to bend over, because he had happened to smell a powerful dose of the stench. In the wave of nausea, he heard a voice that sounded like Eva's. He thought that it sounded as though she had said she was going to go get something. Don just had time to turn around and see her disappear up the stairs. His boots filled with the ice-cold sludge, his socks, inside his pants, all the way to his bare skin.

*"Reboineh shel oilem . . ."*

When Eva finally came back, she showed Don her hand. It was holding a rough gray stone, which she stretched out as far as she could. He waded back to her and took it.

"Are you sure you don't want to come down here?"

The attorney chuckled, but then she held her hand to her mouth to avoid breathing in more than was necessary.

With legs like immobile blocks of ice, Don tried to stagger back to Malraux's plaque again. There wasn't much time left before he wouldn't be able to get anything else done.

He drove the long chisel into the crack and pounded its shaft with the stone. The handle broke on the second attempt, and after a while striking the stone against metal made his hand start to go numb.

Soon he couldn't manage anymore, and he hoped that the chisel was far enough in to be able to withstand a hard blow from the side. He gathered momentum with his whole body and landed the blow so perfectly against the protruding shaft that he continued forward when the plaque suddenly turned and gave way.

Then Don gathered himself again and grasped the edge of the stone with his fingers and began to shift it completely out of its position.

When it finally came loose, the headstone was so heavy that he immediately lost his grip. With a dull clatter, it fell to rest under the surface of the water, just in front of his feet.

Don looked up again and saw that Eva had now directed the flashlight into the long, narrow sarcophagus. The light hit a pale yellow clump, which was covered in grayish black wisps. It took a second before he realized that what he was looking at was the crown of a skull.

"What now?" he asked Eva.

"Can't you try to lift him out?"

*"Gotenyu . . ."*

"Just grab hold of his shoulders and pull."

Don clenched his teeth and looked into the burial compartment. Malraux lay on his back, with his feet turned inward.

He moved his hands carefully along the concrete walls of the sarcophagus to avoid touching the corpse's cheekbones and the remains of what had once been ears. He fumbled around, without being able to see what he was doing, and found something bony which he hoped was the Frenchman's shoulder.

"Careful now," Eva whispered.

Pulling only on one shoulder yielded no results. The corpse's back seemed to have become stuck on the concrete. But when Don also got hold of the other shoulder and yanked, the skeleton came loose from the last bits of skin with a sound like a zipper being pulled down. It came out of the sarcophagus so rapidly that it was only by pure reflex that Don managed to catch the back of the skull in his right hand to stop the skeleton from sliding out.

In the light from the flashlight, the Frenchman's face seemed strangely well preserved. Parts of his parchment-thin cheeks remained, and from his cheekbones ran yellowed sinews that still kept his jaw in place.

"Doesn't he have any injuries?" Eva whispered.

"Probably died from the gas," Don whispered.

He gestured to her to keep shining the light over the face, and with his free left hand he cautiously pried open Camille Malraux's mouth.

And there, in a mouth where all the flesh had long ago rotted away, lay something white that gleamed in the beam of light.

Don stuck in his fingers and worked out the object. It seemed to be made of metal, and it scraped against the dead man's teeth. Then he held it up to Eva.

It was the color of ivory under the yellowed film of grime: the five-pointed star from Eberlein's photographs, what the German had called *seba.* The other part of Nils Strindberg's navigational instrument.

"Give it to me," Eva whispered.

But Don kept holding the star in his hand, and he asked her to aim the flashlight at Malraux's open sarcophagus again. There was something else in there . . . fumbled along the corpse's rib cage and felt himself reach something that was still held by bony fingers.

He shook it from the dead man's grip and pulled his hand out to see what he was holding. A folded piece of paper. Don held it up so Eva could see it too.

"Come here now!" she said, louder. "You might drop it all at any time."

Don looked down at the white star and the paper in his left hand. He felt the weight of the skull in his right hand. He might be able to reach.

"Here!" he hissed to Eva.

Don realized far too late that he had moved too far toward the stairs, and now he could feel the slippery top of the skull start to slide from his grip.

Without support, Malraux's neck slowly bent backward until the back of his head hit the concrete wall under the opening of the burial compartment with a hollow sound. The Frenchman was looking over at Eva with an upside-down face and empty eye sockets. But she was so occupied with the piece of paper that she didn't notice.

"It's some sort of letter," she said. "It's . . ."

Her sentence was interrupted by something that sounded like a chain snapping apart. Don looked over at the opening of the niche and saw that the vertebrae could no longer support the weight of the skull. They snapped one after another, like a string of beads, and when he tried to move, his legs no longer obeyed him.

For an instant the skull remained hanging from one last yellowish sinew, but then Camille Malraux's detached head fell down into the brown sludge with a dismal plop.

The air bubbles from inside the skull caused the surface of the water to roil for a few short seconds.

# 31

# The Telephone

The sound of the lunch rush at Langemark's outdoor seating area trickled in through the gap in the window up on the fourth floor. Inside the hotel room, it stank of the grave, and Don's suit pants and socks lay in a muddy pile on the floor. His boots, which he had made a desperate attempt to rinse off, were in the bathroom, drying in the bathtub.

Last night's rainstorm was long since over, and soft sunlight came in through the thin linen curtains. But Eva and Don hadn't awakened yet. They lay motionless, side by side, under a terrycloth blanket.

Then the blanket began to move as Eva twisted to the side and tried to sit up with stiff joints. When the beam of light from the window shone on her face, she blinked and then shook her head to try to remember where she was.

She remained sitting on the edge of the bed for a while to gather her strength and tried to breathe quietly so that Titelman wouldn't wake up. Finally Eva managed to get her aged body to stand, and she walked with bare feet toward the bathroom.

It all came back to her in there: the feeling of the ivory-colored star she got to hold in her hand down in the crypt, along with the small piece of paper that Don had managed to work out of the Frenchman's grip.

Titelman had been seriously hypothermic after the long time he'd been in the water, and he'd had fits of shivering during the taxi ride back from Saint Charles de Potyze. She had pulled him close to her and held him like a child to try to transfer some human warmth. It felt as though it was the least she could do after everything he'd had to endure.

When Eva had put on her clothes, she walked up to the chair on which Don had hung his jacket. She took the paper from the inner pocket of the jacket, unfolded it carefully, and read the words once more:

My beloved Camille,

The promise I made to you has been fulfilled. The gateway to the underworld is closed.

I wish I could have done more.

From here I travel into my own Niflheim, where the other thing shall be hidden forever.

Your Olaf

Her hand was trembling slightly as she slipped the piece of paper back into Titelman's jacket pocket.

She pulled on her Italian boots, swept her trench coat over her shoulders, and cast one last glance back toward the thin figure in the double bed. He still hadn't wakened from his dreams.

Out in the cramped entryway, she pushed down the handle and closed the door of the hotel room behind her as silently as she possibly could. The brass railing on the stairs was poorly attached, and she balanced with one hand against the wall down the steep steps toward the lobby of the hotel.

The red flags of the museum were waving outside Cloth Hall.

But Eva wanted to get away from the open area and turned onto Boomgaardstraat. As she walked between the storefronts and the cars, her eyes searched the side area for a quiet corner. On a small street she caught sight of a protruding sign that said CHERRY-BLOSSOM TEAROOM in ornate letters.

The window of the café was covered by white lace curtains. A bell over the door tinkled, and a young woman behind the curved counter turned around to face her. Eva ordered a cup of hot chocolate with cream and a waffle. Then she sat down at a table in the back to avoid all eyes.

When she took her cell phone out of her handbag, she was surprisingly gripped by a vague feeling of shame. She dialed the international prefix anyway, and the long number that she had memorized so thoroughly.

Prolonged, echoing rings.

Just when she was about to give up, someone answered. Someone who had the right to know what had just happened.

# 32

# The Tower

Vater had been spinning his spiderweb of contacts for many years. But nothing seemed to have worked this time, even when he'd pulled on all its threads.

Besides the sloppiness of the police in that little border state up in the north, he was most irritated by the apathy and lack of cooperation from the German security service. But then, there had always been a whiff of incompetence behind all of those abbreviations, whether they called themselves BfV, Bundesamt für Verfassungsschutz, LfV, BND, or why not the SS or the Gestapo.

The only truly professional organization he had come across, after the Imperial Police of the German Empire, was the Ministerium für Staatssicherheit, the East German security service, the Stasi. Unfortunately, that had been dismantled long ago, and it had been a big job to remove traces of the foundation from their archives.

How the federal intelligence agency, Bundesnachrichtendienst, had managed to miss the short telephone call was a mystery. Thanks to a complicated legislative process, they now had the same ability to perform radio intelligence as the French did, but they seemed to be completely incapable of doing it.

In a global world, it wouldn't matter where the towers were, they had told him, but still he had to haggle all morning with the bureaucrats at Direction Générale de la Sécurité Extérieure to get them to send over information from Paris. As usual, he had been met with arrogance and superiority, despite all the help the French military industry had received from the foundation throughout the years.

Now the information was finally lying here in front of him, with the coordinates noted in black marker on a satellite image. Rust-colored brick roofs, a cathedral like a supine gray cross, near an open area called Grote Markt. The tower that the cellular signal had passed through was noted with a line consisting of apparently random letters:

Vooruitgangstraat

Where her telephone had gone after that would have to be investigated at the scene. But at least at that point the foundation's agents would be free to act on their own, without any heavy-footed government officers at their side.

# 33

# The Visit

Eva lay alone in the dark of the hotel room on the double bed. The bells of Cloth Hall had just struck midnight, and because it was Sunday, Grote Markt had long been closed down and quiet.

She had sat there at the little café, warming herself with Belgian hot chocolate, for several hours. Lost in memories of the time that had been, and all the hopes she had had for her life that had never come true.

When she had succeeded in shaking off her melancholy and had returned to the hotel room, it had been empty, and Titelman had disappeared. His jacket with the letter and the star had also been missing, and he hadn't left a message about where he'd gone. Eva had asked at the reception desk, but they had only shrugged and hadn't been able to give her an answer.

For the first few hours, she wasn't particularly worried. Just waited and assumed that Titelman had wanted to get new clothes to replace the ones that had been soaked with the smell of Saint Charles de Potyze.

But as time dragged on, she began to wonder anxiously, and then night had fallen without any news. By that time it was too late—she didn't like the idea of going out into the darkness to start looking for him. Instead she decided to get some hours of sleep and wait for the morning light.

Eva closed her eyes and tried to rid herself of the feeling of intense uneasiness. It had sneaked into her in the dreary war museum in Cloth Hall and hadn't really gone away since.

She wanted to stop seeing the flickering black-and-white images from the newsreels inside her head. All those bodies that were torn to shreds time and again. The two maimed and bleeding wax models that lay unconscious in the green cloud of gas in the glass case.

A few steps away, there had been a cold account of the surprisingly quick development of weapons during World War I. One example was grenades with burning white phosphorus, and she recalled the ability of that substance to dig its way through skin and bone in garish color.

She looked up at the ceiling and tried to bring her thoughts back to Titelman. She tried to envision him, bending under the shoulder strap, walking through the alleys of Ypres. Had he been allowed into the small, cute boutiques when he smelled so terribly of graves?

Eva felt something like a smile, and she turned over to lie on her side.

It was impossible for her to fall asleep on her back. There was a painful spot, an area between her fourth and fifth vertebrae, that would never, ever be able to be whole again.

That was where the large needle had been thrust in when the doctors injected the violet liquid into her spinal canal. The scar was still there, even though she had gotten the first injections when she was only fifteen years old.

They had told her that what happened had been only for her own good. Eva felt her hand make a fist over her midriff, where everything had been left lifeless and empty.

But then, finally, a forgiving peace had descended over her. She heard drips coming from the bathroom, but she didn't have the energy to get up. She drifted drowsily into the darkness, and the pitter-patter of the drops of water disappeared more and more until they blended with something that was knocking faintly.

For a brief moment Eva awoke, trying to hear what it could be. She decided she must have misheard, mumbled something to herself, and adjusted the pillow under her head.

Then she heard it again, a heavy knock this time, and it was coming from the door of the hotel room.

"Yes?" Eva had time to say before her mind sharpened enough for her to realize that it would have been better to remain silent.

There was another knock.

Eva sat up as carefully as she could and avoided turning on the lamp by the bed. She thought about where she had placed her boots and her trench coat and caught sight of them over on a chair. She placed her bare feet on the floor.

Without shoes she could sneak silently over the plastic mat, over to the entryway of the hotel room. On her way, Eva had time to consider how long the door would hold if the person who was knocking really wanted to get in. She tried in vain to remember whether the hotel door had felt heavy or light when she had closed it behind herself this morning. The only thing she remembered clearly was that the lock had seemed sturdy, at least.

A beam of light fell into the dark entryway through the peephole in the door. Eva placed her right eye against the round opening and looked out.

Through the distortion of the glass she saw a pair of smoky green eyes looking back. A young woman was standing there, and she seemed to know that Eva had dared to approach.

"Miss Strand?" the woman said in a bright and remarkably friendly voice.

Eva was about to open the door, but then she saw the other shadows out in the corridor: a heavy man in a military coat and another with a pointed, shaved head.

But it seemed to be the woman who was in charge. She was dressed in a motorcycle outfit that was so tight it looked as though it had been painted onto her thin body. She had a shiny integral helmet hanging under one arm and raised her other arm to knock once more, very firmly.

"Miss Strand? Please, open up."

What kind of accent was that? German? No, not German . . . French? Italian? Eva didn't have time to think any further than that before the small hand out there had been tightened into a fist, and the woman banged the door with tremendous strength.

"Miss Strand! You have something in there that belongs to us."

Later, when Eva thought back to the incident, she was surprised that she hadn't moved away from the peephole when that first, adamant punch came. But there was something about the teenager out in the hallway that made it impossible to tear her eyes from her: tremendous energy that had been boiled down into a much-too-small body.

The next double punch was so violent that the hammering sound must have spread throughout all the floors of the hotel.

Again Eva heard her name being called loudly, but now it was as though the young woman's voice had placed itself in the very center of her head. The waves of sound vibrated with such power that Eva's hand, as though of its own accord, began to move down toward the handle of the door.

But just before she reached the handle, the teenager turned around in a kick that was aimed directly at the peephole. Eva just had time to sense how quickly the motorcycle boot was moving before the brass cylinder was kicked right through the hotel room door.

The blow caused Eva to collapse onto the plastic floor of the entryway with her hand against her eye, and she felt something flowing between her fingers. Then she blinked up at the door and was surprised to realize that she could still see. But the cylinder had sliced a deep gash in her eyebrow, and the blood was flowing down onto her face.

Above Eva's head, a smoky green eye looked into the hotel room through the drilled hole where a metal cylinder had once been glued in. Then she heard a soft voice:

"Miss Strand? Is everything all right?"

Eva shook her head down on the floor. Then she quickly began to crawl backward toward the bathroom, where she pulled down a hand towel to at least temporarily stop the flow of blood.

Without really being able to see, she made her way to the hotel room telephone, which she knew was on the nightstand. She held the receiver to her ear, but there was no tone, and it wasn't until that instant that Eva realized how she had been traced. Damn all the cell towers and this continually updated modern technology.

She heard another furious kick outside the door, but the lock seemed for some incomprehensible reason to be withstanding it. The bright voice said something that sounded like an order, and just after that she heard a heavy thud. It was followed by another thud. The hinges were already starting to come loose.

To get as far away from the entryway as possible, she made her way over to the window on the other side of the room. Then she pulled the curtain aside and opened the topmost latch out toward Grote Markt.

Eva could see the wood splinters reflected in the leaded windowpane, and she realized that the hotel door would soon topple in.

"We only want what belongs to us, Miss Strand," the voice whispered, very close.

Eva finally got the lower latch loose, and the window swung open to the inside. She could smell garbage and heard the fans from the outdoor seating down on the square.

She thought that she might be able to scream out into the night, but then Eva cast a glance back at the entryway and lost her voice. A shoulder-size hole had split in the middle of the door, and now the face of a teenager was looking in.

"Miss Strand," said the woman.

Eva was already on her way up into the window in bare feet.

"I'll jump!" she called.

But when she saw the cobblestones fifty feet below, she thought that maybe it wasn't time for that yet.

Instead Eva turned around on the windowsill and started to fumble with her left hand against the brick facade of the hotel. The space between the stones was just large enough for her to get her fingers in the gaps. Her toes could find footing on the protruding tin ledge that continued over to the window of the neighboring room. Eva moved her left foot out and felt her fingers find a grip. The September night breeze swept through her thin blouse.

Balancing with her fingers and toes, Eva cautiously began to clamber sideways with her body pressed as close to the wall as she could get it. A human cross moving high up between the windows on the facade of Hotel Langemark.

When she had managed to turn her face so she was facing forward, with her right cheek scraping against the brick, Eva saw that the tin ledge she was balancing on ran past the next window and over to a drainpipe, which she might be able to climb down.

It was about the same distance there as the drop to the cobblestones of Grote Markt was, but now, hanging by her fingers and toes on the wall, she didn't seem to have a choice. Her wrists had already begun to ache, and her calves shook as she took another small step forward. Eva thought that she was far, far too old for this.

From behind her she heard a bang, which was followed by a crash as the hotel room door cracked. Eva didn't turn around; she just kept taking short, tiny steps. The voice said something again. Something about trying to turn back. But now really wasn't the time to turn around, because Eva had just managed to climb over to the window post of the next room.

She grabbed its upper corner with her hand and felt that it was large enough for her to be able to get a good grip. She managed to wiggle her left foot over onto the wide window ledge, and then her right, and after that she could finally rest.

Something that sounded like breathing made Eva turn her eyes back in the direction she'd come from. She realized that she had to hurry when she saw that the teenager had also climbed out.

But before she continued her escape toward the shining goal of the drainpipe, Eva took a deep breath and happened to glance in through the windowpane. There, just behind the glass, she saw a young man with a pointy, shaved head. As he waved at her, she recoiled, and one foot took a step straight out into the emptiness.

She was far too late in trying to fend off the mistake, and as her body was about to fall, she grabbed an outdoor thermometer that was screwed onto the window frame. But the thermometer was too poorly attached to hold even the weight of a frail woman. Eva swayed, the streetlights glimmering on the stone fifty feet down.

Then she felt herself falling.

But she didn't have time to fall very far before a claw caught her arm. It lifted her gently up toward the window, where she landed again.

As Eva once again balanced on the window ledge, she tried to shake herself loose and get the claw to let go. Then she discovered that the claw was actually a rather small hand. The woman who was holding her so steadily seemed completely unfazed by the situation. She was hanging calmly along the brick facade in her black motorcycle outfit.

"Where is our star?" the woman asked gently.

Then she took a small hop forward and landed next to Eva as though she had suction-cup feet. Bent down and whispered, "And where, Miss Strand, is your friend Don Titelman?"

# 34

# The Login

When the bartender at the gloomy little pub on Minneplein was no longer merely hinting that it was time to go, Don groped for his aviator glasses and slipped down off the tall, rickety barstool. Then his knees immediately gave way, like rubber, and he had to grab the bar just to be able to stay upright.

That last Belgian beer had been absolutely unnecessary, and he had long ago lost count of how many antianxiety barbiturates he had munched on.

With the chipped metal frames of his glasses hanging crookedly on the bridge of his nose, he got his newly purchased velvet jacket off the stool. And as the bartender turned his back on him to start counting the night's takings, Don had enough presence of mind to make sure the star was still in the inner pocket of his jacket.

During his hours in the bar, he had made a few awkward attempts to figure out the inscriptions on the metal. The bartender had let Don borrow a plastic pen to sketch the symbols he thought he could make out in the dusky light of the bar. But it seemed that Nils Strindberg had been right to use a magnifier and a microscope to study the star, because there was only a jumble of lines that mostly looked like abstract art on Don's scribble-covered paper napkin. He had left the short letter to Camille Malraux in the darkness of his inner pocket. There was no reason to read it again, because he could recall its cryptic contents from memory whenever he wanted to:

My beloved Camille,

The promise I made to you has been fulfilled. The gateway to the underworld is closed.

I wish I could have done more.

From here I travel into my own Niflheim, where the other thing shall be hidden forever.

Your Olaf

Those Norwegian words about closed gateways had, in his drunken state, caused Don's thoughts to become self-pitying. If he were just to give up and hand the star over to Eberlein, then surely everything with the Swedish law would work out simply enough. A few weeks in jail, and then they would realize that the man who had been staggering around under the influence of narcotics down by Erik Hall's dock was completely innocent. Someone who had nothing at all to do with the sudden death of that diver. Being indicted and convicted because of an unlucky coincidence—that was something that simply couldn't happen in Sweden.

When Don had gotten this far in his speculations, he heard some sort of snuffling sound in his memory, which came from the Mustache at the police station in Falun. The sound had led him to punch out a few more capsules filled with phenobarbital and decide not to make any hasty decisions, at least not this evening. Besides, he had never heard of anything good having come from a person placing his trust in Germans.

After the bartender had finally pushed him out the door, Don began to walk unsteadily from Minneplein back in the direction of Hotel Langemark. Dressed from head to toe in a brownish black velvet suit, he blended in with the night as he wandered along beside the darkened Gothic windows of Cloth Hall.

When Don looked across Grote Markt at the narrow brick facade of the hotel, his first thought was that some sort of renovation must have begun. Because between two of the windows up on the fourth floor hung a construction mark in the shape of a white cross.

Then, as the white cross slowly began to move to the left, Don blinked to get his eyes under control. He thought about his past experience with antianxiety barbiturates, but this particular hallucination was truly new.

A bit closer to the hotel, Don could see that the illusion had now acquired both arms and legs. Fifty or sixty feet up, someone was clambering along the stones of the facade in a blouse and fluttering white pants. Although Don knew very well who it was, he didn't want to admit that it was Eva who was swaying and about to lose her grip.

His legs began to move him forward instinctively, and he ran toward the hotel's outdoor seating in the hopeless, shortsighted ambition of shouting to the attorney to come down.

But when he had come close enough that Eva might be able to hear him, he saw a shadow pop up in the open window behind her back. It was a thin figure dressed in shiny black, and it got a grip on the brick facade and clambered after Eva. It moved elastically and remarkably quickly toward the attorney, like a spider on its way toward its catch.

Eva had managed to make it to the next window when Don held his hand up to his mouth to bellow out a warning. At that very second, the attorney faltered suddenly, and he could feel in his own body how she lost her balance and fell.

Yet the hair-thin shadow somehow had time to dance its way up to her in a leap along the brick wall. It grabbed one of her two wildly windmilling arms and caught the attorney like a hooked fish. The doubled body weight didn't seem to be a problem; it was as though the shadow's hand and foot had been drilled fast to the stones of the facade.

With a swinging movement, Eva was pushed back up against the window again, and Don let out his breath until he heard her loud scream. She had gotten loose and caught sight of him, and now she was waving her arm in a signal that he should take off. Then Eva was sucked backward; she disappeared inside the hotel, and Grote Markt was once again deserted and quiet.

The shadow in the shiny black costume was still there, and it turned its face in Don's direction and then began to move rapidly down the brick facade. With two stories left to the ground, it prepared for yet another leap.

Don turned around on wobbly legs and began to run as fast as he could, his breath catching in his throat. Cut in onto Rijselsestraat, right on Burchtstraat, followed the glowing trails on the tourist map in his memory. He closed his eyes and rushed between honking cars across the four-lane Oudstrijderslaan.

He didn't stop until he'd reached the tourist buses that stood in the parking lot on the other side of the road. Sank down into the shelter behind the gaudy coaches and looked behind him for the first time. After he'd waited for several clusters of headlights to pass, he realized that no one was following him any longer.

With some sort of half-jogging movement, Don began to move back toward the southern parts of the city. He held his shoulder bag under his arm, pressed against his body like a protective amulet.

Dawn hadn't yet come when he finally reached Ieper Vrachtterminal after an hour or so. He crouched down and slid under the black and yellow gate next to the sentry box, which still seemed to be unstaffed.

He continued forward, half crawling across train tracks and gravel, wondering how long it would take before Eva would be persuaded to tell her abductors about the terminal and the position of the freight car on track number seven.

The bright green Green Cargo car stood deserted in the streams of light, and when Don saw the black letters of the logo on its side, for the first time in a long time, he truly longed to go home.

After unlocking it with his key, he rolled the sliding door a bit to the side and climbed in. He lingered there, quiet for a minute, in the space between the Masonite and the dirty inner wall of the car. Gave a start at the Flemish voice from the loudspeaker, and then he heard a roaring train whistle approach from far away.

Don undid the hinges of the Masonite and pushed his way into the passage that led to the cozy compartment of the sleeping car.

It still smelled stuffy in here, like old sleep, and he fumbled his way through the darkness until he managed to turn on the porcelain lamp above the lower bunk.

In the soft light, he could see that everything was as they had left it about a day ago: the crumpled bedspread and on the small night-stand the open laptop. Prints from his boots were visible on the wall-to-wall carpeting, and now he unlaced them and sank down on the bunk with his head in his hands.

When he returned to the memory of the shadow clambering on the wall and Eva Strand's faltering body, the gravity of her situation finally got to him. Her desperate waves for him to get away, and how she had disappeared, dragged into the darkness of the hotel.

Don reached across the computer keyboard, and it hummed to life with a whispering whirr.

He felt the points of the *seba* star in his inner pocket, above a small, folded piece of paper. The shoulder bag's tempting pantry full of chemical calm . . . But there was no time for sedatives now, nor could he just throw himself down on the bunk and close his eyes forever. Instead he turned his eyes to the monitor, which had finally woken up.

Don tapped in the codes he had once taught attorney Eva Strand, which led to the server that stood in a concrete room under the deserted station at Kymlinge. The idea had been that they would both be able to communicate with Hex if something unexpected happened. And this situation was not a development that Don had counted on, in any case.

When he made contact with his sister's server, the smiley face lit up, and the corners of its mouth indicated that Hex was actually home this time.

But when the happy face had died away and he entered his sister's mirrored desktop, nothing looked the way it usually did. Instead of a crucified Microsoft CEO there was only a black window in which a lone white cursor was blinking in front of an arrow-shaped bracket:

>_

Don's tongue was dry as he listened for sounds outside the car, but he could hear just the clatter of trucks and shouting voices from the new freight train, which was starting to be unloaded.

He hit RETURN and wrote a first message.

**>anyone there?_**

The vertical cursor just continued its slow pulsing. Finally Don impatiently wrote another line:

**>anyone there?**

**>sarah? hex?_**

In a cellar in Kymlinge, someone hit RETURN. Then he could see the letters blink up, one by one:

**>no time, it_**

The cursor remained, pulsating.

It took almost ten minutes before his sister came back:

**>better now what_**

He began to type:

**>you have to move the freight car, eva gone_**

This time the dialogue moved quickly:

**>someone else on the drive can't access**

**>who?**

**>don't know clever has**

**>we have to help eva**

**>left a**

**>we found strindberg's star**

>_

The blinking light of the cursor. Then, in Kymlinge, his sister wrote:

**>i know you found the star_**

Don's rough tongue moving in his mouth. Then he gathered himself and wrote a single symbol:

**>?_**

But Hex was gone.

Outside the car, there was a sudden rustle. Silence followed, and after that, something that could have been a light knock on the metal exterior.

When the steps moved again out there, disappearing in an abating crunch of gravel, Don slowly turned his eyes to the screen. A flickering white line of letters:

**>don. they have left a message here for you_**

# 35

# Mittelpunkt der Welt

The matter had been settled on a foggy day in November 1933.

The seventeenth-century castle in the small Westphalian city of Wewelsburg would be taken over by the SS and converted into the ritual headquarters of all the rapidly proliferating Schutzstaffeln. According to the plans, the north tower of the castle would form the central hub of a future Nazi-dominated world. The project came to be called *Mittelpunkt der Welt*, the Center of the World.

One might think that such a crucial decision would have been made by the leader of the SS himself, Heinrich Himmler. But it was actually put forth by a different, by all accounts even more insane, person.

*

As the head of the SS and the Gestapo, Heinrich Himmler was the shadow prince of the Third Reich. It was his responsibility to take care of all racial and ideological controls, and it was his men who made sure that the ovens in the concentration camps burned steadily.

Himmler had been weak and delicate as a child, with such poor balance that he had never learned to ride a bike. In addition, he had problems with his airways, which caused his voice to become locked into a shrill pitch, and it often cracked with a piercing sound. With his frail body, he became a persistent bookworm, and he loved the German myths and fairy tales. Even as an adult, Himmler considered each word and phrase in them to be true. He thought he saw traces of an ancient Aryan civilization everywhere in these legends. He took it for granted that it had originated in ancient Atlantis, which had sunk to the bottom of the North Atlantic despite its highly advanced technology.

After the National Socialist election victory in 1933, the SS leader began to search for a fitting place where he could advance his theories. He wanted to create an SS college, where the main subjects would be German mythology, archaeology, and astronomy.

Around this time, an older man showed up at Himmler's office out of nowhere. The man introduced himself as Karl Maria Wiligut, and he would soon have a crucial role to play.

Naturally, Himmler tried to investigate his background, but the only thing the SS men found was that Wiligut was financially well-off and had powerful contacts in the German and international weapons industries. What most impressed Himmler was that Wiligut claimed that his Aryan blood went back more than *220,000 years.* An ordinary SS officer only needed to prove his lineage back to 1750—a trifle in comparison, less than 200 years.

Karl Maria Wiligut claimed to be descended directly from the Old Norse god Thor. To prove this, he went into a trancelike state wherein he made contact with his "memory of his Aryan forefathers." From this bank of knowledge, Wiligut related the true history of the Aryans. At first Himmler was taken aback, but after a few hours, his surprise had been exchanged for abounding enthusiasm.

According to Wiligut, the history of the world began 228,000 years ago. At that time, the population consisted of dwarfs, giants, and dragons, and there were still three suns above the earth. The godlike Aryans were also there, of course, led by Wiligut's family.

Through the millennia, Wiligut explained in his trance state, the Aryans had created everything of any worth. Christianity, for example, was actually of German origin, but had been distorted by Jewish exploiters. Jesus was really the Aryan god Balder, who had moved to the Middle East at some point in the dawn of time.

Because of these and even more outrageous stories, Himmler named Wiligut a major-general in the SS and gave him a senior position in the Ahnenerbe's department of prehistory in Munich, as well as a private villa with a household staff in Berlin.

Wiligut's immediate task was to put all of his forefathers' memories to paper. But the old man preferred to mediate defense contracts and sent constant suggestions for construction to Himmler. Wiligut was most interested in creating a great SS castle in Westphalia, which he said was necessary in order to survive the conflict that awaited with the subhumans from the east. He claimed that his forefathers had pointed out the castle in Wewelsburg as the perfect place. The earth there was full of Aryan force lines that contained tremendous psychic energy.

In November 1933, Himmler went along with Wiligut on a journey through the wet, cold forests of Westphalia. The old man showed him Wewelsburg, which sat broodingly on a limestone cliff above the city of the same name. The castle's walls were built in a wedge-shaped triangle. Three towers rose into the autumnal German sky, and Wiligut was of the opinion that this and nowhere else ought to be the location of the Schutzstaffeln's ritual headquarters.

Heinrich Himmler was reluctant at first: Westphalia was far from Berlin and the political power. But Wiligut convinced him by saying that he had seen the Slavic subhumans being crushed right here in a vision. He had even brought along a sheaf of manuscripts, in greasy leather, where it was stated that the battle would take place during the 1940s. Himmler played it safe and rented the castle for the reasonable price of one reichsmark per year.

When the SS took over the keys, the castle had thoroughly deteriorated and was in disrepair. The north tower had begun to lean and was supported only by some rickety iron rods.

Karl Maria Wiligut generously offered to take care of all the practical arrangements for the renovations. Covered trucks soon rolled into the triangle-shaped courtyard of the castle. In the cylinders on the truck beds, there was a compound of materials that Wiligut claimed was the most durable the world had ever seen. With it he recast the inner portion of the north tower, but he didn't care about the rest of Wewelsburg.

In the upper part of the tower, Wiligut constructed a circular room with a floor of light gray marble. A new ceiling was covered with white stucco, and twelve large columns were erected between the floor and the ceiling. There were blind arcades along the walls, from which eight narrow windows gave light.

Wiligut had a mosaic placed in the middle of the floor; it was in the shape of a sun wheel, and it was such a deep shade of green that it looked black in the dim light. It had twelve hook-shaped rays, and in the hub of the wheel was a disc of the purest gold.

When Himmler inspected it, Wiligut explained that this black sun, *die schwarze Sonne,* was actually made up of three entwined swastikas. But the truth was that no one really knew where he had gotten the symbol from.

Directly below the upper room, Wiligut built a crypt. He had the ground under the tower removed and replaced with the strange material from the trucks.

In the middle of the crypt, he built a waterless pool, which is still there today, fifteen feet under the surface of the ground. Around the walls he placed twelve pedestals at a proper height for sitting. From there one could observe the gas pipe that stuck up in the middle of the pool. From that pipe, Wiligut promised, a flame would burn for all time.

In accordance with Himmler's wishes, he reluctantly allowed a swastika to be cast in the hollow roof. But in the arch, alongside the spokes of the swastika, he opened up four angular holes.

These holes in the ceiling somehow distorted the acoustics down in the crypt. Once a word had been spoken, it sounded as though it were immediately sucked up to disappear into the north tower of the castle.

Wiligut left the rest of Wewelsburg's rooms completely alone. And how the old man had planned to use the north tower never became known. A year or so before the war, he was suddenly dismissed by Himmler; the reason given was "failing mental health," and Karl Maria Wiligut disappeared without a trace into the fog and smoke of history.

According to the neo-Nazis, the most lasting memory of him, aside from the north tower of Wewelsburg, was the SS Honor Ring, which Wiligut created for the highest officers of the SS. Himmler had been adamant that the engraving should consist only of Old Norse runes. Still, Wiligut somehow managed to include a star whose shape was strongly reminiscent of an Egyptian hieroglyph.

No one could ask the old man what the meaning of this star was, quite simply because no one knew what had become of him. But a sudden discharge from the SS seldom boded well.

Despite Wiligut's strange ideas about the north tower at Wewelsburg, Himmler was very pleased when he finally took possession of the building. The SS leader could now furnish the empty rooms in the main building as he liked.

Himmler had a round oak table installed in Wiligut's upper room in the north tower. He called that room the Obergruppenführersaal, and he had twelve chairs with pigskin seat cushions made. The twelve highest SS officers would sit in them in a Nazi variation on Arthur's knights of the Round Table. This way they would also avoid seeing the black sun mosaic, which seemed to suck up all the light.

The lower crypt was left empty and unused because no one knew what it was for. Himmler avoided it completely, and if anyone asked, he always claimed that his lungs couldn't handle its chilly atmosphere.

Once the castle came into use, it became the center of the SS leader's two pet projects. These were the Ahnenerbe's historical research and RuSHA, the Schutzstaffeln's Race and Settlement Office.

The task of the Ahnenerbe was to dig up as much evidence of a grandiose German past as possible. The researchers' first expedition was to Backa in Swedish Bohuslän, where they imagined they saw an Aryan alphabet in the rock inscriptions on the granite cliffs. That they also thought they found figures shaped like swastikas made the find even more sensational.

In the Canary Islands, they immediately found remains of what had once been Atlantis, the original home of Aryan civilization. In Tibet and the Himalayas, the researchers looked for traces of the Aryan migration from Atlantis to ancient India.

Iceland was judged to be so interesting and well preserved that it was deserving of the most expensive expedition of all. But the Icelanders never let the German scientists in, because they didn't consider their research to be serious.

Heinrich Himmler was personally involved in the Ahnenerbe's work, particularly when it came to the Aryan people's art of battle. Among other things, he was interested in the Norse gods' thunder-weapon Mjöllnir, and therefore he ordered in his bureaucratic style:

> Investigate the following: Find all areas in the northern Germanic-Aryan cultural sphere in which there is knowledge of lightning,

> thunderbolts, Thor's hammer, or the flying or thrown hammer, as well as all sculptures of the god in which he is depicted with a small hatchet that gives rise to lightning. Please collect all evidence of this in the form of paintings, sculptures, written stories, myths.
>
> I am convinced that this is not based upon natural lightning and thunder but is rather one of our forefathers' early, highly developed weapons of war, which naturally only the Æsir or the gods had and that it implies that they possessed a knowledge of electricity that had never been heard of previously.

When the war began to go badly, Himmler was forced to decrease the activity of the Ahnenerbe. The Führer claimed that the country's resources now had to be concentrated on what was truly important. Himmler consoled himself with the fact that at least this included RuSHA, the Race and Settlement Office.

But the race researchers had gotten stuck by this point. The invasion of the Soviet Union had upended all their theories.

In the well-organized race registry there was no room for the myriad new names. Who had heard of Chuvashes, Mordvins, and Tungus? Who knew which of all these peoples were Jews? Maybe all of them were Aryans? The German officials had no answers.

The question was complicated further because no one could scientifically distinguish between the Jews of their own country from those who were considered Aryans. One unfortunate study had revealed that one in ten Jews in Germany, for example, had such Aryan characteristics as blue eyes and fair hair.

They were forced to realize that only a small number of people matched the formulaic description of the truly Jewish:

short<br>
shuffling gate<br>
flat chest<br>
bent back

weak muscles
fleshy ears
hooked nose
yellowish skin
an intrinsic inclination toward schizophrenia, manic depression, and morphinism

Because the selection of people that fit these criteria was so tiny, they were on a desperate hunt for more measurable differences.

The German officials scrutinized cranial sutures, calf muscles, heart rhythms, fingerprints, and blood types—but found no differences at all. Desperate, they then switched to an examination of the Jews' body odor and earwax, but no matter how they went over and over it, the results were always just as scant.

That was when the thought of creating a special reference collection consisting solely of Jewish skeletons arose. The victims were chosen from the concentration camp Natzweiler-Struthof, and the executions would be done tidily. No parts of the skeleton could be harmed, because that would destroy the scientific worth of the collection. The corpses were shipped by truck to a newly built laboratory, where they were placed in storage tanks filled with alcohol.

In this case, there was a problem that the officials had trouble solving: How would they remove the flesh from the skeletons without leaving unnecessary marks and traces on the surface of the bone?

The first thing they tried was dissolving the muscles away with the help of chemicals. But that process turned out to be time-consuming, and it caused the skeleton to smell horrible.

The next method involved placing the Jews' bodies in a number of closed containers. There, colonies of insects could cleanse the corpse of flesh in peace and quiet. But they changed their minds about this too, because having insects in a newly built laboratory was considered neither clean nor proper.

Finally, the officials decided that the best method would be a form of leaching. When the bodies were lowered into a bath of calcium chloride, all the muscles dissolved. After another period of storage in distilled benzene, the last bits of fat and cartilage had melted away.

The reference collection had already been initiated when the laboratory was taken by the Allies, and in the clinical rooms, the soldiers soon found sixteen bodies of young women and men. They were floating around naked in the large tanks, and none of the German officials seemed to have any idea of how the bodies happened to end up there. On fifteen of the corpses, the skin of the left arm had already been cut away, but on the sixteenth was the blurry blue tattoo that revealed where the bodies came from.

Even in the final stages of the war, Himmler still had grandiose plans for Wewelsburg. He had become so enamored with Wiligut's north tower that he saw it as the core of a gigantic, future SS complex.

The project was called *Mittelpunkt der Welt,* the Center of the World. The drawings were already finished, and it was estimated that the construction would take twenty years. It was thought that it would be finished in the midsixties, with an airport and its own hydroelectric dam.

In order to supply the dam with enough water, large portions of the valley around the city of Wewelsburg would be flooded. The population would be forced to relocate—but when the American troops arrived, all of this was put on ice.

In March 1945, the castle was blown up by SS special forces. They didn't want to leave it in the hands of the Allies, who were only ten or twenty miles away. But no matter how much they tried, the SS men couldn't get the north tower to budge. Just as Karl Maria Wiligut had said, it was durable, and it wasn't at all affected by dynamite.

Immediately after the war, the political elite of Wewelsburg declared that the castle was to be considered a war monument. It was carefully renovated into a museum that concentrated on the years before 1933.

The castle's affairs were handled by a locally established foundation that met once a month in the management office of the large bank building. From its picture window, you can see Wiligut's north tower, if you ever happen to be passing by.

# 36

# Wewelsburg

The vibrations from the taxi's spinning tires spread up through the seat under him. And even if Don tried to hold his legs still, the cardboard box on his lap began to tremble, if only slightly. The box weighed next to nothing. Under its tied-down lid there was only loosely packed cotton and Strindberg's white star, which was forged of such amazingly featherlight material.

He had followed all of Hex's instructions. She had taken over from a distance of seven hundred miles. Yet Don now wondered whether it had been a particularly bright idea.

The message the Germans had left had been short, and it most resembled a polite invitation:

Unser Stern gegen Ihren Freund
Alter Hof, Wewelsburg, Mittwoch mittags

"Our star for your friend, Alter Hof in Wewelsburg, Wednesday at noon."

But the friendly German tone had insincere overtones, because the person who'd left the message had been well on his way to copying and then burning out Hex's server.

When his sister had finally managed to regain control of her computer, she sent the harmful code to one of her online friends, who had a central post in the NSA's cyber-security unit in Maryland in the United States.

The friend had thought that the design of the code was interesting in and of itself and had promised to contact her when he had more answers. At the same time, he didn't know how much he was actually allowed to say, because even at first glance he could see traces of its being manufactured by a familiar, and friendly, German intelligence agency.

Hex had been able to save most of the valuable data on her server, including her access to Green Cargo's logistics system. The freight car was already on its way out of Ieper Vrachtterminal. To be safe, she had also changed its numerical designation through several hours of simple but patience-trying work in a sadly outdated administrative routine file. The car would arrive in Mechelen later that evening.

But anyway, Don was sitting by himself, vibrating gently in the ivory-colored taxi on his way down the Autobahn toward a city he never thought he would have the strength to return to.

When he first saw the loathsome name, he had thought Hex was joking.

But she had been furious and said that this was no fucking joke. Now she would have to change all the addresses and rearrange her whole computer system. And if he was planning on traveling to Wewelsburg and relying on the goodwill of the Germans, that was the most idiotic idea she had ever heard.

At first she hadn't bothered to give him an answer when he tried to explain to her that he couldn't desert the attorney, and that maybe it would be best for everyone if the star ended up in the right hands.

For several hours, his computer had been dark and quiet, but then she had suddenly returned with a simple proposition.

Don carefully adjusted the box and hoped that the last bit of road into Wewelsburg from Salzkotten wouldn't be quite as full of potholes as he remembered it. He didn't see himself as a particularly malevolent person, but his sister had always had good powers of persuasion, especially when she was enraged. And she had certainly been in a terrible mood when she sent her detailed instructions.

*"Blut und Boden,"* came a voice from the front seat.

The bloodshot eyes, which were visible in the rearview mirror, belonged to the taxi driver from the night journey to Saint Charles de Potyze. Don had called the number on the business card he'd received outside the cemetery on that night when it had rained so hard.

Right now he couldn't really remember what he'd been thinking; presumably he had wanted to have a familiar face along the way into Germany. How he had managed to repress the Belgian's horrible driving was more difficult to understand.

"Blood and earth," said the driver again. "Into the heart of the beast."

It had really been a bad idea to call that number on the card.

"Family here in Westphalia?" asked the driver.

"Not very likely," said Don, looking out through the dirt-striped side window.

The dull clouds hung low over Wewelsburg, but it hadn't yet begun to rain. The small city was as he remembered it. First, scattered brick houses in 1950s style, where the destruction had been worst. Then the taxi continued into the rustic center, with timber-frame walls and medieval buildings that hadn't been hit as hard by the Allied bombings.

It was an area that paid tribute to peasants and folklore, and some of the low houses looked as if they had been plucked from a story from the Grimm brothers.

Alter Hof was a restaurant with rustic tables out on Wewelsburg's city hall square, where an abnormally tall bank facade completely dominated the view. Beyond its roof, up on the lime cliff, Don could glimpse the flat upper part of the castle's ailing north tower.

Twining ivy ran along the wavy glass in the restaurant windows, and the tables in the outdoor seating area gaped, half empty. The small group of young men in military jackets and shaved heads truly stuck out.

They didn't look like typical neo-Nazis, Don thought, as the taxi swung in toward the square. They had earpieces in their ears, and one of them was holding something black that could be a weapon, or perhaps more likely a communication instrument.

It seemed as though his arrival was expected, because some of the men got up. One of them had a pointed head, and another one had the rugged body of a wrestler. But he could see no sign of attorney Eva Strand.

The taxi driver pulled the hand brake and turned around. He had parked in the middle of the open square, quite a distance from the restaurant, as Don had instructed.

"Start the car again," Don mumbled quickly. "Keep the motor running, from now on."

The taxi driver rolled his eyes, and then he turned the key in the ignition again.

"So, I'm going to deliver this," said Don, nodding at the cardboard box in his lap. "When my friend has shut the back door, you should already be rolling out of here. Then you drive to Mechelen, as fast as this car can handle."

The driver didn't look particularly inspired. Still, he let the motor idle, rumbling, and he even gave it a little bit of gas.

Through the window of the car, Don could see that all of the men were now standing. One of their dark green backs disappeared into the Alter Hof restaurant.

After a short time, a young woman popped up in the door and looked over toward the rumbling taxi. She had ordinary clothes on, but under her jacket was a glimpse of a holster that had been fastened onto her small body.

She nodded toward the wrestler, but it wasn't until she had begun to move toward the taxi, by herself, that Don thought of the movements of the shadow across the brick facade of Hotel Langemark.

He carefully placed the tied-up cardboard box on the seat beside him, opened the car door, and climbed out onto the cobblestones. There was a scent of spicy sausage and grilled meat on the square, interspersed with the smell of flowing beer.

The woman smiled at him, but Don held up one hand as a signal that she had come close enough. She stopped about thirty feet away from the taxi, but her smile—that was still there.

"Where's the attorney?" Don asked.

"I'm sorry for all this trouble . . ." the woman began, in English with a faint Italian accent.

"Yeah, yeah," Don interrupted. "Where is Eva? I want you to bring her out here right away."

The woman cupped her hand over her soft lips and whispered something up toward her earpiece. Don looked over toward the restaurant, where the taxi was visible in the wavy glass of the windows.

In the freight car in Ypres, the city hall square had sounded like a safe place to hand over the star: an open place, where there ought to be lots of people moving about at noon on a weekday. But now that Don was actually standing here, leaning against the ivory-colored body of the taxi, it didn't feel good at all.

The people closest to him out on the square were the shaved men over by the restaurant table, and there were some schoolchildren doing something with a skateboard near a tobacco stand about fifty yards away.

A disheveled bum was sitting on a park bench, leaning his head back as though the sun were shining, and far over by the stairs up to the entry of the bank, there was a man in a wheelchair, surrounded by a group of men dressed in black. *They sure don't skimp on care for the disabled, the Germans; they look after their own,* Don thought as he saw how the caretakers moved as though they were at the man's beck and call.

But at least the man's bald head was turned in the right direction, and it seemed as though he intended to watch the little scene alongside the taxi—a small assurance that a bystander would react if this entire deal went completely wrong.

Don lost his breath for a second when he saw who was now standing in the doorway to Alter Hof. Eva's face was black-and-blue and swollen, and there was an oval scab under her left eye; it was yellowish brown, on its way to turning black.

"Miss Strand, as you see," said the woman in front of him. "I'm truly sorry, but she gave us no choice."

"She didn't?" asked Don, who really wanted to get out of this sick German city as fast as he possibly could.

"And you have . . . ?" the woman said, taking a few steps forward.

Don tried to keep his eyes on her while at the same time leaning into the backseat of the taxi and grabbing the string around the cardboard box. Behind the woman, he could see that Eva had started to come closer, led brusquely by the arms by the wrestler and another of the foundation's men.

When the attorney was finally standing next to her, the woman asked how he had imagined the exchange would happen. Don held the package in his moist hands and couldn't produce an answer.

"Eva . . ." Don began.

The attorney looked up at him with a grimace.

"What have they done to you?"

She didn't answer, just stared at him.

Instead, alongside Eva, the woman said, "And now, if you could hand over what belongs to us."

When he nodded toward the box, the woman just waved dismissively.

"Just the star, please."

Don undid the bow and let the string fall down onto the cobblestones. Then he opened the lid and gently removed the top layer of cotton. Strindberg's star lay there, resting in the light, and he angled the box so that the woman could see.

"Happy?" he asked when they had been standing like that for a moment.

The woman tore her sooty eyes from the small object.

"I guess we'll see," she said. "May I . . . ?"

She extended a hand and picked up the five-pointed white star from the soft bed of cotton. She held it up before her and, irritated, brushed away a few white specks from the metal. Her mouth moved as she examined its winding inscription.

"You understand what the words mean?" Don couldn't help but ask.

"Yes, but the star seems to be covered in something," said the woman.

"It looked like that when we found it. Is there a problem?"

The woman shook her head and placed the star into the pocket of her jacket. Then her smile was back again.

"Not at all. Everything is as it should be."

She signaled to the men in the military jackets that they should release their grip on the attorney. But Eva was ahead of them; she pulled herself free. Then she threw a glance at the empty box and whispered as she slowly walked past Don, "How could you be so naive?"

Don's mouth suddenly became dry, while at the same time he heard the door close on the other side of the taxi. The car's motor was running, Eva sat in the backseat, but something still felt so wrong. For the woman, the matter seemed to be settled. She was on her way back toward Alter Hof with her hand in her jacket pocket, fingering the star. But the two shaved men were still standing there.

Don heard the woman call out to them to come along, but they didn't seem to care about her instructions anymore. He realized he had forgotten to warn her about the star—everything had gone according to plans—but now he had enough of his own problems.

The wrestler had come very close, and he held a damp linen rag in his hand. Don smelled the sour scent of gas as the rag was suddenly pressed up against his mouth.

The grip on his neck was impossible to throw off, especially now that everything was becoming so foggy. An instant later his legs gave out and everything German mercifully faded away.

# 37

# The Blindness

The Germans' anesthetic seemed to have completely dissolved all the shock absorption inside his skull and left his brain scraping against the walls of the cavity, resulting in a splitting headache.

Don wondered, as he lay there with his cheek against an ice-cold stone floor, if they might have injected him with some type of ketamine after they had put him under with the rag. Because he recognized very well the waves of nausea when he tried to get up on one elbow, and in his mouth was the familiar taste of bitter almond and lemon. But he had never experienced a ketamine intoxication that left him blind. And yet he could see nothing.

There was a sting from his cornea as he tried to reassure himself by way of his fingers that he really had opened his eyes. But the world around him remained black, and in his mouth and nose was the scent of an earthen cellar and stuffy moisture.

He began to massage his knees to get them to loosen up after their stiffness from the cold, and there was a snap as he straightened his crooked back. He had no idea how long he had been lying knocked out on the floor. Presumably it had been several hours, because it took him a number of very painful attempts to get up. When he finally regained some semblance of balance in his legs, Don began to move forward with very small steps.

Held his arms stretched out like a sleepwalker, in the bewildered hope that he would manage to feel his way out of this complete blackness by complete chance. But his fingers ran into a wall after only a few yards.

When he felt along the rough surface, he understood that he was standing at a brick wall. It arched out, as though it were circular, and he began to follow its stones from seam to seam.

While he moved along the wall, trying to keep count of his steps, he began to think about Eva and what had actually happened outside the Alter Hof restaurant. The warning about the star he'd never gotten out before the anesthetizing rag was pressed to his mouth. Don hadn't had time to see what happened to the attorney afterward, and now that he thought about it, he preferred not to guess. He was already ridden with so much guilt about what he had put her through that he didn't have the stamina to try to imagine what had been her final fate.

He had counted thirty steps in a half circle when there was a clatter from something he'd happened upon that seemed to be a large metal chain. He grabbed and managed to catch hold of it—and at the same instant, he knew that he was in the cellar under the west tower of Wewelsburg.

Don tried in vain to stop the suffocating memory from taking over. But he already saw her before him again: the museum guide with her blond hair, drawn-on eyebrows, and wax-red mouth. She had been wearing a colorful scarf on that day so long ago, and he remembered that it had been adorned by a porcelain brooch in the shape of the three-cornered silhouette of the Nazi castle.

The guided tour of the castle's museum had begun with Heinrich Himmler's photography. They had both stood there contemplating the SS leader's face, whose lack of character made it so difficult to recall. His hair shaved high up on the sides, into a wet-combed skullcap. The middle-aged beginnings of a double chin, and above his lip something that looked like a mix between stubble and a mustache.

Under the photograph in the display case, some objects had been preserved like a still life. A belt with the inscription:

*Meine Ehre heißt Treue*

"My honor is called loyalty." Beside the belt lay the SS honor ring and the sharp dagger.

Despite his work on the Ahnenerbe and the symbols of Nazism, Don had tried to avoid Himmler's castle for as long as possible. And now, in hindsight, he wished he had never set foot in its north tower. But because he had come there for a private tour, the museum guide had unlocked it and shown him in.

The first step into the Obergruppenführersaal was the longest one he had ever taken, and the airless room swam before his eyes. It had been so warm, too, July, and the heat had pressed in from the high windows.

He had forced himself to walk across the floor toward the black sun wheel in the mosaic, until he was standing with his boots on its center disc of gold. He looked out toward the twelve columns that ran along the tower room walls and understood that he had reached the core of Bubbe's 1950s house.

Still he had felt absolutely nothing.

At least not until he turned to the museum guide and saw her hushing finger. The respectful gesture had filled him with such distaste that he considered cutting the tour short. But the blond guide must have completely misunderstood his expression, because she had whispered that this was the heroes' indestructible hall.

Then she had led him to the crypt in the lower level of the tower. When his legs began to give way, Don had grabbed for the iron rail of the staircase.

He had dared to approach the grated door to the crypt, but hadn't had the strength to go farther, even though the museum guide offered to open it. Through the grates he had been able to glimpse the swastika on the ceiling, and the guide had pointed out the gas pipe. The place for the eternal flame, he remembered that she had said.

When he had asked her whom the flame had been intended to burn, she had become quiet. Something about his appearance must have caused her to put it together, and she had said that the tour was now over. And he remembered that he had thought, as he walked back up the steep stairs to the upper room, that he had just seen the remains of a madman's creation.

"Wiligut," Don whispered to himself.

He let go of the metal chain and it clattered as it fell back against the stone floor in the cellar of the west tower. Through the sound he thought he heard someone snuffle. At first Don stood stiffly in the damned blindness, but then a hoarse voice asked, "Is someone here?"

With a rush of relief, he took a few steps forward, bent down, and fumbled around in the darkness. Came across fabric with buttons and lapels. Then he found the warm hand, at the end of the trench coat's sleeve.

"Eva?"

She pulled him close without answering, and he felt her catch his head in an awkward hug.

"So you can't see anything either?" he managed to whisper, when he had collected himself a bit.

"No, how could I?" she whispered back. "They've brought us to the castle, haven't they?"

"They've locked us up in their museum," mumbled Don. "At the very bottom of the west tower. I believe you have the informational placard about the concentration camp Buchenwald directly above your head."

"Buchenwald?"

"The SS locked the local Jews in here right after Kristallnacht. They had to crowd in here for a few weeks, until they were sent away to Buchenwald. That was a little footnote on the guided tour."

"Have you been here?"

He sighed.

"Wewelsburg was Himmler's dream of the knights' castle Camelot. It was impossible for me not to travel here."

"Voluntarily?"

"For research. Maybe to honor the prisoners of war who renovated the castle, too. A few thousand people, most of them Russians, who were worked to death, starved, hanged, or shot. *Vernichtung durch Arbeit,* as it was called, annihilation through work."

The attorney just breathed quietly, without saying anything.

"The local concentration camp was called Niederhagen, and it was managed so effectively that the leader was promoted to a commander at Bergen-Belsen. His old gatehouse was converted into a two-family home, I've heard."

"It sounds idiotic to lock someone up in a museum," Eva mumbled.

Don shrugged.

"In any case, it will probably be difficult to get out."

He touched her face lightly with his fingers. There were no longer any traces of the swelling under her eye.

"You really heal fast," Don observed.

"They only beat me for the first few hours," said Eva. "Once they got me to tell them the codes to Hex's server, they seemed to assume they could lure you here. But now . . ."

She let the words glide out into silence, and asked instead, "What was that name you said, by the way?"

"When?"

"Just before you almost stepped on me."

"Wiligut?"

"Yes . . . Wiligut. That sounds familiar somehow."

"It's his fault that the castle is still standing at all. It didn't work to blow up the north tower, not even when the SS men tried themselves. He's some sort of occult shadow figure within Nazism. An old Austrian army officer who was said to have worked in silence within the weapons industry during the interwar period, only to pop up with Himmler like an ancient Aryan oracle in the early thirties. No one knows very much about him, other than that he was once locked up in a mental hospital and that that was the reason Heinrich Himmler fired him. He . . ."

There was a clatter, a key being guided into and turned in a lock. A creaking sound, and then the tone of the darkness shifted. A beam of light was turned on and was directed first down at the floor, and then it swept slowly along the walls of the tower room. When it finally fell on their faces, Eva and Don were caught, blinking, in the powerful light.

"Don Titelman?" They heard a familiar voice.

Then the light out there in the stairwell was turned on and, squinting, Don could see the contours of the nonreflective glasses that could belong to no one other than Reinhard Eberlein. Just behind the German, he could glimpse an unwieldy figure who resembled a toad more than anything.

# 38

# The North Tower

The wind tore at the windows in the hall of the castle, making them clatter behind their pulled curtains. A few yards ahead of them in the shadowy light, the Toad waddled past the busts of Wewelsburg's melancholy prince-bishops, with the tower key swinging from his hand. After him came an attorney from Afzelius in Borlänge who called herself Eva Strand.

Eberlein had taken Don's arm and walked closely next to him. The only thing that was different about the German's catlike appearance from their meeting in Villa Lindarne was the wired earpiece that hung down alongside his pale gray face. But the aged man's lips still shone a shade too red, and under his glasses the inward smile didn't seem to have deserted him yet.

There didn't seem to be any hurry, and the small group moved slowly through the echoing stone hallway.

The Germans paused at a model of Himmler's project *Mittelpunkt der Welt,* and they stood looking at it for a long time. There, inside the glass, was the monstrous SS fortress the Nazis dreamed of in 1941. A wave of giant concrete buildings that would have surrounded the north tower and suppressed any sign of life in the surrounding Westphalian countryside.

"A remarkable person, Karl Maria Wiligut," Don heard Eberlein mumble to himself.

Before he could protest, the German waved dismissively as though he had heard a message from his earpiece. Listened for a moment with his head cocked to one side before the conversation was concluded with a terse nod.

*"Noch eine kleine Weile,"* Eberlein said to the Toad. It will be a little bit longer.

His only answer was a slight shrug from the wide, sloping shoulders. Then the Toad pointed toward a sign that said:

KREISMUSEUM WEWELSBURG REZEPTION

When they walked into the entry hall of the museum, they were met with a muted light. It came from several porcelain ovals that hung above an open fireplace, framed by a marble frieze in Roman style.

A few yards away from the hearth stood a pair of worn leather sofas. Eberlein suggested to Eva and Don that they take the opportunity to rest for a little while. Then he sat down across from them, while the Toad remained waiting in the dark, like a saggy statue.

"As you understand," said Eberlein, "the preparations are not quite finished yet. We are still expecting some guests from far away at tonight's ceremony."

Don pressed his lips together, and Eva curled up in the corner of the sofa with her arms around herself. The bruises on the attorney's face had disappeared, and all that was left of the yellowish brown scab under her left eye was a pale pink circle.

In the long silence that followed, Eberlein looked down at his watch now and again. It was as though he was unsure whether time had stopped or was really still ticking by.

Finally, Don leaned forward and whispered to Eberlein, "You know that we're sitting in the Nazis' old wedding hall, right?"

"I can honestly say that I have no idea what kind of madness Himmler got up to here in Wewelsburg during the war," said Eberlein.

The German's yellow-gray eyes glimmered.

"In that case, I'll tell you," said Don. "In this hall, the Schutzstaffeln had their very own marriage ceremony that was called SS-Eheweihen. It was Heinrich Himmler himself who created the true Aryan marriage ceremony. Before the wedding, the bride had to provide a picture of her cranium from the front and in profile. To this she had to attach a medical certificate stating that her blood was sufficiently pure, and a pedigree had to be sent to RuSHA, the Office of Race and Settlement. If she was suitable, the documents were stamped in a local office here in the castle."

The leather of the sofa creaked as Eberlein squirmed.

"A few doors away," Don continued, "were the clinics for the breeding program Lebensborn. There they fertilized the purebred women who hadn't been successful in finding husbands. Once the pregnancy was over, the newborns were placed in special orphanages where their racial quality was evaluated. Lebensborn . . . do you know what that word means?"

Eberlein sighed.

"It means 'the source of life.'"

"As I said, I know nothing about what the Nazis did here during the war," said Eberlein. "It was unfortunate that they were able to take over our castle at all, especially because we were interested only in renovating the north tower."

The German straightened his glasses, and there was a certain delight in his eyes when he noticed that Don had stiffened.

"Karl Maria Wiligut's task was to create a proper hall of ceremony for the ankh and the star down in the crypt, and a dignified place for the foundation's meetings in the upper hall of the north tower. Nothing more than that. Everything that happened afterward is the responsibility of Heinrich Himmler and the SS."

Don could feel his head swimming, and he sank back against the sofa.

In the dim light, the color of Eberlein's face seemed to have become a shade rosier. Now the German leaned forward a bit, until he sat tottering on the edge of the seat. He cracked his knuckles thoughtfully.

"This is the last time we'll see each other, you and I, Titelman," he said slowly. "You have truly been an invaluable help. It would be a shame if you thought the foundation and I were some sort of . . . *Nazis* in the end."

Don sat silently while Eberlein inspected his nails.

"So what is this all about, then?" he asked at last.

"What this is all about," said Eberlein, "is that you have made further leaps in man's quest for knowledge possible by finding Strindberg's star and then bringing it here. And tonight, when the star and the ankh have been reunited once again, the foundation's interrupted work will be able to continue."

"The foundation's interrupted work . . ." Don repeated.

He sneaked his hand down into his shoulder bag to try to find a pick-me-up. Something that could lift him out of this gathering feeling that he was dreaming.

"The thing is," said Eberlein, "that I may have doctored the story about Nils Strindberg a bit when we met in Stockholm."

"So there were no spheres?" Don mumbled while he looked down in the bag for the right blister pack.

"Strindberg's spheres?" Eberlein scoffed. "You've seen them yourself, photographed in the negatives from the balloon journey, seen sketches of them in Strindberg's stenographic laboratory notes, and followed the expedition diary's coordinates of the ray's movements. What else do you need?

"No, everything I told you there in the library at Villa Lindarne was historically accurate, up until the discovery of the opening down in the underworld," the German continued. "This is about what happened *afterward.* The truth is, you see, that we know who killed Nils Strindberg, Engineer Andrée, and Knut Frænkel out there on the Arctic ice. The foundation has known ever since the spring of 1901, actually."

Eberlein moved back on the sofa and settled himself. Once again it was as though he were slowly being rejuvenated by his own words, and the furrowed lines on his face gradually began to melt away and disappear.

"I don't know if you remember that I showed you Nils Strindberg's last, muddled notes. The ones he wrote on the back of Knut Frænkel's meteorological sheet when he was hiding from his pursuers down in the crevice of the glacier. What Strindberg wrote was that the ankh and the star had been stolen by strangers who attacked the expedition out in the middle of bare expanses of ice. According to Strindberg, Frænkel was already bleeding to death from his gunshot wounds at this point. Engineer Andrée had also been shot, and a slow death awaited Strindberg himself. The gateway to the underworld was open, and then Strindberg mentioned a name. He wrote that 'the older one was called Jansen.'"

Don read the sprawling ink lines in his memory and nodded reluctantly.

"Therefore," Eberlein continued, "it created a stir among the businessmen in the foundation when, in March 1901, a letter arrived that was signed with that very name, or more accurately, 'shipowner J. Jansen.'" The return address was for a law firm in Hamburg. And when the foundation contacted the lawyers there, a rather unbelievable claim was put forth. It turned out that these 'strangers,' as Nils Strindberg called them, were actually a group of destitute Norwegian whalers. They had followed the Swedes' balloon across the sea from

Svalbard, and at the Arctic pack ice they continued their pursuit on skis. How they then managed to navigate correctly across the ice and find their way to the Swedes at the opening of the hole, no one knows. One theory is that Knut Frænkel leaked the story about the Bunsen burner and the sphere's coordinates to the Norwegians back in the camp on Danskøya. We know that their steamer was anchored beside the Andrée expedition's ship *Svensksund* for several weeks, down in Virgohamna. In any case, the Norwegians managed to find their way to the opening only a day or so after Strindberg and Andrée had begun to explore the mouth of the tunnel. According to the Norwegians, the Swedes were needlessly aggressive, and it was entirely their fault that shots were fired. Somehow, Jansen and his men must have gotten Strindberg to tell them how the Bunsen burner and the spheres worked. Because by the time they contacted the foundation, the Norwegians knew all about the movements of the ray and how one could follow its changing position. During the four years that had passed since 1897, the whalers had also gone down into something they called 'the halls of the underworld' on several occasions. They couldn't really explain what was there, but they understood that it was something of great value."

Don let out a cough. "The halls of the underworld?"

"That's what the Norwegians chose to call them," said Eberlein. "They had discovered that even though the hole in the ice moved every third day, it permanently led down to this immense passage of... well, underground halls. But at this point they had also realized that they had neither the financial resources nor the knowledge to make use of what the halls contained. So the Norwegians suggested a kind of exchange. They would remain in control of Strindberg's ankh and star and function as the guardians of the opening. The foundation would send scientific experts to the tunnel, and through their business contacts transform whatever they found down there into a modest economic profit."

"So what was down there?" asked Don.

Eberlein smiled, as the wind was blowing harder outside the castle. Don could see, out of the corner of his eye, that Eva Strand also had begun to listen attentively now.

"At first, nothing that the researchers in the early 1900s could understand," said Eberlein. "It took almost ten years of study before the foundation managed to come up with a method—quite honestly, a rather primitive one—for the extraction of . . . knowledge that had been left behind. Or maybe *knowledge* isn't the right word, actually; more like enigmatic whispers about the ultimate construction of existence, a sort of mental blueprint for how this universe is constructed, in a purely physical sense."

"That sounds like something I've never really had a clear idea of," said Don.

"But to come up with any useful answers, you also have to ask the right questions, don't you?" said Eberlein. "Above all, you yourself have to have at least a vague understanding of the way things are. So the foundation's research began during the first year of the twentieth century, when a concept like a Higgs particle sounded like some kind of dirt that ought to be cleaned up, and it would still be another thirty years before James Joyce made up the word *quark*. Neutrinos, mesons, the astronomical secrets of quasars . . . we're talking about a historical era when the academics of the world hadn't even accepted Darwin's theory of evolution. Steam locomotives were considered advanced. The Mauser rifle, with its smokeless gunpowder—the highest form in the art of war. People had heard of wire spirals, but hardly the DNA spiral. Nor could anyone understand the significance of a discovery like that, even if someone happened to sketch the structure of the double helix from a prophetic vision. And unhappily enough, all such visions ceased in the summer of 1917—that's when the ankh and star disappeared unexpectedly."

"In 1917," said Don.

"When the star was hidden in Malraux's grave," Eva mumbled.

"The last long expedition was carried out in late autumn, 1916.

Weather conditions in the Arctic were difficult, of course, for the technology that the foundation had access to at the time. The recordings from that expedition are the last ones that we still have. In June 1917, the Norwegians sent word that the ankh and star had disappeared without a trace, and with that, the contract with them lost all further meaning for the foundation. All business contacts were severed, and from what I understand, that shipowner, Jansen, died only a few years later, destitute. And yet the Norwegians had managed to earn tremendous amounts of money, just by having control of Strindberg's ankh and star. As I may have mentioned, the businessmen in the foundation worked primarily in the defense industry, and the unexpected scientific discoveries they had managed to extract from the underworld truly had given weapons development a boost. Strindberg's instrument had given them a cutting edge against the competition, one could say."

Don had been seized by a sense of déjà vu, and he could distinctly smell the scent of the airless seminar rooms in Lund where the conspiracy theories never seemed to die out. Still, he couldn't stop listening as Eberlein continued.

"But even if the opening was closed and gone, many of the recorded visions remained. During the twenties and thirties, the foundation's researchers worked hard to investigate the messages they had received there in the darkness of the underworld. Because the primary interest lay in the area of weapons technology, they naturally placed their focus on the structure of the atom. It seemed to contain an almost inexhaustible power if they could just interpret the drawings correctly. But not even the foundation's resources, which were considerable at that time, were enough to fund such a project on their own—they needed a state for that. The most obvious partner was Germany, of course, and the political parties in Berlin. Surprisingly enough, the National Socialists won the election in November 1933, and the foundation found that they suddenly lacked personal contact with the country's new power elite. Nazism was, of course, a right-wing populist movement that no one had taken seriously, and everyone in the defense industry was caught napping. Then Hitler's speedy rearmament came as a consolation, and any progress in weapons technology was met with great respect, no matter how advanced and far-fetched it sounded."

"And Karl Maria Wiligut?" asked Don, who by now had begun to feel a bit dizzy.

"Karl Maria Wiligut"—Eberlein smiled—"was one of the key members of the foundation at the beginning of the thirties. He had experience in spy operations during World War One, and he laid out what he considered to be a brilliant plan. The goal was to seek a closer and more personal collaboration with the Nazis. Above all, with the true leader behind all the smoke-filled rhetoric, namely the SS commander Heinrich Himmler. When Wiligut first suggested to the foundation leadership that he would present himself as an Aryan man with kinship going back 220,000 years, the idea was thrown out as ridiculous. But soon it turned out that he had been right. His success with Himmler was so exceptional that Wiligut became the SS commander's right-hand man. It was in this favorable position that the foundation got the idea of renovating Wewelsburg's north tower. It was a place filled with psychic energy that they'd used throughout the years with good results. Now they wanted something more fitting to their position, and they naively believed that the Nazis and Himmler would turn out to be a reliable help."

"I'd still have to say that their analysis was correct," Don said, blinking into the darkness of the fireplace.

"Yes, the construction of the north tower went as they'd planned. But in 1938, Wiligut was murdered on a backstreet in Munich, and all collaboration with the Nazis was immediately discontinued."

"But surely Karl Maria Wiligut wasn't murdered?" said Don, who lacked even the strength to raise his voice. "He was kicked out of the SS because they discovered he had been in a mental hospital for a long time. They got rid of Wiligut because that proved he was too crazy even for Himmler."

"That was just the Nazis' usual lies," said Eberlein. "He was murdered, as I said, and the reason was that Himmler discovered by chance that, in addition to being openly homosexual, which was bad enough, Wiligut was also a Jew. Himmler could hardly imagine a greater scandal."

"Karl Maria Wiligut. A Jew . . ." Don said. "So what you're saying is that an infiltrating Jew designed the SS ring with the skull, the swastika, the S-rune, and the Germanic Hagal rune? The ring that was given out as a reward to the SS units that commanded the most effective concentration camps?"

"Wiligut never drew a Hagal rune," Eberlein remarked calmly. "What he designed into the SS officers' ring was a representation of the star that Sven Hedin had once found in the ruins in the Taklimakan Desert. Five bars from a hub, in the shape that the ancient Egyptians called *seba*."

Don couldn't think of anything else to say and sat mutely. In the corner of the sofa, Eva was twisting a graying lock of hair in silence. Then Eberlein happened to cast a glance at the clock, and he let out a whistle.

"I think it's time to go."

The German stood up and straightened his suit pants. Don felt all his physical strength run out of him.

"No," Eberlein said, extending his hand down to Don. "After 1938, the foundation is completely blameless for what happened. Besides, from a business standpoint, it was a good choice to leave the Nazis to their fate. Hitler's military power was essentially fully equipped. The business opportunities for the sketches from the underworld were considerably larger on the other side of the Atlantic. The United States had hardly gotten their defense industry started."

Eberlein pulled Don up so he was standing.

"What kind of diabolical help enabled Himmler, Hitler, and Goebbels to hold out for six years is truly a mystery. But in just a little while, Strindberg's ankh and star, with one last contribution on your part, will rediscover the gateway to the underworld for all those questions that still lack answers."

"One last contribution?" Don heard himself say.

But Eberlein had already come to the point where the entry hall opened out to the castle hall, and the Toad stood waiting. And soon they were all following the dim path that Don very well knew led to the north tower of Wewelsburg.

*

In the center of the black sun mosaic in the marble floor sat a bald man in an electric wheelchair. One of his eyes looked like a dead, gray stone, while the other was strikingly alert and sharp.

Outside the windows of the tower room hung a slender crescent moon, behind clouds that were as thin as smoke. A steep staircase led from the upper room down to the crypt, and from it came a puffing noise. The eternal gas flame had been lit for the first time in seventy years.

Elena was standing uncomfortably at Vater's side, in a bloodred evening gown. Two young men with shaved heads were standing there as well; they were so stoical that they seemed to be made of porcelain.

As he began to move into the tower room, Don kept his eyes on the young woman in red to avoid looking down at the rotating sun wheel. Eberlein pulled him in the direction of the stairway that opened into the crypt to show him the glow of the gas flame.

When they had approached Vater in the middle of the hall, Eberlein cleared his throat and opened his mouth.

"Thank you, I know," said Vater, and he extended his long skeletal fingers and nodded at Don to grasp them.

They were as thin as an insect's feelers, and Don let go quickly.

"Don Titelman," Vater said. "And here we have *kleine* Eva, of course . . ."

Eva did not accept the extended hand. Vater chuckled.

"You have traveled far to come here, and you have truly been a great help. Now there is just one thing missing before Strindberg's spheres can come forth again."

Vater pulled on the little joystick on his armrest. Then the hydraulics of the wheelchair lifted his body up until the sharp eye could look straight into Don's.

"We need your help to fulfill a promise."

"A promise," Don whispered. "What will happen then?"

"We are going to fulfill a promise this evening, you see," Vater continued, "or make a sacrifice, if you prefer. Something that was decided just after Karl Maria Wiligut's death, in what was the foundation's most dismal period. I imagine that with your background, you might even be able to see it as a tribute of some sort."

Don shook his head in an attempt to wake up out of this dream. Vater misinterpreted his gesture and continued, irritated: "At a historical moment like this, there is no room for personal doubt. Down in the crypt that the SS and Heinrich Himmler called Walhalla . . ."

Vater spat out the words: "Down in the *crypt,* as you know, there are twelve pedestals along the walls, which will now finally be used for their true purpose. Right now, eleven—what shall we call them—key people from the foundation are sitting in a circle that forms a well-defined telekinetic field. The ankh and the star will be lowered on a chain into the hot flame of the gas pipe. When the objects reach the correct temperature they will fuse into Strindberg's navigational instrument. The stars of the Milky Way will once again shine in the upper sphere, and the North Star's ray will point out the opening of the underworld. And at that instant, Don Titelman, a new and much brighter time will begin."

*"Ich vintsh aych glik,"* Don said. "Then I wish you good luck."

"Us? You will be down there yourself," said Vater. "You can see it as a final favor for the foundation."

Don looked questioningly at the young woman in red, who had taken Strindberg's star from him one day earlier. She met his eyes briefly before she glanced away self-consciously.

"It so happens," Vater continued, "that upon Wiligut's death, the foundation promised a ceremony that honored the triumph of the Jewish blood over the Nazis. And it was intended to take place on the day that the ankh and the star once again fused, in the beautiful tower that was designed for this very purpose."

"The Jewish blood, I don't understand . . ."

Don lurched suddenly, and the young woman in the evening gown took a few quick steps forward to help him.

"*Your* Jewish blood," said Vater. "We need to borrow your Jewish blood. The promise that was given was to fill the hollow down in the crypt. Elena . . . ?" Don could sense the woman hesitating.

"It's time," said Vater.

She didn't move, but then she placed Don's arm over her shoulders and whispered, "If you would be so kind as to come with me."

He could smell the scent of burning gas even at the opening in the marble floor of the upper room. Don closed his eyes and rested against Elena like a rag doll as she helped him down the steep staircase.

When he looked up again, he was standing at the arch that led into the ochre-colored circular crypt. Eleven older men, lit from below by the bluish light that came from the gas flame in the round stone pool, were sitting in an incomplete circle on stone pedestals.

Their yellowed faces turned toward him as he moved toward the steps that led down into the depths of the stone pool. Don walked with support from Elena's shoulder, and when he looked along the wall for help, he saw that both Eberlein and the Toad were among the men in the circle who were carefully following his steps.

The quiet murmuring in the crypt stopped when Don reached the hollow of the pool. High up on the ceiling, above the burning flame, he could glimpse the dirty yellow silhouette of the swastika. Thick chains now ran from the four openings that had been cut around its center. They were linked together into a square net, and on it lay Strindberg's ankh and star.

"Give me your hand," Elena whispered into his ear.

Don was now so close that he could feel the heat from the flame.

"Fall to your knees."

He obeyed, feeling ill, and sank onto the stone slabs in the middle of the pool. There was a flash from some metal object in her hand. Then Don looked away and felt the sharp pain as the edge of the knife cut an incision through the veins along his arm.

"Soon it will be over," Elena whispered, while she held him so he wouldn't fall forward.

The red blood flowed in an arc toward the flame. When the liquid met the heated gas pipe there was a hissing sound followed by a faint scent of iron. Don looked up at the swastika on the ceiling and Strindberg's suspended objects and thought, *So this is* Mittelpunkt der Welt.

He remained on his knees until a pool of blood had formed around the protruding gas pipe. By this point, Elena seemed to have had enough of the ceremony, and there was a disappointed murmur when she helped him get up again.

The last thing Don saw inside the crypt, just as he passed the archway, was Eberlein giving him an appreciative nod. Behind the nonreflecting glasses, the yellow-gray eyes were filled with a peculiar light.

On the stairs up to the upper hall, the woman fastened a bandage around his injured arm with careful fingers.

"I am not to blame for what happened," she whispered.

Don felt himself nod, though he didn't believe her words for a second.

Then he lifted his bandaged arm to his chest and continued unsteadily up to the Obergruppenführersaal, where he collapsed in front of Eva Strand's high-heeled boots.

As though in a fog, Don saw the black-clad, bald men lift Vater out of his wheelchair and carry the spider-thin body down to the crypt.

The woman hesitated, as though she didn't know whether she should follow them or remain in the upper room of the north tower. Finally she made her decision and took a few steps down the stairs. Don opened his mouth to shout a warning. But perhaps he hesitated too long, or else his dry lips couldn't form any words.

*

Down in the crypt, Vater had just taken his place on the twelfth pedestal.

*"Raus bitte."* He waved at the men who had carried him, and they immediately hurried away.

They stopped in the arched opening next to Elena to observe what was going to happen. Eberlein said a few words into his earpiece, and then the chains began to descend from the swastika on the circular ceiling.

The *seba* star, which lay on top of the ankh's crossbar, trembled slightly with the downward movement, and it made a mournful clinking sound. When the wire gauze with the objects only had a few feet left to go to reach the flame, the tension in the crypt increased.

Elena pushed her way closer to see Strindberg's objects fuse together for the first time since 1917, the spheres that Vater had told her about, and the North Star's searching ray. Everything she had only seen pictures of, the unknown reaction that made up the empty center of her life.

A bit lower now.

Elena and the two uniformed men stood crammed on the stairs next to the archway. Eberlein's red mouth and the Toad's eyes, where the gas flame flashed with a distorted, glaring shape. The last thing Elena heard was Vater shouting something about Karl Maria Wiligut and the triumph of the Jewish blood.

In the next instant, she was blinded by the explosive flash that was unleashed from the ankh and the star. The detonation tore the crypt to pieces, a roar that was cut short, and she was thrown headlong backward by the violent force of the shock wave.

# 39

# Brüderkrankenhaus St. Josef

In the instant when Elena happened to wake up out of the fog that the narcotic drip had immersed her in, she woke to screams for help and running footsteps. Then she noticed that everything she heard came from the left, while the right side of her face was paralyzed, disconnected, and stiff. She sank peacefully back into the darkness with the hope that she would never again have to wake up.

The pain was like scissors cutting, clumsily clipping their way in through her right ear canal. With a clenched fist, Elena pressed the bandage as hard as she could to her temple, but whatever was cutting her up in there was impossible to reach.

After the nurses had forced her to wake up, the pain locked her into this spasmodic position. Curled up on the short end of the bottle-green stretcher, she had been able to see them clatter by with emergency carts in the hall of the hospital. The majority of the most serious burns had already been transported to intensive care after the explosion in the north tower of Wewelsburg.

As the hours passed, she heard Eberlein's voice nonstop on the other side of the emergency room wall. Against her will, Elena had been forced to listen to his vain attempts to bring some sort of order into this chaos.

Half of his phone calls seemed to revolve around what it was that had exploded down in the vault of the crypt. The other half involved trying to stop the news reports, which had already started to skid out of control.

A dozen highly placed businessmen involved in Nazi rituals at Schloß Wewelsburg was already a reasonably good story. A dozen businessmen who got *blown up* was truly noteworthy. All of Germany seemed to have come to its feet, although it was still only dawn. The live reports echoed from the TV in the corridor, with continual updates from Brüderkrankenhaus St. Josef in Westphalia, district of Paderborn.

Eberlein's attempts to cite old loyalties, the threat of terror, and the responsibility of the press seemed only to add fuel to the fire of the journalists' enthusiasm. In every report there were speculations of new potential perpetrators, and with each hour, the theories grew wilder and wilder.

But Elena didn't have the strength to wonder about what had caused the crypt to be torn to pieces. She had been forced to perform Vater's errand with the knife like a puppet, with no willpower of her own, and she knew the plans for Titelman and the woman if the ceremony had reached its intended conclusion.

The explosion had been a fitting resolution, and the only thing that bothered her was that her body still so stubbornly refused to give up.

The victims' burned skin was being washed with chlorhexidine to get rid of the debris from the explosion, and now their wailing screams were crowding out the noise from the TV once again. Keeping the wounds clean and moist was of the utmost importance for future plastic surgery.

Elena heard someone go in to Eberlein, and she soon recognized the nasal voice of the senior physician. It seemed to be yet another report about Vater's condition: the old man was getting specialized care in the ICU, burns on his face, full of tubes and needles. The shock had caused his heart to stop, until someone had foolishly gotten it to start pumping again. She let the conversation run on without listening, and if, as his daughter, she was expected to visit him, they would have to drag her there.

Then Elena's thoughts were hacked to pieces by all the sharpness that was cutting deeper and deeper into her ear canal. And she felt that this was exactly what she wanted: that the point of the scissors would short-circuit her life.

She raised her hand to the IV pump that controlled the supply of morphine and increased the rate of infusion as much as she could. Then she sank back with her head on the pillow, waiting for the numbing wave that would wash over her and sweep her away forever.

# 40

# Mechelen–Berlin

They had already cleaned all the surfaces in the freight car once, but Don still felt anxious. He poured dish soap on the rag and opened the spigot of one of the water cans. Then he began once more to polish the counter in the pantry inside the mahogany cabinet. He tried to stand with pliant knees to negate the rocking of the train car.

They were traveling as the last car in the long freight train, which had left Mechelen in the direction of Berlin at dawn. Eva had said that it was better to keep moving, even if the journey would force them back into Germany, past North Rhine–Westphalia and the foundation's castle. They had promised to notify Hex before lunchtime what their destination would be after that. This way Don's sister would at least have a few hours to once again manipulate Green Cargo's archaic logistics system.

Don did actually understand that the cans weren't more dangerous now than when he had taken them off the shelves in the paint store. Still, he picked up the plastic bags marked Boca-Paint, in which the cans sat with their screwed-on safety caps, very cautiously.

"So what are we going to do with all of this?" he asked, turning to Eva.

She was sitting in one of the club chairs in the lounge with a map of the rail lines of northern Europe in her lap. An atlas of the world was open on the round table at her side.

"Throw it all out the window," she suggested, without even bothering to look up.

Don looked at the glazed teak walls and felt his mouth shape itself into a grimace.

*"A bisel komish,"* he muttered. Funny.

"Stop worrying," said Eva.

She had been saying that ever since they managed to get back to Hex's car without being discovered, even though they should have been easy to spot in the freight terminal at Mechelen, in clothes that had been colored ochre yellow from the dust of the explosion.

For his part, Don had been thankful that the freight car was still there at all. He hadn't taken Hex seriously enough when she warned him about the risks of the explosives. A small pile of the white crystals had still been scattered on the counter when they returned from Wewelsburg. He had quickly poured water over them and hoped that they would somehow dissolve.

It had been his sister's idea, all of it. She said that they ought to teach the Germans a lesson if they made trouble. On the other hand, if everything went well, his sister continued, they could always inform them that their rediscovered star should be washed off.

She hadn't even wanted to discuss the purely moral aspects of handing over an object covered in explosives, and as usual, Don had quickly let himself be convinced by her quarrelsome argument.

He had followed the instructions Hex had sent as well as he could. He had found all the necessary ingredients at the paint wholesaler in the industrial area outside of Ieper Vrachtterminal. And the salesman at Boca-Paint hadn't had any objections to selling hydrochloric acid, acetone, and hydrogen peroxide all to one customer.

Back in the lounge of the freight car, he had skimmed through the many discussion sites that Hex had recommended. Making the explosive hadn't seemed very chemically advanced; more like a game for bored teenagers who wanted to see at least something in life sparkle. Following Hex's advice, Don had made ten times the amount of his chosen recipe. The white crystals of explosive looked like coarse grains of salt.

At this point, he had been so stressed that he didn't care about the warnings that TATP could explode at the slightest vibration. Instead he had pressed Strindberg's star against the still-wet crystals that lay on the counter, and they had stuck to the metal like a fine layer of dust.

When the star was dry, he had placed it in the cardboard box, and then he vibrated away in the taxi toward Wewelsburg's city hall square and the outdoor seating at Alter Hof.

Turned away, next to the tips of Eva's boots on the floor of the upper room of the north tower, Don hadn't seen the stairwell flash with the explosion. But the tearing boom from the crypt had taken his breath away.

He had instinctively curled up to shield himself from the shock wave's cloud of stone splinters and blast debris. Afterward, once his deafness had begun to recede, he had been able to hear the distant ringing of an alarm.

He would have liked to think that it was an instinct from his time as a doctor that caused him to find his way down into the cloud of smoke in the steep stairwell. Yet he hadn't cared about the twisted bodies that had once been two uniformed men.

He recalled a few shreds of red fabric that must have been torn from the young woman's evening gown. She had been lying there as pale as a corpse with blood dripping out of her ear and one hand locked on the railing of the stairs in a death grip. There, if anywhere, he really should have stopped to help.

Instead he had staggered farther into the crypt, where there was a strong odor of burned meat. He had hardly been able to see in the yellow haze of pulverized brick and had begun to fumble forward, hunching down.

When he had reached the stone pool, where a gas pipe had once protruded, the air in his lungs was already nearly gone. But then he had caught sight of the shining objects, which lay there side by side. It was as though they had gently floated down to the floor without being affected by the detonation in the least. And when he had picked up the ankh and star, he could feel that they were still as cold as ice.

With the objects thrust under his jacket, Don had rushed back up the stairs. He caught sight of Eva, lost in the growing chaos of the upper room. In the settling smoke from the blast, her face had been covered with small, bleeding wounds where burning splinters of stone had torn her skin open.

They shoved their way through the stone halls of Wewelsburg, past all the ambulance crews and their stretchers. The inner courtyard of the castle was already filled with people who had been lured by the roar of the explosion. By chance he had caught sight of a young man who was standing next to his Vespa with a few girls and pointing up at the tower. Don had dragged Eva up to the small group, which backed away, frightened, leaving the Vespa.

When he had gotten up onto the seat, he turned the key, and the attorney climbed up behind him. She clung to him, her arms around his waist, and Don twisted the throttle toward himself and hurled them away on screeching tires.

"Now it really is clean enough," said Eva.

The freight car had just begun to slow down, and they could hear distant warning bells ringing.

"Come here instead."

Don rinsed the rag clean and threw one last critical glance at the interior of the cabinet. Then he closed its double mahogany doors reluctantly.

Once he had sunk down into the other club chair, she pointed at the railway map, which lay on the table.

"I think we're about there."

The attorney had placed her finger just east of Hannover, next to a small village called Edemissen. Don felt a bit lighter inside when he saw that they had at least managed to get past Westphalia.

"And in about three hours," Eva continued, "we'll be in Berlin. The question is whether you want to stay in Germany, as the situation looks right now. As a wanted terrorist, I mean."

She gave him a brief gaze. Eva's face was still bruised from the explosion.

"I mean, isn't it quite likely that that's what it's going to be considered, a terrorist attack? You just blew up a castle tower and a bunch of innocent people. Who knows how many of them are still alive? I think the search efforts after a terrorist attack in Germany will be considerably more intensive than after an isolated murder in an insignificant country up north. I am quite certain that your picture and information are already in Berlin."

Don suddenly felt a powerful homesickness, and he looked up at Malmö, Lund, and Stockholm. And besides, he was so unimaginably, horribly tired.

"Aren't the Germans looking for *two* terrorists, in that case?" he tried.

Eva didn't answer.

Instead she moved the railway map off of the table. Under it, the atlas of the world was still open, and in it he could see the Polish borders of Lithuania, Belarus, and Ukraine.

"I imagine that they won't look as hard here as they would in the heart of Europe," she said. "And up here . . ."

She turned a few pages and found the outline of a coast that Don couldn't place at all, at first. Then he saw the name of the city, and the geography fell slowly into place.

"Up here," Eva continued, "I would imagine that they won't look at all. And also, from here we can find out whether Strindberg's objects really work, with their spheres and constellations."

Don looked at the attorney, but it didn't look as though she meant her suggestion only as a joke.

# 41

# Healed

The morphine had pushed away all light, but still the pain just dug deeper and deeper into her ear canal. The pointed scissors cut tirelessly, with a rasping, scraping sound.

Elena no longer knew whether she was awake. The only thing she was completely certain of was that she couldn't see anything.

She pressed her hands down by her sides to reassure herself that the hospital bed, at least, was still there. But the only thing below her was emptiness, and the peculiar feeling that she was falling.

When she opened her eyes, she was blinded by intense sunshine that beamed at her from all directions. Squinting, she could make out the horizon like a faint streak between the white sky and the snow. The thin line ran in a half circle around her, but whether it was close or far away, she couldn't see. Everything around her had transformed into an expanse of ice, which seemed to have neither a beginning nor an end. Then Elena noticed that someone was standing nearby, breathing just behind her back. And in her left ear, where she could still hear, there was a hissing sound that spread into a voice.

"Elena . . ."

She closed her eyes, and there was another breath.

"Elena. *Devi ascoltare.* You must listen, Elena. You are the only one we can reach."

*"Madre?"*

"*Questo deve finire.* It must end."

"I . . . don't have the ankh anymore. It has . . ."

"*Devi portarcela.* You must take it to us. *Questo deve finire.* You are the only one we can reach."

A soft hand moved at her ear. The gentle stroke continued along Elena's cheek. At the same time, all her pain dissipated, and she finally drifted off into dreamless sleep.

# 42

# Changing Tracks

Berlin, Kostrzyn, Gorzów, Krzyż, Poznań, Kutno, Warsaw, Łuków, Terespol. At the Polish border with Belarus, they were towed into a hut and a few men in work overalls crept under the axles of the freight car in the dark.

Through the bunk in the sleeping compartment Don listened to the hammers striking against the undercarriage of the car, and then the vibrations from the pounding caused the china in the lounge compartment to start rattling.

When the tools had finally become silent, Eva pressed him close to her, while at the same time they heard the jacks pressing the car off of its western European wheels.

The books fell in piles from their shelves over in the lounge, and from the mahogany cabinet came the sound of breaking glass. With the next lift, the compartment door began to slide back and forth, in time with the jerky upward movements.

When the car had been lowered again, it was screwed onto the wider axles that fit the railroad tracks in the former Soviet republics. The gauge that had once slowed the Nazis' weapons transports to Stalingrad and Kursk.

After the wheel change, the journey continued with the monotonous rhythm of the rail joints, and soon Eva and Don fell asleep again. Sleeping, they were carried from Brest, via Baranovichi and Minsk, to the border crossing that lay right between the Belarusian city of Orsha and the Russian forest that had become infamous under the name Katyn.

There they stood, in the light of dawn.

The stillness made Don wake up and swing his feet down onto the soft carpet of the sleeping compartment. Behind him, Eva still lay sleeping with one arm stretched out across the warm spot where his body had been resting a moment ago.

He stretched, feeling slightly nauseated after the bumpy journey, and padded in his stocking feet over to the lounge, then sank down in one of the lounge's easy chairs to gather enough strength to make himself a cup of morning tea.

The railway map was still on the table. The only thing they'd had to go on was the timetable that Hex sent via the Internet, a clock, and a very poorly sharpened pencil. Still, the notes from Germany were written with great confidence.

The first crossed-out place came twelve miles or so before Warsaw, and after that, the journey had gone increasingly jerkily and slowly. Near a small, forgotten village there was a final, resigned mark which consisted of a long row of blunt question marks.

Don looked at the clock and saw that it was nearly quarter to four in the morning. He tried to figure out how far they could have come by this time. The tip of the pen moved uncertainly toward the point where the Dnieper flowed out of Russia, but just as he was about to cross it out he heard violent pounding from the outside of the freight car's sliding door. After a short silence, the pounding was briskly repeated, as though whoever was standing out there actually expected someone to come open up.

Don sat frozen, with the tip of his pencil pressing right through the dark blue stripe of the Dnieper.

Then he heard quick steps from out in the Masonite hallway, and Eva was standing in the door to the compartment, newly awakened and with red eyes. It looked as though she were silently trying to mime a question, then there was more pounding, and someone pulled on and started tampering with the lock on the sliding door.

Don managed to get his fingers to release the pencil and got his body to move again, shaking itself out of the muscle lock that his panic had so quickly caused. But when he got up on his feet, he could feel the walls of the lounge closing in on him, in time with all the scraping sounds and bangs coming from outside.

"The outer hidden wall is closed, right?" she whispered. "The panels can't have slid apart, can they?"

He signaled: I don't know.

"Should I look?" Eva tried again. "The wall can be locked together again from the inside, right? Maybe it's just a routine check; maybe they'll be satisfied with a quick peek."

Don didn't have time to give an answer, because now they could hear a voice outside the sliding door hissing in thick Russian:

"Откройте дверь!"

"We can just . . ." Don began, before he was once again interrupted by the voice:

"Вы здесь?"

Don swallowed a few times, and then he finally got his legs to start moving forward. He was blocked by Eva, who was standing there in front of the compartment door like a human barrier.

"Move," he said. "We have to open up."

"Эй, вы здесь?" came the voice.

The attorney didn't seem to want to give up. She held tight to the edges of the door frame with whitening fingers.

Don broke through Eva's grip with a bit of force and shoved her aside to get out into the narrow Masonite corridor. He reached the small metal catches near the ceiling, which were still holding the hidden walls in place, closed.

After he'd opened them so that he could see the sliding door ahead of him, Don began to fumble in his pocket to take out the key.

"Откройте, пожалуйста!"

The pounding sounded a lot louder now that the wooden wall had been moved aside. Don sank to his knees and placed the key in the lock of the sliding door. He rotated it two turns and then slowly got up to wait for what would happen.

Someone immediately pulled the sliding door a bit to the side, and the first patch of light streamed in over Don's face. There was only one person standing outside: a soldier with a sparse beard in a worn grayish green uniform. Alongside the shaft of his boot a German shepherd was prowling around with its ears back. It began to bark immediately, and it didn't obey the soldier's hushing noises. But then came a hard tug on the leash, which choked the dog into panting yips.

"Господин? Sir?"

There was a certain embarrassment in the Russian soldier's questioning manner.

"Well . . . what do you want?" Don blinked.

He was glad that he couldn't see himself, newly awakened up on a freight car in the dawn light.

"Shh . . ." the soldier hushed again.

Then the Russian quickly looked over his shoulder and nodded toward something that seemed to be hidden under the wagon. When Don bent down he caught sight of a narrow wooden box that was sticking out near the closest axle.

"Package for you. Посмотрите. Have a look."

Don didn't really know how he should act, and the only thing he could think of was to ask, "Do you need help?"

The soldier shook his head and adjusted the leather strap of his

Kalashnikov. Then he crouched down and pulled the box out into the light. He heaved it up onto the edge of the car in front of the opening of the Masonite door, where there was just enough room to push it in.

Don stood and watched the spectacle without having any idea what he should say. Finally he managed to mumble a sheepish "Why, thank you."

The Russian nodded but still seemed nervous. He lingered there in the vicinity of the car and rocked a bit on his boots.

"And . . . a little something? Немного денежек?"

After quickly rooting around in his pockets, Don produced a few crumpled bills, which he handed over. The Russian took them and peered up at him with a crooked smile.

"Thank you. Счастливого пути!"

Then the door of the car rolled shut before Don's face in a single, forceful motion, which ended in a noisy good-luck thump from the outside. And it wasn't until the soldier's steps had disappeared off over the gravel and were replaced by the sound of his own breathing that Don began to realize that this delivery had been the soldier's only errand.

With Eva's help he managed to squeeze the wooden box into the lounge. It stood there on the red wall-to-wall carpet like a sealed and ominous mystery.

It was elaborately secured with white plastic bands, and the metal seal on its lid was still unbroken. Don and Eva hesitated for a long time, just standing there and observing the wooden box skeptically at a distance of a few steps.

Finally Don gave a resigned sigh and went to dig a knife out of the drawers of the mahogany cabinet. With it, he cut away the plastic strips so that they fell to the floor in coils, and with a final cut he broke the seal.

He placed the knife under the edge of the lid, cracked it open, and backed away so that Eva would also be able to see what it contained. But all that was visible was protective black plastic, which seemed to be covering something puffy and soft.

Eva moved back as he began to slit open the plastic inch by inch with the tip of the knife. He hesitantly took hold of a flap and ripped away the protective cover, and up poked a fluffy polar jacket made of neon-yellow Gore-Tex.

He found yet another jacket packed down tightly on top of rolled-up winter clothes. He took out long underwear, hats, and gloves and spread them on the floor of the lounge car. There was an ice axe, ice cleats made of stainless steel, and after that a couple of flashlights and a small box of tools. Wrapped tightly in several layers of plastic wrap lay a pale green loaf of dollar bills in shockingly high denominations.

At the very bottom was something that could have been stolen from the chemistry room of a school: a Bunsen burner with a chromium-plate base, an air regulator for fine adjustments of the gas, and a cylinder of propane with a rubber hose fastened to it.

When Don had lifted the Bunsen burner out onto the floor and looked down once again, he caught sight of the envelope that was still lying on the bottom of the wooden box. It contained two expertly falsified Swedish passports and a short letter written in remarkably poor handwriting.

to Don
for successful exploration of the underworld
zayn mit mazel
your Hex, Chana Sarah Titelman

# 3

# 43

# Мурманск

Murmansk. The sixty-eighth parallel. Northwestern Russia, on the coast of the Kola Peninsula, north of the Arctic Circle. A city surrounded by low mountains that were already covered by snow. The great harbor that opened out to the black water of the Arctic Ocean. The wide piers that were only lit here and there in the predawn darkness.

A single trolley bus clattered its way along a dilapidated row of apartment houses, the last remains of Soviet Communism, broken by the facade of a skyscraper. Hotel Russlandia was completely dark in the early morning, until a window on the tenth floor emitted a flickering glow.

The flame illuminated Don Titelman's face; then he lowered the lighter toward the Bunsen burner's hissing gas. At first the flame flickered golden yellow, but then he expertly adjusted the regulator and the burning gas changed to a hotter white.

He lifted up the wire gauze on which Strindberg's star lay resting on top of the ankh, and placed it on the tripod so it was in the very middle of the flame. Then Don took a step back and waited. And after a minute or so came the reaction that he would never truly be able to get used to.

Nils Strindberg's sketches had proven to be largely correct. But they couldn't do justice to the beauty that was appearing here: the star sinking into place in the crossbar of the ankh when the metal fused together, and how the object became transparent so that it looked as though it were made of blown glass.

Then the first star lit up above the ankh, and the sparkling arc of the Little Dipper. The North Star at its apex, which grew into a ball of fire a half inch in diameter. Don thought that the celestial sphere, which Nils Strindberg had drawn as bluish gray, was more like a winter night, frosty and black.

Under this winter night, the shadow of the northern hemisphere would soon be visible, and it always began with the single point of the North Pole. The point expanded into an ice cap out toward the sea and turned into the spiny silhouette of Greenland. The coastline of Svalbard, the fjords of northern Norway, and the creamy yellow tundra of Siberia, which ran over toward the Bering Strait. And just then, when the dome of the hemisphere had finished expanding, the North Star flashed, as it always did, into a ray of light.

It seemed that the tip of the ray was hot, because when it hit the ice outside of Svalbard, there was a sizzling sound. Then it stood still and continued to indicate its position. Don looked down at his open map of the Arctic. Took the red ink pen to draw in another X.

They had been staying at Hotel Russlandia for almost a month now, and each day they had lit the Bunsen burner and done the same experiment. The ray had moved at three-day intervals, just as Nils Strindberg had predicted in his laboratory notes, and Don and Eva had been able to follow its jumping steps on their Arctic map.

Don let the pen move over the grid of the map. Then he placed the tip at the eighty-third parallel, twenty-eight degrees and forty minutes east. The X ended up in the middle of the area just north of Svalbard that was already covered in red ink marks. Through this area, Eva had drawn a line in marker that ran all the way from Murmansk to the North Pole of Earth.

Don looked up from the map and saw the spheres mirrored in the window of the hotel room. He shut off the gas, and the flame went out with a clicking sound. He let the crystal-clear ankh remain on the bed of wire gauze, and there was a clink as the star came loose from the middle of the crossbar.

The star and the ankh were once again white and cold as ice when Don placed them among the tightly packed winter clothes. Then Don wound the rubber hose around the gas cylinder and the Bunsen burner. Stuffed it all down in the backpack together and pulled the straps tight.

He threw a glance at the X he'd just marked on the Arctic map. It would be the last X Don would draw in while they were still in Murmansk. The next time they lit the Bunsen burner they would already be far out over the bottomless water of the Arctic Ocean. When the attorney was finished with her morning shower, they would leave Hotel Russlandia to go aboard.

Don took a few steps up to the window and looked down at the Russian icebreaker. It was sitting there in the harbor like a floating high-rise, under cones of light.

There were two white ellipses on the black hull; they formed the shape of an atom. *Yamal,* as the ship was called, was driven by a nuclear reactor—the only force that was strong enough to break through the pack ice of the Arctic in October.

The body of the ship was painted orange and had cavernous window openings; they ran in long rows along the superstructure of steel. Really, Don thought, he should be relieved that it was finally time to depart. But the only thing he felt was a dull pain in his stomach, which was completely and definitely due to fear. The treacherous sea was out there, ready to swallow him. He thought that it was just waiting to pull the ankh and star down in its ice-cold belly.

A month ago, in the freight car, the attorney's suggestion had sounded hypothetical: hiding up in Murmansk and then maybe trying to go farther north. Far away from all the European police, they would both be able to search for the answer to Nils Strindberg's secret: the opening down into the underworld that they had now heard so much talk about.

Don hadn't really taken her seriously, but then Eva had opened the computer and shown him all the North Pole cruises that left Murmansk regularly. The journey that the attorney had finally managed to book them on was the Early Fall Arctic Cruise offered by Bailey Expeditions.

Hex's dollar bills had been only just enough for the tickets, and after using fake passport numbers, they had received their travel documents via fax. There they could read their new names: Samuel and Anna Goldstein, a middle-aged Swedish Jewish couple. The wife had blond hair and a noticeably blurry passport photograph.

It would take seven days to get up to the ninetieth parallel, but now that autumn had begun, they would be traveling under a polar sky that was always black.

They hadn't figured out how they would get the icebreaker to stop once they had reached the latitude that the position of the ray indicated. But Eva hadn't seemed particularly interested in discussing all the problems; the only thing she had been able to talk about in Murmansk was getting on their way as quickly as possible. Don had tried to point out that the Green Cargo car was still waiting on the slushy tracks of the freight terminal on the outskirts of Murmansk. Maybe his sister could send them off to Southeast Asia or somewhere else that the police couldn't find them and where the climate was considerably warmer. But Eva had just pointed out all the ordeals she'd already had to endure and said that in that case, she would travel up north by herself to search for the answers to the mystery.

When Don heard the shower shut off over in the bathroom, it felt as though the final hourglass had run out. He assumed that the attorney would choose to put on her clothes there in the steam again this time. She had always seemed very careful to hide her body.

And as he stood still in the pitch-black dawn, waiting for Eva to be ready, the only thing Don Titelman could think about was that he never should have traveled to Falun and opened the door to Erik Hall's glass veranda.

# 44

# *Yamal*

It had been one thing to see the nuclear icebreaker from the window up on the tenth floor of Hotel Russlandia. Completely different, Don thought, to crawl along like a puny beetle in the shadow of *Yamal*'s sky-high hull. Way up on the steel-plated prow he could see the grin of a red painted shark mouth, and from inside the vessel came the dull rhythm of Russian marching music.

The harbor stank of rotting seaweed, and the sun still hadn't managed to come up over the gray-black waters of Kola Bay. Murmansk had already begun to descend into the polar darkness that would linger until the end of the six months of winter. It was with an increasing sense of panic that Don stumbled along there in the snowdrifts. The dawn chill had tightened his throat, and with each breath it became more difficult to get air.

The backpack hung like a lump over one of his shoulders, and over the other he carried his bag of antianxiety medications. With each step forward, the edge of the Bunsen burner dug deeper and deeper into his back, and Don could see the glowing red jackets from far away in the misty light that came from the lights of the quay. There were perhaps fifty passengers standing in a group around the baggage carts. When he came closer, Don noticed a sunburned man who seemed to be some sort of guide. The man was carrying a megaphone in his hand, and with the other he continually smoothed his fluffy hair.

"I'm David Bailey," said the man, extending his hand to greet them.

"Samuel Goldstein," Don said, "and this is . . . Anna, my wife. We were the ones who booked our cruise so late."

"Better late than never," Bailey said with a crooked smile. "Besides, you're not the only ones who made a last-minute decision."

Later the guide made sure that Eva and Don each received a red expedition jacket. On the backs and breast pockets was a round logo that said EARLY FALL ARCTIC CRUISE. Bailey opened a binder with plastic pockets that contained name tags for all the passengers. Don received one and pinned it to his jacket: SAMUEL GOLDSTEIN, SWEDEN, CABIN 43.

As they were standing there waiting, Don looked around and noticed that most of the people who were going to be freighted into the dark of the North Pole seemed to be retirees. It sounded as though most of them were Americans, and many of them were wearing baseball caps.

A group of teenagers speaking French and Italian gathered in a circle around their bags with World Wide Fund for Nature logos on them.

Then Don stiffened as he heard the singsong intonation that could only be Swedish. It was coming from a boy with a cell phone, who was now turning in his direction.

They stood there on the edge of the quay for a drawn-out moment, just staring at each other. He looked about sixteen, and he had a knitted cap and a kaffiyeh. He continued his conversation in a quiet voice and just nodded slightly at Don's Swedish name tag. The boy must have missed all the photographs on the newsbills, or else he didn't care.

At exactly 7:00, *Yamal*'s foghorn let out a roaring whistle. When the sound had finally faded away, Bailey shouted into his megaphone that it was now time to board. The retirees began to move in toward the elevators that would lead them to the icebreaker's quarterdeck. Eva took hold of Don's arm, and he hesitantly let himself be dragged along. A member of the crew stopped him brusquely just as he was about to go in. He pointed at the backpack, which apparently had to be placed on the baggage cart. The cart rolled off immediately after Don had bewilderedly handed the backpack over, and Eva asked if he had remembered to take out Strindberg's star and ankh. Don looked at her vacantly, and then he began to wave and shout after the cart, which was being towed away along the harbor pier. But his shouts disappeared in the wind, and it was far too late.

He looked for David Bailey, to find out where his backpack would end up and whether it would be searched, but had to get in line behind another passenger who also seemed to want to keep his luggage.

He could glimpse the lines AGUSTO LYTTON and ARGENTINA on the old man's name tag. He had a few long-haired men with him; they had stern faces and angry eyes. They seemed to follow the South American's every wave, and they were vigilantly guarding the group's baggage. There were several heavy crates, and printed on the metal were yellow warning symbols that said FRAGILE. While the old man argued with David Bailey in a mixture of Spanish and English, Don became more and more taken by how strange he looked.

Lytton's face was like a bare skull, with skin so thin that it could have been painted on and transparent enough to show the triangle of his nasal bone and the cartilage that still formed the contour of a hook nose. The color of his eyes was so pale there in the sockets that at first Don thought it was due to blindness. But once Lytton had gotten what he wanted, he immediately began to indicate where the crates should be placed. The surly men freed themselves from the wet snow and started to carry them, and David Bailey turned to Don with a long, drawn-out sigh. After having assured Don that the backpack was in good hands, the guide led him in toward the elevators that would carry them aboard. There he pushed on a switch box that was hanging loose on cables, and with a clatter they left the safety of Murmansk.

A hundred feet above the swells of the sea, on the quarterdeck of the icebreaker, stood a helicopter. It had drooping rotor blades and was painted in Russian colors: white roof, blue cabin, and an underbelly of flaking red.

When Bailey came out of the elevator, he explained that the helicopter would be used to scout for cracks in the Arctic pack ice to ensure a comfortable journey.

Then the guide raised his megaphone like a flag and took all the retirees in toward *Yamal*'s towering superstructure. Don could see the radar masts and a satellite dish sticking out on the roof, some sixty feet up.

Inside the giant ship, the corridors turned out to be claustrophobically narrow. Bailey pointed out a shabby relaxation area where they would find a sauna and a small pool. A low-ceilinged dining room with plain long tables awaited them farther on. There was also a small bar with a printed plastic sign that displayed the limited Russian menu for the next few weeks.

The control room for the icebreaker's nuclear reactor was on the next deck, and it had out-of-date monitors. After that came airless walkways with cabins, where the passengers' names had been stuck on in stamped tape. Don's door was right across from Eva Strand's.

On the fourth floor, Bailey pointed out the captain's suite, which had wide windows that looked onto the icebreaker's foredeck. Then came a wide staircase up to a tinted glass door that fit tightly in front of *Yamal*'s navigation bridge.

After Bailey knocked a few times, a man who had a bearlike physique and black sunglasses opened up. There were badges on the epaulets of his naval shirt, and his beard was scrubby and gray.

The guide introduced the man as Captain Sergei Nicolayevich. The captain just mumbled something inaudible in reply, but after him came the thin chief engineer of *Yamal,* who gave a mini-lecture about the icebreaker's ten-year tradition of being a charter ship, followed by a short safety demonstration.

In order to lighten the mood, the guide ended by mentioning the small motorboat for zoological expeditions. On previous journeys, they'd seen walruses and polar bears, and perhaps the passengers would have that kind of good luck this time.

Don found his way to his cabin as fast as he could to see where the Russians had put his backpack. On the other side of the door he found a room that smelled musty and didn't seem to have been cleaned.

The light came from two windowpanes and a fluorescent light on the ceiling. He immediately caught sight of his backpack alongside the bolted-down legs of the sofa. He opened it on the plastic floor and dug around for the ankh and the star. Then he felt the objects and could finally let out his breath.

Behind a purple-striped curtain was a small sleeping area. On the bed was a blanket that was the same shade as *Yamal*'s orange hull. There was a sign above the pillow stating that the light inside the cabin couldn't be turned off. But the Russians could offer full-coverage eye masks if the curtain wasn't enough.

Inside the bathroom hung a robe that was embroidered with the text Ямал—*Yamal.* Russian Muzak hummed through the loudspeaker system, and it was like being locked up in a cell.

The air in the cabin was thick as syrup, and Don could feel the walls pressing in. He sat on the sofa and tried to get something calming out of the pockets of his shoulder bag.

But then he caught sight of the map of the Arctic Ocean that lay in front of him on the side table. The icebreaker's route from Murmansk up to the red point of the North Pole was drawn out on it.

As he traced the winding line with his finger, he tried to remember the last X he'd marked on his own Arctic map. He began to suspect that the distance between the icebreaker and the opening at the eighty-third parallel would be far too great.

A shudder went through the floor of the cabin. Don went to the window and realized that *Yamal* had already begun to be hauled out to the open sea.

# 45

# The Seventy-seventh Parallel

Vater was sitting in his electric wheelchair in the management office of the bank building, in front of the panorama window. It was difficult to tell that he was smiling because one side of his face was completely blotchy, burned beyond recognition by an exploding star.

Under the suppurating blisters on his eyebrow was something that looked like a gray stone, while the eye on the uninjured side of his face was alert and black as coal.

It was directed down toward the desk, where there was passport documentation indicating that a Mr. and Mrs. Goldstein had just passed the seventy-seventh parallel on their way to the North Pole. The woman's picture was conspicuously blurry, but the man's face had immediately been identified by the computers' image search. The profile of the nose, the tired eyes, the weak jawline: Don Titelman.

Vater hadn't slept very much during the past few weeks. He had devoted all his strength to searching for the foundation's lost ankh. Because of all his burns, the doctors had said he ought to take it very easy. But he refused to let himself be ruled by anything as frail as his body.

He had avoided cooperating with the European police. Giving them Don Titelman's name would only have caused problems. If they were to arrest the Swede by chance, it would be difficult to regain control, both of Titelman's continued fate and of Strindberg's star and ankh.

Instead, Vater had relied on his usual channels, the military powers that the foundation had helped through the years. This way they had also been able to use some resources that wouldn't have been available to the regular police.

What had finally gotten results was the continual radar monitoring that had been furnished by German intelligence. It had been directed at all vessels that passed the seventy-seventh parallel and then continued to the north.

The passenger lists had been scrutinized carefully, and when in doubt they got out the passport documentation. So now it had become caught in their net—the Russian icebreaker, which, according to the latest information, appeared to be named *Yamal.*

# 46

# The Third Day

He hadn't been able to sleep more than a few hours during the night, despite the small wads of toilet paper he'd stuffed in his ears to avoid hearing all the canned music, which couldn't be turned off. And the walls were so thin that he had been able to hear the South Americans whispering. A few of Lytton's men were staying in the cabin next to his, and their words had been woven into his dreams as a mumbling hiss.

Don pulled the bed curtain aside and went to look out the cabin's window. Through the stripes of dirt he could see that the ship was now approaching the edge of the pack ice. They cruised past broken-off icebergs, which shone in the light from *Yamal*'s spotlights.

He put on his velvet suit and the red expedition jacket and knocked at the attorney's door, but as usual no one opened it. Eva had become withdrawn during the past few days, and he didn't really know how she was spending her time on board. When they spoke, she seemed dejected somehow, but she didn't want to talk about whatever was weighing on her.

Out on the promenade deck, it was very windy, and the polar air cut right through the velvet fabric of his pants. Don pulled up the zipper at his throat and looked out into the darkness toward the infinite wall of pack ice.

The Russians seemed to be looking for a crack where the jets could take hold and blast an opening so the ship could keep bearing north. Over by the railing, an older couple was standing and staring silently off at the mass of ice, and Don could see that they were holding each other's hands tight.

Finally it got so cold that his body began to go numb, and on stiff legs he found his way back into the ship again. He was in the habit of sitting in the drab library that was in a corner on the third deck. And that was what Don did on this long day, too.

Once there, he took out the letter he'd found in Malraux's grave and read once again through its short lines of Norwegian. But who this Olaf was, or what he meant by Niflheim—Don still didn't know.

At lunchtime he sneaked back through the halls. In his cabin he took more Haldol and liquor. Don had just had time to swallow when he heard a knock. As he opened the door for the attorney, the whole ship shook. Then the floor under them suddenly began to vibrate. *Yamal* had just begun to push its way through the wall of ice.

Don had hidden the Bunsen burner under the bed, and now he set it up on the table in front of the sofa. The gas pipe fell over several times before he managed the trick of securing its base.

The attorney lit the flame and then all they could do was glumly establish that the ray still hadn't moved. Don opened the notebook and wrote:

October 4th, 12:20
lat. 83 degrees 50 minutes north
long. 28 degrees 40 minutes east

Eva had brought along a scrap of paper with the ship's most recent coordinates. On the map she drew out its planned route. Using a ruler, she tried to estimate the distance to the opening. Finally she said:

"We're going way too far east. We're going to pass it at a distance of at least fifty nautical miles."

Don repeated her measurement, and he could only nod.

"It's not even one hundred kilometers," Eva said. "How much time could the icebreaker lose? A few hours?"

"No, we'll just have to go up to the command bridge and ask the Russians to change course," Don said.

Eva turned down the flame of the Bunsen burner and it went out.

"Maybe we can wait," she said. "Maybe the ray will have time to change position again, and there's no point in talking to David Bailey and the Russians before we know exactly where the opening is."

"Presumably it won't just end up right in front of the icebreaker," Don said. "So what had you planned to do to convince them?"

But the attorney just shrugged. Then she pulled on her jacket and left his cabin.

As usual, Don sat alone at dinner, picking at his borscht. It was hard to get any beet soup down in the mournful noise as the icebreaker pushed its way through the ice. The retirees were sitting in silence, as were the WWF teenagers. The grating sound lay over the dining room like a dull, grumbling threat.

The only people who could be heard speaking were the South Americans over with Agusto Lytton. Don recognized Moyano and Rivera, the two men who were staying in the cabin next to his. Moyano had a long torso and scarred cheeks. A tattoo wound across Rivera's throat like a long, narrow demon.

Like the other men who surrounded Lytton, they had coal black hair that fell far down onto their backs. Native American looks, with broad cheeks and copper-colored skin. This made the pale old man, in his elegant suit, stand out in a way that was almost comical. But there was no doubt about who directed the conversation at the South Americans' table.

The only thing available to drink, besides water, was Russian Stolichnaya. Don poured another glass of vodka, for his seasickness. After a while he began to feel quite intoxicated and staggered up out of his chair. Despondently he made his way back to his cabin again.

In the narrow room, Don felt infinitely exhausted, and in his drunkenness he heard himself sniffle. He made a vain attempt to hold back his tears, but it was like finding himself in a tunnel with no end.

To calm himself, he took two clonazepam, which he hoped would make everything go dark within a few minutes. But after several hours, he was still awake, and then, late at night, he happened to think that perhaps the ray had changed position by this point. His hand unsteady from the liquor, he managed to get a few sparks out of the lighter, and in an instant the gas transformed into a lick of fire.

He adjusted the regulator and picked up Strindberg's ankh and star. Then he moved the objects into the flame, and above them, the spheres began to appear once more.

As the ray pointed down, Don immediately saw that it had changed position. In the notebook he noted its new location:

October 4th, 11:20 P.M.
lat. 82 degrees, 45 minutes north
long. 31 degrees, 15 minutes east

When he placed the ruler on the map, he realized with a dizzy feeling that the opening was already more than thirty-five miles *behind* the icebreaker. The ray had moved quite far to the south, and they had already passed it.

Don banged on Eva's door, but she didn't open up, even though it was so late. He went to look for her, lurching around, lost in *Yamal*'s steep staircases.

He pushed open the doors onto the quarterdeck and came out by the helicopter. Next to its sloping blades, Don took several deep breaths to try to filter the alcohol out of his body.

The frosty Arctic sea air bit into his lungs and made it nearly impossible to breathe. He stood there coughing, thinking that he was sinking. At the same time, it was far too annoying to just stand there, so close to the opening, without even having made an attempt to get the Russians to change the icebreaker's course.

In the dining room, the South American men were still sitting at their long table, and Don could feel Agusto Lytton following him with his gaze.

David Bailey and *Yamal*'s gray-bearded captain, Sergei Nicolayevich, were standing at the small bar. They turned to Don as he came reeling in their direction.

"Mr. Goldstein," David Bailey said, looking at him with hazy eyes. "You're up late; is something troubling you?"

The Russian captain was drinking vodka from a beer glass.

"Yes, you could say that," Don mumbled.

Then he didn't really know how he should begin. In the silence, the captain poured another glass of vodka, which he thrust over to Don.

"It's like this, Mr. Bailey," Don began, wobbling, "the . . ."

Bailey nodded and waited for him to continue.

"It's like this: the icebreaker has to turn around immediately. I have the new coordinates in my pocket, so you can see . . ."

He dug around in his expedition jacket and found the crumpled paper. He slammed it down on the bar in front of Bailey, and then took a burning gulp from his glass.

"Mr. Goldstein." Bailey smiled. "I think you mostly need to sleep."

"Not at all," Don said. "On the contrary, it's very important that I'm awake right now."

He pointed at the smeared coordinates on the paper. The captain grinned behind his scrubby beard. Don wondered whether Sergei Nicolayevich understood English, but he didn't dare ask. Instead he continued to Bailey:

"We have to turn around immediately, do you understand? It will only delay us by a few hours."

"So what is it that's so terribly interesting right there?" Bailey asked, showing the scrap of paper to the captain with a smile.

"There's . . ."

Don didn't know how he should put it, and he could feel his knees buckling.

"Like I said," said David Bailey, "I think it's best that you go to bed. Tomorrow evening we're going to approach the North Pole, and you want to be well rested then, don't you? It's not unusual for it to be a drain on the nerves when you experience our first meeting with the ice."

"There's a tunnel straight down into the underworld," said Don, "and we're leaving it behind us."

"I'm sure there is," Bailey said soothingly. "But as you know, the captain is the one who determines our course. When you're on board, you're under his command, it's as simple as that."

"We have to turn around . . ."

Bailey moved Don's glass of vodka away.

"Mr. Goldstein, that's enough," said the guide.

Don turned around hesitantly and met Agusto Lytton's eyes. As he staggered away from the bar, he heard the captain shout after him, "Mr. Goldstein! I wish you a good night!"

But when the laughter came, Don was already on his way out through the doors of the dining room. His lungs were aching for cleansing air.

The wind was blowing hard on the quarterdeck; it blew away some of his drunkenness, and Don suddenly realized that he had just given up. He grabbed the railing so hard his knuckles turned white. *A shvartsen sof,* Don thought, so this was the sad end of the journey.

His eyes slowly began to fill with tears, which hardened into frozen streaks against his cheeks, and without any hope whatsoever, Don turned around and looked in toward the light of the ship.

# 47

# Agusto Lytton

With his hands still clenching the railing, Don had to squint to be able to see. The old man behind him was lit up by the powerful lights that ran like a string of pearls along *Yamal*'s ice-covered hull.

Agusto Lytton was not wearing the obligatory expedition jacket but rather something that resembled a fur. And other than that, in the backlighting that prevailed around the edge of the ship, Don could only make out the hook-nosed profile of his face.

"A death without pain, Señor Goldstein," said Agusto Lytton, nodding down toward the wake the icebreaker was plowing up. "The shock of the cold will cause you to lose consciousness in less than thirty seconds, and then it takes an hour for you to sink to rest at a depth of thirteen thousand feet." Don noticed his eyes beginning to adjust to the light, and he tried to get his tongue to form an answer.

"Yet you hesitate?" Lytton continued, taking a step closer. Don got his head to bend in an affirming nod. "You want us to . . . turn around? If I heard correctly there in the dining room? You said that . . ."

Don swayed suddenly, but just as he was about to fall, Lytton caught his arm. Sharp fingertips, a hard grip, which didn't give in to his weight.

When Don finally got control of his legs, he began to fumble through his shoulder bag without really knowing what he wanted to find. No sedative would be able to bring him out of this state of inebriation.

"Do you need help with anything, Señor Goldstein?" asked Lytton, who was still holding on to his arm.

Don tried to get a smile out, but it just turned into a stiff grimace. Because now he had found the chewable tablets of dextroamphetamine, and he took a fistful and tossed them in his mouth. He pressed his teeth together and as though he were chewing cud he began to crush the dry amphetamine derivative, which might make him perk up.

"You're helping yourself, I see," said Lytton. "But it seems as though you're freezing. Perhaps you should warm up for a bit?"

Don made an attempt to pull away from the fingers, but they didn't release their firm grip.

Finally he slouched along, resigned, as Lytton guided him away from the railing. They walked toward the iced-over ladder that ran up to *Yamal*'s upper deck.

"From darkness to light," Don heard Lytton mumble when they had come into the warmth of the ship again.

He could see the double doors of the captain's suite some distance away through the dimly lit corridor. Lytton took a small key from the pocket of his fur coat and stuck it into the lock of the door.

Captain Sergei Nicolayevich was apparently still off with David Bailey in the bar, because the large suite in front of them was dark and quiet. When Lytton turned on the lights, Don saw that the icebreaker was more than just plastic wallpaper and poor cleaning. Before him here was a room that could have belonged to a nineteenth-century admiral.

Wall panels of polished hardwood and furniture with gilded detailing. The floor was covered with a sound-muffling carpet, and the sound of the ice floe breaking under *Yamal* could hardly be heard.

There was a large drink cabinet with doors of crystal, and through the long row of windows that looked onto the foredeck, Don could see the beams of the spotlights playing over the ice.

Where the windows ended, at the far wall, stood an open writing desk, which seemed to be used as a worktable. Piles of papers were spread out on it; manuscripts in old-fashioned binders and an antique-looking magnifying glass. But Don really only had eyes for the inviting leather sofa that stood waiting in the center of the room.

He staggered forward, sank down, and leaned back so that he was half reclining, finally able to rest his legs. He placed his feet up on the low glass table that stood next to the sofa. Then Don moved them a little bit so he wouldn't dirty the large Arctic map that was spread out across the glass of the table.

"Señor Goldstein," Lytton said behind him, "I didn't bring you to my suite for you to lie down and sleep."

There was a clatter from the china, and then there was the gurgling noise of something being poured.

The old man walked around Don's boots and placed the steaming teacup on the table. The scent of poppy and cinnamon made Don think of Eberlein and the library at Villa Lindarne.

He wiggled into a sitting position and looked over toward Lytton, who was now sitting in the easy chair across from Don.

"You need to get something warm in you, Señor Goldstein," Lytton said. "Please, drink."

"You can call me . . . Samuel," said Don.

"Agusto Lytton, Lytton Enterprises."

Don nodded and extended his hand in a hesitant greeting.

"So, Señor Goldstein . . ."

Lytton opened a small silver case. He took out a cigarillo, which he lit with his bony hand.

"The North Pole is a remarkable place, I can guarantee it. Are you nervous that *Yamal* won't manage to cut through all the ice?"

Don took a sip of the tea and felt himself gradually beginning to wake up.

Lytton's contours became sharper and sharper over in the easy chair. Watery, shrunken eyes in a skull covered with paper-thin skin. Don thought that it would take only a slight scratch to lay bare the bone of his forehead. Then he looked down at the narrow lips and the sparse mustache. It bobbed up and down as Lytton began to speak again in his soft voice.

"I asked if you were nervous."

"Not at all," said Don. "It's not that . . ."

He took another warming sip.

"I understand from Captain Nicolayevich that you booked your journey late as well," Lytton said, taking a deep drag of his cigarillo.

"Yes, it was a coincidence, you could say," Don said.

"I understand," said Lytton, "but I don't think you'll come to regret it."

He formed a ring of smoke with his lips.

"Do you know the Russian captain personally?" Don asked.

"Not at all, but I have learned to recognize his needs," said Lytton. "The constant Russian need for money, to be precise. We have made a small business agreement about the suite, the captain and I. I didn't feel at home in the cabin they gave me. My men are also dissatisfied; I don't know how it is with you."

"No, it's . . . a bit tight, perhaps," said Don.

"Yes, isn't it?" said Lytton. "This is much better. Cleaner, too, and the view is, as you can see, quite spectacular."

Don looked out at the Arctic sea and didn't really know what he should say. But it seemed as though Lytton wished to have a nighttime conversation, so he made a lame attempt.

"Lytton Enterprises, you said. That doesn't sound particularly South American."

"No, it's been an international company for many years."

"So what does . . ."

"Import-export, you could say," said Lytton. "Mostly exports, to be honest."

"Exports of what?"

"Oh, it's a dirty branch that you don't want to know about. Believe me, Señor Goldstein."

It hadn't only come from the tea, Don thought. The exhilarated feeling inside of him definitely had traces of dextroamphetamine. The alcohol intoxication had dispersed like a fog, and the old man in the easy chair now appeared absurdly sharp.

Don looked from Lytton down to the glass table and the large map of the Arctic ice cap that was spread out there. The icebreaker's route ran in a red line up toward the North Pole. A silver Russian coin lay at the point of *Yamal*'s current position.

"Only seven degrees of latitude left," said Lytton. "In a few days, we can have a toast at the North Pole, you and I."

"Señor Lytton," Don began carefully, without really knowing why himself. "What would you say about doing me a favor?"

"If it's just a matter of helping you back to your cabin, I can . . ."

"No, it's something that's probably considerably more difficult," said Don.

He looked up at the contours of the skull over there in the easy chair. The remarkable thing was that Lytton's face gave him such a strong sense of déjà vu.

Don shook his head. The ashy tip of the cigarillo glowed as the old man inhaled.

"This . . ." Don pointed at the silver coin. "This is where we are right now."

Lytton sat quietly, waiting.

"And here," Don said, moving his finger an inch or so to the southwest, "is something I think you will find very interesting to see. Something that everyone aboard this icebreaker would find amazing."

"Something that everyone can see can hardly be worth anything,"

Lytton said. But he had moved to the edge of the easy chair, and now he was bending over the map and examining the position where Don had placed his finger.

Then Lytton took out a pen, pushed the fingertip aside, and drew a black X.

"You still want the icebreaker to turn around, I see," said the old man after a while. "It would probably be an expensive affair, if it's even possible, and you would likely need a very good reason."

"There's a hole," Don began.

Lytton laughed.

"There's a hole? A huge hole in the ice, you mean? Well, that sounds sensational."

"I thought maybe you could help me with David Bailey . . ."

Lytton coughed, irritated, and blew out a cloud of smoke.

"You truly understand nothing, Señor Goldstein. Talk to *el americano,* the guide? Do you really think he has any say in this? If the course were to be changed, it would be handled by the Russians, but I can promise you that in that case it would be a very costly affair."

"You are sitting in the captain's suite, after all," Don tried. "Perhaps you can . . ."

"You want me to help you. Pay and get the icebreaker to turn around, so you can investigate something you say is a hole? Is it deep, Samuel Goldstein? Deep enough to contain something surprising?"

Then Lytton laughed again.

"You are funny, Señor Goldstein. And besides, what does your wife say about this?"

The piercing eyes were buried deep in his face.

"My . . . wife?" Don said. "You could say that all of this is her idea."

"Really?" said Lytton, sounding a bit more interested. "So what are the two of you willing to bet on it, in that case?"

The old man rapped his knuckles against the X on the map. Then he sat there in silence, as though he were waiting for Don's decision.

"I would probably have to discuss that with her, I guess," Don mumbled. He got up from the sofa, and although he hadn't really had time to consider, he heard himself add, "Maybe we can show you something that really is amazing, Señor Lytton. Something you have never seen before."

Lytton looked searchingly up at Don from the map.

"I have lived for a very long time, I can tell you, so I rather doubt that."

Don could feel the dextroamphetamine making him smile; he turned around one last time and said, "Just give me half an hour, Señor Lytton. I'll come back soon."

"I'm more worried about how you will find your way back to your cabin, but in any case I wish you good luck."

Lytton took a drag of the cigarillo and raised his hand in farewell. Then his eyes returned to the Arctic map and locked onto the position that Don had pointed out just a moment ago.

# 48

# Eva Strand

The dextroamphetamine had carried Don down the steep stairs to Eva Strand's cabin with light steps. Outside the door he glanced at his watch and saw that it was long past midnight. Hesitated for a second, and then he knocked.

The door was opened so quickly that he got the feeling the attorney had been standing there waiting in the dark. Maybe she had been out on some errand too, because she already had her coat on.

Don saw Eva look questioningly at the Bunsen burner, which he was holding in his hand, and he cleared his throat and said, "I think maybe I've found someone who can solve our problem."

If he'd been expecting a long discussion, he had been mistaken. Just a few minutes later, they were out in the polar night, on their way back to Agusto Lytton's lounge.

Don could feel Eva wind her way under his arm to seek shelter from the severe cold. The wind caused the icicles on the railing to break off and fall down into the dark furrow that *Yamal* was plowing in the chalk white ice. Above them, the radar masts shook in the wind as the ship continued to force its way on to the north.

Agusto Lytton had remained awake and left the doors to the captain's suite ajar. When Don cautiously pushed them open, the old man was still hunched over the Arctic map on the glass table, lost in thought.

Lytton realized that they were standing there in the doorway, and in the thin corners of his mouth, a smile began to take shape.

"So you are Señora Goldstein?"

Lytton had stood up, and he waved at them to come in.

Don noticed that the top buttons of his silk shirt were unbuttoned now, and through the yellowed skin he could glimpse the bones of the man's rib cage.

"Or do I dare call you Anna?" asked Lytton.

Eva Strand looked a bit strained as she greeted him. But the South American had already taken his eyes from her and was looking instead at the Bunsen burner and the plastic bag dangling at its side in Don's hand.

"What is it you've brought with you?" Lytton asked. "Equipment for some kind of scientific experiment?"

Don didn't really know what to say, so he just nodded slightly. Then he walked to the middle of the lounge with the Bunsen burner, which he placed on the glass table.

The star and the ankh clinked as he took them out of the bag, and then he began to assemble the gas cylinder's hose.

"You know that it's forbidden to even smoke aboard the icebreaker," said Lytton. "If one follows the captain's orders."

The old man sat down in the easy chair and observed Don's movements while he lit yet another cigarillo.

When the rubber hose was firmly attached to the valve on the burner, Don turned up the gas. Then the flame sparked to life, and he adjusted it to glowing white.

"I promised you something you've never seen before," Don said, looking at Lytton.

"And I'm still doubtful," said Lytton, taking another drag.

Don laid the ankh and star on the tripod's wire gauze and then placed it above the flame from the burner. He could make out the South American's face through the spheres that were slowly beginning to take shape.

When the North Star flashed to life, he heard a gasp from Lytton. Don moved closer so he could see the position that the ray pointed to on the white Arctic ice.

"You seem to have measured correctly," said Lytton, when he had compared it to the black X on the map.

He picked up a compass to measure the distance from the X to the silver coin that marked the ship.

"To get there, *Yamal* must immediately turn onto a southwesterly course. We have already gone ten or twenty miles past it."

As the flame went out and the spheres faded away, Lytton looked up at Don and said, "But I must ask you, Señor Goldstein . . . do you really know what it is the ray is pointing at?"

Don felt his mouth becoming increasingly dry. This speedy resolve was not something he'd counted on. Inside of him, the exhilaration slowly trickled away.

"It's supposed to be some sort of opening into the underworld," he said hesitantly.

"The important thing," Eva said, "is whether you can help us get the icebreaker to turn south and take us there."

"Getting the Russians to turn *Yamal*," Lytton said, "is probably just a question of money. But of course we must also get the ship to wait at an adequate distance in order to investigate whatever is down in the opening in peace and quiet."

Lytton leaned over the map.

"I can probably convince Sergei Nicolayevich. The icebreaker will have to stay a few nautical miles away, here . . ." Lytton pointed down at a dot that he'd already drawn on the map, just beyond the black X. "Then we'll take the helicopter and fly out to investigate whatever it is that's out there in the ice. It will have to take as long as it takes; the North Pole can wait."

The Bunsen burner was still standing on the glass table, and the objects had fallen apart on the wire gauze of the tripod. Out of pure instinct, Don wanted only to pack up all the equipment and leave Lytton and the captain's lounge. But it was already too late, for now the old man reached out and picked up the ankh in his hand.

"It's so light," Lytton said, letting his fingers glide across the inscriptions on the ankh, "and strangely enough, completely cold."

"It's probably best to . . ." Don began, but he was interrupted by Lytton:

"Do you know what? I think I would like to see the experiment once more. That star ray was truly beautiful, and maybe we could determine where it's pointing even better if we try once more."

Don got up from the sofa to start disassembling the Bunsen burner. Lytton grabbed his hand and said, "I really insist, Señor Goldstein. I can light it myself, if you don't want to."

Then he moved the tip of his cigarillo toward the opening of the gas pipe. Adjusted the regulator, and soon the white flame was burning again.

Don stood there, at a loss, and watched Eva help get the ankh and the star in place. The attorney didn't seem particularly concerned about Lytton's snap decision.

He turned his back to them and walked away a bit to try to figure out what was actually going on. Through the row of windows in the captain's suite, Don could see the spotlights shining against the heavily falling snow.

After he'd stood there for a while listening to the dull sound of the ice breaking under the ship, he looked back at the glass table where the spheres had now begun to appear once more.

Lytton and Eva didn't seem particularly interested in what he was doing, so Don continued toward the open writing desk that stood against the far wall of the lounge.

He began to fumble through the piles of paper, but Lytton must have had excellent hearing, because from behind him Don could hear the South American say, "Don't touch anything there, please, Señor Goldstein."

Don lifted something that looked like a blueprint. He threw a glance over his shoulder to see if Lytton would react, but at this point the old man was looking intently at the searching light of the North Star.

Lytton Enterprises seemed to have broad business interests, Don thought as he paged further through the papers on the writing desk. Chemical formulas and physical calculations were mixed in with financial cost-estimate sheets and texts of an almost New Age nature. After a blueprint with a technical description of an MRI scanner, his attention was caught by a picture from an awards ceremony. There was a German name that he couldn't help but recognize:

"Fritz Haber . . . ?" Don mumbled.

*"¿Disculpe?"* Lytton said, without taking his eyes from the spheres. "Excuse me, what did you say?"

"I see here that your company, Lytton Enterprises, has given a 'Scholarship of Fritz Haber' to a Luis Flores?"

"Every year, for many years, Señor Goldstein. Luis Flores is a very gifted young chemist. We are happy to be able to help him."

"Is this scholarship named for the famous Fritz Haber?"

"For the winner of the Nobel Prize, yes. Haber was actually one of the founders of Lytton Enterprises, you could say. Why?"

"You mean Fritz Haber? The researcher who received the Nobel Prize for the Haber process?"

"Yes, it was a completely groundbreaking way to create ammonia. A very receptive chemist, Fritz Haber," said Lytton, who was now looking over at Don.

But Don was back in Ypres and the war museum, at the display case about chemical warfare.

"You *are* aware that Fritz Haber's wife committed suicide after the gas attack at Gravenstafel? She couldn't stand knowing that her husband had not only invented the gas used in the war, but also insisted upon being there at the front to open the spigots himself. She shot herself in the heart when she found out what Fritz Haber had done. He set off that same morning for the eastern front to supervise fresh attacks against the Russians. That time, the Germans used a type of nerve gas that no one had seen before."

Don looked at Lytton.

"It was Fritz Haber's research that led to the Nazis' favorite gas, Zyklon B."

"Zyklon B was created to get rid of insects," said Lytton in a measured tone. "It was never meant to be used against people. Besides, Fritz Haber has presumably saved more lives than anyone."

"You think so?" Don muttered, continuing to page through the piles of paper on the writing desk.

"Well, you see," Lytton said, "the Haber process made the industrial production of ammonia possible, as well as cheap fertilizers for agriculture. Without that fertilizer, a third of the world's population would starve to death. Stopping Haber's research would have made all these lives impossible. Would that have been a more humane choice, Señor Goldstein?"

Lytton turned his back toward the Bunsen burner, drawn by the fizzling sound of the ray. And Don didn't answer, because now he had caught sight of a different black-and-white photograph.

At first he had paged past it, because it looked like the cover of an advertising brochure. But there was something about that picture that . . .

The gas flame was turned down and shut off.

"An experience. *Muchas gracias,* Señora Goldstein. I'll help you pack up."

Lytton stopped talking. There was a clatter as Eva began to disassemble the Bunsen burner. Don realized that he only had a few short seconds.

It was difficult to really make out the faces in the grainy picture, but one of the men there was definitely Agusto Lytton. As the South American must have looked in his prime, before all the softness melted away from his cheekbones.

Next to Lytton in the picture were three people dressed in black, and in the row below them sat several more men and a young woman in a white blouse whose knees were turned modestly to the side.

LYTTON ENTERPRISE—BOARD OF DIRECTORS—BUENOS AIRES
1936

Don began to count from 1936. Judging by his face, Lytton must have been at least fifty years old when this picture was taken. If that were the case, now Lytton would have to be . . .

Don counted again, thinking that he must have read wrong.

He turned the brochure over. On the back the names were listed in the order in which they sat:

K. Fleischer—F. Haber—J. Jansen—M. Trujillo
N. Weiß—J. Maier—E. Jansen

Fleischer, Haber . . . *J. Jansen*?

Don quickly turned back to the cover again. He met Agusto Lytton's stern gaze from the middle of the back row. Lytton? Jansen? Had he changed his name?

And hadn't there been another Jansen?

Front row, third from the left. Yes, *E. Jansen*.

The young woman, pale hair, but he would need a magnifying glass in order to really be able to see . . . Hadn't Lytton had a magnifying glass? There it was—quickly, now, third from the left, the slanting legs, the face, the cold eyes, and she really did look remarkably similar. E. Jansen—*Eva Jansen?*

*Eva . . .*

Don felt a warm breath on the back of his neck. The attorney had moved so silently that he hadn't heard a thing.

"I married into the name Strand two years after that photograph," Eva whispered. "A Swedish man. He died in 1961."

Don didn't turn around. Suddenly he was back in the interrogation room in Falun. He remembered that the attorney from Afzelius had reminded him of someone as she sat there in the clicking fluorescent light. And now he knew who it was Eva had reminded him of: the pictures in the evening papers of the dead man as he was carried out, the long hair that framed the face like a halo. Eva Strand resembled the man in the mine with the gash on his forehead. The man who, according to the letter in Malraux's grave, had been named Olaf . . .

*Olaf Jansen?*

# 49

# Jansen

Outside, the snow had begun to fall heavily, and the wind whipped the cloud of white flakes against the windows of the captain's suite. Sweeping clouds of whirling white covered the windowpanes, and the lounge became unmoored from all its ties to space and time. When Don tried to look out, all he saw was himself, reflected in the pale glass. How he was standing there with his back bent over the piles of paper on the writing desk, the attorney's hazy figure behind him.

He avoided meeting Eva's eyes as he walked back to the table and the Bunsen burner. He sank down into the sofa in front of Agusto Lytton's empty easy chair.

The old man had prepared himself to go, and he was standing over by the doors out to the hall of the icebreaker with his fur over his shoulders. Then Don saw that Eva got Lytton to stop, and soon he heard a whispered conversation in Spanish. For a while he tried to hear what the conversation was about, but soon he zoned out, resigned.

He leaned his head against the cushions of the sofa, and in his memory, he returned to the pictures from the evening papers.

Olaf Jansen's lifeless face was once again staring up at him from the stretcher at the opening of the mine shaft. Don wondered how he could have avoided noticing what now seemed so obvious. The arch of the temples, the cheekbones, the same chin . . . all these features that connected Olaf with Eva Strand. But the man in the mine had died in 1918, of course, and belonged to another time.

When Don looked up at the dim ceiling light of the suite again, he could hear that the whispering by the doors had stopped. Instead there was a clattering noise from the large drink cabinet. A few steps.

"I think you might need this, Don."

He took the glass of vodka from Eva's hand.

"Drink, now."

Don swallowed a few sips and laid his head back against the pillows again, and he studied the attorney from below. Now all he could see, in her face, was everything that reminded him of the dead man.

"So . . . Olaf Jansen. He must have been your . . . grandfather? Right?"

Eva looked at him for a long time, and then she said tonelessly, "No, Don. Olaf Jansen, he was my only brother."

"But . . . how . . . ?"

Then the black-and-white photograph came flickering back. The blond woman sitting there with her modestly turned knees. In his memory, Don could see the caption shining up at him:

LYTTON ENTERPRISES—BOARD OF DIRECTORS—BUENOS AIRES
1936

"The last time I saw Olaf, I was only eleven years old," Eva said.

"So you've met him?" said Don. "But didn't he commit suicide down in the mine almost a hundred years ago?"

Eva nodded, and the corners of her mouth tightened. Don felt the nausea wash over him. He could no longer think clearly.

There was a creak from the easy chair as Agusto Lytton came and sat down. Then he sighed in Eva's direction.

"*Su amigo tiene quince minutos.* Your friend can have fifteen minutes, no more. Then we must wake up the men and set the operation in motion. We're already delayed, you know that."

"The operation . . . ?" Don began, but Lytton interrupted:

"There's quite a bit you're wondering about, I imagine, Señor Titelman."

The old man opened his silver case and took out another cigarillo. Tapped its tip against the glass table.

"I have promised my daughter I will give you fifteen minutes as a thank-you for all you've done. But as far as I'm concerned, even shorter than that would be best."

"Your daughter?" said Don. "Eva?"

Agusto Lytton lit his cigarillo and nodded slightly. Don looked at Eva, then back at the old man, and felt himself sagging.

"Well, Señor Titelman?" said Lytton, after blowing another smoke ring.

In the silence, Don could hear Eva sitting down at his side. She took his arm and helped him sit up on the sofa again. Lytton drummed his fingers impatiently on the arm of the easy chair.

"Eva, what is the point in . . ."

A glance from her caused the old man to become silent. Then she helped Don take another few drops of vodka from his glass.

"So you . . ." Don tried.

Didn't really know where he should start.

"So you're Jansen? That Norwegian who once stole Strindberg's star and ankh? Andrée's murderer?"

Lytton stared without giving an answer.

"Father?" Eva's urging voice.

"Yes, yes," Lytton sighed. "Yes, it's true, Señor Titelman. Once I was called Jansen. But in time, that name became . . . how should I put it . . . ? A burden. I had to make a complete break from my past in order to keep my business going."

"So why did you choose the name Lytton?"

The old man rolled his eyes.

"Señor Titelman, I urge you to think of the time. With every minute we are farther away from the opening that Strindberg's ray has indicated."

Don set his glass down on the table and fixed his eyes on it. He felt that he somehow had to find at least one point of focus.

"So in other words, you're Olaf's . . . So you claim to be the father of that dead man in the mine? The one who died in 1918?"

"Yes, but when it comes to my son I would prefer not to . . . That is a different matter, and I don't know whether . . ."

Lytton looked at Eva, but she didn't let him escape.

"Olaf, well . . ." Lytton began hesitantly. "I truly loved that boy. But it . . ."

His voice constricted unexpectedly. Lytton himself looked surprised.

"You promised," Eva said harshly.

The old man took another drag from the cigarillo. Blinked in a cloud of yellow-gray smoke. Sat in silence for a minute, as though he were trying to collect himself.

"My Olaf . . ." Lytton tried again, in a whisper. "He was born at the end of the seventies. By the time he was a teenager, he had learned to handle the harpoon better than my father and me. We were whalers, three generations back. Can you understand what it feels like to work out at sea, along with your own son?"

Lytton's eyes closed. His voice began to grow steady again.

"We had our ships at Lofoten and Svalbard. A modest little firm, and the business had just barely paid for itself. When my father died in the fall of ninety-five, there was almost no money left. The boy was only seventeen, so . . ."

"Ninety-five?" Don interrupted. "You're talking about 1895?"

"Yes, yes, of course, 1895!" Lytton said, irritated.

"All these lies," Don said, trying to gather the strength to get up.

"Señor Titelman?"

"You're trying to get me to believe that you are well over one hundred fifty years old. I don't understand why, but . . ."

Eva's voice: "Just listen to what Father has to say, Don."

"And you, Eva, that would make you about a hundred, right? I beg your pardon, but . . ." Don stood up, swaying. "It doesn't seem particularly credible," he said.

Eva took hold of his arm.

"In the twenties, Father's chemists developed a method of slowing down the aging process. But it has proven to have a price, particularly for women. For me. The telomeres in DNA have bonds that . . ."

"As far as I'm concerned, we can just let this be," Lytton interrupted. "What is the point of digging up old sorrows?"

Don bent back down to the table and picked up his empty vodka glass. Then he walked over to the drink cabinet and poured more. He took a few sips, and finally the temptation became too great to resist.

"In that case, Lytton, or Jansen, or whatever I should call you, I would really like to know what happened to Nils Strindberg, Knut Frænkel, and Engineer Andrée."

The crash from a huge ice floe being crushed out in the darkness. Lytton looked questioningly at Eva, and after another sigh came the beginning of an answer.

"I was the one who convinced the boy that we should follow them when the Swedes' balloon took off. It was about money; nothing has ever been about anything other than that."

Don leaned against the drink cabinet. The vibrations from *Yamal*'s hull trembled up through his legs.

"We were not financially well-off, as I said," Lytton continued. "Not just us; that went for everyone on Svalbard at that time. And of course Andrée and his Swedes, with their German marks, needed all the help they could get. We took care of some of their shipments back and forth from Danskøya. My boy, Olaf, got to be close friends with Knut Frænkel during those weeks. *Admired* him, Señor Titelman. You know how boys can be. A few days before the expedition took off, Olaf heard the secret of the ankh and the star in confidence. The ray that pointed out . . . well, you know about all of that. When he told me about it, I immediately realized that the secret could be worth incomprehensible amounts of money. Even though the boy didn't want to, I forced him to come along when we followed the balloon across the sea. It was Olaf and me and several of my closest men."

Don was still holding the bottle of smooth Russian vodka. *Es macht nisht oys*, what did that matter? He unsteadily poured another glass. Took it with him back to the sofa and sank down.

"So was it you yourself or your son who murdered Engineer Andrée and Strindberg?"

"Murdered?" Lytton sneered. "You should really watch what you say."

"Murdered, shot, executed? Which one fits best?"

Lytton threw a furious glance at Eva.

"Eva, *mí hija*, must I really . . . ?"

She nodded, and Don could hear that Lytton's breathing was choked. After a glance at the clock, though, the South American chose to continue.

"Andrée's hot air balloon was much faster than our steam-powered ship, of course, but we knew the winds and could predict which direction it would go. By the time the balloon came in over the pack ice it had already lost speed. We reached the ruined gondola on skis, barely twenty-four hours after the Swedes had taken off. From there we followed Andrée, Strindberg, and Frænkel's tracks all the way to the opening of the tunnel."

"And there . . . ?" Don asked.

"There . . . well, when we arrived it was completely empty—only the desolate ice, and in it there was a circular, gaping hole."

"It was empty?"

"Well, maybe not exactly empty," Lytton said, puffing on his cigarillo. "The Swedes had put up their tent before they went down into the tunnel itself, of course. Our plan was to find the ankh and star in their packs and then leave quickly. But when the Swedes suddenly returned . . . everything became so chaotic. Andrée was the first who realized what we were up to, and behind him came Strindberg and Frænkel. There was a snowstorm, just like tonight, and I don't think even Andrée could see our faces through the storm. We tried to shout to the Swedes that we only wanted the ankh, but Andrée had already taken his rifle off. Then—it was so strange, because he suddenly grabbed his throat, and then he just collapsed. We never heard a shot, because it was so horribly windy. But when I turned around, Olaf was throwing down his rifle. The boy had happened to shoot Andrée in the throat—an accidental shot, Señor Titelman. He had only wanted to show them that we had weapons too, nothing more than that."

Don rubbed the crystal edge of the vodka glass. Once again he saw Eberlein's black negative, in the library at Villa Lindarne. The falling snow, Andrée's figure at the sharp-edged mouth of the hole.

"An accidental shot, you say. Does that go for Knut Frænkel and Nils Strindberg, too?"

Lytton squirmed, troubled.

"Yes, of course you know about Frænkel's injuries, too. Well, Frænkel . . ."

"Father," Eva said sternly.

Lytton looked away.

"I shot Knut Frænkel, Señor Titelman. I shot Knut Frænkel in the back when he and Nils Strindberg tried to run away."

"In the back," Don said skeptically. "Strindberg wrote that Frænkel was bleeding from the stomach."

"The bullet went right through his body. In his back, out through Frænkel's belly."

Lytton leaned forward and placed the cigarillo in the ashtray on the glass table to go out on its own.

"But Nils Strindberg was stubborn. He managed to drag Frænkel all the way up to that crack in the ice. They must have managed to slide down along its walls, because we saw them moving in the dark, a hundred feet down. Olaf was crying and screaming that we should help them. But Frænkel was already a lost cause, and Strindberg would have reported us as soon as he got back to Svalbard. We would all have been hanged if I had let it happen."

"So you just let them slowly freeze to death down there instead," said Don.

He looked over at Eva, but her face was rigid, her eyes fastened on her hands in her lap.

"So what happened after you killed the Swedes?"

"Well, then . . ." Lytton mumbled. "Then we went down into the opening, and down there . . ."

The old man closed his eyes.

"Down there was a world that was impossible for us to understand. We were simple Norwegian sailors, Señor Titelman. It was . . . it was incomprehensible. But we did manage to figure out enough to realize that Strindberg's star and ankh functioned as some sort of key to the underworld. And to see what that key was worth, we contacted the expedition's German financiers through a proxy . . ."

Don was transported back to the SS hall in Wewelsburg, where he heard Eberlein's words once again. The Norwegians' demands to the foundation that they receive payment to open the tunnel down to the underworld.

"Not just *open,*" Lytton snorted. "Is that what the foundation wanted you to think? Maybe that's how it was at first, but later the collaboration between us and the Germans became equal. And our own researchers were at least as successful as the foundation's at turning dim visions into new chemical compounds and useful military technology. Just the advances that Fritz Haber made . . ."

Don felt the nausea roll over him as he thought of the gas displays in Ypres, Camille Malraux, *Tué à l'ennemi.* Once again he saw, in the Frenchman's dried mouth, the star that Olaf had placed there.

"If you were so successful," Don muttered, "then why did your own son hide the star in a grave?"

Before Lytton could answer, Eva whispered:

"My brother never forgave Father for murdering the Swedes. The fact that Father shot Frænkel in the back and let Strindberg die is the only reason we're sitting here today."

"Olaf never forgave anyone for anything," Lytton hissed. "Above all, he never forgave himself for accidentally shooting at Engineer Andrée. For a long time, we thought he would regain his reason and come to his senses. That he would help us to make use of everything we had found down there. But the boy didn't want to have anything to do with the opening; he seemed to believe that it was a limbo before hell itself. As soon as we got back to Svalbard, he left and severed all contact."

"Niflheim," Don whispered.

Lytton grinned.

"We never let him disappear completely. Olaf was still my son, after all. He was allowed to live his life, discreetly monitored, so he didn't start to spread rumors about the foundation's and our secret. After a while he got back on his feet, and he became a teacher of Old Norse at the Sorbonne in Paris. Because he seemed completely uninterested in our business, we gradually reduced our monitoring. So we never heard anything about any Camille Malraux, or that Olaf had become so upset when he learned who manufactured the gas that was released over the trenches in Ypres."

The old man stuck out the grayish black tip of his tongue and moistened his lips. Then he continued, fumblingly.

"It was at the end of the war . . . he showed up in the middle of January 1917 at our base at Spitsbergen."

"Olaf?"

Lytton nodded.

"He wanted to join the business again, he said. And you see, Señor Titelman, that was just what I had been waiting for all those years. After our successes in the war, everything looked so bright. The business had just kept growing, and we dared to do more and more. Our researchers had found hints about the mystery of aging down there in the depths: the double helix of nucleic acids that are the basis of modern science's primitive theories of DNA. But instead of helping us advance science, Olaf stole Strindberg's star and ankh. The boy must have planned it carefully, because in his flat in Paris he had left enough clues to drive us all mad."

Lytton got up from his easy chair and walked over to the writing desk, which was reflected in snow-covered windows. There he paged through the piles of paper until he found what he was looking for. Leaning forward, he read:

I know a hall that stands far from the sun
On the shore of the dead. The doors face north.
Drops of venom fall in through the smoke-hole.
This hall is braided with the backs of snakes.

Perjurers and outlawed murderers
Must wade through heavy streams there.

The memory of the front page of an evening paper that was nearly black. Erik Hall's pixelated photograph of straggling lines of chalk on a wall far down in a mine shaft.

"Niflheim," Don said again.

The old man turned to him.

"Yes, isn't it strange? You look through all the literature in the world, all the myths of the world, but forget your own. Niflheim, the realm of Hel, the portal to the Nordic hell of cold. The thing was . . ."

Lytton looked out at the long row of windows. The snowstorm raged, the winds of the Arctic sea tore and howled.

"The thing was that Olaf left us one last challenge. He knew that we would search through his flat in Paris. There, among the piles of documents and maps, was a sort of will, a final mystery addressed to his own father. There he wrote that he had given the ankh and the star two different graves so that they would always be separated. And if I wanted to look for these tools of the devil, then I could search for them at one of the many gates of hell, where they would lie until the end of time."

"The many gates of hell," Don mumbled. "Did he give any directions?"

"Diabolically enough, Señor Titelman, you could say that he actually did. In his flat there were notes about Etruscan necropolises, the Mato cave in Brazil, Rama in India, the entrance under Mount Epomeo on the island of Ischia outside Naples, a well in Varanasi, the Great Pyramid of Giza, Cueva de los Tayos in Ecuador, the passages under Mount Shasta in California . . . Yes, he gave us endless alternatives where we could hunt for the opening of a tunnel down to hell. But not a single word about Niflheim, Falun, or a French second lieutenant by the name of Camille Malraux. And we searched, Señor Titelman. God knows we have dug, detonated, and drilled without ever having found the right gate."

"The star in the mouth of his beloved in a grave at Saint Charles de Potyze," Don said. "The cross in his own hand at the gates of hell in a mine shaft outside of Falun."

"He must have relied on sources that placed the entrance to Niflheim right there. He was precise, Olaf was."

Don closed his eyes. He scanned through the headlines in the newspapers, the prints on the awl that came from the dead man's own fingers. One question left: "So why did Olaf take his own life?"

Lytton just shook his head, but Eva said quietly, "I think he was looking for a place to be alone with his torment over his beloved. Someplace far from the sun, where outlawed murderers like himself wade in the rivers of the dead without any hope."

"Yes, who knows what happened down there," Lytton said curtly. Don sank back against the sofa cushions.

"So when you heard about the discovery in the Swedish mine, you sent your daughter Eva there?"

"Yes, she speaks perfect Swedish and knows the country because she lived with a Swedish attorney in the middle of the century."

"My husband had to die childless," Eva said quietly.

"But by the time she got there, Erik Hall had already been murdered, and the ankh was gone, so she . . ."

"I heard on the radio that a perpetrator had been apprehended, and I assumed that person came from the foundation," Eva said. "In order to investigate what had happened more closely, I presented myself as an attorney. After that, I just had to remember the correct legal phrases."

She tried to smile but didn't get a reaction from Don. Instead he asked Lytton, "That was your idea, Murmansk and the icebreaker?"

"The easiest way to get to the Arctic without attracting attention," Lytton said. "I would have been happy to pay for your cruise ticket, but from what Eva's told me, your sister got to take care of that expense. And now . . ."

Lytton left the window and walked back to the glass table, where he had thrown off his fur coat earlier. After he'd wrapped it over his shoulders again, he turned to Don with one last smile.

"You've had twenty minutes, Señor Titelman. And now, if you'll excuse me, we must end this."

Lytton picked the ankh and the star up off the table and was just about to let them slide into his pocket when Don grabbed his arm. The old man laughed.

"I don't think that hold will be enough . . ."

"You forgot a war," said Don. "If you were all so capable of making use of the discovery of the underworld—what happened once you had lost the ankh and the star?"

Lytton made an attempt to wrench himself loose.

"It was only a matter of survival, Señor Titelman. Only that."

"You took over the collaboration with the Nazis once the foundation had left them, didn't you? In Wewelsburg, Eberlein said that their business transactions with Hitler stopped before the war."

"Like I said, Señor Titelman. It was only a matter of survival."

"Your Fritz Haber gave the Nazis Zyklon B. What else did you manage to make for them? The V-2 rockets? The jet motor?"

Lytton wrenched himself loose with a hiss.

"They didn't want to listen to us! That was the problem. Their never-ending race hatred and the Jewish question. They should have realized that we had come much further than the foundation when it came to controlling the power of the atom."

Don looked at him skeptically.

"The Nazis never had any atomic weapons. Maybe a test program, but nothing advanced."

"No, that's what I'm saying," Lytton snorted. "They were completely obsessed. They didn't believe the theories, because there were so many Jewish researchers who were working on nuclear physics. The Nazis wanted to create their own 'German physics' that would be completely Aryan. It didn't matter what we said; our top man, Heisenberg, was harassed by the SS and couldn't get any funding for his work. When we finally got them to build a nuclear reactor and start up small-scale production of enriched uranium and heavy water, it was far too late. The war had already been lost."

"So that was why you established Lytton Enterprises in Argentina? To avoid being extradited after the war?"

"Señor Titelman . . . we established ourselves in Argentina when we broke away from the foundation in 1917. It was a way to go underground. Lytton Enterprises was created as a front, a livestock company, and neither the foundation nor the Allies knew where the Nazis had received their help. Even if they perhaps suspected. But now . . ."

Lytton placed the ankh and the star in the pocket of his fur coat.

"Now a completely different era awaits us. This time we aren't just going down into the underworld to try to decipher vague whispers. We are going to open the gate to another world."

Don looked up at the old man's deep eye sockets with mistrust. Then Lytton turned his face away from him and disappeared toward the doors of the captain's suite.

There was a rattling noise as the lock turned twice from the outside.

# 50

# Under the Surface

Just over seven hundred nautical miles north of the North Cape, the German Navy's submarine had finally caught up with the icebreaker. It had switched from diesel motors over to vibrationless atomic-hydrogen power and then continued to glide forth, sixty-five feet under the hull of *Yamal,* like a silent shadow.

Down in the submarine, Elena could hear the jets above them cutting through the sheet of Arctic ice and the ship breaking its way forward with heavy propeller blades.

Although they weren't giving out any radar signal, the crew had advised the foundation's men not to take any risks at all. It was impossible to know with any certainty what sort of measuring instruments a Russian atomic icebreaker might have on board.

The filtered air and the excess pressure had given Elena a constant headache. She lay in one of the narrow hammocks that stretched like coffins along the concave wall of the mess.

In the other compartments lay the commandos that the German security service had helped Vater pick out. The primary requirement had been combat experience in Arctic conditions. Beyond that they had judged the men's ability to remain silent about what they might see.

Elena could feel the cabin tilting as the X-rudder balanced the direction of their journey. Then she turned her head and looked down at Vater and Eberlein, who were whispering to each other over the map table in the middle of the cabin.

They had flown up to the northernmost tip of Scandinavia in a jet plane in order to meet the submarine at the naval base outside of Tromsø. They'd had to hurry, because the icebreaker was fast approaching the area that the spheres indicated. But now, twenty-four hours later, Vater seemed to have begun to doubt that Titelman and Eva Strand were really on board.

From what he was hissing at Eberlein, Elena understood that they were about to pass the eighty-fourth parallel and the icebreaker still hadn't changed course. And there was nothing to suggest that it was slowing down. Above them, *Yamal* kept on breaking the ice at the same sluggish pace.

Silently, she listened to the increasingly heated discussion. But Elena didn't say anything, because she no longer wished to offer Vater clues and answers.

The hand that had so magically healed her after the explosion had also stirred up other things inside her. Looking at Vater still evoked revulsion, but her fear was no longer as intense. It was as though the bonds that forced her were coming loose, as though that hand had brought to life everything that had been slumbering inside her for so long. Her senses were becoming sharp again, and soon they would be as sensitive as a six-year-old child's.

Vater seemed to suspect something, because she wasn't allowed to move freely on the submarine, even though it was only 184 feet long and filled with men in uniform. Maybe he thought she would attempt to sink it as a belated act of revenge.

But he didn't need to worry about that. On the inside, Elena was roaming in entirely different places.

Her mother's gentle voice pulled her along all the time, guiding her through the bright rooms that had once been her home. There she listened, like a child, to her sisters' laughter and voices. There were no troubles there; she was completely safe. Elena knew for certain that the ankh was up on the icebreaker. Because now, when she closed her eyes, she could see its silhouette so clearly before her. It floated about two hundred feet above them, at the top of a ladder, and the person who was carrying the ankh and the star was a very old man. For the past few hours, she had followed the experiments with the flame of the Bunsen burner, and Elena already knew the final position of the ray.

When she closed her eyes like this and listened, her mother's voice was so close. All the whispers she had heard from the ankh earlier had now run together into one. It had been speaking to her ever since they had begun to approach the icebreaker. And Elena wanted so badly to let herself be swept away, to disappear off into space and time. In her aching head, the tone of the voice was starting to change. It sounded increasingly urgent, as though it were searching for some sort of reaction. Time and again she heard its now so familiar words:

"*Devi portarcela,* Elena, bring it to us. *Questo deve finire,* this has to end."

But Elena didn't know what she was expected to answer.

"*Devi portarcela,* Elena," the voice interrupted.

Her mother's eyes were sad.

"*Deve finire,* this must end."

And for the first time, Elena heard herself mumble:

"*Ti sento,* I hear you. *Ti sento, madre.*"

The wave that came flowing from the ankh, through the hull of the icebreaker and the freezing water, was so warm that she immediately lost her breath.

# 51

# Changing Course

Maybe it was the howling wind or the perpetual scraping of the ice floe, but something was making it hard for guide David Bailey to get any rest. He wondered how long he'd been lying there, tossing and turning in his bed, and he started to fumble with one hand across the cabin's nightstand.

Even before he pulled off his eye mask, he had managed to get hold of his small black PDA. He woke it up to see what time it was, but as he realized that it was nearly three o'clock, there was something else on the glowing green screen that caught his eye.

There must be something wrong with the location of the satellite, Bailey thought, and he shook his hand, but the digital GPS numbers refused to change. For a little while the guide just lay there, staring suspiciously, but finally he conceded to himself that the icebreaker really had changed course.

It had made a half turn on its own axis, and instead of heading for the North Pole, *Yamal* was breaking through the ice and going straight south.

When Bailey had managed to get up the staircase and reach the navigation bridge, he discovered that its tinted glass doors were locked. He hesitated for a second, but then he knocked.

The Russian sailor who opened them didn't look particularly impressed by the guide's little GPS. Instead he pointed grimly at the captain and the chief engineer, who were standing in the cold blue glow of the control console.

It was nearly impossible to make out the foredeck of the icebreaker through the window in front of them, even though all the spotlights were shining into the whirling clouds of the snowstorm.

The captain didn't even look up when Bailey stood right next to him. The line of the radar circled around below his bearded face.

"Captain Sergei Nicolayevich," David Bailey said, "why have we turned? Is there something the passengers ought to know?"

The captain turned to him, inscrutable, his lips sealed. Bailey could see his own face reflected in the black sunglasses, and then he heard the chief engineer's thin voice.

"The journey to the North Pole is going to be somewhat delayed because of a snowstorm and a few other factors. We're going to stay in one place for a few days in a position about fifty nautical miles to the southwest."

"Stay in one place?" David Bailey panted. "South? But the contract . . ."

"Our highest priority, as I'm sure you understand, is the safety of everyone on board."

When the chief engineer had stopped speaking and the captain didn't give any further explanation, Bailey began to look around the room with all its blinking instruments.

Among the Russian uniform coats he glimpsed a gaunt face. He immediately recognized the stubborn old man who had wanted to carry his luggage aboard himself.

Several of Lytton's long-haired men were standing alongside him with glaring eyes. David Bailey tried to produce something that looked like his usual, self-confident smile, and he extended a hand in greeting.

But Lytton kept standing there with his arms crossed, and he was the one who spoke first.

"Señor Bailey, I was just planning to come and wake you. You must immediately take a message to all your passengers. There are a few new rules on this ship, and it's important to be aware of them."

"Oh," said David Bailey, confused, "but it's nearly four o'clock. I assume everyone is sleeping, and . . ."

"Señor Bailey, I'm not asking you. You don't even need to think, just contribute your reassuring voice."

Bailey had time to see on their name tags that it was Moyano and Rivera who were lifting him by the arms. The South Americans carried him a bit above the floor over to the console, where there was a microphone with a flexible shaft.

Lytton pulled it down in front of the guide's mouth and placed his index finger on the speaker button.

"This is what you will say, and I think it will be best for you to keep to the text."

A handwritten paper that contained only a few short phrases was placed on the table in front of Bailey.

"They have to hand in all electronic equipment?" the guide stammered. "Telephones and cameras? But surely that isn't necessary."

He looked beseechingly over at Nicolayevich, but the captain's face was still expressionless.

Then Agusto Lytton pressed the button and from the PA system came static that turned to a tinny whistling. David Bailey coughed, cleared his throat, and looked down at the first syllables on the paper. Then he began to read in an unsteady voice.

⁎

Eva had begun to wonder whether Don Titelman had fallen asleep, because she couldn't see his eyes where he was half lying on the sofa.

The captain's suite had been uncannily silent for an hour or so, in the rhythm of the icebreaker's motion.

Don hadn't asked her any questions after Lytton's long story. He had just turned away in silence. She could hardly imagine what he thought about what he'd heard, but that he was skeptical—that, she assumed.

Yet it was true, everything he'd been told. Even if the years seemed to blend together now, she and her father had lived far too long. The injections during her teen years had left scars and pain, but just as with Lytton, they had fulfilled their intended purpose.

They had slowed the genetic countdown that is built into each person. The biological clock, which is set at birth to run out at a given time. Ninety years after the first trials, her cells were still successfully copying themselves without the slightest defect or mutation.

Her skin may have become slightly thinner, and she had some joint and skeletal problems. Otherwise, Eva's body was completely preserved, just like her brother's in the mine. It was almost ironic that this underworld opening had, in such different ways, placed both siblings outside the course of time.

Sterility was the price she'd had to pay, but no one could have guessed at the time that it would be a consequence. Her father had always told her that this gift had been so incomprehensible that she could never repay it, and in that way he had kept her under his control.

Sometimes Eva wondered whether she'd even existed, because if you exist you must surely have the ability to make your own decisions, right? Certainly she'd had her own life in Stockholm for a few decades around the war, along with a husband, before she had returned to her father and her life in his shadow.

The only thing they actually shared was the loss of Olaf—Lytton had never really been able to get over that grief. Yet she still didn't know what her father had mourned the most: the loss of his son or of Strindberg's white star and ankh.

Once, at the beginning of the century, he had taken her along down into the opening. Eva had been about ten years old, and she remembered it as a journey to hell. The sound down there had never left her, but she couldn't remember any mystical visions.

She had never returned, nor had she become involved with the military research. She ended up as a silent assistant, taking care of the practical details of her father's life. Of those who had gone down into the underworld with him, she was the only one who was still alive, the only one who knew where all of Lytton's knowledge came from.

As far as she knew, her father's research had gone into a more experimental phase during the past few years. It seemed as though he now hoped to be able to make contact with the other side, which he'd been keeping at bay for so long via the injections.

Lytton considered the men he had brought along on the icebreaker to have enough mental strength to be able to open the portal down in the underworld. The goal was total knowledge, to get past all hints and intimations. To reach the clarity for which he had been searching for so long. She had followed her father's instructions and traveled to Falun, where she met this Don Titelman. He had reminded her so much of the brother she'd lost that she had thought it couldn't be a coincidence.

During their journey together, Eva had become increasingly uncertain of what she actually wished to achieve by recovering both of Strindberg's objects. She didn't know anymore whether it was about helping her father or whether she actually wanted to obliterate his underworld.

She still couldn't say for certain, sitting there next to Don on the sofa. The only thing she knew was that she very much wanted to protect him from the unavoidable end of the journey. She straightened his velvet jacket, and then she just sat there listening to the sound of his slow breathing.

When Don felt her touching him, he thought that he should try to catch her hand. Demand answers to all the questions that he hadn't had time to ask yet.

For being over one hundred years old, Eva had a remarkably agile mind, and she must have had astounding luck playing the attorney. But as they said: *A mentsh on mazel iz vi a toyter mentsh.* A person who isn't lucky might as well be dead.

Then Don couldn't help but smile as he thought of all the meanderings that had come between the interrogation room in Falun and the captain's suite. In his memory, they would always wander through Ypres and Saint Charles de Potyze, and he could already feel a sense of loss, even though Eva was sitting only a few feet away.

He looked up and tried to find a way to ask the first question, but at that very moment it became inconceivably quiet. Then the glasses over in the drink cabinet shook, and with a sucking tug the icebreaker *Yamal* began to slow down.

# 52

# The Opening

Out in the snowstorm and the wind, the blades of the helicopter had just begun to turn. Don tried to cover his ears to protect himself from the roaring noise of the machine. But it was difficult because Moyano kept yanking him by the arm as he dragged him along toward the helipad on the ship's quarterdeck.

Alongside them, Eva pressed her way forward through the wind. She had shoved her hands into the pockets of her jacket, and in the spotlight her eyes appeared to be red-rimmed. She hadn't bothered to cover her head, and the gray strands of hair were hardly visible under the growing layer of snow.

Agusto Lytton hadn't bothered to come fetch them from the captain's suite himself. The old man was already standing by the open door of the helicopter's cabin, where his shouts were drowned out by the choppy roar of the rotor blades.

Then Lytton waved at his men to load the last steel chest. Don recognized his cabin neighbor Rivera, who was currently grabbing the front handle and heaving the heavy box into the helicopter's freight area.

A small metal staircase had been folded out from the cabin. Its lowest step had disappeared in four inches of snow. The old man gave Don one last shove up toward the greenish yellow light of the cabin door.

Eva sat close beside Don and huddled up to shield herself from the cold. The interior of the helicopter was stripped down, and large roses of ice were growing across the glass. She blew into her hands and stamped her feet on the floor. One by one, the South Americans took their places, their breath like clouds of frozen smoke.

Finally only Agusto Lytton was standing out in the storm. But suddenly he too came up the metal stairs, which then were reeled in. The old man knocked on the window of the cockpit and gave the pilot a bony thumbs-up.

With its rotors whipping at maximum speed, the helicopter gave a lurch and then began to lift unsteadily from the deck. The wind caught them about thirty feet above the helipad and threw the machine sideways. They could hear the metal crates sliding and scraping down in the freight area. Eva tumbled toward Don, and he could feel himself bite his tongue so hard his mouth filled with the taste of blood.

At the last second, the South American pilot managed to correct the angle, and they soared up until they were level with the ship's radar masts. Then came a sudden slip backward, out over the path of sea that the keel had broken free from the Arctic ice.

Down there in the spotlight, Don caught sight of something that made him catch his breath. A spool-shaped, shining fuselage that was breaking its way up through the black surge of the waves. But the farther they got from the icebreaker, the more certain Don was that it must have been a reflection of light, an optical illusion that just showed how tired he was. For a few minutes, they could still see *Yamal* from the helicopter, like a distant star, far off in the darkness. Soon even that glow went out, and they continued in blackness and heavily falling snow.

Lytton's men sat in their red expedition jackets in the glow of the emergency lighting. The noise in the cabin was so loud that they couldn't speak to one another.

Don let his eyes slide across the row of Native American faces and gleaming eyes. Moyano, who was sitting directly across from him, had a firm grip on the magazine of an automatic weapon. Next to Moyano sat Rivera, fingering something that looked like a rubber mask, a full-coverage hood with openings for the nose and mouth.

Eva's eyes were shut tight, and the thin skin above the bridge of her nose was creased. The only person who seemed to be completely unconcerned about the situation was Agusto Lytton, who sat looking at the ankh and the star.

Don let his eyes stop there, because by now the lurching had caused him to feel quite motion sick. Strindberg's objects seemed to be the only fixed point in the helicopter.

But as the minutes passed, it was as though the ankh began to change. Its metal became increasingly transparent, and soon it glowed with a shimmering light.

When the glow passed into the star, the two objects began to fuse together again. The reaction that Don had seen so many times when the gas flame burned hot enough.

In the next instant, it was as though an air pocket had opened under the helicopter. Don could feel a sinking in his stomach as they fell down toward the expanse of ice.

He pulled his shoulder bag close and looked at Eva in the darkness. But the light was too poor for him to make out the expression on her face.

*

Nothing could have prepared Don for what awaited them once the helicopter had landed. Yet he had seen the exact same sight in Eberlein's glass-encased negatives.

Lytton's men had brought him up to an enormous abyss that had opened in the ice, like a chasm, straight down into the underworld. Its edges were totally smooth, as though they had been cut with a flame. The vertical opening of the tunnel was so wide that it was impossible to see its other side.

The helicopter had landed about a hundred yards away, and dragged tracks led through the snow toward the opening. The South Americans had fetched their metal crates and lined them up on the edge of the abyss.

Don pulled his jacket tighter around himself as a shield against the howling wind. Then he saw Rivera and Moyano taking hold of one of the boxes and dangling it over the edge of the hole. When the metal touched the inner wall of the tunnel, they let go of the handles, and in an instant the box had disappeared downward.

"*Éste es el final.* We've reached our final destination," Agusto Lytton shouted through the storm. "I'm sorry to say this, but for you, Señor Goldstein, the long journey will end right here."

Lytton waved at Moyano, who had to lower his huge body so he could hear the instructions. Don could see the pockmarked face contort into an expression of disappointment.

"You'll have to stay up here and keep watch with Moyano," Lytton shouted. "I hope you both find some way to occupy the time." Then the old man pulled Eva up to the opening. They took a big step over the edge, as though the abyss didn't exist, and when Don looked again neither Lytton nor Eva was there.

He could hear some nervous voices among the South American men. But they soon followed, falling one after another down into the gaping emptiness.

Don and Moyano stood there alone, in the clouds of whirling snow.

*

After more than an hour had passed, Moyano seemed to have grown tired of his task. The South American had begun to move around the opening, leaving Don sitting by himself.

And as Don sat there, looking down into the chasm, he could think only of Nils Strindberg. That this was what he, Andrée, and Frænkel had seen on that July day in 1897.

The inner walls of the tunnel shimmered blue and purple, and glistening strings ran down toward the underworld. Its walls held tight, with no cracks, defying the tremendous pressure of the billions of tons of water in the ocean. A tentacle that stretched down to the bottom through mile after mile of freezing sea. Don couldn't understand how someone could manage such a fall, and yet Lytton and Eva . . .

His thoughts were interrupted by crunching footsteps.

It was Moyano, who had completed yet another circle in the roaring wind. Don looked up at the South American, who was now also leaning over the tunnel.

"*¿Es un milagro, no?* It's a miracle, isn't it?" Moyano whispered.

Don felt himself nod. Then he plodded through the snow on his knees, to get a better look at all the glittering light.

Moyano took off one of his gloves and crouched down beside Don. Then the South American felt along the inner edge of the tunnel with his fingers.

Suddenly his hand was stuck, as though the wall was made of glue. Moyano yanked and tugged, and there was a smacking sound as he finally managed to pull himself loose.

"Try it yourself," he whispered to Don, who now also hesitantly extended his hand toward the edge.

In the next instant his glove had been sucked down into the depths of the tunnel.

The walls were flowing somehow, like a quickly melting glass surface.

Beside him, Moyano had taken another step forward and was balancing unsteadily on the very edge of the opening. There was something about the figure at the abyss, Don thought, that felt threatening. He got up so that he wouldn't be caught in the South American's fumbling grasp.

Moyano lifted one boot at the prospect of one last step out into the nothingness. He held his arms out from his long torso, which was swaying in the gusts of wind.

Just when it seemed as though he was going to make a decision, the South American clapped his hand to the side of his throat.

At first it looked as though he had succeeded in crushing some sort of insect, but then the blood spurted out between his fingers and in cascades across ice and snow like a red shower. For a few seconds Moyano managed to remain standing, but then his legs gave way over the mouth of the tunnel, and he fell.

Don turned toward the darkness, with his face straight into the wind. It was nearly impossible to keep his eyes open in the heavy snow, and he couldn't put together what little he could make out.

Had the ice out there become *alive* somehow? It moved toward him like a billowing wave of grayish white. The whole block of snow came rolling, towering up like ghosts and spirits. It came rushing toward him in fluttering whitish gray camouflage.

That was all Don saw before he was thrown down onto the ice. He lay there with a body on top of him, feeling his mouth fill with snow. An elbow against the back of his neck pressed the rest of the air out of his lungs. He desperately managed to twist a little bit and take a few short breaths.

Don lay there gasping and saw a pair of studded wheelchair wheels slowly rolling up.

"Don Titelman," said a familiar voice from above the wheels. "I must say, you are really starting to be a pain."

Finally the elbow moved, and Don could roll onto his back and look up, blinking. Through the snowfall he saw Vater's face, which was half burned off.

"You were in a real hurry to leave us last time, in Wewelsburg. But I never gave up hope that we would meet again."

His one eye dead; the other alert and sharp.

"Pick him up," said Vater.

Don felt his arms being clasped and the soldiers lifting him until he was standing. His boots slid in the snow as he tried to shake himself loose. Eberlein stood at Vater's side in a camouflage uniform and nonreflective glasses. Behind him, the Toad was approaching with waddling steps.

"So close to the solution of the mystery, and yet you still haven't gotten to see anything," said Vater. "Elena?"

One of the soldiers detached from the row: a small figure that approached Don with fluid movements. When she took off her hood, Don saw the woman's smoky eyes, which he recognized from the north tower at Wewelsburg.

"Yes, Vater?" said Elena.

"We'll take Titelman down with us," said Vater. "This will be a fitting end for him."

Don saw one arm being placed in a handcuff.

"And you'll be responsible for him down there, Elena," said Vater.

She extended her wrist and Vater put a cuff on it, locking her to Don.

With his thin back sticking up out of the electric wheelchair, Vater rolled up to the edge. He looked down at the shimmering blue opening. Then he said, "From now on, no more talking."

Elena moved her boot toward the inner wall of the tunnel and nodded at Don to do the same. When she put her weight down there was a slurping sound, and her heel was immediately stuck.

It looked as though a hand had caught her and was now trying to drag her down. The green eyes looked up at him. "*Venga,* Signor Don. Come."

Don hesitantly took off his aviator glasses and heard the wall encircle his own boot. Then Elena yanked on the handcuff, and in the next instant they had both tumbled down.

# 53

# The Black Sun

The wall of the tunnel sucked him downward with a speed that only increased. The sticky grip that had caught Don's boot like flypaper had also pasted itself onto his back. But even though he was hanging there like an insect, unable to move, he was presumably traveling faster than if he had been freefalling into the depths of the underworld.

The rush of air pressed so hard against Don's face that he was forced to look upward in order to be able to see at all. His hair stuck out from his head like a broom from the resistance of the air, and his velvet suit flapped and strained, as though it was going to be ripped to pieces. The snowstorm had become a shrinking white point during the first few seconds of his fall. Now it was long since gone, and yet the tunnel hadn't gone dark or dim.

Shimmering lights pulsed from the blue-violet walls like stars in the night sky. Hanging above him were all the camouflage-clad figures that were tumbling down along with Don.

The one he could see best was Vater, who dangled, stuck in his wheelchair, only about thirty feet higher up. Alongside Vater he could see Eberlein, who looked like a butterfly nailed to the wall of the tunnel, and something that resembled a white cue ball: the familiar shape of the Toad.

Don had always thought of hell as something that was eternally burning, but strangely enough, it became colder the farther down they went. He managed to turn his head toward Elena in the strong wind, and he saw that her eyes were closed but her mouth was moving, as though she were in some sort of trance.

Don wondered whether he should try to wake her, but her face seemed so peaceful that he chose to let her be. Instead he hugged the bag tighter, and he, too, closed his eyes. Then he continued to fall without worrying about looking.

He kept his eyes closed for so long that in the end it felt as though his eyelids had grown rigid. He could hardly move his mouth, his cheeks, his forehead, frozen by all the biting winds.

But suddenly in the rushing sound Don sensed a slight change of tone. The fall had finally begun to slow down. The pull of the wind subsided into a quiet murmur, and soon he was falling as slowly as a feather down toward the bottom, which lay hidden in a gray cloud of mist.

"They're waiting for us," said Elena.

There was a haze that surrounded them, and the cold was razor sharp. Don grimaced to try to get his face out of its frozen paralysis.

As quickly as the wall had glued itself to him, it let him go just as gently now. Don felt himself floating the last few yards to the bottom, where his boots sank into a deep layer of dust.

Elena had also landed, and the chain of the handcuffs jangled as she pulled him closer. He didn't know why, but something made him grope for her hand, which seemed to be the only warm point in their landing spot.

A path that was arched like the ceiling of a Gothic church ran through the fog in front of them. Its walls radiated the same blue-violet light as the tunnel, but they undulated in a completely different way, like lightweight fabric moving in the wind. But the air down here was still, humid, and raw.

Behind him, the soldiers were gathering with their automatic weapons and their night-vision goggles. Eberlein had bent down at Vater's side, and the two of them were conversing quietly.

The electric wheelchair had sunk so far down into the dust that its wheels were no longer visible, and then Don was dragged along by the handcuff as Elena began to move through the mist toward the nearest wall of the vaulted path.

His boots plowed up clouds of dust, and he had trouble keeping his balance as he was yanked along. When they approached the billowing surface, Don saw that it was made of a strangely free-flowing material. In place of the glasslike walls of the tunnel, the vaulted path was composed of flowing dust, which fell in rippling streams. This cloven waterfall of ash seemed to be the only thing standing between him and the crushing weight of the masses of stone.

Don hesitantly stretched out his fingers to feel it, and his hand sank into the wall up to the elbow with no resistance. There didn't seem to be anything behind it, just clouds of flakes and granules that fell slowly over his hand.

And as he stood there looking in at all the stars of light that sparkled in the violet-blue cascade, he began to wonder what he really knew about the cold hell of the myths.

The two Old Norse words *nifl* and *heim* literally meant "the mist-shrouded world." A place where dusk was always falling, without night ever coming. According to the Icelandic sagas, a bitter cold would prevail here, filled with poisonous vapors and venom. The Inuit believed that it would lie far below the Arctic Ocean, in a place called Adlivun. It was Hades, the Greek realm of shadows, and his own grandmother would have said . . .

"Sheol," Don mumbled. *"Geyen in Sheol."*

But Elena didn't see hell when she touched the rippling wall. Ever since she had fallen from the edge of the hole, she had been comforted by her mother's whispering voice.

Now, standing there, she was seized with the impulse to take a step forward and walk into the falling dust. Far behind the points of light she thought she saw the contours of faces that were urging her in with their eyes.

She saw mouths, mumbling words she couldn't hear. It was as though they wanted something from her, as though there was something that only she could give.

Elena put her hand in, and in the rain of millions of violet-blue specks, she thought it was starting to become remarkably transparent. A yellowish red aura formed within her skin, where muscles and tendons ran like luminous tracks. She cupped her hand and carefully brought some of the material out.

At first, it lay dead in her hand, like a lifeless grayish black powder. Then the sparks began to wake up, and her face was gradually illuminated with their light.

Elena thought of Wewelsburg and of the dust that the foundation had managed to salvage in sealed glass capsules. The material she'd had to start from, to dream up visions of the ultimate foundations of physics and chemistry. Now the sparks were talking to her again, showing her strings of molecules and patterns of atomic bonds. But she didn't intend to try to produce any sketches of what the basic design of the world looked like.

Instead she held the granules up to Don and showed him their beautiful glittering surface. But the Swede just looked scared—his eyes were like dashes behind the foggy lenses of his aviator glasses. Don and Elena plodded side by side, some distance behind the snow-white figures. The soldiers in their camouflage uniforms glided forward along the walls like sharp contours of light.

Vater was sailing in his electric wheelchair at the very front, his hairless head bobbing like a single lantern. There was a soft buzz as the wheels plowed ahead.

Don could see Eberlein and the Toad just behind Vater's long, narrow back. Sometimes the nonreflective glasses were aimed back, as though it was important for Don in particular to experience what was hiding down here. After a long silence, there was a distant rumble, which came rolling toward them through the passage. The noise grew louder and louder the farther in they came, and soon it crashed against them in booming blows. When Don sneaked a look at Elena he saw that the white smoke from her mouth came in rhythmic exhalations. At the same time, his own breathing felt increasingly panting and weak.

Vater's wheelchair braked, and farther on one of the soldiers had raised his hand in a signal to stop. There was another boom, and its rumbling echo vibrated through Don's chest and back.

Once again he sought Elena's warmth as they stood there in the mists of the underworld. She gripped his fingers, and they looked out over the gigantic hall into which the passage opened.

Elena didn't know what she should think about this place, which had been described to her so many times. It had seemed like a palace in a fairy tale, a magical source of wisdom and understanding.

But now, as the mist dissipated, she realized that Vater's words had not been true. They hadn't come to a place of light and reason; they were standing before a mausoleum that welcomed only those who were already dead.

The space before them was so large that it wasn't possible to see where its walls ended, and when Elena leaned her head back, it was like looking up at a starry sky with small pinpricks of light. Slender pillars stretched up toward the ceiling, completely filling the cave, like an endless forest of branchless trees.

Elena was just about to take a step forward when she felt a firm grip around her wrist. It clamped down and spun her around, where she was met by Vater's one-eyed gaze.

"This labyrinth is far too large for you, Elena," said Vater. "You had better follow my tracks."

Then he pushed the lever forward and his electric wheelchair began to roll once again. With a hum it made tire tracks through the sea of dust, down toward the outer edge of the pillars. The white-clad soldiers followed in a crouch, as though they were expecting some form of resistance. Alongside Eberlein walked the Toad, who disappeared among the columns with carefully waddling steps.

Don's head swam as he realized that all contact with reality had been interrupted. He searched for the rush of nitrazepam inside himself, to make it easier to accept that he found himself inside a hallucination.

Elena jerked him along with her tugs on the handcuff, and he came stumbling along behind her. He could not for the life of him understand why the Germans would drag him down into the underworld.

The pillars they waded past were very narrow and stood like glittering blue torches in the darkness. Don wondered how these thin stalks could bear the unimaginable weight of the rock.

The air was stale and murky down here. It bore the scent of stuffy closets and mothballs, and suddenly he was back in the 1950s house with Bubbe. He saw the glass table he'd lain under, when she had talked him into sharing her prison of fear. That was a prison he would never get out of, he thought, no matter where the Germans were leading him now.

What had she wanted from him, anyway, whispering those gruesome stories? He had been only eight years old, and surely she couldn't have expected him to heal her pain.

Yet he had given her all he had to offer: the boundless worship and love of a child.

He remembered the daydreams he had had during those long summers. He had dreamed about reaching into the mechanics of the world itself. How he, Don, by some magical fluke, would be able to turn back the tides of time.

As soon as he had discovered how this could be done, he had promised himself to take his grandmother by the hand. Then, together, they would have traveled to some place of existence long before the terror of Ravensbrück.

And in these memories of gloom, Don came to question what he himself had been to his grandmother. Then, all of a sudden, he knew that the dreadful answer was that she probably hadn't cared about him at all.

Elena, who was walking there beside him, had also begun to let her thoughts wander. She was guided forward through the cavity by her mother's comforting voice. It whispered about warm sunlight that fell on a balcony in the southern suburbs of Naples. It promised that she would finally be able to come home.

This was not a peaceful place, Elena thought; she sensed shadows around it. Not even the foundation's researchers had been able to say what kind of hall this was. She wanted to believe that she found herself in an intersection of time, where the wall between this world and the next was infinitely weak.

But Elena's thoughts were interrupted as Vater slowed down among the pillars. She saw him start to whisper with the officer who had led the soldiers here.

The officer unslung his automatic weapon from his shoulder and placed it in Vater's hands. With the weapon, Vater pointed toward a clearing about a hundred yards away. Then he gestured to indicate that the soldiers should start spreading out. There was a buzz as the electric wheelchair resumed its journey.

With a feeling of pure resignation and gloom, Don had finally submitted to his surroundings: the dust with its sparks and the glittering columns that towered toward the distant ceiling of the cave. The mists of Niflheim that wound around him with all their raw moisture and cold. But as they approached the clearing beyond the pillars, his heart began to beat so quickly that nothing in his bag would be able to get it to calm down.

The thing that was standing there in the mist resembled a stone ship: rough-hewn blocks of stone that formed a circle. But it was the object in the center of the circle that made Don's body buckle forward with the vomit reflex he'd been trying to control all his life.

Hanging in the center of the stone circle was a giant floating black sun, and from its round disc extended twelve hook-shaped rays. It was *die schwarze Sonne* that rose there above the tiny particles, weightless between the blocks of stone, and it defied gravity.

Elena recognized the black sun too. It was the portal to something completely different, *etwas ganz anderes,* and the strongest visions occurred next to it. It was the antenna that brought whispers from another world. But now that Elena saw it in front of her in real life for the first time, it wasn't the black disc with its spokes that caught her attention.

Instead she looked at the long-haired men who were in the process of assembling a device in the shape of a giant metal frame. It consisted of six seats, linked together by thin tubes, and in front of one of the seats stood a man whose facial skin was so thin that she could make out the yellowish bone of his skull.

Don squinted at the South Americans to avoid looking at the floating black sun. Lytton's men had now begun to pull on rubber hoods, with openings for their noses and mouths. Otherwise, the hoods were full coverage, and they clung to the men's heads. Then the rubber hoods began to shimmer through the darkness, in time with the electrical energy of the men's brain waves.

Rivera attached a tube to the socket at his temple. It coiled over to the next seat, and then up to the next South American. After all six of them had connected themselves to the chairs' cables, they sat there in their metal frame like a series-connected human machine.

Agusto Lytton signaled to Rivera, as though to let the procedure begin. In the roar of the underworld, the tubes began to pulse with a greenish glow.

Don turned to Elena, but she didn't seem to understand either.

Vater was screwing a sight onto the top of his automatic weapon, and the German soldiers had begun to take cover behind the stone blocks. Without a sound, they sank down onto their knees in the deep drifts of dust.

Don began to search for Eva, but the only people in the circle between the blocks of stone were Agusto Lytton and his six interconnected men.

The black sun had begun to change in front of their glowing skulls. Its disc had become soft, like clay, a clay that began to move around and around in a sluggish rotation.

As it spun faster and faster, the sun began to resemble a black vortex. Hovering in front of the men in the metal frame, it looked as if it wanted to suck up the last traces of light. In addition, the rays of the sun wheel seemed to be growing longer and longer. One of them almost reached the woman who had once called herself attorney Eva Strand.

She must have been hiding behind the disc of the sun, but now she was wading toward Lytton. In her hand she held the object that had brought Don so far away from Lund.

Strindberg's ankh was still transparent, and it shone against Eva's red jacket, but Lytton seemed uninterested in his daughter. His eyes didn't want to leave the black sun of the underworld.

When Eva had walked past her father, she continued away from the South American men. She came to a halt so she was standing right between the metal frame and the Germans.

The soldiers had their sights on her from behind the stone blocks, but they seemed to be waiting for a signal from Vater. He directed his one eye toward Eva and observed her as she bent down toward the surface of the dust.

She scooped up a handful and inspected the gray-black powder. Then Don saw Eva's aged face light up as the sparks came to life. She lifted her eyes straight at him and nodded and smiled slightly at Don. She didn't seem at all surprised to find him there.

Behind her, he saw the sucking vortex and the South Americans' shimmering heads. Around her lay the gray sea, the piles of lifeless powder. Eva moved her lips, as though she were trying to say something to him, but her words were drowned out by yet another drawn-out, booming roar.

After the roar had passed into silence, there was a tug on Don's handcuff. He turned around and saw that Elena was also looking at Eva Strand now.

Behind Elena, Vater was adjusting his automatic weapon, and when the red dot flashed to life, Don realized that he had attached a laser sight. The other Germans were doing the same as they crouched behind the blocks of stone. The threads of the laser sights' lights were soon visible in the misty air.

Don turned to Eva again, and he couldn't understand why she still hadn't moved. She must have figured out what was going on, of course, but she was still standing there without warning the others.

The tubes between the glowing skulls pulsed faster and faster, and the vortex that had formed in the middle of the sun was now bulging inward like a ravenous hole.

It was like a maelstrom, a spiral that sucked everything toward it, and when Don looked at it, he felt his body becoming heavier and heavier. He thought that it was about to pull everything that made up his heart and soul out of him, that what made him *him* was on its way into the whirling depths of the sun.

Elena had also begun to feel the intense force of gravity, but for her, the worst part wasn't the increasing heaviness. It was that her mother's voice had disappeared, drowned out by the ominous roar of the maelstrom.

Then she discovered that Vater's laser had begun to move, and that its beam of light was slowly swinging toward Eva Strand. Elena tried to get her mouth to form a warning, but she couldn't find her voice in all the growing chaos.

The beam stopped in a red dot on the attorney's pale forehead. It was motionless, like a caste mark, for a final, drawn-out second.

Don never heard the shot. The only thing he saw was that Eva collapsed like a marionette whose strings had suddenly been cut.

Don barely got the scream that rose within him out of his lips. He tore at the chain of the handcuffs and dragged Elena out from the block of stone, away toward the attorney's horizontal body.

Over by the black sun, Lytton had finally discovered what was happening, and now he threw himself behind the shield of the metal frame. The tubes stopped glowing with a hissing sound. One after another, the South Americans tumbled off their seats and dropped to shelter behind Lytton's construction.

Don sank to his knees and carefully lifted Eva's head with one hand. With the fingers of his other hand, he tried to stop the blood that flowed out of the hole in the back of her head where the bullet had forced its way out.

There was a coin-size hole in Eva's forehead where Vater's shot had hit her. A third eye, like her brother's gashed wound. In death they were alike, Don thought, Eva and Olaf. In death, all time between the siblings had been erased.

He heard himself trying to shout at Eva that she should wake up. Then he leaned down, so close that he could feel her shallow breaths.

There was a weak flame flickering deep inside, behind her pupils. Don tried to find something to say, but no matter how hard he tried, he could find no words.

"Don Titelman," Eva breathed. "That was a really great . . . train car you had."

"Eva . . ."

"But it wasn't . . . it wasn't right. That it should bring you all the way here."

"Eva," Don whispered, "try to breathe."

She just looked at him for a long time, until a puff of air blew out the light in her eyes.

Elena saw how the pale face became wrapped in veils of dust. The fine lines in Eva's face had softened and were slowly smoothed out. Don was still trying to hold back the blood, and when he looked up at Elena, she could see his jaw moving mutely.

Behind the metal structure, the South Americans had begun to move, while at the same time the vortex was weakening. Without the men's brain waves, the maelstrom seemed to be gradually slowing down. It spun more and more weakly now, and at last the black sun hung as bright and motionless as it had before Lytton's strange experiment.

The lasers from the Germans danced through the mist, and more and more red points of light were aimed at the metal frame. Elena looked down at the ankh, which Eva was still holding in her hands. It sparkled in the darkness as she gently lifted it from the dead woman's fingers, exposing the star in the center of the object. On the other side of the body, Don was sitting with his head bowed, and his shoulders were shaking. Elena grasped the cold metal and lifted the ankh to her breast.

She sneaked a look at Vater, who she knew was watching her from behind his block of stone. Then Elena turned toward the South Americans' metal frame and slowly stood up.

"Jansen!" Vater's hissing voice through the haze. A movement was visible in the dust beyond the tubes, but there was no answer.

"It is you, isn't it, Jansen, back from the dead?" shouted Vater. "It will be a short visit, in that case. You see how it went for your daughter here."

"What did she have to do with us?" Lytton shouted back, lying behind his protective frame. "Your damned underworld has taken the lives of both my children."

"The darkness demands its sacrifices. You of all people should know that," Vater said.

The seat of the electric wheelchair slowly began to lift him up. Elena could see Vater's half-burned face rising over the edge of the stone block.

"This is what your daughter did to me, Jansen. No one asked her and Titelman to blow up the foundation's tower. If you dare to show yourself, you are welcome to continue with your promising experiment."

"And what if we succeed in opening the portal?" Lytton shouted back. "If we make contact with whatever is behind it?"

Vater didn't answer, and more lasers lit up, one by one. But this time they came from the South Americans, who had by now taken positions behind the metal frame. The lasers from the two groups crossed in the mist and formed a web of searching lights.

"I have a different suggestion," Lytton shouted. "You ask your daughter to come over here with the ankh. Then you all disappear quietly so we can complete our task here."

Elena looked at the red dot that was wandering over her chest. It came from one of the weapons that was now aimed at her by Lytton's men.

At the same time, Don saw that another red dot had begun to shine on the back of her head, from the weapon that Vater was balancing in his hand.

Elena pressed the ankh to her forehead to feel its cold clarity, and concentrated as hard as she could to search for her mother's voice. She looked over at the black sun, which hung there weightless and unfathomable. In its smooth disc, Elena could see her own face emerge.

By now Don had also begun to move, after having placed Eva's head to rest in the soft dust. When he had stood up, he followed Elena's eyes toward the underworld's hovering sun.

It looked as though it was changing again, and its disc had become a shade lighter. He could hear Elena mumbling syllables that sounded like Italian words by his ear. With each syllable she produced, the sunlight gradually increased.

"Elena!" Vater shouted.

But it seemed as though she couldn't hear anything.

"Elena!" Vater hissed again. "I expect you to bring the ankh here." Don saw Elena's mouth moving faster and faster, in time with the growing sunlight. So that he wouldn't be blinded, he held up a hand for shade. He caught sight of Agusto Lytton, who was lying there under the shining sun. The way the light shadowed his face, his eyes looked like two black, empty sockets, but his skull was now covered with brilliant light.

Elena could feel something tugging and yanking inside her, as though one last action were demanded of her. She was standing next to a portal that led away from the darkness, but she didn't know how she could get it to open. "I want it, *lo voglio,*" she mumbled. "I want you to take the ankh from us."

At that instant, something like a breath came from the white disc of the sun. A cloud of light, of shining particles, detached itself from its center and came sailing over the grayish black drifts. Don saw the cloud coming toward them, and how it enveloped Elena. Her eyes closed, she extended the ankh, and he could hear her whisper:

"I want you to take me, too."

When Elena opened her eyes, she could no longer see any part of the underworld. The mist was gone, the stone blocks, and the cold that had been so bitter and hard. The only thing that remained was the light, which shimmered around her, and it felt as though she were being held in a warming embrace.

"Take me too," she whispered.

As an answer, from within the flowing brightness, there was a sudden motion, a swirling breeze of shining particles that gently loosened her fingers from the cross. The breeze turned into slender hands holding the ankh above her. Elena looked up toward a face that so resembled her own: the high cheekbones, the wide mouth, and the eyes that she hadn't gazed into since she was a child.

"Elena, your time hasn't come yet."

Her mother's voice had hardly faded away before Elena saw the ankh begin to burn. It was slowly consumed by the fire emanating from the hands of the glowing creature, until the cross and its star had turned as black as coal.

Don, who was standing at Elena's side, could feel the warmth too, but what he saw inside the shimmering cloud was impossible to understand.

To him the figure of light appeared crooked and twisted; it was bent into the shape of a very old woman. Her long, graying hair was tied up in a familiar knot. Then he looked down at the woman's calves, which were twined with knotty scars, and he realized that he must reach the center of the cloud himself, that Elena must let him come in.

"Bubbe . . ." Don mumbled.

Elena was jostled as Don moved closer, and the handcuffs clattered as they swayed in front of the glittering being. At the same time there were deafening cracks from the thousands of pillars, which were starting to bend, and somewhere one of them snapped from the weight and crashed down, broken.

Now that he was so close to what appeared to be his grandmother, Don was filled with a tremendous sense of relief, a feeling of complete lightness. He didn't care about the terrible din as the columns cracked and fell. Nothing outside the radiance of the cloud meant anything anymore.

The creature took hold of the chain that linked him to Elena. In the next instant, Don's black boots floated up from the floor of the cavern. The creature pulled them up above the circle of stones, away from the brilliant sun wheel.

Stones and gravel rained from the high ceiling over all the men, who were fighting to get out. Don could see Agusto Lytton rushing between the falling pillars. Vater, in his electric wheelchair, was being carried through the masses of debris by camouflage-clad soldiers.

The only ones who were standing perfectly still were Reinhard Eberlein and the Toad. They remained side by side before the furious glow of the underworld sun.

The chain of the handcuffs carried Don and Elena higher and higher. It was as though the figure of light had grown wings, as they could hear a flapping sound.

The last thing Don saw as he looked back was something white pouring out of Eva Strand's forehead. It seemed as if her soul trickled out of her like a stream, back toward the white-hot embrace of the sun.

Then their speed increased so quickly that the rush of air forced his face down. Don fought to breathe as he and Elena were hauled out of the collapsing cavern.

# 54

# The North Star

The wave of pressure emanating from the collapsing vaulted passage pushed the creature of light forward at breakneck speed. When Don looked down, he saw that the tips of his boots were cutting through the dust, and the handcuff yanked and tore at his arm until he thought it would be ripped off.

Elena was somewhere in the blinding glow around him, but she was nearly impossible to see. Don could hear her careening back and forth as they turned and began to be hauled up through the vertical tunnel that led back to the surface of the earth again.

The wings were growing broader and broader above them, and they beat and lashed. All the sparkling strings went dark under Don's feet, and the walls of the tunnel began to narrow and squeeze together.

In the whistling wind, he could still feel a peculiar serenity as he hung dangling under the shining creature. Bubbe's voice was still speaking inside him, like a healing power that moved through the labyrinths of his memory, where she extinguished the pictures of terror and pain.

He could see her there, walking through her 1950s house, closing the cupboard he never should have opened. When its door closed, the swastika and the Schutzstaffeln's daggers disappeared in the dark, and Don wanted to believe that they were gone for good.

*"S'iz nisht dain gesheft, mein nachesdik kind,"* Bubbe whispered. Bearing all of this sadness, that should never have been your business, my beloved child.

At that second, it was as though a grip around his throat loosened; a strangling noose had finally been cut loose.

When they reached the mouth of the tunnel, the being's wings got caught in downward suction, like a vacuum. For an instant they were pressed back down toward the depths, and Don thought that they would never be released. Elena's body came tumbling toward him, and he lost his breath as they fell together. But then the Arctic wind swept in and gave the wings the support to lift, and suddenly the creature was soaring up high in freedom, above the expanses of ice.

The snowstorm must have died down a long time ago, and when Don looked up at the vault of black velvet, he saw only the cream white arch of the Milky Way. The flame that burned brightest of all was the North Star, which came closer and closer with its flashing light. But the farther the being lifted them from the tunnel, the more it seemed to lose its strength. The radiance around it faded until almost nothing was left, and Don felt one last twitch from the handcuff.

Then he and Elena came loose and fell, joined together, from the aura that was now fading gradually. Don saw her camouflage jacket fluttering in the wind as she tried to keep her balance.

Falling through the sky, he was filled with a childlike feeling of freedom. During the short seconds when he was tumbling down, the beating of his heart stopped, and the peace that filled him extended beyond time and space. The lingering chain that had bound his life to his grandmother's had finally been cracked and broken. Somehow this creature had opened the door of Bubbe's house and let him go.

But then the glittering of the North Star was drowned in a cloud of whirling snow. The strong wind had caused them to land at an angle, and they bounced across the ice like a ball of yarn. Don felt Elena's arms holding him and their bodies each taking every other thud. Finally they were sliding across a surface as smooth and slippery as soaped glass.

When their movement had subsided and everything became still, Don fell onto his back. Elena lay beside him, and he could hear that she, too, was gasping for breath. Then their breathing gradually slackened, becoming slower and slower. They lay close to each other under a distant sky.

Don squinted up at the North Star and thought how similar it was to the spark of light he had once watched appear above Nils Strindberg's white ankh. Then he loosened his shoulder strap a bit, got hold of his bag, and began to grope through it out of habit. But as he rooted around among bottles and syringes, he had a feeling he wasn't used to. Don took a deep breath and decided to take the risk of remaining in something that resembled a state of normalcy for a little while.

In all probability, not even dextroamphetamine could make the stars way up there above him any clearer. And he had never experienced from Valium the calm he felt in his chest right now.

Elena lay listening to the blowing wind, and through their linked hands, she felt the warmth that radiated from Don. She wondered if he had seen her mother down there too, or if he had met someone else entirely in the underworld's sun. The figure of light that had taken the ankh from her had done it for her own good. There was something behind the disc of that sun, through that portal, that a living person wasn't prepared to see.

The frosty air and the ice under her made everything feel comfortably soft. Elena thought that she could lie here forever, gazing up at the vault of stars, and just let time go by.

For the first time since she was a child, there was no one who would demand answers from her. Maybe when her time was up, she would find out, but as it was now, she could just rest quietly here.

# 55

# Gone with the Wind

Don felt his arm being dragged along by the handcuff as Elena finally stood up. She crouched down and began to inspect the tiny lock of the cuffs.

Then she asked whether he had anything with him that they could use, preferably something pointed and narrow. Don couldn't help but smile as he dug around in his shoulder bag with his hand, and soon he produced a small syringe that was sealed in plastic.

Elena took the needle and worked it in with practiced fingers, and only a few seconds later, she had succeeded in freeing his wrist. His skin was chafed and bloody where the cuff had been, and once Elena had freed herself, she took out a small bandage. She wound it around Don's wrist, and then she said, "We have to get out of here before the weather has time to get worse."

Don looked despondently out over the endless ice.

"You mean we should walk all the way back to the icebreaker? Isn't that really far?"

"Eleven miles," said Elena. "But considering the questions that would await us there, I don't think that's a very good choice. But over there . . ."

She pointed toward the Russian helicopter.

"It's only a few hundred yards over there, isn't it?"

Elena brushed the snow off herself, and before he could say anything, she had begun to walk away. Don stood up on trembling legs. Then he began to follow her as quickly as he could, because in spite of her baggy camouflage clothing, Elena was moving with lithe steps.

But she stopped suddenly by one of the snowdrifts and bent down as though she had found something. When Don came closer he saw that the thing she had picked up out of the snow was Strindberg's star and ankh, burned black.

Elena seemed remarkably confident behind the controls of the helicopter. She tossed one helmet over to Don and helped him put on his headset and visor. Then, through the tinted glass, he was able to follow what looked like practiced movements as she looked through all those meters and systems.

The rotor blades began to revolve, and the helicopter soared up over the chalk white expanses of the Arctic. She guided them forward without lurching despite the wind, and they sailed low over the tunnel, which was no more than a hole a yard in diameter by now. When Don looked down, he could see that the downdraft from the rotors was causing the rest of the opening to be covered over, and all that was left was the drifting snow.

Elena adjusted the pitch of the rotors, and as their lift increased, the craft rose up toward the stars again. In the roar of the motor, his headset crackled with static, and Don heard her shout that she was planning to fly them toward Longyearbyen on Svalbard, about three hundred miles away.

Elena tilted the helicopter's nose down, and once the blades caught, it finally surged ahead. Don sat with his head against the window, looking down at the ice as it flew by; and vibrating in his lap were the remains of a star and an ankh.

The white metal, which had turned black, had also become noticeably frail and brittle. Don took off his gloves and let his fingers glide over the ankh's rough surface, where all the inscriptions had melted away.

He thought of a place they ought to visit on their journey south, and he began to search for the right coordinates on the map. Once he'd called them out to Elena via his microphone, he only had to explain them with a few concise words.

When they had reached the edge of the pack ice, they flew out over the Arctic Ocean. Black swells, which were becoming increasingly gray in the light of dawn. The polar night receded with every nautical mile south, and far off on the horizon, there was a glimpse of something that resembled a sunrise. From inside the visor, Don could see the sunlight breaking, but then he closed his eyes and returned to the underworld and Eva Strand.

She was still lying there in the darkness, wrapped in the veils of pulverized dust. Once again he saw the sudden shine above her eyes, and in the rhythm of the rotors he tried to force himself to fall asleep.

*

Don had lost all sense of time when Elena finally shook him awake. She pointed over at something that looked like floating ice, and it wasn't until the helicopter had descended that he could see the jagged cliffs sticking up.

The island was covered in snow except for a small strip of beach, and Don shouted that they should land on the southwestern part. That was where the stone had been erected, as far as he could remember, and he was seldom wrong when it came to such things.

He grabbed the edge of the seat as Elena balanced the skids in the correct position, and soon they had landed on frozen gravel.

Don pulled off his helmet and wrapped himself in the red jacket that said EARLY FALL ARCTIC CRUISE. At the bottom of the helicopter's metal stairs, he looked up at Elena, who waved at him to hurry.

He began to jog up the sharp stone cleft in the slope, and he came up onto the hill where the monument stood. After he had read the names on the brass plate, he looked down at what he had brought along: the burned objects that had once been Strindberg's star and ankh.

The two objects looked so unassuming in his hand, and he wondered how they could have brought him all the way here. Then Don placed the star and the ankh to rest on top of the cement monument.

When he returned to the cockpit, Elena was leaning comfortably backward and had taken off her helmet. He was struck by how green her eyes were when she directed them at him and said, "There's something I've been sitting here thinking about."

Don listened skeptically as she told him her suggestion. It was certainly not his experience that something so difficult could be so simple. But Elena didn't seem to see any risks, at least not on her part. It was doubtful that she even existed officially; Vater had seen to that a long time ago.

They continued to discuss the matter as the blades of the helicopter began to rotate, and soon the skids lifted from frozen ground. The blades of the rotor beat their way up over the hill, and they hung there motionless for a second, above the lonely monument on the island.

The draft under them caused the ankh and the star to tremble, but then the helicopter lifted higher and higher and sailed away.

The only things left, in the sunshine at the expedition's final camp on Kvitøya, were two blackened objects and the names on the memorial stone:

S. A. ANDRÉE

N. STRINDBERG

K. FRÆNKEL

. 1897 .

# The Letter

A few weeks later, in a drizzly Falun, the entrance doors of the Åhléns department store closed with a hiss behind a retiree with heavy bags. Outside of Systembolaget, the liquor shop, a few guys were messing around with a moped; and none of them was probably thinking it, but Falun's shopping street, Åsgatan, was really terribly dismal.

If you were to cross the river, you would reach the part of town that was closest to the Great Copper Mine, built upon centuries-deep layers of slag. On that side, right after the bridge, was Falun's police station, and in one of its interrogation rooms, a fluorescent light was buzzing. Leaning against the back of a chair sat a crooked figure in a velvet suit and aviator glasses. Directly across from him sat a policeman with a mustache. A letter with a German postmark lay between them on top of a notebook. The only sound was the monotonous buzzing from the ceiling and the hum of the ventilation system. Then the Mustache cleared his throat to bring the conversation to an end.

"So you mean to say you don't know anything about who sent this to us? Yet you return to Sweden just a few days after it lands on our desk?"

Don straightened his glasses.

"I assume I'll have to explain this to Säpo, too," he said. The policeman blew his nose.

"I don't think you'll have to do that. They don't seem to be very interested anymore, and from what I've heard, there's an internal investigation in progress about why you were taken from here in the first place. And this so-called attorney . . ."

Don waved his hand dismissively.

"Well, what a damned mess," the Mustache mumbled to himself.

"And the fingerprints on the bottle you found?" Don asked.

"We will search the international registries as well, but here in Sweden, we haven't found a match. And being able to hit like that, with such a small hand . . . You almost start to wonder whether Erik Hall was killed by a child. But of course, whoever wrote this letter was able to point out exactly where the bottle was and give a technical description of how the blow was dealt besides. So it was a letter from a murderer, but nothing about why . . ."

"Maybe there are some parts of this thing that you still don't know," Don said.

The policeman gave him a look that was meant to be piercing.

"Oh, really? Has something happened that you still haven't told us?"

Don shook his head vigorously.

"Well, we should keep in touch, anyway," the Mustache said tentatively. "I mean, in case something turns up."

In the silence that followed, all that was audible was the occasional clicking of the fluorescent light. Finally, Don pushed his chair back and pulled on the strap of his bag.

"So I'm free to go, then?"

The Mustache nodded reluctantly, and Don stood up. When he reached the door, he heard the policeman's voice.

"I'm sorry if we happened to involve you in this mess unnecessarily, Titelman. Do you perhaps have a legal representative we can contact if there are any more questions?"

Don looked at the Mustache, sitting there in the fluorescent light. Then he said, "No, I think I can take care of myself from now on."

# Acknowledgments

Therese Uddenfeldt—without you, nothing would have been possible.

Thanks also to:

Stephen Farran-Lee and Karin Lundwall;

Michael Kucera, Anna-Karin Ivarsson, Daniel Öhman, Sara Hallgren Öhman, Lars Pahlman, Judit Ek, Niklas Möller, Pier Franceschi, and Margit Silberstein;

Anna Hedin, Katarina Wallentin, Lars Wallentin, Mikael Uddenfeldt, and Astrid Uddenfeldt;

Peter Giesecke, Ricardo Gonzalez, Elias Hedberg, Olov Hyllienmark, Roger Jansson, Håkan Jorikson, Olle Josephson, Daniel Karlsson, Johanna Mo, Margareta Regebro, Lotta Riad, Thomas Roth, Salomon Schulman, and Katja Östling;

In the few places where the novel diverges from reality, it's reality that ought to change.